Thomas Dekker, Richard Herne Shepherd

Dramatic Works

now collected with illustrative notes and a memoir of the author - Vol. 3

Thomas Dekker, Richard Herne Shepherd

Dramatic Works

now collected with illustrative notes and a memoir of the author - Vol. 3

ISBN/EAN: 9783337093204

Printed in Europe, USA, Canada, Australia, Japan

Cover: Foto ©Andreas Hilbeck / pixelio.de

More available books at **www.hansebooks.com**

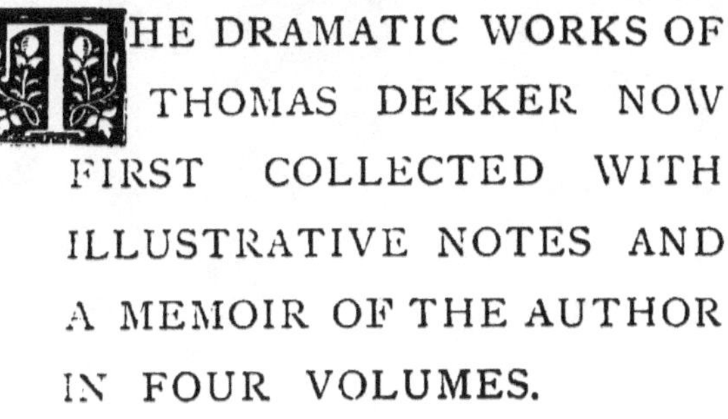

THE DRAMATIC WORKS OF THOMAS DEKKER NOW FIRST COLLECTED WITH ILLUSTRATIVE NOTES AND A MEMOIR OF THE AUTHOR IN FOUR VOLUMES.

VOLUME THE THIRD

LONDON
JOHN PEARSON YORK STREET COVENT GARDEN
1873

NORTH-VVARD

HOE.

Sundry times Acted by the Children
of Paules.

By Thomas Decker, and
Iohn Webſter.

Imprinted at London by G. ELD.
1607.

NORTH-WARD HOE.

ACTVS PRIMVS.

Enter Luke Greene-ſhield with Fetherſtone booted.

Feth. ART ſure old *Maybery* Innes here to night.

Gree. Tis certaine the honeſt knaue Chamberleine that hath bin my Informer, my baud, euer ſince I knew *Ware* aſſures me of it, and more being a *Londoner* though altogether vnacquainted, I haue requeſted his company at ſupper.

Feth. Excellent occaſion : how wee ſhall carry our ſelues in this buſines is onely to be thought vpon.

Gree. Be that my vndertaking : if I do not take a full reuenge of his wiues puritanicall coyneſſe.

Feth. Suppoſe it ſhe ſhould be chaſt.

Gree. O hang her : this art of ſeeming honeſt makes many of our young ſonnes and heires in the Citty, looke ſo like our prentiſes,—Chamberlaine.

Cha. Heare Sir.			*Enter Chamberlaine.*

Gree. This honeſt knaue is call'd *Innocence,* iſt not a good name for a Chamberlaine ? he dwelt at *Dun-ſtable* not long ſince, and hath brought me and the two Butchers Daughters there to interuiew twenty times & not ſo little I proteſt : how chance you left dunſtable Sirra ?

Cha. Faith Sir the towne droopt euer ſince the peace in *Ireland,* your captaines were wont to take their leaues of their *London* Polecats, (their wenches I meane Sir) at Dunſtable : the next morning when they had broke their faſt togeather the wenches brought them to Hockly 'ith hole, & ſo the one for *London* the other for *Weſtcheſter,* your onely rode now Sir is *Yorke Yorke* Sir.

Gree. True, but yet it comes ſcant of the Pro-pheſy ; *Lincolne* was, *London* is, and *Yorke* ſhall-be.

Cha. Yes, Sir, tis fullfild, *Yorke* ſhalbe, that is, it ſhalbe *Yorke* ſtill, ſurely it was the meaning of the prophet : will you haue ſome Cray-fiſh, and a Spitch-cocke.

Enter Maybery with Bellamont.

Feth. And a fat Trout.

Cham. You ſhall Sir ; the Londoners you wot of.

Green. Moſt kindly welcome—I beſeech you hold our bouldneſſe excuſed Sir.

Bella. Sir it is the health of Trauailers, to inioy good company : will you walke.

Feth. Whether Trauaile you I beſeech you.

May. To *London* Sir we came from *Sturbridge.*

Bel. I tel you Gentlemen I haue obſeru'd very much with being at ſturbridge ; it hath afforded me mirth beyond the length of fiue lattin Comedies ; here ſhould you meete a Nor-folk yeoman ful but ; with his head able to ouer-turne you ; and his pretty wife that followed him, ready to excuſe the ignorant hardneſſe of her huſbands forhead, in the gooſe markt number of freſhmen ; ſtuck here and there, with a graduate :

like cloues with great heads in a gammon of bacon :
here two gentlemen making a mariage betweene their
heires ouer a wool-pack ; there a Minifters wife that
could fpeake falfe lattine very lifpingly ; here two in
one corner of a fhop : Londoners felling their wares,
& other Gentlemen courting their wiues ; where they
take vp petticoates you fhold finde fchollers & townf-
mens wiues crouding togither while their hufbands
weare in another market bufie amongft the Oxen ;
twas like a campe for in other Countries fo many
Punks do not follow an army.   I could make an excellent difcription of it in a Comedy : but whether are
you trauailyng Gentlemen ?

Feth.   Faith Sir we purpofed a dangerous voiage,
but vpon better confideration we alterd our courfe.

May.   May we without offence pertake the ground
of it.

Green.   Tis altogither triuial in-footh : but to paffe
away the time till fupper, Ile deliuer it to you, with
proteftation before hand, I feeke not to publifh
euery gentle-womans difhonor, only by the paffage
of my difcource to haue you cenfure the ftate of our
quarrel.

Bel.   Forth Sir.

Green.   Frequenting the company of many marchants wiues in the Citty, my heart by chance leapt
into mine eye to affect the faireft but with al the
falfeft creature that euer affection ftoopt to.

May.   Of what ranck was fhe I befeech you.

Feth.   Vpon your promife of fecrefie.

Bel.   You fhall clofe it vp like treafure of your
owne, and your felfe fhall keepe the key of it.

Green.   She was and by report ftill is wife to a moft
graue and well reputed Cittizen.

May.   And entertaind your loue.

Green.   As Meddowes do Aprill : the violence as
it feemed of her affection—but alas it proued her dif-
fembling, would at my comming and departing be-dew

her eyes with loue dropps; O fhe could the art of
woman moft feelingly.

Bel. Moft feelingly.

May. I fhould not haue lik'd that feelingly had
fhe beene my wife, giue us fome fack heare and in
faith—we are all friends; & in priuate—what was her
hufbands name—Ile giue you a caroufe by and by.

Green. O you fhall pardon mee his name, it
feemes you are a Cittizen, it would bee difcourfe
inough for you vpon the exchange this fort-night
fhould I tell his name.

Bel. Your modefty in this wiues commendation;
on fir.

Green. In the paffage of our loues, (amongft other
fauours of greater valew) fhe beftowed vpon me this
ringe which fhe protefted was her hufbands gift.

May. The poefie, the poefie—O my heart, that
ring good infaith:

Green. Not many nights comming to her and being
familiar with her.

May. Kiffing and fo forth.

Green. I Sir.

Ma. And talking to her feelingly.

Gre. Pox on't, I lay with her.

May. Good infaith, you are of a good com-
plexion.

Green. Lying with her as I fay: and rifing fomewhat early from her in the morning, I loft this ring in
her bed.

May. In my wiues bed.

Feth. How do you Sir.

May. Nothing: lettes haue a fire chamberlaine;
I thinke my bootes haue taken water I haue fuch a
fhudering: ith' bed you fay;

Green. Right Sir, in Miftris *Maiberies* fheetes.

May. Was her name *Maybery.*

Green. Befhrew my tongue for blabbing, I prefume
vpon your fecrefy.

May. O God Sir, but where did you find your loofing.

Green. Where I found her falfneffe : with this Gentleman ; who by his owne confeffion pertaking the like inioyment ; found this ring the fame morning on her pillowe, and fham'd not in my fight to weare it.

May. What did fhee talke feelingly to him too ; I warrant her hufband was forth a Towne all this while, and he poore man trauaild with hard Egges in's pocket, to faue the charge of a baite, whilft fhe was at home with her Plouers, Turkey, Chickens ; do you know that *Maibery.*

Feth. No more then by name.

May. Hee's a wondrous honeft man ; lets be merry ; will not your miftriffe ?—gentlemen, you are tenants in common I take it.

Feth. Gree. Yes.

May. Will not your Miftreffe make much of her husband when he comes home, as if no fuch leger-demaine had bin acted.

Green. Yes fhe hath reafon for't, for in fome countries, where men and women haue good trauailing ftomackes, they begin with porredge ; then they fall to Capon or fo-forth : but if Capon come fhort of filling their bellies, to their porridge againe, tis their onely courfe, fo for our women in *England.*

May. This wit taking of long iourneys : kindred that comes in ore the hatch, and failing to Weftminfter makes a number of Cuckolds.

Bell. Fie what an idle quarrell is this, was this her ring ?

Green. Her ring Sir.

May. A pretty idle toy, would you would take mony for't.

Feth. Green. Mony fir.

May. The more I looke on't, the more I like it.

Bell. Troth 'tis of no great valew, and confidering the loffe, and finding of this ring made breach into your friendſhip, Gentlemen, with this trifle purchaſe his loue, I can tell you he keepes a good Table.

Green.   What my Miſtris gift ?

Feth.   Faith you are a merry old Gentleman; Ile giue you my part in't.

Green.   Troth and mine, with your promiſe to conceale it from her husband.

May.   Doth he know of it yet ?

Green.   No Sir.

May.   He ſhall neuer then I proteſt : looke you this ring doth fitte me paſſing well.

Feth.   I am glad we haue fitted you.

May.   This walking is wholeſome, I was a cold euen now, now I ſweat for't.

Feth.   Shalls walke into the Garden *Luke.* Gentlemen weele downe and haſten ſupper.

May.   Looke you, we muſt be better acquainted that's all.   *Exeunt Green. and Feth.*

Green.   Moſt willingly; Excellent, hee's heat to the proofe, lets with-draw, and giue him leaue to raue a little.

May.   Chamberlaine, giue vs a cleane Towell.

Enter Chamberlaine.

Bell.   How now man ?

May.   I am fooliſh old *Maybery*, and yet I can be wiſe *Maybery* too ; Ile to London preſently, begon Sir.

Bell.   How, how ?

May.   Nay, nay, Gods pretious you doe miſtake mee Maiſter *Bellamont* ; I am not diſtempered, for to know a mans wife is a whore, is to be reſolu'd of it, and to be reſolued of it, is to make no queſtion of it, and when a caſe is out of queſtion ; what was I ⌐ ſaying ?

Bell.   Why looke you, what a diſtraction are you falne into ?

May. If a man be deuorſt, do you ſee, deuorſt *forma Iuris,* whether may he haue an action or no, gainſt thoſe that make hornes at him?

Bell. O madneſſe! that the frailty of a woman ſhould make a wife man thus idle! yet I proteſt to my vnderſtanding, this report ſeemes as farre from truth, as you from patience.

May. Then am I a foole, yet I can bee wife and I liſt too : what ſayes my wedding ring?

Bell. Indeed that breeds ſome ſuſpition : for the reſt moſt groſe and open, for two men, both to loue your wife, both to inioy her bed, and to meete you as if by miracle, and not knowing you, vpon no occaſion in the world, to thruſt vpon you a difcourſe of a quarrell, with circumſtance ſo diſhoneſt, that not any Gentleman but of the countrie bluſhing, would haue publiſht. I and to name you : doe you know them?

May. Faith now I remember, I haue ſeene them walke muffled by my ſhop.

Bell. Like enough; pray God they doe not borrow mony of vs twixt *Ware* and *London* : come ſtriue to blow ouer theſe clowdes.

May. Not a clowd, you ſhall haue cleane Moone-ſhine, they haue good ſmooth lookes the fellowes.

Bell. As Iet, they will take vp I warrant you, where they may bee truſted; will you be merry?

May. Wonderous merry; lets haue ſome Sack to drowne this Cuckold, downe with him : wonderous merry : one word & no more; I am but a fooliſh tradeſman, and yet Ile be a wife tradeſman. *Exeunt.*

Enter Doll lead betweene Leuer-poole, *and* Chartley, *after them* Philip *arreſted.*

Phil. Arreſt me? at whoſe ſute? *Tom Chartley, Dick Leuerpoole,* ſtay, Ime arreſted.

Omn. Arreſted?

1. *Ser.* Gentlemen breake not the head of the

peace; its to no purpofe, for hee's in the lawes clutches, you fee hee's fangd.

Doll. Vds life, doe you ftand with your naked weapons in your hand, and doe nothing with em? put one of em into my fingers, Ile tickle the pimple-nofed varlets.

Phil. Hold *Doll*, thruft not a weapon vpon a mad woman, Officers ftep back into the Tauerne, you might ha tane mee ith ftreete, and not ith' Tauerne entire, you Cannibals.

Ser. Wee did it for your credit Sir.

Chart. How much is the debt? Drawer, fome wine.

Enter Drawer.

1. *Ser.* Foure fcore pound: can you fend for Baile Sir? or what will you doe? wee cannot ftay.

Doll. You cannot, you pafty-footed Rafcalls, you will ftay one day in hell.

Phil. Foure fcore pounds drawes deepe; farewell *Doll*, come Serieants, Ile ftep to mine Vncle not farre off, here-by in Pudding lane, and he fhall baile mee: if not, *Chartly* you fhall finde me playing at Span-counter, and fo farewell. Send mee fome Tobacco.

1. *Ser.* Haue an eye to his hands.

2. *Ser.* Haue an eye to his legges.   *Exeunt.*

Doll. Ime as melancholy now?

Chart. Villanous fpitefull luck, Ile hold my life fome of thefe fawfie Drawers betrayd him.

Draw. Wee fir! no by Gad Sir, wee fcorne to haue a *Iudas* in our company.

Leuer. No, no, hee was dogd in, this is the end of all dycing.

Doll. This is the end of all whores, to fall into the hands of knaues. Drawer, tye my fhoe pry thee: the new knot as thou feeft this: *Philip* is a good honeft Gentleman, I loue him becaufe heele fpend, but when I faw him on his Fathers Hobby, and a brace of

Punkes following him in a coach, I told him hee
would run out, haſt done boy ?

Draw. Yes forſooth: by my troth you haue a
dainty legge.

Doll. How now good-man rogue.

Draw. Nay ſweete Miſtreſſe *Doll.*

Doll. *Doll* ! you reprobate ! out you Bawd for
ſeauen yeares by the cuſtome of the Citty.

Draw. Good Miſtris *Dorothy* ; the pox take mee,
if I toucht your legge but to a good intent.

Doll. Prate you : the rotten toothd raſcall, will for
ſixe pence fetch any whore to his maiſters cuſtomers :
and is euery one that ſwims in a Taffatie gowne Lettis
for your lippes ? vds life, this is rare, that Gentlewomen
and Drawers, muſt ſuck at one Spiggot : Doe you
laugh you vnſeaſonable puck-fiſt ? doe you grin ?

Chart. Away Drawer : hold pry thee good rogue,
holde my ſweete *Doll*, a pox a this ſwaggering.

Doll. Pox a your gutts, your kidneys ; mew : hang
yee, rooke : I'me as melancholy now as Fleet-ſtreete
in a long vacation.

Leuer. Melancholy ? come weele ha ſome muld
Sack.

Doll. When begins the terme ?

Chart. Why ? haſt any ſuites to be tryed at Weſtminſter ?

Doll. My Sutes you baſe ruffian haue beene tryed
at Weſtminſter already : ſo ſoone as euer the terme
begins, Ile change my lodging, it ſtands out a the way ;
Ile lye about Charing-croſſe, for if there be any ſtir-
rings, there we ſhall haue 'em : or if ſome Dutch-man
would come from the States ! oh ! theſe *Flemmings*
pay ſoundly for what they take.

Leuer. If thou't haue a lodging Weſt-ward *Doll*,
Ile fitte thee.

Doll. At Tyburne will you not ? a lodging of your
prouiding ? to bee cal'd a Lieutenants, or a Captaines
wench ! oh ! I ſcorne to bee one of your Low-country
commodities, I ; is this body made to bee mainteined

with Prouant and dead pay? no: the Mercer muſt
bee paide, and Sattin gownes muſt bee tane vp.

Chart. And gallon pots muſt be tumbled downe.

Doll. Stay: I haue had a plot a breeding in my
braines—Are all the Queſt-houſes broken vp?

Leuer. Yes, long ſince: what then?

Doll. What then? mary then is the wind come
about, and for thoſe poore wenches that before Chriſt-
maſſe fled Weſt-ward with bag and baggage, come
now ſailing alongſt the lee ſhore with a Northerly
winde, and we that had warrants to lie without the
liberties, come now dropping into the freedome by
Owle-light, ſneakingly.

Chart. But *Doll*, whats the plot thou ſpakſt off?

Doll. Mary this: Gentlemen, and Tobacco-ſtinck-
ers, and ſuch like are ſtill buzzing where ſweete meates
are (like Flyes) but they make any fleſh ſtinke that
they blow vpon: I will leaue thoſe fellowes therefore
in the hands of their Landreſſes: Siluer is the Kings
ſtampe, man Gods ſtampe, and a woman is mans
ſtampe, wee are not currant till wee paſſe from one
man to another.

Both. Very good.

Doll. I will therefore take a faire houſe in the
Citty: no matter tho it be a Tauerne that has blowne
vp his Maiſter: it ſhall be in trade ſtill, for I know
diuerſe Tauernes ith Towne, that haue but a Wall betweene them and a hotte-houſe. It ſhall then bee
giuen out, that I'me a Gentlewoman of ſuch a birth,
ſuch a wealth, haue had ſuch a breeding, and ſo
foorth, and of ſuch carriage, and ſuch qualities, and
ſo forth: to ſet it oft[a] the better, old *Iack Hornet* ſhall
take vppon him to bee my Father.

Leuer. Excellent, with a chaine about his neck
and ſo forth.

Doll. For that, Saint *Martins* and wee will talke:
I know we ſhall haue Gudgions bite preſently: if they
doe boyes, you ſhall liue like Knights fellowes; as
occaſion ſerues, you ſhall weare liueries and waite, but

when Gulls are my winde-falls, you fhall be Gentlemen, and keepe them company : feeke out *Iack Hornet*
incontinently.

Leuer. Wee will : come *Charely*, weele playe our
partes I warrant.

Dell. Doe fo :—
The world's a ftage, from which ftrange fhapes we
    borrow :
To day we are honeft, and ranke knaues to morrow.

Exeunt.

Enter Maybery, Bellamont, *and a Prentice.*

May. Where is your Miftris, villaine ? when went
fhe abroad ?

Pren. Abroad Sir, why affoone as fhe was vp Sir.

May. Vp Sir, downe Sir, fo fir : Maifter *Bellamont*,
I will tell you a ftrange fecret in Nature, this boy is
my wiues bawd.

Bell. O fie fir, fie, the boy he doe's not looke like
a Bawde, he has no double chin,

Pren. No fir, nor my breath does not ftinke, I
fmell not of Garlick or *Aqua-vitæ* : I vfe not to bee
drunke with Sack and Sugar : I fweare not God dam
me, if I know where the party is, when 'tis a lye and
I doe know : I was neuer Carted (but in harueft)
neuer whipt but at. Schoole : neuer had the Grincoms : neuer fold one Maiden-head ten feuerall times,
firft to an *Englifhman*, then to a *Welfhman*, then to a
Dutchman, then to a pockie *Frenchman*, I hope Sir I
am no Bawd then.

May. Thou art a *Baboune*, and holdft me with
trickes, whilft my Wife grafts grafts, away, trudge, run,
fearch her out by land, and by water.

Pren. Well Sir, the land Ile ferret, and after that
Ile fearch her by water, for it may be fhees gone to
Brainford. *Exit.*

Mayb. Inquire at one of mine Aunts.

Bell. One of your Aunts, are you mad ?

Mayb.   Yea, as many of the twelue companies are, troubled, troubled.

Bel.   Ile chide you : goe to, Ile chide you foundly.

May.   Oh maifter *Bellamont !*

Bel.   Oh Maifter *Maybery /* before your Seruant to daunce a Lancafhire Horne-pipe : it fhewes worfe to mee, then dancing does to a deafe man that fees not the fiddles : Sfoot you talke like a Player.

Mayb.   If a Player talke like a mad-man, or a foole, or an Affe, and knowes not what hee talkes, then Ime one : you are a Poet Maifter *Bellamont,* I will beftow a piece of Plate vpon you to bring my wife vpon the Stage, wud not her humor pleafe Gentlemen.

Bella.   I thinke it would : yours wud make Gentlemen as fatt as fooles : I wud giue two peeces of Plate, to haue you ftand by me, when I were to write a iealous mans part : Iealous men are eyther knaues or Coxcombes, bee you neither : you weare yellow hofe without caufe.

May.   With-out caufe, when my Mare beares double : without caufe ?

Bell.   And without wit.

May.   When two Virginall Iacks skip vp, as the key of my inftrument goes downe !

Bel.   They are two wicked elders.

May.   When my wiues ring does fmoake for't.

Bell.   Your wiues ring may deceive you.

May.   O Maifter *Bellamont* ! had it not beene my wife had made me a Cuckold, it fhould neuer haue greeued mee.

Bel.   You wrong her vpon my foule.

Mai.   No, fhe wrongs me vpon her body.

Enter a Seruingman.

Bel.   Now blew-bottle ? what flutter you for Sea-pye ?

Ser.   Not to catch fifh Sir, my young Maifter, your fonne maifter *Philip* is taken prifoner.

Bel.   By the *Dunkirks*.
Ser.   Worfe : by Catch-polls : hee's encountred.
Bel.   Shall I neuer fee that prodigall come home.
Ser.   Yes Sir, if youle fetch him out, you may kill a Calfe for him.
Bel.   For how much lyes he?
Ser.   The debt is foure fcore pound, marry he chargde mee to tell you it was foure fcore and ten, fo that he lies onely for the odde ten pound.
Bel.   His childs part fhal now be paid, this mony fhalbe his laft, & this vexation the laft of mine : if you had fuch a fonne maifter *Maiberie.*
Mai.   To fuch a wife, twere an excellent couple.
Bel.   Releafe him, and releafe me of much forrow, I will buy a Sonne no more : goe redeeme him.

Enter Prentice and Maiberies wife.

Prent.   Here's the party Sir.
Mai.   Hence, and lock faft the dores, now is my prize.
Prent.   If fhe beate you not at your owne weapon, wud her Buckler were cleft in two peeces.   *Exit.*
Bel.   I will not haue you handle her too roughly.
Mai.   No, I will like a Iuftice of peace, grow to the point : are not you a whore : neuer ftart : thou art a Cloth-worker, and haft turnd me.
Wife.   How Sir, into what Sir, haue I turn'd you?
May.   Into a Ciuill Suite : into a fober beaft : a Land-rat, a Cuckold : thou art a common bed-fellow, art not? art not?
Wif.   Sir this Language, to me is ftrange, I vnder-ftand it not.
May.   O ! you ftudie the french now.
Wife.   Good Sir, lend me patience.
May.   I made a fallade of that herbe : doeft fee thefe flefh-hookes, I could teare out thofe falfe eyes, thofe Cats eyes, that can fee in the night : punck I could.

Bel.   Heare her anfwer for her felfe.

Wif.   Good Maifter *Bellamont,*
Let him not do me violence : deere Sir,
Should any but your felfe fhoote out thefe names,
I would put off all female modefty,
To be reueng'd on him.

May.   Know'ft thou this ring ? there has bin old
running at the ring fince I went.

Wife.   Yes Sir, this ring is mine, he was a villayne,
That ftole it from my hand : he was a villayne :
That put it into yours.

May.   They were no villaynes,
When they ftood ftoutly for me : tooke your part :
And ftead of collours fought vnder my fheetes.

Wife,   I know not what you meane.

May.   They lay with thee : I meane plaine dealing.

Wife.   With me ! if euer I had thought vncleane,
In deteftation of your nuptiall pillow :
Let *Sulpher* drop from Heauen, and naile my body
Dead to this earth : that flaue, that damned fury
(Whofe whips are in your tongue to torture me)
Cafting an eye vnlawfull on my cheeke,
Haunted your thre-fhold daily, and threw forth
All tempting baytes which luft and credulous youth,
Apply to our fraile fex : but thofe being weake
The fecond feige he layd was in fweete wordes.

Mai.   And then the breach was made.

Bel.   Nay, nay, heare all.

Wife.   At laft he takes me fitting at your dore,
Seizes my palme, and by the charme of othes
(Back to reftore it ftraight) he won my hand,
To crowne his finger with that hoope of gold.
I did demand it, but he mad with rage
And with defires vnbrideled, fled and vow'd,
That ring fhould mee vndo : and now belike
His fpells haue wrought on you. But I befeech you,
To dare him to my face, and in meane time
Deny me bed-roome, driue me from your board,
Difgrace me in the habit of your flaue,

Lodge me in fome difcomfortable vault
Where neither Sun nor Moone may touch my fight,
Till of this flander I my foule acquite.
    Bel. Guiltleffe vpon my foule.
    May. Troth fo thinke I.
I now draw in your bow, as I before
Suppof'd they drew in mine : my ftreame of ielozy,
Ebs back againe, and I that like a horfe
Ran blind-fold in a Mill (all in one circle)
Yet thought I had gon fore-right, now fpy my error :
Villaines you haue abuf'd me, and I vow
Sharp vengeance on your heads : driue in your
      teares
I take your word ya're honeft, which good men,
Very good men will fcarce do to their wiues.
I will bring home thefe ferpents and allow them,
The heate of mine owne bofome : wife I charge you
Set out your hauiours towards them in fuch collours,
As if you had bin their whore, Ile haue it fo,
Ile candy o're my words, and fleeke my brow,
Intreate 'em that they would not point at me,
Nor mock my hornes, with this Arme Ile em-
    brace 'em
And with this—go too.
    Wife. Oh we fhall haue murder—you kill my
    heart.
    May. No : I will fhed no bloud,
But I will be reueng'd, they that do wrong
Teach others way to right : Ile fetch my blow
Faire and a far off and as Fencers vfe
Tho at the foote I ftrike, the head Ile bruize.

Enter Philip *and feruant.*

    Bel. Ile ioyne with you : lets walke : oh ! heres
    my Sonne.
Welcome a fhore Sir : from whence come you pray.
    Phil. From the houfe of praier and fafting—the
Counter.

Bel.   Art not thou afham'd to bee feene come out of a prifon.

Phil.   No Gods my Iudge, but I was afham'd to goe into prifon.

Bel.   I am told fir, that you fpend your credit and your coine vpon a light woman,

Phil.   I ha feene light gold fir, paffe away amongft Mercers.

Bel.   And that you haue layd thirty or fortie pounds vpon her back in taffaty gownes, and filke petticoates.

Phil.   None but Taylors will fay fo, I nere lay'd any thing vpon her backe : I confeffe I tooke vp a petticoate and a raiz'd fore-part for her, but who has to do with that ?

May.   Mary that has euery body Maifter *Philip.*

Bel.   Leaue her company, or leaue me, for fhee's a woman of an ill name.

Phil.   Her name is *Dorothy* fir, I hope thats no il name.

Bel.   What is fhee ? what wilt thou do with her ?

Phil.   Sbloud fir what does he with her ?

Bel.   Doeft meane to marry her ? of what birth is fhee ? what are her commings in, what does fhe liue vpon ?

Phillip.   Rents fir, Rents, fhee liues vpon her Rents, and I can haue her.

Bel.   You can.

Phil.   Nay father, if deftiny dogge mee I muft haue her : you haue often tould mee the nine Mufes are all women, and you deale with them, may not I the better bee allowed one than you fo many ? looke you Sir, the Northerne man loues white-meates, the Southery man Sallades, the Effex man a Calfe, the Kentifhman a Wag-taile, the Lancafhire man an Egg-pie, the Welfhman Leekes and Cheefe, aud your Londoners rawe Mutton, fo Father god-boy, I was borne in London.

Bella.   Stay, looke you Sir, as hee that liues vpon

Sallades without Mutton, feedes like an Oxe, (for hee
eates graffe you knowe) yet rizes as hungry as an
Affe, and as hee that makes a dinner of leekes will
haue leane cheekes, fo, thou foolifh Londoner, if
nothing but raw mutton can diet thee, looke to liue
like a foole and a flaue, and to die like a begger and
a knaue, come Maifter *Maiberie*, farewell boy.

    Phil.   Farewell father Snot . . . Sir if I haue her,
Ile fpend more in muftard & vineger in a yeare, then
both you in beefe.

    Both.   More faucy knaue thou.   *Exeunt.*

Actus 2. *Scena* 1.

Enter Hornet, Doll, Leuerpoole *and* Chartly *like
feruingmen.*

    Horn.   AM I like a fidlers bafe violl (new fet
vp,) in a good cafe boies? ift neate,
is it terfe ! am I hanfome ? ha !

    Omn.   Admirable, excellent.

    Dol.   An vnder fheriffe cannot couer a knaue more
cunningly.

    Leuer.   Sfoot if he fhould come before a Church-
warden, he wud make him peu-fellow with a Lords
fteward at leaft.

    Horn.   If I had but a ftaffe in my hand, fooles
wud thinke I were one of *Simon* and *Iudes* gentlemen
vfhers, and that my apparell were hir'd : they fay three
Taylors go to the making vp of a man, but Ime fure
I had foure Taylors and a halfe went to the making of
me thus : this Suite tho' it ha bin canuaft well, yet tis
no law-fuite, for twas difpatcht fooner than a poffet on
a wedding night.

    Dol.   Why I tel thee Jack *Hornet*, if the Diuel and
all the Brokers in long lane had rifled their wardrob,
they wud ha beene dambd before they had fitted
thee thus.

C 2

Horn. Punck, I fhall bee a fimple father for you : how does my chaine fhow now I walke.

Dol. If thou wert hung in chaines, thou couldft not fhow better.

Chart. But how fit our blew-coates on our backes.

Dol. As they do vpon banckrout retainers backes at Saint *Georges* feaft in *London* : but at *Weftminfter*, It makes 'em fcorne the badge of their occupation : there the bragging velure-caniond hobbi-horfes, praunce vp and downe as if fome a the Tilters had ridden 'em.

Hor. Nay Sfoot, if they be banckrouts, tis like fome haue ridden 'em : and there-vpon the Cittizens Prouerbe rifes, when hee fayes ; he trufts to a broken ftaffe.

Doll. *Hornet*, now you play my Father, take heed you be not out of your part, and fhame your adopted Daughter.

Horn. I will looke grauely *Doll*, (doe you fee boyes) like the fore-man of a Iury : and fpeake wifely like a Lattin Schoole-maifter, and be furly and dogged, and proud like the Keeper of a prifon.

Leuer. You muft lie horribly, when you talke of your lands.

Horn. No fhop-keeper fhall out lye mee, nay, no Fencer : when I hem boyes, you fhall duck : when I cough and fpit gobbets *Doll.*

Doll. The pox fhall be in your lungs *Hornet.*

Hor. No *Doll*, thefe with their high fhoes fhall tread me out.

Doll. All the leffons that I ha prickt out for 'em, is when the Wether-cock of my body turnes towards them, to ftand bare.

Horn. And not to be fawcie as Seruing-men are.

Char. Come, come, we are no fuch creatures as you take vs for.

Dol. If we haue but good draughts in my peeter-boate, frefh Salmon you fweete villaines fhall be no meate with vs.

Horn. Sfoot nothing mooues my choller, but that my chaine is Copper : but tis no matter, better men than old *Jack Hornet* haue rode vp Holburne, with as bad a thing about their neckes as this : your right whiffler indeed hangs himfelfe in Saint *Martins*, and not in *Cheape-fide.*

Doll. Peace, fome-body rings : run both, whilft he has the rope in's hand, if it be a prize, hale him, if a man a war, blow him vp, or hang him out at the maine yeards end.

Horn. But what ghofts (hold vp my fine Girle) what ghofts haunts thy houfe ?

Doll. Oh ! why diuerfe : I haue a Clothiers Factor or two ; a Grocer that would faine Pepper me, a *Welfh* Captaine that laies hard feege, a *Dutch* Mar-chant, that would fpend al that he's able to make ith' low countries, but to take meafure of my Holland fheetes when I lye in 'em : I heare trampling : 'tis my Flemifh Hoy.

Enter Leuerpoole, Chartly, *and* Hans van Belch.

Hans. Dar is bor pou, and bor pou : een, twea, drie, bier, and biue fkilling, drinke Skellum bpfie freefe : nempt, dats b drinck gelt.

Leuer. Till our crownes crack agen Maifter *Hans van Belch.*

Hans. How ift met pou, how ift bro ? brolick ?

Doll. Ick bare well God danke pou : Nay Ime an apt fcholler and can take.

Hans. Datt is good, dott is good : Ick can neet ftap long : for Ick heb en fkip come now bpon de bater : O minu ſchoonen bro, wee ſall danœ lanteera, teera, and ſing Ick drincke to you min here, ban :—wat man is dat bro.

Hor.   Nay pray ſir on.

Hans. Wlat honds foot is dat Doro=thy.

Doll.   Tis my father.

Hans. Gotts Sacrament! your bader! why ſeyghen gou niet ſo to me! mine heart tis mine all great deſire, to call you mine bader ta for Ick loue dis ſchonen bro your dochterkin.

Hor.   Sir you are welcome in the way of honeſty.

Hans. Ich bedanck you: Ick heb ſo ghe founden bader.

Horn.   Whats your name I pray.

Hans. Mun nom bin Hans van Belch.

Horn.   Hans Van Belch!

Hans. Yau, yau, tis ſo, tis ſo, de dronken man is alteet remember me.

Horn.   Doe you play the marchant, ſonne *Belch.*

Hans. Yau bader: Ick heb de ſkip ſwim now bpon de bater if you endouty, goe bp in de little Skip dat goe ſo, and bee puld bp to Wlapping, Ick ſal beare you on my backe, and hang you about min neck into min groet Skip.

Horn. He Sayes *Doll,* he would haue thee to Wapping and hang thee.

Doll. No Father I vnderſtand him, but maiſter *Hans*, I would not be ſeene hanging about any mans neck, to be counted his Iewell, for any gold.

Horn. Is your father liuing Maiſter *Hans.*

Hans. Yau, yau, min bader heb ſcho-non huſen in Ausburgh groet mine heare is mine baders broder, mine bader heb land, and bin full of fee, dat is beaſts, cattell.

Char. He's lowzy be-like.

Hans. Min bader bin de groteſt fooker in all Ausbrough.

Dol. The greateſt what ?

Leuer. Fooker he ſaies.

Dol. Out vpon him.

Hans. Yaw yaw, fooker is en groet min here hees en elderman bane Citty, gots facrament, wat is de clock ? Eck niet ſtay.

A watch.

Hor. Call his watch before you, if you can.

Doll. Her's a pretty thing : do theſe wheeles ſpin vp the houres ! whats a clock.

Hans. Acht : yaw tis acht.

Doll. We can heare neither clock, nor Iack going, wee dwell in ſuch a place that I feare I ſhall neuer finde the way to Church, becauſe the bells hang ſo farre ; Such a watch as this, would make me go downe with the Lamb, and be vp with the Larke.

Hans. Seghen you ſo, dor it to.

Doll. O fie : I doe but ieſt, for in trueth I could neuer abide a watch.

Hans. 𝕲𝖔𝖙𝖙𝖘 𝖋𝖆𝖈𝖗𝖆𝖒𝖊𝖓𝖙, 𝕴𝖈𝖐 𝖓𝖎𝖊𝖙 𝖍𝖊𝖇 𝖎𝖙 𝖆𝖓𝖞 𝖒𝖔𝖗𝖊.

Exeunt Leuer-poole *and* Chartly.

Dol. An other peale ! good father lanch out this hollander.

Horn. Come Maifter *Belch*, I will bring you to the water-fide, perhaps to Wapping, and there ile leaue you.

Hans. 𝕴𝖈𝖐 𝖇𝖊𝖉𝖆𝖓𝖈𝖐 𝖞𝖔𝖚 𝖇𝖆𝖉𝖊𝖗.   *Exit.*

Doll. They fay Whores and bawdes go by clocks, but what a Manaffes is this to buy twelue houres fo deerely, and then bee begd out of 'em fo eafily ? heele be out at heeles fhortly fure for he's out about the clockes already : O foolifh young man how doeft thou fpend thy time ?

Enter Leuer-poole *firft, then* Allom *and* Chartly.

Leuer. Your grocer.

Dol. Nay Sfoot, then ile change my tune : I may caufe fuch leaden-heeld rafcalls ; out of my fight : a knife, a knife I fay : O Maifter *Allom*, if you loue a woman, draw out your knife and vndo me, vndo me.

Allo. Sweete miftris *Dorothy*, what fhould you do with a knife, its ill medling with edge tooles, what's the matter Maifters ! knife God bleffe vs.

Leu. Sfoot what tricks at noddy are thefe.

Do. Oh I fhal burft, if I cut not my lace : I'me fo vext ! my father hee's ridde to Court : one was about a matter of a 1000. pound weight ; and one of his men (like a roague as he is) is rid another way for rents, I lookt to haue had him vp yefterday, and vp to day, and yet hee fhowes not his head ; fure he's run away, or robd & run thorough ; and here was a fcriuener but euen now, to put my father in minde of a bond, that wilbe forfit this night if the mony be not payd Maifter *Allom*. Such crofle fortune !

Allo.   How much is the bond ?

Chart.   O rare little villaine.

Dol.   My father could take vp, vpon the bareneffe of his word fiue hundred pound : and fiue toe.

Allom.   What is the debt ?

Dol.   But hee fcornes to bee . . . and I fcorne to bee . . .

Allom.   Pree thee fweete Miftris *Dorothy* vex not, how much is it ?

Dol.   Alas Maifter *Allom,* tis but poore fifty pound.

Allo.   If that bee all, you fhall vpon your worde take vp fo much with me : another time ile run as far in your bookes.

Dol.   Sir, I know not how to repay this kindneffe : but when my father——

All.   Tufh, tufh, tis not worth the talking : Iuft 50 pound ? when is it to be payd.

Dol.   Betweene one and two.

Leue.   That's wee thre.

Allom.   Let one of your men goe along, and Ile fend fifty pound !

Dol.   You fo bind mee fir, . . . goe firra : Maifter *Allom,* I ha fome quinces brought from our houfe ith Country to preferue, when fhall we haue any good Suger come ouer ? the warres in Barbary make Suger at fuch an excefliue rate ; you pay fweetely now I warrant, fir do you not.

Al.   You fhal haue a whole cheft of Suger if you pleafe.

Dol.   Nay by my faith foure or fiue loaves wil-be enough, and Ile pay you at my firft child Maifter *Allom.*

Allom.   Content ifaith, your man fhall bring all vnder one, ile borrow a kiffe of you at parting.

Enter Captaine Iynkins.

Dol.   You fhall fir, I borrow more of you.

Ex. Allo. & Leu.

Chart. Saue you Captaine.

Dol. Welcome good captaine *Fynkins.*

Captaine. What is hee a Barber Surgeon, that dreſt your lippes ſo.

Dol. A Barber! hee's may Taylor; I bidde him meaſure how hie, hee would make the ſtanding coller of my new Taffatie Gowne before, and hee as Tailors wilbe ſawcie and lickeriſh, laid mee ore the lippes.

Captaine. Vds bloud ile laie him croſſe vpon his coxcomb next daie.

Dol. You know tis not for a Gentlewoman to ſtand with a knaue, for a ſmall matter, and ſo I wud not ſtriue with him, onelie to be rid of him.

Capt. If I take Maiſter prick-louſe ramping ſo hie againe, by this Iron (which is none a gods Angell) Ile make him know how to kiſſe your blind cheekes ſooner: miſtris *Dorothy* Hornet, I wud not haue you bee a hornet, to licke at Cowſherds, but to ſting ſuch ſhreds of raſcallity: will you ſing a Tailor ſhall haue mee my ioy?

Dol. Captaine, ile bee lead by you in any thing! a Taylor! foh.

Capt. Of what ſtature or fiſe haue you a ſtomach to haue your huſband now?

Dol. Of the meaneſt ſtature Captaine, not a ſize longer than your ſelfe, nor ſhorter.

Cap. By god, tis wel ſaid all your beſt Captaine in the Low-countries are as taller as I: but why of my pitch Miſtris Dol?

Dol. Becauſe your ſmalleſt Arrowes flie fartheſt; ah you little hard-fauord villaine, but ſweete villaine, I loue thee beecauſe thou't draw a my ſide, hang the roague that will not fight for a woman.

Cap. Vds blould, and hang him for vrſe than a roague that will ſlaſh and cut for an oman, if ſhe be a whore.

Dol. Pree the good Captaine *Fynkins,* teach mee

to fpeake fome welch, mee thinkes a Welchmans tongue is the neateft tongue !——

Cap. As any tongue in the vrld, vnlefle *Cra ma trees,* that's vrfe.

Dol. How do you fay, I loue you with all my heart.

Cop. *Mi cara whee, en hellon.*

Dol. *Mi cara whee, en hel-hound.*

Cap. *Hel-hound, o mondu, my cara whee, en hellon.*

Dol. *O, my cara whee en hellon.*

Cap. Oh ! and you went to wryting fchoole twenty fcore yeare in *Wales,* by Sefu, you cannot haue better vtterance, for welch.

Dol. Come tit mee, come tat me, come throw a kiffe at me, how is that ?

Cap. By gad I kanow not, what your tit mees, and tat mees are, but *mee uatha*——Sbloud I know what kiffes be, afwel as I know a Welch hooke, if you will goe downe with Shropfheere cariers, you fhal haue Welch enough in your pellies forty weekes.

Dol. Say Captaine that I fhould follow your collours into your Country how fhould I fare there ?

Cap. Fare ? by Sefu, O there is the moft abominable feere ? and wider filuer pots to drinck in, and fofter peds to lie vpon & do our neceffary pufines, and fairer houfes and parkes, & holes for Conics, and more money, befides tofted Sees and butter-milke in *Northwales* diggon : befides, harpes & Welch Freeze, and Goates, and Cowheeles, and Metheglin, ouh, it may be fet in the Kernicles, wil you march thither ?

Dol. Not with your Shrop-fheire cariers, Captaine.

Cap. Will you go with Captaine *Ienkin* and fee his Couzen *Maddoc* vpon *Ienkin* there, and ile run hedlongs by and by, & batter away money for a new Coach to iolt you in.

Dol. Beftow you Coach vpon me, & two young whlte Mares, and you fhall fee how Ile ride.

Cap. Will you ? by all the leckes that are wornc

on Saint Dauies daie I will buy not only a Coach,
with foure wheeles, but alfo a white Mare and a ftone
horfe too, becaufe they fhal traw you, very luftily, as
if the diuill were in their arfes.   *Exit.*
How now, more Tailors————*Meetes Phillip.*

 Phi.   How fir ; Taylors.
 Dol.   O good Captaine, tis my Couzen.

   Enter Leuerpoole at another dore.

 Cap.   Is he, I will Couzen you then fir too, one
day.
 Phil.   I hope fir then to Couzen you too.
 Cap.   By gad I hobe fo, fare-well *Sidanien.*   *Exit.*
 Leuer.   Her's both money, and fuger.
 Dot   O fweete villaine, fet it vp.
       Exit, and Enter prefently.
 Phil.   Sfoot, what tame fuaggerer was this I met
Doll.
 Dol.   A Captaine, a Captaine : but haft fcap't the
Dunkerks honeft *Philip ? Philip* ryalls are not more
welcome : did thy father pay the fhot ?
 Phil.   He pai'd that fhot, and then fhot piftolets
into   my   pockets :   harke wench :   chinck chink,
makes the punck wanton and the Baud to winck.
         Capers.

 Chart.   O rare mufick.
 Leuer.   Heauenly confort, better than old *Moones.*
 Phil.   But why? why *Dol,* goe thefe two like
Beadells in blew ? ha ?
 Doll.   Theres a morrall in that : flea off your skins,
you pretious Caniballs : O that the welch Captaine
were here againe, and a drum with him, I could march
now, ran, tan, tan, tara, ran, tan, tan, firra *Philip* has
thy father any plate in's houfe.
 Phil.   Enough to fet vp a Gold-fmithes fhop.
 Dol.   Canft not borrow fome of it ? wee fhall
haue guefts to morrow or next day, and I wud ferue

the hungry rag-a-muffins in plate, tho twere none of
mine owne.

Phil. I fhall hardly borrow it of him but I could
get one of mine Aunts, to beate the bufh for mee,
and fhe might get the bird.

Dol. Why pree the, let me bee one of thine Aunts,
and doe it for me then. As Ime vertuous and a
Gentlewoman ile reftore.

Phil. Say no more tis don.

Dol. What manner of man is thy father? Sfoote
ide faine fee the witty Monky becaufe thou fayft he's
a Poet: ile tell thee, what ile do: *Leuer-poole* or
Chartly, fhall like my Gentleman vfher goe to him,
and fay fuch a Lady fends for him, about a fonnet or
an epitaph for her child that died at nurfe, or for fome
deuice about a maske or fo: if he comes you fhall
ftand in a corner, and fee in what State ile beare my
felfe: he does not know me, nor my lodging.

Phil. No, no.

Doll. Ift a match Sirs? fhalls be mery with him
and his mufe.

Omn. Agreed, any fcaffold to execute knauery
vpon.

Doll. Ile fend then my vant-currer prefently: in
the meanetime, marche after the Captaine, fcoundrels,
come hold me vp:
Looke how *Sabrina* funck ith' riuer *Seuerne*,
So will we foure be drunke ith' fhip-wrack Tauerne.
Exeunt.

Enter Bellamont, Maybery, *and Miftreffe* Maybery.

May. Come Wife, our two gallants will be here
prefently: I haue promift them the beft of entertainment, with proteftation neuer to reueale to thee their
flander: I will haue thee beare thy felfe, as if thou
madeft a feaft vpon *Simon* and *Judes* day, to country
Gentlewomen, that came to fee the Pageant, bid them
extreamly welcome, though thou wifh their throats
cut; 'tis in fafhion.

Wife.   O God I fhall neuer indure them.

Bell.   Indure them, you are a foole: make it your cafe, as it may be many womens of the Freedome ; that you had a friend in priuate, whom your husband fhould lay to his bofome: and he in requitall fhould lay his wife to his bofome: what treads of the toe, falutations by winckes, difcourfe by bitings of the lip, amorous glances, fweete ftolne kiffes when your husbands backs turnd, would paffe betweene them, beare your felfe to *Greenefhield* as if you did loue him for affecting you fo intirely, not taking any notice of his iourney: theile put more tricks vpon you: you told me *Greenefhield* meanes to bring his Sifter to your houfe, to haue her boord here.

May.   Right, fhee's fome crackt demy-culuerin, that, hath mifcaried in feruice: no matter though it be fome charge to me for a time, I care not.

Wife.   Lord was there euer fuch a husband ?

May.   Why, wouldft thou haue me fuffer their tongues to run at large, in Ordinaries and Cockpits ; though the Knaues doe lye, I tell you Maifter *Bella-mont*, lyes that come from fterne lookes, and Sattin out-fides, and guilt Rapiers alfo, will be put vp and goe for currant.

Bell.   Right fir, 'tis a fmall fparke, giues fire to a beautifull womans difcredit.

May.   I will therefore vfe them like informing knaues, in this kinde, make up their mouthes with filuer, and after bee reuenged vpon them: I was in doubt I fhould haue growne fat of late: and it were not for law fuites: and feare of our wiues, we rich men fhould grow out of all compaffe: they come, my worthy friends welcome: looke my wiues colour rifes already.

Green.   You haue not made her acquainted with the difcouery.

May.   O by no meanes: yee fee Gentlemen the affection of an old man; I would faine make all whole agen. Wife giue entertainment to our new acquaintance, your lips wife, any woman may lend her lips without her husbands priuity tis alowable.

Wife. You are very welcome, I thinke it be neere dinner time Gentlemen : Ile will the maide to couer, and returne prefently.

Bell. Gods pretious why doth fhe leaue them?

Exit.

May. O I know her ftomack : fhee is but retirde into another chamber, to eafe her heart with crying a little : it hath euer bin her humor, fhe hath done it 5. or 6. times in a day, when Courtiers haue beene heare, if any thing hath bin out of order, and yet euery returne laught and bin as merry : & how is it Gentlemen, you are well acquainted with this roome, are you not?

Gree. I had a dellicate banquet once on that table.

May. In good time : but you are better acquainted with my bed chamber.

Bell. Were the cloath of gold Cufhins fet forth at your entertainement?

Feth. Yes Sir.

May. And the cloath of Tiffew Valance.

Feth. They are very rich ones.

May. God refufe me, they are lying Rafcols, I haue no fuch furniture.

Green. I proteft it was the ftrangeft, and yet withall the happieft fortune that wee fhould meete you two at *Ware,* that euer redeemed fuch defolate actions : I would not wrong you agen for a million of *Londons.*

May. No, do you want any money? or if you be in debt, I am a hundreth pound ith' Subfidie, command mee.

Feth. Alas good Gentleman ; did you euer read of the like pacience in any of your ancient *Romans?*

Bel. You fee what a fweet face in a Veluet cap

can do, your citizens wiues are like Partriges, the
hens are better then the cocks.

Feth.   I beleeue it in troth, Sir you did obferue how
the Gentlewoman could not containe her felfe, when
fhe faw vs enter.

Bell.   Right.

Feth.   For thus much I muft fpeake in allowance of
her modeftie, when I had her moft priuate fhe would
blufh extreamely.

Bell.   I, I warrant you, and aske you if you would
haue fuch a great finne lie vpon your confcience, as to
lie with another mans wife.

Feth.   Introth fhe would.

Bell.   And tell you there were maides inough in
london, if a man were fo vitioufly giuen, whofe Por-
tions would helpe them to hubsbands though gentlemen gaue the firft onfet.

Feth.   You are a merry ould gentlemen infaith
Sir : much like to this was her langwage.

Bell.   And yet clipe you with as voluntary a
bofome ; as if fhe had fallen in loue with you at fome
Innes a court reuels : and inuited you by letter to her
lodging.

Fet.   Your knowledge Sir, is perfect without any
information.

May.   Ile goe fee what my wife is doing gentlemen, when my wife enters fhew her this ring ; and
twill quit all fufpition.   *Exit.*

Feth.   Doft heare *Luke Greenfhield* wil thy wife be
here prefently.

Green.   I left my boy to waight vpon her, by this
light, I thinke God prouides ; for if this cittifen had
not out of his ouerplus of kindnes proferd her, her
diet and lodging vnder the name of my fifter, I could
not haue told what fhift to haue made ; for the greateft
part of my mony is reuolted ; weele make more vfe of
him, the whorefon rich Inkeeper of *Doncafter* her
father fhewed himfelfe a ranke oftler : to fend her vp

at this time a yeare ; and by the carier to, twas but a
iades trike of him.

Feth. But haue you inſtructed her to call you
brother.

Green. Yes and ſhele do it, I left her at Boſomes
Inne, ſheele be here, preſently.

Enter Maybery.

May. Maiſter *Greencſheild* your ſiſter is come ;
my wife is entertaining her, by the maſſe I haue bin
vpon her lips already.   Lady you are welcome, looke
you maiſter *Greencſhield*, becauſe your ſiſter is newly
come out of the freſh aire, and that to be pent vp in
a narrow lodging here ith' cittie may offend her health
ſhe ſhall lodge at a garden houſe of mine in Morefeilds
where if it pleaſe you and my worthy friend heare to
beare her company your ſeuerall lodgings and Ioint
commons (to the poore ability of a cittizen) ſhal be
prouided.

Feth. O God Sir.

May. Nay no complement your loues comand it :
ſhalls to dinner Gentlemen, come maiſter *Bellamont*
Ile be the Gentleman vſher to this faire Lady.

Gree. Here is your ring Miſtris ; a thouſand
times,—— and would haue willingly loſt my beſt of
maintenance that I might haue found you halfe ſo
tractable.

Wif. Sir I am ſtill my ſelfe, I know not by what
means you haue grown vpon my husband, he is much
deceaued in you I take it : will you go in to dinner—
O God that I might haue my wil of him & it were
not for my husband ide ſcratch out his eyes preſently.
Ex.

Fet. Welcome to London bonny miſtris Kate, thy
husband little dreams of the familiarity that hath paſt
betwene thee & I Kate.

Kate. Noe matter if hee did : he ran away from
me like a baſe ſlaue as he was, out of *Yorke-ſhire*, and

pretended he would goe the Iland voiage, fince I
neere heard of him till within this fortnight: can the
world condemne me for entertayning a friend, that
am vfed fo like an Infidel?

Fe. I think not, but if your husband knew of this
he'd be deuorft.

Kat. Hee were an affe then, no wifemen fhould
deale by their wiues as the fale of ordinance paffeth in
England, if it breake the firft difcharge the workman
is at the loffe of it, if the fecond the Marchant, & the
workman ioyntly, if the third the Marchant, fo in our
cafe, if a woman proue falfe the firft yeare, turne her
vpon her fathers neck, if the fecond, turne her home
to her father but allow her a portion, but if fhe hould
pure mettaile two yeare and flie to feueral peeces, in
the third, repaire the ruines of her honefty at your
charges, for the beft peece of ordinance, may bee
crackt in the cafting, and for women to haue cracks
and flawes, alas they are borne to them, now I haue
held out foure yeare, doth my husband do any things
about *London* doth he fwagger?

Feth. O as tame as a fray in Fleeteftreete, when
their are nobody to part them.

Ka. I euer thought fo, we haue notable valiant
fellowes about Doncafter, theile giue the lie and the
ftab both in an inftant.

Feth. You like fuch kind of man-hood beft
Kate.

Kat. Yes introth for I think any woman that
loues her friend, had rather haue him ftand by it then
lie by it, but I pray thee tel me, why muft I be quar-
terd at this Cittizens garden houfe, fay you.

Fe. The difcourfe of that wil fet thy bloud on fire
to be reuengd on thy husbands forhead peece.

Ent. Bella & *Maift.* Maybe.

Wif. Wil you go in to dinner fir?
Kat. Wil you lead the way forfoth?

Wif.   No fweete forfothe weele follow you.

O Maifter *Bellamont* : as euer you tooke pitty vpon the fimplicity of a poore abufed gentlewoman : wil you tell me one thing.

Bell.   Any thing fweet Miftris *Mayberrie.*

Wife.   I but will you doe it faithfully ?

Bell.   As I refpect your acquaintance I fhall doe it.

Wife.   Tell me then I befeech you, doe not you thinke this minx is fome noughty packe whome my husband hath fallen in loue with, and meanes to keepe vnder my nofe at his garden houfe.

Bell.   No vpon my life is fhe not.

Wife.   O I cannot beleeue it, I know by her eies fhe is not honeft, why fhould my husband proffer them fuch kindnes ? that haue abufed him and me ; fo in-tollerable : and will not fuffer me to fpeake ; theres the hell ont not to fuffer me to fpeake.

Bell.   Fie fie, he doth that like a vferer, that will vfe a man with all kindnes, that he may be careleffe of paying his mony, vpon his day, and after-wards take the extremitie of the forfature ; your iealoufie is Idle : fay this were true, it lies in the bofome of a fweete wife to draw her husband from any loofe imper-fection, from wenching, from Iealoufie, from couituouf nes from crabbednes, which is the old mans common difeafe, by her politicke yealding.

Bell.   She maye doe it from crabednes, for example I haue knowne as tough blades as any are in England broke vpon a fetherbed—come to diner.

Wife.   Ile be ruled by you Sir, for you are very like mine vncle.

Bell.   Sufpition workes more mifchiefe growes more
       ftrong,
To feuer chaft beds then aparant wrongs.   *Exit.*

ACTVS 3. SÆNA I.

Enter Doll, Chartly, Leuerpoole *and* Phillip.

Phil.   Come my little Punke with thy two Com-
pofitors to this vnlawfull painting houfe, thy pounders
a my old poeticall dad wilbe here prefently ; take vp
thy State in this chayre, and beare thy felfe as if thou
wert talking to thy pottecary after the receipt of a
purgation : looke fcuruily vpon him : fometimes be
merrie and ftand vppon thy pantoffles like a new
elected fcauinger.

Doll.   And by and by melancholicke like a Tilter
that hath broake his ftaues foule before his Miftriffe.

Phil.   Right, for hee takes thee to bee a woman of
a great count : harke vpon my life hee's come.

Doll.   See who knocks : thou fhalt fee mee make a
a foole of a Poet, that hath made fiue hundred
fooles.

Leuer.   Pleafe your new Lady-fhip hee's come.

Doll.   Is hee ?   I fhould for the more ftate let him
walke fome two houres in an vtter roome : if I did
owe him money, 'twere not much out of fafhion ; but
come enter him : Stay, when we are in priuate con-
ference fend in my Tayler.

Enter Bellamont *brought in by* Leuerpoole.

Leuer.   Looke you my Ladie's a fleepe, fheele wake
prefently.

Bell.   I come not to teach a Starling fir God-boy-
you.

Leuer.   Nay in trueth Sir, if my Lady fhould but
dreame you had beene heare.

Doll.   Who's that keepes fuch a prating ?

Leuer.   'Tis I Madam.

Doll.   Ile haue you preferd to be a Cryer : you

haue an exlent throate for't: pox a the Poet is he not come yet?

Leuer. Hee's here Madam.

Doll. Crie you mercy: I ha curſt my Monkey for ſhrewd turnes a hundred times, and yet I loue it neuer the worſe I proteſt.

Bel. Tis not in faſhion deere Lady to call the breaking out of a Gentlewomans lips, ſcabs, but the heate of the Liuer.

Dol. So ſir: if you haue a ſweete breath, and doe not ſmell of ſwetty linnen, you may draw neerer, neerer.

Bel. I am no friend to Garlick Madam.

Doll. You write the ſweeter verſe a great deale ſir, I haue heard much good of your wit maiſter Poet: you do many deuiſes for Cittizens wiues: I care not greatly becauſe I haue a Citty Laundreſſe already, if I get a Citty Poet too: I haue ſuch a deuiſe for you, and this it is.

Enter Tayler.

O welcome Tayler: do but waite till I diſpatch my Tayler, and Ile diſcouer my deuice to you.

Bell. Ile take my leaue of your Ladiſhip.

Doll. No: I pray thee ſtay: I muſt haue you ſweate for my deuice Maiſter Poet.

Phil. He ſweats already beleeue it.

Dol. A cup of wine there: what faſhion will make a woman haue the beſt bodie Taylor.

Tay. A ſhort dutch waſt with a round cathern-wheele fardingale: a cloſe ſleeue with a cartooſe col-lour and a pickadell.

Dol. And what meate will make a woman haue a fine wit Maiſter Poet.

Bel. Fowle madam is the moſt light, delicate, & witty feeding.

Dol. Fowle ſayſt thou: I know them that feede of it euery meale, and yet are as arrant fooles as any are

in a kingdome of my credit : haft thou don Taylor?
now to difcouer my deuice fir : Ile drinck to you
fir.

Phil. Gods pretious, wee nere thought of her
deuice before, pray god it be any thing tollerable.

Dol. Ile haue you make 12. poefies for a dozen
of cheefe trenchers.

Phil. O horrible !

Bel. In welch madam?

Dol. Why in welch fir.

Bel. Becaufe you will haue them feru'd in with
your cheefe Ladie.

Dol. I will beftow them indeede vpon a welch
Captaine : one that loues cheefe better than venfon,
for if you fhould but get 3. or 4. Chefhire cheefes and
fet them a running down Hiegate-hill, he would make
more haft after them than after the beft kennell of
hounds in *England;* what think you of my deuice?

Bel. Fore-god a very ftrange deuice and a cunning
one.

Phil. Now he begins to eye the goblet.

Bel. You fhould be a kin to the *Bellamonts*, you
giue the fame Armes madam.

Dol. Faith I paid fweetely for the cup, as it may
be you and fome other Gentleman haue don for their
Armes.

Bel. Ha, the fame waight : the fame fafhion : I
had three neft of them giuen mee, by a Nobleman at
the chrifting of my fonne *Philip.*

Phil. Your fonne is come to full age fir : and hath
tane poffeffion of the gift of his Godfather.

Bel. Ha, thou wilt not kill mee.

Phil. No fir, ile kill no Poet leaft his ghoft write
fatires againft me.

Bel. Whats fhe? a good common welthes woman,
fhee was borne.

Phil. For her Country, and has borne her Country.

Bel. Heart of vertue? what make I here?

Phil. This was the party you rail'd on : I keepe no worſe company than your ſelfe father, you were wont to ſay venery is like vſery that it may be allowed tho it be not lawfull.

Bel. Wherefore come I hither.

Dol. To make a deuice for cheeſe-trenchers.

Phil. Ile tell you why I ſent for you, for nothing but to ſhew you that your grauity may bee drawne in : white haires may fall into the company of drabs aſwell as red beardes into the ſociety of knaues : would not this woman deceiue a whole camp ith Low-countries, and make one Commander beleeue ſhe only kept her cabbin for him, and yet quarter twenty more in't.

Dol. Pree the Poet what doeſt thou think of me.

Bel. I thinke thou art a moſt admirable, braue, beautifull Whore.

Dol. Nay ſir, I was told you would raile : but what doe you thinke of my deuice ſir, nay : but you are not to depart yet Maiſter Poet : wut ſup with me ? Ile caſhiere all my yong barnicles, & weele talke ouer a peice of mutton and a partridge, wiſely.

Bel. Sup with thee that art a common vndertaker ? thou that doeſt promiſe nothing but watchet eyes, bumbaſt calues and falſe perywigs.

Dol. Pree the comb thy beard with a comb of black leade, it may be I ſhall affeᵈt thee.

Bel. O thy vnlucky ſtarre ! I muſt take my leaue of your worſhippe I cannot fit your deuice at this inſtant : I muſt deſire to borrow a neſt of goblets of you : O villanie ! I wud ſome honeſt Butcher would begge all the queanes and knaues ith Citty and cary them into ſome other Country they'd ſell better than Beefes and Calues : what a vertuous Citty would this bee then ! mary I thinke there would bee a few people left int, vds foot, guld with Cheeſe-trenchers and yokt in entertainment with a Taylor ? good, good.

Exit.

Phil. How doeſt *Doll* ?

Doll. Scuruie, very ſcuruie.

Leuer. Where fhalls fuppe wench ?

Doll. Ile fuppe in my bedde : gette you home to your lodging and come when I fend for you, ô filthy roague that I am.

Phil. How ! how, miftris *Dorothy* ?

Dol. Saint Antonies fire light in your Spanifh flops : vds life, i'le make you know a difference, betweene my mirth and melancholy, you panderly roague.

Om. We obferue your Ladifhip.

Phi. The puncks in her humer—pax.   *Exit.*

Dol. Ile humor you and you pox mee : vds life haue I lien with a *Spaniard* of late, that 1 haue learnt to mingle fuch water with my Malago, O ther's fome fcuruie thing or other breeding ; how many feuerall loues of Plaiers of Vaulters, of Lieutenants haue I entertain'd befides a runner a the ropes, and now to let bloud when the figne is at the heart ? fhould I fend him a letter with fome Iewel in't, he would requite it as lawiers do, that returne a woodcock pie to their clients, when they fend them a Bafon and a Eure, I will inftantly go and make my felfe drunke, till I haue loft my memory, liue a fcoffing Poet?   *Exit.*

Enter Lep-frog *and* Squirill.

Frog. Now *Squirill* wilt thou make vs acquainted with the ieft thou promift to tell vs of ?

Squi. I will difcouer it, not as a Darby-fhere women difcouers her great teeth, in laughter ; but foftly as a gentleman courts a wench behind an Arras : and this it is, yong *Greenefheild* thy Maifter with *Greenefheilds* fifter lie in my maifters garden-houfe here in More-fields.

Frog. Right, what of this ?

Squir. Mary fir if the Gentlewoman be not his wife, he commits inceft, for Ime fure he lies with her euery night.

Fro. All this I know, but the reft.

Squir. I will tell thee, the moſt pollitick trick of a woman, that ere made a mans face looke witherd and pale like the tree in Cuckolds Hauen in a great ſnow : and this it is, my miſtris makes her huſband belieue that ſhee walkes in her ſleepe a nights, and to con-firme this beleefe in him, ſondry times ſhee hath rizen out of her bed, vnlockt all the dores, gon from Cham-ber to Chamber, opend her cheſts, touz'd among her linnen, & when he hath wakte & miſt her, comming to queſtion why ſhe coniur'd thus at midnight, he hath found her faſt a ſleepe, mary it was Cats ſleepe, for you ſhall heare what prey ſhe watcht for.

Frog. Good ; forth.

Squir. I ouer-heard her laſt night talking with thy Maiſter, and ſhe promiſt him that aſſoone as her hus-band was a ſleepe, ſhe would walke according to her cuſtome, and come to his Chamber, marry ſhee would do it ſo puritannically, ſo ſecretly I meane, that no body ſhould heare of it.

Frog. Iſt poſſible ?

Squir. Take but that corner and ſtand cloſe, and thine eyes ſhall witneſſe it.

Frog. O intollerable witte, what hold can any man take of a womans honeſty.

Squir. Hold ? no more hold then of a Bull noynted with Sope, and baited with a ſhoale of Fidlers in Staffordſhire : ſtand cloſe I heare her com-ming.

Enter Kate.

Kate. What a filthy knaue was the ſhoo-maker, that made my ſlippers, what a creaking they keepe : O Lord, if there be any power that can make a womans husband ſleepe ſoundly at a pinch, as I haue often read in fooliſh Poetrie that there is, now, now, and it be thy will, let him dreame ſome fine dreame or other, that hee's made a Knight, or a Noble-man,

or fome-what whilft I go and take but two kiffes, but
two kiffes from fweete *Fetherftone.*   *Exit.*

Squir.   Sfoot hee may well dreame hees made a
Knight: for Ile be hangd if fhe do not dub him.

Green.   Was there euer any walking fpirit, like to
my wife? what reafon fhould there bee in nature
for this; I will queftion fome Phifition: nor heare
neither: vdflife, I would laugh if fhe were in Mafter
Fetherftones Chamber, fhee would fright him, Maifter
Fetherftone, Maifter *Fetherftone.*

Within Fether.   Ha, how now who cals?

Green.   Did you leaue your doore open laft
night?

Feth.   I know not, I thinke my boy did.

Green.   Gods light fhee's there then, will you know
the ieft, my wife hath her old tricks, Ile hold my life,
my wife's in your chamber, rife out of your bed, and
fee and you can feele her.

Squi.   He will feel her I warrant you?

Gree.   Haue you her fir?

Feth.   Not yet fir, fhee's here fir.

Enter Fetherftone *and* Kate *in his armes.*

Green.   So I faid euen now to my felfe before God
la: take her vp in your armes, and bring her hether
foftly, for feare of waking her: I neuer knew the like
of this before God la, alas poore *Kate,* looke before
God; fhees a fleepe with her eyes open: prittie
little roague, Ile wake her, and make her afhamd
of it.

Feth.   O youle make her ficker then.

Green.   I warrant you; would all women thought
no more hurt then thou dooft, now fweet villaine, *Kate,*
Kate.

Kate.   I longd for the merry thought of a phefant.

Green.   She talkes in her fleepe.

Kate.   And the foule-gutted *Tripe-wife* had got it,

& eate halfe of it: and my colour went and came, and my ſtomach wambled: till I was ready to found, but a Mid-wife perceiued it, and markt which way my eyes went; and helpt mee to it, but Lord how I pickt it, 'twas the fweeteſt meate me thought.

Squi. O pollitick Miſtriſſe.

Green. Why *Kate, Kate*?

Kate. Ha, ha, ha, I befhrew your hart, Lord where am I?

Green. I pray thee be not frighted.

Kate. O I am fick, I am fick, I am fick, O how my fleſh trembles: oh fome of the *Angelica* water, I fhal have the Mother prefently.

Gree. Hold downe her ſtomach good maiſter *Fetherſtone*, while I fetch fome.   *Exit.*

Feth. Well diſſembled *Kate.*

Kate. Piſh, I am like fome of your Ladies that can be fick when they haue no ſtomack to lie with their husbands.

Feth. What mifchiuous fortune is this: weel haue a iourney to *Ware Kate*, to redeeme this misfortune.

Kate. Well, Cheaters do not win all wayes: that woman that will entertaine a friend, muſt as well prouide a Cloſet or Back-doore for him, as a Fetherbed.

Feth. Be my troth I pitty thy husband.

Kate. Pitty him, no man dares call him Cuckold; for ſhe weares Sattin: pitty him, he that will pull downe a mans figne, and fet vp hornes, there's law for him.

Feth. Be fick againe, your husband comes.

Enter Greeneſhield *with a broken ſhin.*

Green. I haue the worſt luck; I thinke I get more bumps and fhrewd turnes ith' darke, how do's fhee maiſter *Fetherſtone*.

Feth. Very ill fir, fhees troubled with the moothe.

extreamly, I held downe her belly euen now, and I
might feele it rife.

Kate.   O lay me in my bed, I befeech you.

Gree.   I will finde a remedy for this walking, if all
the Docters in towne can fell it ; a thoufand pound to
a penny fhe fpoile not her face, or breake her neck,
or catch a cold that fhee may nere claw off againe,
how dooft wench ?

Kate.   A little recouerd : alas I haue fo troubled
that Gentleman.

Feth.   None ith' world *Kate*, may I do you any
farther feruice.

Kate.   And I were where I would be in your bed :
pray pardon me, waft you Maifter *Fetherftone*, hem, I
fhould be well then.

Squi.   Marke how fhe wrings him by the fingers.

Kate.   Good night, pray you giue the Gentleman
thankes for patience.

Green.   Good night Sir.

Feth.   You haue a fhrewd blow, you were beft haue
it fearcht.

Green.   A fcratch, a fcratch.   *Exit.*

Feth.   Let me fee what excufe fhould I frame, to
get this wench forth a towne with me : Ile perfwade
her husband to take Phifick, and prefently haue
a letter framed, from his father in law, to be deliuerd
that morning for his wife, to come and receiue fome
fmall parcell of money in *Enfield* chafe, at a Keepers
that is her Vncle, then fir he not beeing in cafe to trauell, will intreate me to accompany his wife, weele
lye at *Ware* all night, and the next morning to *London*, Ile goe ftrike a Tinder, and frame a Letter prefently.   *Exit.*

Squi.   And Ile take the paines to difcouer all
this to my maifter old *Maybery*, there hath gone a
report a good while, my Maifter hath vfed them
kindly, becaufe they haue beene ouer familiar with
his wife, but I fee which way *Fetherftone* lookes.
ffoote ther's neare a Gentleman of them all fhall gull a

Citizen, & thinke to go fcot-free : though your commons fhrinke for this be but fecret, and my Maifter
fhall intertaine thee, make thee infteed of handling
falfe Dice, finger nothing but gold and filuer wagge,
an old Seruing-man turnes to a young beggar, whereas
a young Prentife may turne to an old Alderman, wilt
be fecret?

Leap.   O God fir, as fecret as rufhes in an old
Ladyes Chamber.   *Exit.*

ACTVS 4.   *SCENA I.*

Enter Bellamont, *in his Night-cap, with leaues in his
     hand; his* man *after him with lights, Standifh,
     and Paper.*

Bel.   Sirrah, Ile fpeake with none.
Seru.   Not a plaier?
Bel.   No, tho a fharer ball ;
I'll fpeak with none, although it be the mouth
Of the big company; I'll fpeak with none : away.
Why fhould not I bee an excellent ftatefman?   I can
in the wryting of a tragedy make *Cæfar* fpeake better
than euer his ambition could ; when I write of *Pompey*,
I have *Pompey's* foul within me : and when I perfonate
a worthy Poet, I am then truly myfelf, a poore vnpre-
ferd fcholler.

Enter his Man haftily.

Seru.   Here's a fwaggering fellow, fir, that fpeakes
not like a man of gods making, fweares he muft fpeake
with you, and wil fpeake with you.
Bell.   Not of gods making? what is he? a Cuckold?
Seru.   He's a Gentleman fir, by his clothes.
Bel.   Enter him and his clothes : clothes fometimes are better Gentlemen than their Mafters.

Enter the Captaine & and the Ser.

Is this he ?—Seeke you me, fir.

Cap.   I feek, fir, (god pleffe) you for a Sentillman
that talkes befides to himfelf when he's alone, as if
hee were in Bed-lam ; and he's a Poet.

Bel.   So, fir, it may bee you feeke mee, for Ime
fometimes out a my wits.

Cap.   You are a Poet, fir, are you.

Bel.   I'me haunted with a Fury, fir.

Cap.   Pray, Mafter Poet, fhute off this little pot-
gun, and I wil coniure your Fury : 'tis well lay you,
fir.   My defires are to haue fome amiable and amorous fonnet or madrigall compofed by your Fury, fee
you.

Bell.   Are you a louer fir of the nine Mufes.

Cap.   Ow, by gad, out a cry.

Bell.   Y'are, then, a fcholler, fir.

Cap.   I ha pickt vp my cromes in Sefus colledge in
Oxford, one day a gad while agoe.

Bell.   Y'are welcome, y'are very welcome. Ile borrow your Iudgement : looke you, fir, I'me writing a
Tragedy, the Tragedy of Young *Aftianax.*

Cap.   *Styanax* Tragedy ! is he liuing, can you tell ?
was not *Styanax* a *Monmouth* man ?

Bell.   O, no, fir, you miftake ; he was a *Troyane*
great *Hectors* Son.

Cap.   *Hector* was grannam to *Cadwallader* : when
fhee was great with child, God vdge me, there was
one young *Styanax* of *Monmouthfheire* was a madder
greek as any is in al *England.*

Bell.   This was not he, affure yee. Looke you, fir,
I will haue this Tragedy prefented in the *French* court
by *French* Gallants.

Cap.   By God, your *Frenchmen* will doe a Tragedy-
enterlude poggy well.

Bell.   It fhall be, fir, at the marriages of the Duke
of *Orleans* and *Chatilion* the admiral of *France*, the
ftage.

Cap. Ud's blood, does *Orleans* marry with the Admirall of *France*, now.

Bell. O, fir, no, they are two feuerall marriages. As I was faying, the ftage hung all with black veluet, and while tis acted, myfelf will ftand behind the Duke of *Biron*, or fome other cheefe minion or fo, who fhall, I they fhall take fome occafion, about the mufick of the fourth Act, to ftep to the *French* King, and fay, *Sire voyla, il eft uotre treſhumble feruiteur, le plu fage à diuine efprit, monfieur Bellamont*, all in French thus, poynting at me, or, Yon is the learned old *Englifh* Gentleman, Mafter *Bellamont*, a very worthie man to bee one of your priuy Chamber or Poet Lawreat.

Cap. But are you fure Duke Pepper-noone wil giue you fuch good vrds, behind your back to your face.

Bel. O I, I, I man, he's the onely courtier that I know there : but what do you thinke that I may come to by this.

Cap. God vdge mee, all *France* may hap die in your debt for this.

Bel. I am now wryting the defcription of his death.

Cap. Did he die in his ped.

Bel. You fhall heare : fufpition is the Mynion of great hearts,

no : I will not begin there : Imagine a great man were to be executed about the 7. houre in a gloomy morning.

Capt. As it might bee *Sampfon* or fo, or great *Golias* that was kild by my Countriman.

Bel. Right fir, thus I expreffe it in yong *Aftianax*. Now the wilde people greedy of their griefes, Longing to fee, that which their thoughts abhord, Preuented day, and rod on their owne roofes.

Cap. Could the little horfe that ambled on the top of Paules, cary all the people ; els how could they ride on the roofes !

Bel. O fir, tis a figure in Poetry, marke how tis
    followed,
Rod on their owne roofes,
Making all Neighboring houfes tilde with men ;
tilde with men I ift not good.

Cap. By Sefu, and it were tilde all with naked
Imen twere better.

Bel. You fhall heare no more ; pick your eares,
they are fowle fir, what are you fir pray ?

Cap. A Captaine fir, and a follower of god *Mars.*

Bel. *Mars, Bachus,* and I loue *Apollo* ! a Captaine ! then I pardon you fir, and Captaine what wud
you preffe me for ?

Cap. For a witty ditty, to a Sentill-oman, that I
am falne in with all, ouer head and eares in affections,
and naturall defires.

Bel. An Acroftick were good vpon her name me
thinkes.

Cap. Croffe fticks : I wud not be too croffe
Maifter Poet : yet if it bee beft to bring her name
in queftion, her name is miftris *Dorothy Hornet.*

Bel. The very confumption that wafts my Sonne,
and the Ayme that hung lately vpon mee : doe you
loue this Miftris *Dorothy* ?

Cap. Loue her ! there is no Captaines wife in
England, can haue more loue put vpon her, and yet
Ime fure Captaines wiues, haue their pellies full of
good mens loues.

Be. And does fhe loue you ? has there paft any
great matter betweene you ?

Cap. As great a matter, as a whole coach, and
a horfe and his wife are gon too and fro betweene
vs.

Bel. Is fhee ? ifayth Captaine, bee valiant and tell
trueth, is fhe honeft ?

Cap. Honeft ? god vdge me, fhee's as honeft,
as a Punck, that cannot abide fornication, and
lechery.

Bel. Looke you Captaine, Ile fhew you why I

aſke, I hope you thinke my wenching daies are paſt, yet Sir, here's a letter that her father, brought me from her and inforc'd mee to take this very day.

Enter a Seruant and Whiſpers.

Cap. Tis for ſome loue-ſong to ſend to me, I hold my life.

Bel. This falls out pat, my man tells mee, the party is at my dore, ſhall ſhe come in Captaine ?

Cap. O I, I, put her in, put her in I pray now.

Exit Seru.

Bel. The letter ſaies here, that ſhe's exceeding ſick, and intreates me to viſit her : Captaine, lie you in ambuſh behind the hangings, and perhaps you ſhall heare the peece of a Commedy : ſhe comes, ſhe comes, make your ſelfe away.

Cap. Does the Poet play *Torkin* and caſt my *Lucrœſies* water too in hugger muggers : if he do, *Styanax* Tragedy was neuer ſo horrible bloudy-minded, as his Commedy ſhalbe,— *Tawſons* Captaine *Jenkins.*

Enter Doll.

Doll. Now, maſter Poet, I ſent for you.

Bell. And I came once at your Ladiſhips call.

Doll. My Ladiſhip and your Lordſhip lie both in one manner ; you have conjur'd up a ſweete ſpirit in mee, haue you not, Rimer ?

Bell. Why, *Medea !* what ſpirit ! wud I were a young man for thy ſake.

Doll. So wud I, for then thou couldſt doe mee no hurt : now thou doeſt.

Bell. If I were a yonker, it would be no Imodeſty in mee to be ſeene in thy company ; but to have ſnow in the lap of Iune, vile, vile ! yet come ; garlick has a white head and a greene ſtalke, then why ſhould not I ? lets bee merry : what ſaies the deuill to al the world ? for Ime ſure thou art carnally poſſeſt with him.

E

Doll. Thou haſt a filthy foot, a very filthy cariers foote.

Bell. A filthy ſhooe, but a fine foote : I ſtand not upon my foote I.

Cap. What ſtands he upon then ? with a pox, god bleſs us ?

Doll. A legge and a Calfe ! I haue had better of a butcher fortie times for carrying a body !—not worth begging by a Barber-ſurgeon.

Bell. Very good, you draw me and quarter me : fates keepe me from hanging.

Doll. And which moſt turnes up a womans ſto-mach, thou art an old hoary man ; thou haſt gon ouer the bridge of many years, and now art ready to drop into a graue : what doe I ſee then in that withered face of thine ?

Bell. Wrinkles ; grauity.

Doll. Wretchednes, griefe : old fellow thou haſt bewitch me ; I can neither eate for thee, nor ſleepe for thee, nor lie quietly in my bed for thee.

Cap. Vdsblood ! I did never ſee a white flea before I will clinge you ?

Doll. I was borne ſure, in the dog-dayes, Ime ſo unluky ; I, in whome neither a flaxen haire, yellow beard, French doublet, nor Spaniſh hoſe, youth nor perſonage, rich face nor mony, cold euer breed a true loue to any, euer to any man, am now beſotted, doate, am mad, for the carcas of a man ; and, as if I were a baud, no ring pleaſes me but a deaths head.

Cap. Seſu, are Imen ſo arſy-varſy.

Bell. Mad for me ? why, if the worme of luſt were wrigling within mee as it does in others, doſt thinke Ide crawl upon thee ; wud I low after thee, that art a comon calfe-bearer ?

Doll. I confeſſe it.

Cap. Doe you ? are you a towne cowe, and confeſſe you beare calues ?

Doll. I confeffe I haue bin an Inne for any gueft.

Cap. A pogs a your ftable-room ; is your Inne a baudy-houfe now ?

Doll. I confeffe (for I ha bin taught to hide nothing from my Surgeon, and thou art he,) I confeffe that old ftinking Surgeon like thyfelfe whom I call father, that *Hornet*, neuer fweat for me ; Ime none of his making.

Cap. You lie he makes you a punke *Hornet minor.*

Doll. Hees but a cheater, and I the falfe die hee playes withall, I power all my poifon out before thee, becaufe heareafter I will be cleane : fhun me not, loath me not, mocke me not. Plagues confound thee, I hate thee to the pit of hell, yet if thou goeft thither, ile follow thee, run, ayde doe what thou canft, ile run and ride ouer the world after thee.

Cap. Cockatrice : You, miftris *Salamanders,* that feare no burning, let my mare and my mares horfe, and my coach come running home agen ; and run to an hofpitall, and your Surgeons, and to knaues and panders, and to the tiuell and his tame to.

Doll. Fiend, art thou raifed to torment me ?

Bell. She loves you, Captain, honeftly.

Cap. Ile haue any man, oman, or cilde, by his eares, that faies a common drab can love a Sentillman honeftly, I will fell my Coach for a cart to have you to puncks hall, Pridewell.—I farge you in *Apollos* name, whom you belong to, fee her forthcoming, till I come and tiggle her, by and by, Sbloud, I was neuer Cozened with a more rafcall peece of mutton, fince I came out a the Lawer Countries.   *Exit.*

Bell. My dores are open for thee: be gon : woman !

Doll. This goates-peezle of thine—

Bell. Away I love no fuch implements in my houfe.

Doll. Doeft not ? am I but an implement ? by all

the maidenheads that are loſt in *London* in a yeare
(and thats a great oth), for this trick, other manner of
women than myſelfe ſhall come to this houſe only to
laugh at thee ; and if thou wouldſt labour thy heart
out, thou ſhalt not do withal.   *Exit.*

Enter Seruant.

Bell. Is this my poetical fury : how now, ſir !

Serv. Maſter *Maybery* and his wife ſir i'th next
roome.

Bell. What are they doing ſir ?

Serv. Nothing, ſir, that I ſee ; but only wud ſpeake
with you.

Bell. Enter 'em : this houſe will be too hot for
mee, if this wench caſt me into theſe ſweates, I muſt
ſhifte myſelfe for pure neceſſity. Haunted with
ſprites in my old daies !

Enter Maybery *booted, his Wife with him.*

May. A Commedy, a Canterbury tale ſmells not
halfe ſo ſweete as the Commedy I haue for thee, old
Poet : thou ſhalt write vpon't, Poet.

Bell. Nay, I will write vpon't, ift bee a Commedie,
for I have beene at a moſt villanous female Tragedie :
come, the plot, the plot.

May. Let your man give you the bootes preſently :
the plot lies in *Ware,* my white Poet.—Wife thou and
I this night will have mad ſport in *Ware*; marke me
well, Wife, in *Ware.*

Wif. At your pleaſure, ſir.

May. Nay, it ſhal be at your pleaſure, Wife.—
Looke you, ſir, looke you : *Fetherſtones* boy, like an
honeſt crack-halter, layd open all to one of my prentices ; (for boys, you know, like women, love to be
doing.)

Bell. Very good : to the plot.

May. *Fetherſtone*, like a crafty mutton-monger, perſuades *Greenſhield* to be run through the body.

Bell. Strange ! through the body !

May· Ay, man, to take phiſick : he does ſo, he's put to his purgation ; then, ſir, what does me *Fetherſtone* but counterfits a letter from an inn-keeper of Doncaſter, to fetch *Greenſhield* (who is needy you know) to a keepers lodge in Enfeild-chace, a certain vncle, where *Greenſhield* ſhould receiue mony due to him in behalfe of his wife.

Bell. His wife ! is *Greenſhield* married ? I haue heard him ſweare he was a bachiler.

Wife. So haue I a hundred times.

May. The knaue has more wiues than the Turke, he has a wife almoſt in euery ſhire in *England*, this parcel-Gentlewoman is that In-keepers Daughter of *Doncaſter*.

Bell. Hath ſhe the entertainement of her fore-fathers ? wil ſhe keepe all commers company ?

May. She helps to paſſe away ſtale Capons, ſower wine, and muſty prouander : but to the purpoſe, this traine was laid by the baggage herſelf, and *Fetherſtone*, who it ſeems makes her huſband a vnicorne, and to giue fire to't, *Greenſheild*, like an Arrant wittall intreates his friend to ride before his wife, and fetch the money, becauſe taking bitter pills, he ſhould proue but a looſe fellow if he went, and ſo durſt not go.

Bell. And ſo the poore Stag is to bee hunted in *Enfeild chace*.

May. No ſir, Maiſter poet there you miſſe the plot, *Fetherſtone* and my Lady *Greenſheild* are rid to batter away their light commodities in *Ware, Enfeild-chace* is to cold for 'em.

Bell. In *Ware* !

May. In durty *Ware* : I forget my ſelfe wife, on with your ryding ſuite, and cry *North-ward hoe*, as the boy at Powles ſaies, let my Prentice get vp before thee, and man thee to *Ware*, lodge in the Inne I told thee, ſpur cut and away.

Wife. Well fir.   *Exit.*

Bell. Stay, ftay, whats the bottom of this riddle? why fend you her away?

May. For a thing my little hoary *Poet*: looke thee, I fmelt out my noble ftincker *Greenfheild* in his Chamber, and as tho my heart ftringes had bin crackt, I wept, and fighd, & thumpd, and thump'd, and rau'd and randed, and raild, and told him how my wife was now growne as common as baibery, and that fhee had hierd her Taylor to ride with her to *Ware*, to meete a Gentleman of the Court.

Bel. Good; and how tooke he this drench downe.

May. Like Egs and Mufcadine, at a gulp: hee cries out prefently, did not I tell you old man, that fheed win my game when fhe came to bearing? hee railes vpon her, wills me to take her in the Act; to put her to her white fheete, to bee diuorc'd, and for all his guts are not fully fcourd by his Pottecary, hee's pulling on his bootes, & will ride along with vs; lets mufter as many as wee can.

Bel. It wilbe excellent fport, to fee him and his owne wife meete in *Ware*, wilt not? I, I, weele haue a whole Regiment of horfe with vs.

May. I ftand vpon thornes, tel I fhake him bith hornes: come, bootes boy, we muft gallop all the way, for the Sin you know is done with turning vp the white of an eye, will you ioyne your forces.

Bel. Like a *Hollander* againft a *Dunkirke*.

May. March then, this curfe is on all letchers throwne,

They giue hornes and at laft, hornes are their owne.

                                    Exit.

Enter Captaine Ienkins, *and* Allom.

Allo. Set the beft of your little diminitiue legges before, and ride poft I pray.

Allo. Is it poffible that miftris *Doll* fhould bee fo bad?

Cap. Poffible ! Sbloud tis more eafie for an oman to be naught, than for a foldier to beg, and thats horrible eafie, you know.

Al. I but to connicatch vs all fo grofly.

Cap. Your *Norfolke* tumblers are but zanyes to connicatching punckes.

Allom. Shee gelded my purfe of fifty pounds in ready money.

Cap. I will geld all the horfes in fiue hundred Sheires, but I will ride ouer her, and her cheaters, and her *Hornets*; Shee made a ftarke Affe of my Coach-horfe, and there is a putter-box, whome fhee fpred thick vpon her white bread, and eate him vp, I thinke fhee has fent the poore fellow to *Gelderland*, but I will marfe prauely in and out, and packe againe vpon all the low countries in Chriftendom, as *Holland* and *Zeland* and *Netherland*, and *Cleueland* too, and I will be drunke and caft with maifter *Hans van Belch*, but I will fmell him out.

Allom. Doe fo and weele draw all our arrowes of reuenge vp to the head but weele hit her for her villany.

Cap. I will traw as petter, and as vrfe weapons as arrewes vp to the head, lug you it fhal be warrants to giue her the whippe deedle.

Allom. But now fhe knowes fhees difcouered, fheele take her bells and fly out of our reach.

Cap. Fle with her pells ! ownds I know a parifh that fal tag downe all the pells and fell em to Capten *Ienkens*, to do him good, and if pelle will fly, weele flie too, vnles, the pell-ropes hang vs : will you amble vp and downe to maifter Iuftice by my fide, to haue this rafcall *Hornet* in corum, and fo, to make her hold her whoars peace.

Allom. Ile amble or trot with you Capten : you told me, fhe threatened her champions fhould cut for her ; if fo, wee may haue the peace of her.

Cap. *O mon du* ! *u dguin* ! follow your leader, *Ienken* fhall cut, and Slice, as worfe as they : come I

fcorne to haue any peace of her, or of any onam, but
open warres.   *Exeunt.*

Enter Bellamont, Maybery, Greenſheild, Phillip,
      Leuerpoole, Chartley : all booted.

Bell. What ? will theſe yong Gentlemen to helpe
vs to catch this freſh Salmon, ha ? *Phillip* ! are they
thy friends.

Phil. Yes Sir.

Bell. We are beholding to you Gentlemen that
youle fill our conſort I ho ſeene your faces me thinkes
before ; and I cannot informe my ſelfe where.

Both. May be ſo Sir.

Bell. Shalls to horſe, hears a tickler : heigh : to
horſe.

May. Come Switts and Spurres ! lets mount our
Cheualls : merry quoth a.

Bell. Gentlemen ſhall I ſhoote a fooles bolt out
among you all, becauſe weele be ſure to be merry.

Omn. What iſt ?

Bell. For mirth on the high way, will make vs rid
ground faſter then if theeues were at our tayles, what
ſay yee to this, lets all practiſe ieſts one againſt
another, and hee that has the beſt ieſt throwne vpon
him, and is moſt gald, betweene our riding foorth
and comming in, ſhall beare the charge of the whole
iourney.

Omn. Content ifaith.

Bell. Wee ſhall fitte one a you with a Cox-combe
at *Ware* I belieue.

May. Peace.

Green. Iſt a bargen.

Omn. And hands clapt vpon it.

Bel. Stay, yonders the Dolphin without Biſhops-
gate, where our horſes are at rack and manger, and
wee are going paſt it : come croſſe ouer : and what
place is this ?

May. Bedlam iſt not ?

Bell. Where the mad-men are, I neuer was amongſt them, as you loue me Gentlemen, lets ſee what Greekes are within.

Green. Wee ſhall ſtay too long.

Bell. Not a whit, *Ware* will ſtay for our comming I warrant you : come a ſpurt and away, lets bee mad once in our dayes : this is the doore.

Enter Full-moone.

May. Saue you ſir, may we ſee ſome a your mad-folkes, doe you keepe em ?

Full. Yes.

Bell. Pray beſtow your name ſir ʋpon vs.

Full. My name is *Full-moone.*

Bell. You well deſerue this office good maiſter *Full-moone*: and what mad-caps haue you in your houſe.

Enter the Phiſition.

Ful. Diuerſe.

May. Gods ſo, ſee, ſee, whats hee walkes yonder, is he mad.

Full. Thats a Muſition, yes hee's beſides him-ſelfe.

Bell. A Muſition, how fell he mad for Gods ſake ?

Ful. For loue of an *Italian* Dwarfe.

Bell. Has he beene in *Italy* then ?

Full. Yes and ſpeakes they ſay all manner of languages.

Enter the Bawd.

Omn. Gods ſo, looke, looke, whats ſhee.

Bell. The dancing Beare : a pritty well-fauourd little woman.

Full. They ſay, but I know not, that ſhe was a Bawd, and was frighted out of her wittes by fire.

Bel.   May we talke with 'em maifter *Ful·moone.*

Full.   Yes and you will; I muft looke about for
I haue vnruly tenants.   *Exit.*

Bell.   What haue you in this paper honeft friend ?

Gree.   Is this he has al manner of languages, yet
fpeakes none.

Baud.   How doe you Sir *Andrew*, will you fend for
fome aquauite for me, I haue had no drinke neuer
fince the laft great raine that fell.

Bell.   No thats a lie.

Baud.   Nay, by gad, then, you lie, for all you're Sir
Andrew.   I was a dapper rogue in Portingal voyage,
not an inch broad at the heele and yet thus high : I
fcornd, I can tell you, to be druncke with rain-water
then, fir, in thofe golden and filuer dayes ; I had fweet
bits then, fir *Andrew.*   How doe you, good brother
Timothy ?

Bell.   You haue been in much trouble fince that
voyage.

Baud.   Neuer in bridewell, I proteft, as I'm a virgin, for I could neuer abide that bridewell, I proteft,
I was once fick, and I took my water in a bafket, and
carried it to a doctors.

Phil.   In a bafket ?

Baud.   Yes, fir : you arrant foole there was a vrinall
in it.

Phil.   I cry you mercy.

Baud.   The doctor told me I was with child.   How
many Lords, Knights, Gentlemen, Cittizens, and
others, promifed me to be godfathers to that child !
'twas not God's will : the prentifes made a riot vpon
my glaffe windows, the Shrove-tuefday following, and
I mifcarried.

Omn.   O do not weep !

Baud.   I ha' caufe to weep : I truft gintlewomen
their diet fometimes a fortnight : lend gentlemen holland fhirts, and they fweat 'em out at tennis ; and no
reftitution, and no reftitution.   But Ile take a new
order : I will haue but fix ftewed prunes in a difh, and

fome of Mother Wall's cakes; for my beft cuftomers
are taylors.

Omn.   Taylors! ha, ha!

Baud.   I taylors: giue me your London prentice; your country gentlemen are growne too
politicke.

Bell.   But what fay you to fuch young gentlemen
as thefe are?

Baud.   Foh! they, as foon as they come to their
lands, get vp to London, and, like fquibs that run
vpon lyncs, they keep a fpitting of fire and cracking
till they ha fpent all; and when my fquib is out, what
fays his punk? foh, he ftinks.

Enter the mufition.

Methought, this other night I faw a pretty fight,
    Which pleafed me much.
A comely country mayd, not fqueamifh nor afraid,
    To let Gentlemen touch:
I fold her maidenhead once, and I fold her
        maidenhead twice,
    And I fold it laft to an alderman of *York*:
And then I had fold it thrice.

Mus.   You fing fcuruily.

Baud.   Marry, muff, fing thou better, for Ile go
fleepe my old fleepes.   *Exit.*

Bell.   What are you a-doing, my friend.

Mus.   Pricking, pricking.

Bell.   What doe you meane by pricking?

Mus.   A Gentleman-like quality.

Bell.   This fellow is fome what prouder and fulliner
then the other.

May.   Oh; fo be moft of your mufitions.

Mus.   Are my teeth rotten?

Omn.   No, fir.

Mus.   Then I am no comfit-maker nor vintner

I do not get wenches in my drinke.—Are you a
mufition ?

Bell. Yes.

Mus. Wele be fworn brothers, then, looke you,
fweet rogue.

Green. Gods fo, now I think vpon't, a ieft is crept
into my head : fteale away, if you loue me.

Exeunt : mufition fings.

Mufi. Was euer any marchants baud fet better I
fet it : walke Ime a cold, this white fattin is too thin
vnles it be cut, for then the Sunne enters : can you
fpeake Italian too, *Sapete Italiano.*

Bell. *Vn poco.*

Mufi. Sblood if it be in you, Ile poake it out of
you ; *vn poco*, come March lie heare with me but till
the fall of the leafe, and if you haue but *poco Italiano*
in you, Ile fill you full of more *poco* March.

Bell. Come on.   *Exeunt.*

Enter Maybery, Greenefhilde, Philip, Full-moone,
Leuerpoole, *and* Chartely.

Gree. Good Maifter *Mayberie, Philip*, if you be
kind Gentlemen vphold the ieft : your whole voiage is
payd for.

May. Follow it then.

Ful. The old Gentleman fay you, why he talkt
euen now as well in his wittes as I do my felfe, and
lookt as wifely.

Gree. No matter how he talkes, but his Pericra-
nion's perifht.

Ful. Where is he pray ?

Phil. Mary with the Mufition, and is madder by
this time.

Char. Hee's an excellent Mufition himfelfe, you
muft note that.

May. And hauing met one fit for his one tooth :
you fee hee fkips from vs.

Green. The troth is maifter *Full-moone,* diuers traines haue bin laide to bring him hither, without gaping of people, and neuer any tooke effect till now.

Ful. How fell he mad?

Green. For a woman, looke you fir: here's a crowne to prouide his fupper: hee's a Gentleman of a very good houfe, you fhall bee paid well if you conuert him; to morrow morning, bedding, and a gowne fhall be fent in, and wood and coale.

Ful. Nay fir, he muft ha no fire.

Green. No, why looke what ftraw you buy for him, fhall returne you a whole harueft.

Omnes. Let his ftraw be frefh and fweet we befeech you fir?

Green. Get a couple of your fturdieft fellowes, and bind him I pray, whilft wee flip out of his fight.

Ful. Ile hamper him, I warrant Gentlemen. *Exit.*

Omnes. Excellent.

May. But how will my noble Poet take it at my hands, to betray him thus.

Omn. Foh, tis but a ieft, he comes.

Enter Mufition and Bellamont.

Bell. *Perdonate mi, fi Io dimando del voftro nome:* oh, whether fhrunke you: I haue had fuch a mad dialogue here.

Omn. Wee ha bin with the other mad folkes.

May. And what fayes he and his prick-fong?

Bell. Wee were vp to the eares in *Italian* ifaith.

Omn. In *Italian*; O good maifter *Bellamont* lets heare him.

Enter Full-moone, *and two Keepers.*

Bell. How now, Sdeath what do you meane? are you mad?

Ful. Away firra, bind him, hold faft: you want a wench firra, doe you?

Bell. What wench ? will you take mine armes from me, being no Heralds ? let goe you Dogs.

Ful. Bind him, be quiet: come, come, dogs, fie, & a gentleman.

Bell. Maifter *Maibery*, *Philip*, maifter *Maibery*, vds foot.

Ful. Ile bring you a wench, are you mad for a wench.

Bell. I hold my life my comrads haue put this fooles cap vpon thy head : to gull me : I fmell it now : why doe you heare *Full-moone*, let me loofe ; for Ime not mad ; Ime not mad by Iefu.

Ful. Aske the Gentlemen that.

Bel. Bith Lord I'me afwell in my wits, as any man ith' houfe, & this is a trick put vpon thee by thefe gallants in pure knaucry.

Ful. Ile trie that, anfwer me to this queftion : loofe his armes a little, looke you fir, three Geefe nine pence ; every Goofe three pence, whats that a Goofe, roundly, roundly one with another.

Bel. Sfoot do you bring your Geefe for me to cut vp.   *ftrike him foundly, and kick him.*

Enter all.

Omn. Hold, hold, bind him maifter *Full-moone.*

Ful. Binde him you, hee has payd me all, Ile haue none of his bonds not I, vnleffe I could recouer them better.

Gre. Haue I giuen it you maifter Poet, did the Lime-bufh take.

Ma. It was his warrant fent thee to *Bedlam*, old *Iack Bellamont* : and, Maifter *Full-i'-the-moon*, our warrant difcharges him.—Poet, wele all ride vpon thee to *Ware*, and backe againe, I feare, to thy coft.

Bell. If you do, I muft bear you,—Thank you, Maifter *Greenfhield* ; I will not die in your debt.— Farewell, you mad rafcalls.—To horfe, come.—'Tis well done, 'twas well done. You may laugh, you fhall

!augh, gentlemen. If the gudgeon had been fwallowed by one of you, it had been vile ; but by Gad, 'tis nothing, for your beft Poets, indeed, are mad for the moft part.—Farewell, good-man *Full-moone.*

Full. Pray, gentlemen, if you come by, call in.

Exit.

Bell. Yes, yes, when they are mad.—Horfe your felues now, if you be men.

May. Hee gallop muft that after women rides, Get our wiues out of Towne, they take long ftrides.

Exeunt.

ACTVS 5. *SCÆNA* 1.

Enter old Maybery *and* Bellamont.

May. But why haue you brought vs to the wrong inn, and withal poffeft *Greenfhield* that my wife is not in town ? when my projeét fhas, that I would haue brought him vp into the chamber where young *Fether-ftone* and his wife lay, and fo all his artillery fhould haue recoiled into his own bofome.

Bell. O, it will fall out farre better : you fhall fee my reuenge will haue a more neat and vnexpeéted conueyance. He hath been all vp and downe the towne to enquire for a Londoners wife : none fuch is to be found, for I haue mewd your wife vp already. Marry, he hears of a *Yorkfhire* gentlewoman at next inn, and that's all the commodity *Ware* affords at this inftant. Now, fir, he very politickly imagines that your wife is rode to *Puckridge*, fiue mile further ; for, faith he, in fuch a town, where hofts will be familiar, and tapfters faucy, and chamberlains worfe then theeues' intelligencers, they'll neuer put foot out of ftirrop ; either at *Puckridge* or *Wades-Mill*, faith he, you fhall find them ; and becaufe our horfes are weary, he's gone to take vp poft-horfe. My counfel is only this, —when he comes in, faign your felfe very melancholy, fweare you will ride no further ; and this is your part

of the comedy : the fequel of the ieft fhall come like
money borrowed of a courtier, and paid within the
day, a thing ftrange and vnexpected.

Enter Greenfhield.

May. Enough, I ha't.

Bell. He comes.

Green. Come, gallants, the poft-horfe are ready ;
'tis but a quarter of an hours riding ; weele ferret them
and firk them, in-faith.

Bell. Are they growne politick ? when do you fee
honefty couet corners, or a gentleman thats no thief
lie in the inn of a carrier ?

May. Nothing hath vndone my wife but too much
riding.

Bell. She was a pritty piece of a poet indeed, and
in her difcourfe would, as many of your goldfmiths'
wiues do, draw her fimile from precious ftones fo
wittily, as redder then your ruby, harder then your
diamond, and fo from ftone to ftone in leffe time then
a man can draw on a ftraight boot, as if fhe had been
an excellent lapidary.

Green. Come, will you to horfe, fir ?

May. No, let her go to the deuil, and fhe will : Ile
not ftir a foot further.

Green. Gods precious, ift come to this ?—Perfuade
him, as you are a gentleman : there will be ballads
made of him, and the burthen thereof will be,—If you
had rode out 5 mile forward, he had found the fatal
houfe of *Brainford* northward ; O hone, hone, hone,
o nonero !

Bell. You are merry, fir.

Green. Like your citizen, I neuer thinke of my
debts when I am a horfeback.

Bell. You imagin you are riding from your
creditors.

Green. Good, in faith.—Will you to horfe ?

May. Ile ride no further.

Green. Then Ile difcharge the poſtmaſter.—Waſt
not a pretty wit of mine, maiſter poet, to haue had him
rod into *Puckridge* with a horn before him? ha,
waſt not?

Bell. Good ſooth, excellent: I was dull in appre-
hending it: but come ſince we muſt ſtay: wele be
mery, chamberlaine call in the muſick, bid the
Tapſters & maids come vp and dance, what weel
make a night of it, harke you maiſters, I haue an excellent ieſt to make old *Maibery* merry, Sſoote weele
haue him merry.

Green. Lets make him drunke then, a ſimple catch-
ing wit I.

Bel. Go thy waies, I know a Nobleman would take
ſuch a delight in thee.

Green. Why ſo he would in his foole.

Bell. Before God but hee would make a difference,
hee would keepe you in Sattin, but as I was a ſaying
weel haue him merry: his wife is gon to *Puckridge*,
tis a wench makes him melancholy, tis a wench muſt
make him mery: we muſt help him to a wench.
When your cittizen comes into his Inne, wet & cold,
dropping, either the hoſtis or one of her maids,
warmes his bed, puls on his night-cap, cuts his cornes
puts out the candle, bids him command ought, if he
want ought: and ſo after maiſter cittiner ſleepes as
quietly, as if he lay in his owne low-country of *Holland*, his own linnen I meane ſir, we muſt haue a
wench for him.

Gree. But wher's this wench to be found, here are
al the moueable peticotes of the houſe.

Bil. At the next Inne there lodged to night——

Gree. Gods pretious a *Yorkeſhire* Gentlewoman;
I ha't, Ile angle for her preſently, weele haue him
merry.

Bel. Procure ſome Chamberlaine to Pander for
you.

Gree. No Ile be Pander my ſelfe, becauſe weele
be merry.

F

Bell. Will you, will you?

Gree. But how? be a Pander as I am a gentleman? that were horrible, Ile thruſt my ſelf into the
out-ſide of a Fawlconer in towne heere: & now I
thinke on't there are a company of country plaiers,
that are to come to towne here, ſhall furniſh mee with
haire and beard: if I do not bring her, . . . wilbe
wondrous merry.

Bel. About it looke you ſir, though ſhe beare her
far aloofe, and her body out of diſtance, ſo her mind be
comming 'tis no matter.

Green. Get old *Maiberry* merry: that any man
ſhould take to heart thus the downe fall of a woman,
I thinke when he comes home poore ſnaile, heele
not dare to peepe forth of doores leaſt his hornes
vſher him.   *Exit.*

Bel. Go thy wayes, there be more in *England*
weare large eares and hornes, then Stagges and
Aſſes: excellent hee rides poſte with a halter about
his neck.

May. How now wilt take?

Bel. Beyond expeſtation: I haue perſwaded him
the onely way to make you merry, is to helpe you
to a wench, and the foole is gone to pander his owne
wife hether.

May. Why heele know her?

Bel. She hath beene maskt euer ſince ſhe came
into the Inne, for feare of diſcouery.

May. Then ſheele know him.

Bel. For that his owne vnfortunate wit helpt my
laſie inuention, for he hath diſguiſd himſelfe like a
Fawkner, in Towne heare, hoping in that procuring
ſhape, to doe more good vpon her, then in the out-
ſide of a Gentleman.

May. Young *Fetherſtone* will know him?

Bel. Hee's gone into the towne, and will not returne this halfe houre.

May. Excellent if ſhe would come.

Bel. Nay vpon my life ſheele come: when ſhe

enters remember fome of your young bloud, talke as
fome of your gallant commoners will, Dice and
drinke: freely: do not call for Sack, leaft it betray
the coldneffe of your man-hood, but fetch a caper
now & then, to make the gold chinke in your pockets:
I fo.

May. Ha old Poet, lets once ftand to it for the
credit of *Milke-ftrecte.* Is my wife acquainted with
this.

Bel. She's perfect, & will come out vpon her qu,
I warrant you.

May. Good wenches infaith: fils fome more
Sack heare.

Bel. Gods pretious, do not call for Sack by any
meanes.

May. Why then giue vs a whole Lordfhip for life
in *Rhenifh,* with the reuerfion in Sugar.

Bell. Excellent.

May. It were not amiffe if we were dancing.

Bell. Out vpon't, I fhall neuer do it.

Enter Greenfheild *difguifed, with miftreffe* Greenfheild.

Green. Out of mine noftrils tapfter, thou fmelft
like *Guild-hall* two daies after *Simon* and *Iude,* of
drinke moft horribly, off with thy mafke fweete finner
of the North: thefe maskes are foiles to good faces,
and to bad ones they are like new fatin outfides to
loufy linings.

Kate. O, by no means, fir. Your merchant will
not open a whole peece to his beft cuftomer: he that
buys a woman muft take her as fhe falls. Ile vnmask
my hand; heres the fample.

Green. Goe to, then, old Poet. I haue tane her
vp already as a pinnis bound for the ftraights; fhe
knows her burden yonder.

2 F

Bell. Lady, you are welcome. Yon is the old gentleman ; and obferue him, he's not one of your fat city chuffs, whofe great belly argues that the felicity of his life confifts in capon, fack, and fincere honefty ; but a leane fpare bountiful gallant one that hath an old wife and a young performance ; whofe reward is not the rate of a captain newly come out of the Low-Countries, or a *Yorkfhiere* attorny in good contentious practice, fome angel, —no, the proportion of your welthy citizen to his wench is her chamber, her diet, her phifick, her apparel, her painting, her monkey, her pandar, her everything. Youle fay, your young gentleman is your only feruice, that lies before you like a calues head, with his braines fome halfe yeard from him: but, I affure you, they muft not onely haue variety of foolery, but alfo of wenches : whereas your confcionable greybeard of Farrington-within will keep himfelf to the ruins of one caft waiting-woman an age : and perhaps, when he's paft all other good works, to wipe out falfe waights and twenty i' the hundred, marry her.

Green. O, well bould *Tom* (   ) we haue prefedents for't.

Kate. But I haue a hufband fir.

Bell. You haue ? If the knaue thy hufband be rich, make him poor, that he may borrow money of this merchant, and be laid vp in the Counter or Ludgate ; fo it fhall bee confcience in you old gentleman, when he hath feized all thy goods, to take the horne and maintain thee.

Green. O, well bould, *Tom* (   ) we haue prefedents for't.

Kate. Well, if you be not a nobleman, you are fome great valiant gentleman by your bearth and the fafhion of your beard, and do but thus to make the citizen merry, becaufe you owe him fome money.

Bell. O, you are a wag.

May. You are very welcome.

Green. He is tane; excellent, excellent! theres
one will make him merry. Is it any imputation to
help ones friend to a wench?

Bell. No more than at my lords entreaty to help
my lady to a pretty waiting-woman. If he had giuen
you a gelding, or the reuerfion of fome monopoly, or
a new fute of fatin, to haue done this, happily your
fatin would haue fmelt of the pander: but what's
done freely, comes, like a prefent to an old lady, without any reward: and what is done without any reward, come like wounds to a foldier, very honourably
notwithftanding.

May. This is my breeding, gentlewoman: and
whether trauel you?

Kate. To London, fir, as the old tale goes, to feeke
my fortune.

May. Shall I be your fortune, lady?

Kate. O, pardon me, fir; Ile haue fome young
landed heir to be my fortune, for they fauour fhe-
fooles more than citizens.

May. Are you married?

Kate. Yes, but my hufband is in garrifon i' the
Low-Countries, is his colonels bawd, and his captain's
iefter: he fent me word ouer that he will thriue, for
though his apparel lie i' the Lombard, he keeps his
confcience i' the mufter-book.

May. He may doe his country good feruice,
lady.

Kate. I as many of your captains do, that fight,
as the geefe faued the Capitol, only with prattling.
Well, well, if I were in fome noblemans hands now,
may be he would not take a thoufand pounds for
me.

May. No.

Kate. No, fir; and yet may be at years end would
giue me a brace of hundreth pounds to marry me to
his baily or the folicitor of his law-fuits.—Whofe this,
I befeech you?

Enter Miſtreſs Mayberry, *her hair looſe, with the Hoſtice.*

Hoſt.　I pray you, forſooth, be patient.

Bell.　Paſſion of my heart, Miſtreſs Mayberry.

　　　　　　　　　　　　Exeunt Fiddlers.

Green.　Now will ſhee put ſome notable trick, vpon her cuckoldly huſband.

May.　Why, how now, wife! what means this? ha?

Miſt. May.　Well, I am very well. O my vnfortunate parents would you had buried me quick, when you linkt me to this miſery.

Ma.　O wife, be patient! I haue more cauſe to raile wife.

Miſt. May.　You haue, proue it, proue it: wheres the Courtier, you ſhould haue tane in my boſome: Ile ſpit my gall in's face, that can tax me of any diſhonour: haue I loſt the pleaſure of mine eyes, the ſweetes of my youth, the wiſhes of my bloud: and the portion of my friends, to be thus diſhonord, to be reputed vild in *London*, whilſt my huſhand prepares common diſeaſes for me at *Ware*, O god O god.

Be.　Prettily well diſſembled.

Hoſt.　As I am true hoſtice you are to blame ſir, what are you maiſters: Ile know what you are afore you depart maiſters, doſt thou leaue thy Chamber in an honeſt Inne, to come and inueagle my coſtomers, and you had ſent for me vp, and kiſt me and vſde me like an hoſtice, twold neuer haue greeued mee, but to do it to a ſtranger.

Kate.　Ile leaue you ſir.

May.　Stay, why how now ſweete gentlewoman, cannot I come forth to breath my ſelfe, but I muſt bee haunted, raile vpon olde *Bellamont*, that he may diſcouer them, you remember *Fetherſtone Greenſheild*.

Miſt. May.　I remember them, I, they are two as coging, diſhonorable dambd forſworne beggerly gentle-

men, as are in al London, and ther's a reuerent old
gentleman to, your pander in my confcience.

Bel. Lady, I wil not as the old goddes were wont,
fweare by the infernall *Stix*; but by all the mingled
wine in the feller beneath, and the fmoke of Tobacco
that hath fumed ouer the veffailes, I did not procure
your husband this banqueting difh of fuckket looke
you behold the parenthefis.

Hoft. Nay Ile fee your face too.

Kat. My deare vnkind husband; I proteft to
thee I haue playd this knauifh part only to be
witty.

Gree. That I might bee prefently turned into a
matter more fodllid then horne, into Marble.

Bel. Your husband gentlewoman: why hee neuer
was a fouldier.

Kat. I but a Lady got him prickt for a Captaine,
I warrant you, he wil anfwere to the name of Captaine, though hee bee none: like a Lady that wil not
think fcorne to anfwere to the name of her firft husband; though he weare a Sope-boyler.

Green. Hange of thou diuill, away.

Kat. No, no, you fled me tother day,
When I was with child you ran away,
But fince I haue caught you now.

Green. A pox of your wit and your finging.

Bel. Nay looke you fir, fhe muft fing becaufe weele
be merry, what though you rod not fiue mile forward,
you haue found that fatall houfe at *Brainford* North-
ward. O hone, ho ho na ne ro.

Green. God refufe mee Gentlemen, you may laugh
and bee merry: but I am a Cockold and I thinke you
knew of it, who lay ith fegges with you to night wild-
ducke.

Kat. No body with me, as I fhall be faued; but
Maifter *Fetherftone*, came to meete me as far as *Roi-
ftone.*

Green. Fetherftone.

May. See the hawke that firft ftoopt, my phefant

is kild by the Spaniell that firſt ſprang all of our ſide
wife.

Bel. Twas a pretty wit of you ſir, to haue had
him rod into Puckeridge with a horne before him ; ha :
waſt not ;

Green. Good.

Bel. Or where a Cittizen keepes his houſe, you
know tis not as a Gentleman keepes his Chamber for
debt, but as you ſayd euen now very wiſely, leaſt his
hornes ſhould vſher him.

Green. Very good *Fetherſtone* he comes.

Enter Fetherſtone.

Feth. Luke *Greeneſhield* Maiſter *Maybery*, old
Poet : *Mol* and *Kate*, moſt hapily incounterd, vdſlife
how came you heather, by my life the man lookes
pale.

Green. You are a villaine, and Ile mak't good
vpon you, I am no ſeruingman, to feede upon your reuerſion.

Feth. Go to the ordinary then.

Bel. This is his ordinary ſir & in this ſhe is
like a London ordinary : her beſt getting comes by
the box.

Green. You are a dambd villaine.

Feth. O by no means.

Green. No, vdſlife, Ile go inſtantly take a purſe,
be apprehended and hang'd for't, better then be a
Cockold.

Feth. Beſt firſt make your confeſſion ſirra.

Green. 'Tis this thou haſt not vſed me like a
gentleman.

Feth. A gentleman ! thou a gentleman ! thou art
a taylor.

Bell. Ware preaching.

Feth. No, ſirrah, if you will confeſs ought, tell how
thou haſt wronged that vertuous gentlewoman : how
thou laieſt at her two yeare together, to make her

difhoneft ; how thou wouldft fend me thither with letters ; how duly thou wouldft watch the citizens'-wiues' vacation, which is twice a-day. namely the Exchange-time, twelue at noon, and fix at night ; and where fhe refufed thy importunity and vowd to tell her hufband, thou wouldft fall down vpon thy knees, and entreat her for the loue of heauen, if not to eafe thy violent affeſtion, at leaft to conceal it,—to which her pity and fimple vertue confented ; howthou tookeft her wedding-ring from her; met thefe two gentlemen at *Ware*; fained a quarrel; and the ref. is apparent. This only remains,—what wrong the poor gentlewoman hath fince receaued by our intolerable lye, I am moft heartily forry for, and to thy bofom will maintain all I haue faid to he honeft.

May. Viſtory, wife ! thou art quit by proclamation.

Bell. Sir you are an honeft man : I haue known an arrant thief for peaching made an officer; giue me your hand, fir.

Kate. O filthy abhominable hufband, did you all this ?

May. Certainly he is no captain ; he blufhes.

Mift. May. Speak fir, did you euer know me anfwer your wifhes ?

Green. You are honeft ; very vertuoufly honeft.

Mift. May. I will, then, no longer be a loofe woman : I haue at my husbands pleafure tane upon me this habit of jelofy. Ime forry for you ; vertue glories not in the fpoil, but in the victory.

Bell. How fay you by that goodly fentence ? Look you, fir, you gallants vifit citizens houfes, as the *Spaniard* firft failed to the *Indies* : you pretend buying of wares or felling of lands ; but the end proues 'tis nothing but for difcouery and conqueft of their wiues for better maintenance. Why, look you, was he aware of thofe broken patience when you met him at *Ware* and poflefled him of the downfall of his wife ? You are a cuckold ; you have panderd your own wife

to this gentleman; better men haue done it, honeſt
Tom ( ), we haue preſidents for't. Hie you to *London.*
What is more catholick i'the city than for husbands
daily for to forgiue the nightly ſins of their bedfellows ?
If you like not that courſe, but to intend to be rid of
her, rifle her at a tauern, where you may ſwallow
down ſome fifty wiſeacres, ſons and heirs to old tenements and common gardens, like ſo many raw yeolkes
with muſcadine to bedward.

Kate. O filthy knaue, doſt compare a woman of
my carriage to a horſe ?

Bell. And no diſparagement; for a woman to
haue a high forehead, a quicke eare, a full eye, a wide
noſtril, a ſleeke ſkin, a ſtraight back, a round hip, and
ſo forth, is moſt comely.

Kate. But is a great belly comely in a horſe, ſir ?

Bell. No, lady.

Kate. And what think you of it in a woman, I
pray you ?

Bell. Certainly I am put down at my own weapon :
I therefore recant the rifling. No, there is a new trade
come up for caſt gentlewomen, of peeriwip-making :
let your wife ſet vp i'the Strand; and yet I doubt
whither ſhe may or no, for they ſay the women haue
got it to be a corporation. If you can, you may make
good vſe of it, for you ſhall haue as good a coming-in
by hair (though it be but a falling commodity), and
by other fooliſh tiring, as any between Saint *Clements*
and *Charing.*

Feth. Now you haue run yourſelf out of breath,
hear me. I proteſt the gentlewoman is honeſt : and
ſince I have wronged her reputation in meeting her
thus priuately, Ile maintain her.—Wilt thou hang at
my purſe, *Kate,* like a paire of barbary buttons, to
open when 'tis full, and cloſe when 'tis empty ?

Kate. I'll be diuorced, by this Chriſtian element :
and becauſe thou thinkeſt thou art a Cockold, leſt I
ſhould make thee an infidel in cauſing thee to belieue
an vntruth, I'll make thee a Cockold.

Bell. Excellent wench.

Feth. Come, lets go, fweet ; the Nag I ride upon bears double : weele to London.

May. Do not bite your thumbs, fir.

Kate. Bite his thumb !
I'll make him do a thing worfe than this :
Come loue me where as I lay.

Feth. What, *Kate* !

Kate. He fhall father a child is none of his,
O, the clean contrary way.

Feth. O lufty Kate. *Exeunt.*

May. Methought he faid even now you were a taylor.

Green. You fhall hear more of that hereafter : I'll make *Ware* and him flink ere he goes : if I be a taylor, the rogues naked weapon fhall not fright me ; I'll beat him and my wife both out a the towne with a taylors yard. *Exit.*

May. O valiant Sir *Triftram*—Room there !

Enter Philip, Leuerpool, *and* Chartly.

Phi. News, father, moft ftrange news out of the Low-Countries : your good lady and miftris, that fet you to work upon a dozen of cheefe-trenchers, is new lighted at the next inn, and the old venerable gentle-mans father with her.

Bell. Let the gates of our inn be locked up clofer than a noblemans gates at dinner-time.

Omn. Why, fir, why ?

Bell. If fhe enter here, the houfe will be infected : the plague is not halfe fo dangerous as a fhe-hornet.—
Philip, this is your fhuffling a the cards, to turn up her for the bottom card at *Ware*.

Phi. No, as Ime vertuous, fir : afk the two gentle-men.

Leuer. No, in troth, fir. She told vs, that, in-quiring at *London* for you or your fon, your man chalked out her way to *Ware*.

Bell. I wud *Ware* might choke em both.—Maifter *Maybery*, my horfe and I will take our leaues of you : Ile to Bedlam again rather than ftay her.

May. Shall a woman make thee fly thy country? Stay, ftand to her, though fhe were greater than Pope *Joan*. What are thy brains conjuring for, my poetical bay-leaf-eater?

Bell. For a fprite o'the buttery, that fhall make us all drink with mirth, if I can raife it. Stay, the chicken is not fully hatched.—hit, I befeech thee! fo, come?—Will you be fecret, gentlemen, and affifting?

Omn. With brown bills, if you think good.

Bell. What will you fay if by fome trick we put this little hornet into *Fetherftones* bofom, and marry 'em together?

Omn. Fuh! 'tis impoffible.

Bell. Moft poffible. Ile to my trencher-woman ; let me alone for dealing with her : *Fetherftone*, gentlemen, fhall be your patient.

Omn. How, how?

Bell. Thus. I will clofe with this country pedler, Miftris *Dorothy*, that trauels vp and down to exchange pins for conyfkins, very louingly ; fhe fhall eat of nothing but fweatmeats in my company, good words ; whofe tafte when fhe likes, as I know fhe will, then will I play vpon her with this artillery,—that a very proper man and a great heir (naming *Fetherftone*) fpied her from a window, when fhe lighted at her inn, is extremely fallen in loue with her, vows to make her his wife, if it ftand to her good liking, even in *Ware* ; but being, as moft of your young gentlemen are, fomewhat bafhful, and afhamed to venture vpon a woman,——

May. City and fuburbs can juftify it : fo, fir.

Bell. He fends me, being an old friend, to undermine for him. I'll fo whet the wenches ftomach, and make her fo hungry, that fhe fhall haue an appetite to him, feare it not. *Greenfhield* fhall haue a hand in it too ; and, to be revenged of his partner, will, I know, ſtrike with any weapon.

Leuer. But is *Fetherſtone* of any means ? elſe you undo him and her.

May. He has land between *Foolham* and *London :* he would haue made it ouer to me.—To your charge, poet : giue you the aſſault vpon her ; and ſend but *Fetherſtone* to me, Ile hang him by the gills.

Bell. He's not yet horſed, ſure.—*Philip*, go thy ways, giue fire to him, and ſend him hither with a powder preſently.

Phil. He's blowne vp already.   *Exit.*

Bell. Gentlemen, youle ſtick to the deuice, and look to your plot ?

Omn. Moſt poetically : away to your quarter.

Bell. I march : I will caſt my rider, gallants. I hope you ſee who ſhall pay for our voyage.   *Exit.*

Enter Phillip *and* Fetherſtone.

May. That muſt hee that comes here : Maiſter *Fetherſtone*, O Maiſter *Fetherſtone*, you may now make your fortunes weigh ten ſtone of Fethers more then euer they did : leape but into the ſaddle now, that ſtands empty for you, you are made for euer.

Leuer. An Aſſe Ile be ſworne.

Feth. How for Gods ſake ? how?

May. I would you had, what I could wiſh you, I loue you, and becauſe you ſhall be ſure to know where my loue dwels, looke you ſir, it hangs out at this ſigne : you ſhall pray for *Ware*, when *Ware* is dead and rotten : looke you ſir, there is as pretty a little Pinnas, ſtruck ſaile hereby, and come in lately ; ſhee's my kinſe-woman, my fathers youngeſt Siſter, a warde, her portion three thouſand ; her hopes if her Grannam dye without iſſue, better.

Feth. Very good ſir.

May. Her Gardian goes about to marry her to a

Stone-cutter, and rather than fheele be fubiect to fuch
a fellow, fheele dye a martyr, will you haue all out?
fhee's runne away, is here at an Inne ith' towne, what
parts fo euer you haue plaide with mee, I fee good
parts in you, and if you now will catch times hayre
that's put into your hand, you fhall clap her vp
prefently.

Feth. Is fhe young? and a pretty wench?

Leuer. Few Cittizens wiues are like her.

Phil. Yong, why I warrant fixteene hath fcarce
gone ouer her.

Feth. Sfoot, where is fhe? if I like her perfonage,
afwell as I like that which you fay belongs to her perfonage, Ile ftand thrumming of Caps no longer, but
board your Pynnis whilft 'tis hotte.

May. Away then with thefe Gentlemen with a
French gallop, and to her : *Phillip* here fhall runne for
a Prieft, and difpatch you.

Feth. Will you gallants goe along : wee may be
married in a Chamber for feare of hew and crie
after her, and fome of the company fhall keepe the
doore.

May. Affure your foule fhee will be followed ;
away therefore. Hees in the *Curtian* gulfe, and
fwallowed horfe and man : hee will haue fome body
keepe the doore for him, fheele looke to that: I am
yonger then I was two nights agoe, for this phifick.—
how now ?

Enter Captaine, Allom, Hans, *and others booted.*

Capt. God pleffe you ; is there not an arrant
scuruy trab in your company, that is a Sentill-woman
borne fir, and can tawg *Welch*, and *Dutch*, and any
tongue in your head?

May. How fo? Drabs in my company : doe I
looke like a Drab-driuer?

Capt. The Trab will driue you (if fhe put you
before her) into a pench hole.

Allom. Is not a Gentleman here one Maifter *Bel-lamont* fir of your company.

May. Yes, yes, come you from *London*, heele be here prefently.

Capt. Will he ? *tawfone*, this oman, hunts at his taile like your little Goates in *Wales* follow their mother, wee haue warrants here from maifter Suftice of this fhire, to fhew no pitty nor mercie to her, her name is *Doll*.

May. Why fir, what has fhe committed ? I thinke fuch a creature is ith' towne.

Capt. What has fhe committed : ownds fhee has committed more then man-flaughters, for fhee has committed her felfe God pleffe vs to euerlafting prifon : lug you fir, fhee is a punke, fhe fhifts her louers (as Captaines and *Welfh* Gentlemen and fuch) as fhe does her Trenchers when fhe has well fed vpon't, and there is left nothing but pare bones, fhee calls for a cleane one, and fcrapes away the firft.

Enter Bellamont, *and* Hornet, *with* Doll *betweene them*, Greenefhield, Kate, Mayberies *wife*, Phillip, Leuerpoole, *and* Chartley.

May. Gods fo Maifter *Fetherftone*, what will you doe ? here's three come from *London*, to fetch away the Gentlewoman with a warrant.

Feth. All the warrants in *Europe* fhall not fetch her now, fhe's mine fure enough : what haue you to fay to her ? fhee's my wife.

Cap. Ow ! Sbloud doe you come fo farre to fifhe and catch Frogs ? your wife is a Tilt-boate, any man or oman may goe in her for money ; fhee's a Cunny-catcher : where is my moueable goods cald a Coach, and my two wild peafts, pogs on you wud they had trawne you to the gallowes.

Allom. I muft borrow fiftie pound of you Miftris Bride.

Hans. 𝕳𝖆𝖜 𝖇𝖗𝖔, 𝖆𝖓𝖉 𝖞𝖔𝖚 𝖒𝖆𝖐𝖊 𝖒𝖊 𝖉𝖊

**gheck, de groet foole, pou heb mine gelt
to : war is it ?**

Doll. Out, you bafe fcums ! come you to difgrace
me in my wedding-fhoes ?

Feth. Is this your three-thoufand-pound ward ? ye
told me, fir, fhe was your kinfwoman.

May. Right, one of mine aunts.

Bell. Who pays for the northern voyage now,
lads ?

Green. Why do you not ride before my wife to
London now ? The woodcocks i'th fpringe.

Kate. O, forgive me, dear husband ! I will neuer
loue a man that is worfe than hangd, as he is.

May. Now a man may haue a courfe in your
park ?

Feth. He may, fir.

Doll. Neuer, I proteft : I will be as true to thee as
Ware and *Wade's-Mill* are one to another.

Feth. Well, it's but my fate. Gentlemen, this is
my opinion, its better to fhoot in a bowe that has
been fhot in before, and will neuer ftart, then to draw
a fair new one, that for euery arrow will be warping.
—Come wench, we are joind, and all the dogs in
France fhall not part us.—I haue fome lands : thofe
Ile turn into money, to pay you, and you, and any.—
Ile pay all that I can for thee, for Ime fure thou haft
paid me.

Omn. God giue you ioy.

May. Come lets be merry, lye you with your
owne Wife, to be fure fhee fhall not walke in her
fleepe ; a noyfe of Mufitians Chamberlaine.

This night lets banquet freely : come, weele dare,
Our wiues to combate ith' greate bed in Ware.

Exeunt.

FINIS.

THE
F A M O V S

Hiſtory of Sir Tho-
mas Wyat.

With the Coronation of Queen Mary,

and the coming in of King
Philip.

As it was plaied by the Queens Maieſties
Seruants.

Written by *Thomas Dickers*,
And *Iohn Webſter*.

LONDON
Printed by E. A. for *Thomas Archer*, and are to be
folde at his ſhop in the Popes-head Pallace,
nere the Royall Exchange.
1607.

3   G

[There is a later edition of this play with the following title : *The Famous Hiſtory of Sir Thomas
Wyat &c.   Written by Thomas Deckers, and Iohn
Webſter. London Printed for Thomas Archer &c.*
1612. The differences in the text are few and unim-
portant.]

THE

Famous Hiſtorie of

Sir Thomas Wyat.

Enter Northumberland and
Suffolke.

Suff. Ow fares the King, my Lord ?
  ſpeaks he cheerely ?
Nor. Euen as a dying man, whoſe life
  Like to quicke lighting, which is
no ſooner ſeene, but is extinct.
Suff. Is the Kings will confirm'd ?
Nor. I, thats the point that we leuel at.
But oh, the confirmation of that will, tis all, tis all.
  Suff. That will confirme my Daughter Queene.
  Nor. Right, & my Sonne is marryed to your
  daughter.
My Lord, in an euen plaine way, I will
Deriue the Crowne vnto your Daughters head.
What though the King hath left behinde,
Two Siſters, lawfull and immediate heires,
To ſucceed him in his Throane, Lyes it not
In our powers to contradict it ?
Haue we not the King and Counſels hands vnto it ?

Tut, wee ftand high in mans opinion,
And the worldes broad eye.

Enter Sir Thomas Wyat.

Suff.	Heere comes Sir Thomas Wyat.
Nor.	Sir Thomas booted and fpur'd, whether away
	fo faft ?
Wiat.	It bootes me not to ftay,
When in this land rebellion beares fuch fway.
Gods will, a Court ! Tis chang'd
Since Noble Henries daies.
You haue fet your handes vnto a will.
A will you well may call it :
So wils Northumberland :
So wils *Suffolke,*
Againft Gods will, to wrong thofe Princely Maides.
	Nor.	Will you not fubfcribe your hand with other
		of the Lords ?
Not with me, that in my handes,
Surprife the Soueraigntie.
	Wyat.	Ile damb'd my foule for no man, no for no
		man,
Who at doomes day muft anfwere for my finne :
Not you, nor you my Lordes,
Who nam'de Queene Iane in noble Henries daies,
Which of you all durft once difplace his iffue ?
My Lords, my Lords, you whet your kniues fo fharp,
To carue your meate,
That they will cut your fingars.
The ftrength is weakeneffe that you builde vpon,
The King is ficke, God mend him, I, God mend
	him :
But where his foule from his pale body free,
Adieu my Lords, the Court no court for me.
					Exit Wyat.

	North.	Farwell, I feare thee not.
The Fly is angrie, but hee wants a fting,
And all the Counfell : onely this peruerfe

And peeuifh Lord, hath onely deny'd his hand
To the inuefting of your princely Daughter.
Hee's idle and wants power.
Our Ocean fhall thefe petty brookes deuoure,
Heere comes his Highneffe Doctor.

Enter Doctor.

Suff.   How fares his Highneffe ?
Doct.   His body is paft helpe.
We haue left our practice to the Diuines,
That they may cure his foule.
　　Aru.   Paft phifickes helpe, why then paft hope of
　　life,
Heere comes his Highneffe Preacher :
Life reverent man.

Enter Preacher.

　　Pre.   Life, life, though death his body doe dif-
　　feuer,
Our King liues with the King of heauen for euer.
　　Nor.   Dead ! fend for Heralds, call me Purfe-
　　uants,
Wher's the King at armes ? in euerie market towne
Proclaime Queene *Iane.*
　　Suff.   Beft to take the opinion of the Counfell,
　　Nort.   You are too timorous.   We in our felues
Are power fufficient : the King being dead.
This hand fhall place the crowne on Queene *Ianes*
　　head.
Trumpets and Drums, with your notes refound,
Her royal name, that muft in ftate be crown'd.
　　　　　　　　　　　　　　　　Exeunt Om.

Enter Guilford and Jane.

　　Guil.   Our Coufen King is dead.
　　Jan. Alaffe, how fmall an Vrne containes a King ?

He that ruld all, euen with his princely breath,
Is forc'd to ſtoöpe now to the ſtroake of death.
Heard you not the proclamation ?
 Gui. I heare of it, and I giue credit to it
What great men feare to be,
Their feares grow greater.
Our Fathers grow ambitious
And would force vs ſaile in mightie tempeſts,
And are not Lordes of what they doe poſſeſſe.
Are not thy thoughts as great ?
  Ʒan. I haue no thoughts ſo ranke, ſo growne to
   head,
As are our Fathers pride.
Troth I doe inioy a Kingdome hauing thee.
And ſo my paine be proſperous in that,
What care I though a Sheep-cote be my Pallace
Or faireſt roofe of honour.
 Gui. See how thy blood keepes courſe with mine :
Thou muſt be a Queene, aye me ! a Queene,
The flattering belles that ſhrilly ſound
At the Kings funerall with hollow heartes,
Will cowardly call thee Soueraigne :
For indeed thou wouldſt prooue but an Vſurper.
  Ʒan. Who would weare fetters though they were
   all of golde ?
Or to be ſicke, though his faint browes
For a wearing Night-cap, wore a Crowne.
Thou muſt aſſume, a tytle that goes on many feet,
But tis an office, wherein the heartes of Schollers,
And of Souldiers will depend vppon thy Hearſe.
Were this rightly ſcand,
Wee ſcarce ſhould finde a King in any Land.

    Enter Arundell.

 Arun. Honor and happy reigne
Attend the new Maieſtie of England.
 Ʒan. To whome my Lord bends this your aue.
 Arun. To your grace dread Soueraigne,

You are by the Kings will, and the confent
Of all the Lords, chofen for our Queene.
   Jan.   O God ! me thinkes you fing my death,
In parts of muſickes lowdnes,
Tis not my turne to rife.

Enter Northumberland, Suffolke with the Purſe and the
Mace, with others.

   Nor.   The voice of the whole Land ſpeakes in my
      tongue
It is concluded your Maieſtie muſt ride,
From hence vnto the Tower : there to ſtay
Vntill your Coronation.
   Jan.   O God !
   Suff.   Why fighes your Maieſtie?
   Jan.   My Lord and Father, I pray tell me,
Was your Fathers Father ere a King?
   Suff.   Neuer, and it like your grace.'
   Jan.   Would I might ſtill continue of his lyne,
Not trauell in the cloudes.
It is often feene, the heated blood
That couets to be royall, leaues off ere it be noble,
My learned carefull King, what muſt we goe ?
   Gui.   We muſt.
   Jan.   Then it muſt be fo.
   Nor.   Set forward then.

A dead march, and paſſe round the ſtage, and
Guilford ſpeakes.

The Towre will be a place of ample ſtate,
Some lodgings in it, will like dead mens fculs,
Remember vs of frailty.
   Gui.   We are led with pompe to prifon,
O propheticke foule.
Lo we afcend into our chaires of State,
Like funerall Coffins, in fonie funerall
Pompe defcending to their graves.   But we muſt on.

How can we fare well, to keep our Court :
Where Priſoners keepe their caue ?
      A floriſh. Exeunt Omnes.

*Enter Queene Mary with a Prayer Booke in her hand,
like a Nun.*

 Mary. Thus like a Nun, not like a Princeſſe
  borne,
Deſcended from the Royall Henries loynes :
Liue I inuirond in a houſe of ſtone,
My Brother *Edward* liues in pompe and ſtate,
I in a manſion here all ruinate.
Their rich attire, delicious banquetting :
Their ſeuerall pleaſures, all their pride and honour,
I haue forſaken for a rich prayer Booke.
The Golden Mines of wealthy India,
Is all as droſſe compared to thy ſweetneſſe.
Thou art the ioy, and comfort of the poore,
The euerlaſting bliſſe in thee we finde.
This little volume incloſed in this hand,
Is richer then the Empire of this land.

   Enter Sir Henry Beningfield.

 Ben. Pardon me Madam, that ſo boldly
I preſſe into your Chamber. I ſalute your
Highneſſe with the high ſtile of Queene.
 Mar. Queene ! may it be ?
Or ieſt you at my lowring miſerie.
 Ben. Your Brother King is dead,
And you the catholicke Queene muſt now ſuccede.
 Mar. I ſee my God at length hath heard my
  prayer.
You Sir Harry, for your glad tydings,
Shall be held in honour and due regard.

   Enter ſir Thomas Wyat.

 Wiat. Health to the Lady Mary.

Mar.   And why not Queene, Sir Thomas?
Wia.   Aske that of Suffolke duke, & great Nor-
   thumberland
Who in your fteede hath Crown'd another.
Mar.   another Queene, Sir Thomas wee aliue,
The true immediate heires of our dread Father?
Wia.   Nothing more true then that:
Nothing more true then you are the true heire,
Come leaue this Cloyfter and be feene abroad,
Your verie fight will ftirre the peoples hearts,
and make them cheerely, for Queene Marie crie.
One comfort I can tell you: the tenants of the
Dukes Northumberland and Suffolke denide their
   ayde,
In thefe unlawful armes:
To all the Counfell I denide my hand,
And for King Henries Iffue ftill will ftand.
Mary.   Your Counfel, good fir Thomas, is fo
   pithy
That I am woon fo like it.
Wia.   Come let vs ftreight from hence,
From Framingham:
Cheere your fpirits.
Ile to the Dukes at Cambridge, and difcharge them
   all:
Profper me God in thefe affaires,
I lou'd the Father wel, I lou'd the Sonne,
And for the Daughter I through death will run.
                              Exeunt Omnes.

Enter Northumberland, Suffolke, Bret and fouldiers.

Nor.   wher's Captaine Bret?
Bre.   Heere my Lord.
Suff.   Are all our numbers full!
Bre.   They are my Lord.
Suff.   See them arain'd, I will fet forward ftreight.
Nor.   Honorable friends, and natiue peeres,
That haue chofen me to be the leader of thefe martiall

troopes, to march againſt the ſiſter
Of our late dead Soueraigne.
Beare witneſſe of my much vnwillingneſſe,
In furthering theſe attemps
I rather ioy to thinke vpon our ancient victories
Againſt the French and Spaniard,
Whoſe high pride we leueld with the waues of brittiſh
    ſhore
Dying the hauen of Brit. with guiltie blood,
Till all the Harbor ſeem'd a ſanguine poole :
Or we deſire theſe armes, we are now to warre
Gainſt the perfidious northern enemie,
Who trembling at our firſt ſhocke voice and ſight,
Like cowards turn'd their backes with ſhamefull flight
But thoſe rich ſpoiles are paſt : we are now to goe,
Being natiue friends, againſt a natiue foe.
In your hands we leaue the Queene elected,
She hath ſeiſure of the Tower,
If you be confident, as you haue ſworne
Your ſelues true liege men to her highneſſe
She no doubt, with royall fauour will remunerate
The leaſt of your deſertes.   Farwell
My teares into your boſomes fall,
With one imbrace I doe include you all.
   Aru.   My Lord, moſt lou'd with what a mourning
      heart
I take your farwell, let the after ſignes
Of my imployment witneſſe.   I proteſt
Did not the ſacred perſon of my Queene ;
Whoſe weale I tender as my ſoules cheefe bliſſe,
Vrge my abode, I would not thinke it ſhame
To traile a pike where you were generall.
But wiſhes are in vaine, I am bound to ſtay,
And vrgent buſineſſe calls your grace away.
See, on my knees I humbly take my leaue,
And ſteep my wordes with teares.
   Nor.   Kinde Arundell, I bind thee to my loue.
Once more farwell.
   Arun.   Heauens giue your grace ſucceſſe.

Commend vs to the Queene and to your Sonne,
Within one weeke, I hope war will be done.
   Bre. Come my Lords, ſhall vs march.
Exit. Northumb.

   Nor. I, I, for Gods ſake on.
Tis more then time my friendes, that we were gone.
Exeunt Omnes.

Enter Treaſurer and Porter.

   Tre. What ho Porter ! open the gate.
   Por. I beſeech your honour to pardon me,
The Counſell hath giuen ſtrict commaund
Not any ſhall paſſe this way.
   Tre. Why you idle fellow, am I not ſent vppon
the Queenes affaires, commanded by the Lords ? and
know you not that I am Treaſurer ? come open the
Gate, you doe you know not what.
   Por. Well my Lord, I doe aduenture on your
     word,
The Dukes diſpleaſure`: all the Counſell boord
Beſides, may be my heauie enemies,
But goe a Gods name, I the worſt will proue,
And if I die, l die for him I loue.
   Tre. I thanke thee, and will warrant thee from
     death.
Is my Horſe ready ?
   Por. It is my Lord.
   Tre. Then will I flie this fearefull Counſell boord.
Exit Tre.

   Por. My heart miſgiues me, I haue done amiſſe,
Yet being a Counſellor one of the number
Nothing can prooue amiſſe.
Now ſhall I know the worſt.
Heere comes my Lord of Arundell.

Enter Arundell.

   Arun. Porter, Did the Lord Treaſurer paſſe this
way ?

Por. But now my gratious Lord.

Arun. Vngratious Villaine, follow,
Bring him backe againe.
If not, by faire meanes bring him backe by force :
And heare you firra, as you goe, will the Lord Maior
and fome Aldermen of his Bretheren, and fome
efpeciall Cittizens of note, to attend our further
pleafures prefently. The Treafurer fled : the Duke is
but newly arrefted, fome purpofe, on my life, to croffe
their plots : weele fet ftrong watches, fee Gates and
walles well mand :
Tis ten to one but princely innocence,
Is thefe ftrange turmoiles wifeft violence.

*Enter Winchefter, Arundell, and other Lords : the
Lord Treafurer kneeling at the Counfell Table.*

Arun. Though your attempt, Lord Treafurer be
  fuch,
That hath no colour in thefe troublous times,
But an apparant purpofe of reuolt,
From the deceaft Kings will, and our decree,
Yet, for you are a Counfellor of note,
One of our number, and of high degree,
Before we any way prefume to iudge,
We giue you leaue to fpeake in your behalfe.

Tre. My Lord, the bufineffe of thefe troublous
  times,
Binding vs al, ftill to refpect the good of common
  weale :
Yet doth it not debar priuate regard of vs & of our
  own
The generall weale is treafur'd in your breft,
And all my ableft powers haue bin imployed
To ftir them there, yet haue I borne a part,
Laying the commons troubles next my heart,
My ouerfight in parting without leaue :
Was no contempt, but onely for an houre.
To order home affaires, that none of mine,
In thefe nice times fhould vnto faction clime.

Aru. Nay my good Lord, be plaine with vs, I
    pray,
Are you not grieu'd that we haue giuen confent
To Lady Ianes election?
   Tre. My Lords I am not.
   Arun. Speake like a Gentleman, vpon your word
Are you not difcontent?
   Tre. Troth to be plaine, I am not pleaf'd,
That two fuch princely Maides lineally defcended
From our royall King, and by his teftimonie,
Confirmed heyre, if that their Brother dying Iffules,
And one that neuer dream't, it neuer defired
The rule of Soueraignetie,
But with virgins teares hath oft bewaild her miferie,
Should politickly by vs be nam'd a Queene.
   Arun. You haue faid nobly, fit and take your
    place.

Enter Porter.

   Por. My Lords, Sir Thomas Wyat craues acceffe
vnto your honours.
   Arun. Let him come neare.

Enter Wyat.

   Por. Roume for Sir Thomas Wyat.
   Wiat. A diuine fpirit teach your honours truth,
Open your eyes of iudgement to beholde
The true Legitimate, Mary your vndoubted foue-
    raigne.
   Arun. Arife, fir Thomas, fit and take your place.
Now to our former bufineffe :
The obligation wherein we all ftood bound
To the deceafed late Kings will and our decree,
His coufen Iane, and the two abfent Dukes
Cannot be conceal'd without great reproach
To vs and to our Iffue.
We haue fworn in prefence of the facred hoft of
    heauen

Vnto our late young Lord, to both the Dukes,
That no impeachment ſhould diuert our heartes
From the impeachment of the Lady Jane.
To this end we haue ceaſed her in the tower,
By publike proclamation made her Queene :
To this end we haue armed the Duke, with power
Giuen them commiſſion vnder our owne handes
To paſſe againſt the Lady. You performe in hoſtile
     maner
And no doubt, the ſpleene of the vndanted ſpirit
Of Northumbers Earle, will not be called
With writings of repeale.
Aduice in this, I holde it better farre
To keepe the courſe we runne then ſeeking change,
Hazard our liues, our heires, and the Realmes.
     Wiat.   In actions roauing from the bent of truth,
We haue no perſident thus to perſiſt
But the bare name of worldly policie.
If others haue ground from Iuſtice, and the law,
As well diuine as politicke agreeing,
They are for no cauſe to be diſinherited.
If you not ſeauen yeares ſince to that effect,
Swore to the Father to maintaine his ſeede,
What diſpenſation hath acquited you
From your firſt ſacred vowes ?
Youle ſay, the will extorted from a childe.
O ! let mine eyes in naming that ſweete youth,
Obſerue their part.
Powring downe teares, ſent from my ſwelling heart.
Gods mother, I tearme childe ? but ile goe on,
Say that the will were his, forced by no tricke,
But for religions loue his ſimple act,
Yet note how much you erre.
You were ſworne before to a mans will,
and not a will alone,
But ſtrengthned by an act of Parliament.
Beſides this ſacred proofe. The Princely Maides,
Had they no will nor act to prooue their right ?

Haue birthrights no priuiledge, being a plea fo
    ftrong,
As cannot be refeld, but by plaine wrong?
Now were you toucht. The Lady in [the] tower
alaffe fhee's innocent of any claime.
Truft me, fhee'd thinke it a mofte happy life,
To leaue a Queenes, and keepe a Ladies name.
And for the Dukes, your warrants fent them foorth,
Let the fame warrant call them backe againe.
If they refufe to come, the Realme, not they
Muft be regarded. Be ftrong and bold:
We are the peoples factors. Saue our Sonnes
From killing one another, be affraide,
To tempt both heauen and earth, fo I haue faid.
    Arun. Why then giue order that fhe fhall be
      Queene,
Send for the Maior, her errors wele forget,
Hoping fhe will forgiue.
    Wiat. Neuer make doubt,
Setting her ceremonious order by.
She is pure within, and mildly chaft without.
    Arun. Giue order to keepe faft the Lady Iane,
Diffolue the Counfell. Let vs leaue the Tower,
and in the Citie hold our audience.
    Wyat. You haue aduifed well honorable Lordes,
So will the Cittizens be wholly ours,
and if the Dukes be croffe, weele croffe their powers.
                    Exeunt Omnes.

        Enter Bret, Clown, and Souldiers.

    Br. Lance perfado, quarter, quarter.
    Clo. What fhall we quarter Captaine?
    Bre. Why the Souldiers?
    Clo. Why they are not hang'd nor drawne yet?
    Bre. Sir I meane quarter them, that the offended
multitude, may paffe in fafetie.
    Clo. May we not take tooles of the pies & the
aple-women.

Bre. Not in any ſorte, the Dukes pleaſure will
paſſe free.

Clo. The Commons ſhal be vſed with al common
curteſie.   That goes in rank like beanes and cheeſe-
cakes on their heads in ſteade of Cappes.

Bre. Sirra, this is a famous Vniuerſitie, and thoſe
ſchollers, thoſe lofty buildings and goodly houſes,
Founded by noble Patrons.   But no more.
Set a ſtrong watch.   That be your cheefeſt care.

Enter a Countryman and a Maide.

Man.   Whats heere Souldiers?

Bre.   Feare not, good ſpeech, theſe rude armes I
     beare,
Iſt not to fight?   Sweet, gentle Peace away,
But to ſuccour your liues, paſſe peaceibly away.

Clo.   Crie God ſaue the Queene as you goe, and
God ſend you a good market.

Man.   God ſaue the Queene, what Queene? there
     lies the ſenſe.
When we haue none, it can be no offence.

Clo.   What carry you there in your basket?

Mai.   Egs forſooth.

Clo.   Well, crie God ſaue Queene Iane as you goe,
and God ſend you a good Market.

Mai.   Is the right Queene called Iane? alacke for
     woe,
at the firſt ſhe was not chriſtened ſo.   *Exit.*

Br.   Thus olde and young, ſtill deſcant on her
     name,
Nor lend no eare, when wee her ſtile proclaime.
I feare, I feare.   Fear Bret, what ſhouldſt thou feare?
Thou haſt a breſt compoſ'd of adamant.
Fall what ill betide;
My anchor is caſt, and I in Harbor ride.

Enter Northumberland and Wyat.

Wia.   My Lord tis true, you ſent vnto the Counſell

for frefh fupplies, what fuccour, what fupplies ?
Happie is he can draw his necke out of the coller,
and make his peace with Marie.
   Nor. How ftands the Treafurer addicted to vs ?
   Wya. I had forgot : when we weare at counfell,
He ftole away, and went home to his houfe,
And by much intreatie was woon to returne,
In briefe they all incline to Queene Mary
My Lord farwell,
Each haftie houre will coulder tydings tell.
Exit Wyat.

   Nor. Come they in thunder, we will meete with
     them ;
In the loudeft language that their ordinance fpeakes,
Ours fhall anfwere theirs.
Call me a Herald, and in the market-place Proclaime
Queene Iane. The ftreetes are full,
The towne is populous, the people gape for noueltie.
Trumpets fpeake to them,
That they may anfwere with an echoing crie,
God faue Queene Iane, God faue her Maieftie.

A Trumpet founds, and no anfwere.

The Herald foundes a parlee, and none anfwers.

   Nor. Ha ? a bare report of Trumpets !
Are the flaues horfe, or want they arte to fpeake ?
O me ! This Towne confifts on famous Colledges,
Such as know both how, and what, and when to
     fpeake,
Well, yet wee will proceede,
and fmother what clofe enuie hath decreed.
Ambrofe my Sonne, what newes ?

Enter Ambrofe.

   Amb. O my thrice honoured Father.
   Nor. Boy, fpeake the worft,

H

That which foundes deadlyeft, let me heare that firft.
  Amb. The Lords haue all reuolted from your
    faction.
  Nor. Wee in our felues are ftrong.
  Am. In Baynards Caftle was a counfell held,
Whether the Maior and Sheriffes did refort,
And twas concluded to proclaime Queene Mary.
  Nor. Then they reuolt the allegiance from my
    Daughter,
And giue it to another :
  Am. True my thrice honoured Father,
Befides, my brother Guilford and his wife
Where fhe was proclaimde Queene, are now
Clofe Prifoners, namely in the Tower.
  Nor. God take them to his mercie, they had
    neede,
Of grace and patience, for they both muft bleede,
Poore Innocent foules, they both from guilt are free.
  Am. O my thrice honoured Father ! might I ad-
uife you, flie to your manner, there ftuddie for your
faftie.
  Nor. Boy, thou faift well,
And fince the Lords haue all reuolted from me,
My felfe will now reuolt againft my felfe.
Call me a Herald to fill their emptie eares,
Affift me Sonne, my good Lord Huntingdon,
Euen in this market Towne proclaime Queene Mary.

  A trumpet foundes a parley, the Herald proclaimes.

  He. Mary by the grace of God, Queene of England, France and Ireland, defendres of the Faith.
Amen.

    Within a fhoute and a flourifh.

  Nor. Amen, I beare a part,
I with my tongue, I doe not with my heart,
Now they can crie, now they can baule and yell,
Bafe minded flaues, fincke may your foules to hell.

Enter Maifter Roofe with Letters.

Roo.   My honored Lord, the Counfell greetes you
    with thefe Letters.
Nor.   Stay Maifter Roofe, ere you depart receiue
an anfwere and reward.   *He readeth the Letter.*
In the Soueraigne name of Mary our Queene
You fhall vppon the fight hereof,
Surceafe your armes, difcharge your Souldiers,
And prefently repaire vnto the Court,
Or elfe to be held as an Arch-Traitor.
No.   Tis fhort & fharp, Maifter Roofe, we do obey
your warrant : but, I pray tel mee, how doth all our
friendes at Court ? is there not a great mortalitie
amongft them ?
Is there not a number of them deade of late fince I
came thence ?
Ro.   My gratious Lord not any.
Nor.   O maifter Roofe, it cannot bee, I will affure
    you
At my departure thence, I left liuing there at leaft
Fiue hundred friendes, and now I haue not one,
Simply not one : friendes ! ha, ha, ha, Commiffion
Thou muft be my friend.
And ftand betwixt me and the ftroake of death,
Were thy date out, my liues date were but fhort,
They are colde friends, that kil their friendes in fport.
Am.   Heere comes your honoured friend the Earle
    of Arundell.

Enter Arundell.

Nor.   My honourd friend !
Arun.   I am no friend to Traitors :
In my mofte high & Princely Soueraignes name,
I doe arreft your honour of high Treafon.
Nor.   A traitor Arundell ? haue I not your hand
in my commiffion ? let me perufe it : as I tak't tis
heere, and by your warrant haue fo ftrict proceeded.

Is the limits of my warrant broke ? anſwere me.

 Arun. It may be that it hath pleaſed her Maieſtie
To pardon vs, and for to punniſh you.
I know no other reaſon, this I muſt,
I am commaunded, and the act is Iuſt.

 Nor. And I obey you : when we parted laſt
My Lord of Arundel, our farwell was
Better then our greeting now.
Then you cride God ſpeede,
Now you come on me ere you ſay take heede :
Then you did owe me your beſt bloods : nay greeu'd
You could not ſpend them in my ſeruice.
O then it was a double death to ſtay behinde,
But I am ouertooke and you are kinde,
I am, beſhrew you elſe, but I ſubmit,
My crime is great, and I muſt anſwere it.

 Arun. You muſt with your three Sons, be guarded
  ſafe
Vnto the Tower : with you, thoſe Lords and Knights
That in this faction did aſſociate you.
For ſo I am inioyn'd.
Then peaceably, let vs conduct you thither.

 Nor. O my Children ! my ſoule weepes endleſſe
  teares for you.
O at the generall Seſſions, when all ſoules
Stand at the bar of Iuſtice,
And hold vp their new immortalized handes,
O then let the remembrance of their tragick endes
Be rac'd out of the bed-rowle of my ſinnes :
When ere the blacke booke of my crime's vnclaſpt,
Let not theſe ſcarlet Letters be found there :
Of all the reſt, onely that page be cleere.
But come to my arraignement, then to death,
The Queene and you haue long aim'd at this head,
If to my Children, ſhe ſweet grace extend,
My ſoule hath peace, and I imbrace my end. *Exeunt.*

   Enter the Duke of Suffolke.

 Suff. Three daies are paſt, Monday, Tueſday, and
  Wedneſday too

Yet my protefting feruant is not come.
Himfelfe conducted me to this hard lodging,
A fimple Cabin, for fo great a Prince,
And then he fwore, but oathes you fee are vaine,
That he would hourely come and vifite me :
I that was wont, to furfeit in eftate,
And now through hunger almoft defolate.

Enter Homes fweating with bottell and Bag.

Hom.   My Lord.
Suff.   Ned Homes, fpeake haft thou brought me
  meate ?
Hom.   With much a doe, my Lord, meat, bread &
  wine,
While you refrefh your felfe, I will recorde
The caufe of my long ftay.
Suff.   I prethee doe, neede bids me eate,
Neede bids me heare thee too.
Hom.   The night I left you in the hollow tree,
My houfe was fearched.
Suff.   Goe on, goe on.
Hom.   And I no fooner entred but attached,
Threatned the Rack : and if I did not yeeld
Your gracious felfe into their gracelefle hands.
Suff.   And thou haft don't, thou haft betraied me.
Hom.   Done it ! o betraie you ? O noe !
Firft would I fee my loued wife and Children
Murdered, and tof'd on fpeares, before I would
Deliuer your grace vnto their handes,
For they intend your death.
Suff.   Goe on, goe on.
Hom : and offer'd a thoufand Crownes to him that
  can
Bring newes of your abode, twas offer'd in my
  hands :
Which I befeech may ftop my Vital breath,
When I am feede with golde to worke your death.

Enter Sheriffe and Officers.

Sher.   See yonder fits the Duke.

Suff.   I kiffe thee in requitall of this loue.

Hom.   and in requitall of fo great a grace,
I kiffe your hand that dares to kiffe my face.

She.   So Iudas kift his Maifter : ceaze the Duke.

Suff.   Ah me ! Ned Homes we are vndone,
Both thou and I betraide.

She.   My Lord, late Duke of Suffolke, in her
highneffe name I doe arreft you of high Treafon.

Suff.   I doe obey, and onely craue this kindneffe,
You would be good vnto my Seruant Homes,
Where in releeuing me, hath but performde
The duetie of a feruant to his Lord.

She.   You are deceiu'd fir in your feruant much,
Hee is the man that did betray you.
Heere Maifter Homes, towards your thoufand pounds,
Heere is a hundred markes,
Come to the Exchequer, you fhall haue the reft.

Suff.   Haft thou betraide me ? yet with fuch a
     tongue,
fo fmoothly oilde, flight of my dangers feare,
O break my heart, this griefe's too great to beare.

Ho.   Pardon me my Lord.

Suff.   God pardon thee, and lay not to thy foule
This greeuous finne : Farwell.
And when thou fpendeft this ill got golde
Remember how thy Maifters life was folde.
Thy Lord that gaue thee Lordfhips, made thee great,
Yet thou betraidft him as he fat at meate.
On to my graue, tis time that I were dead,
When he that held my heart betraies my head.

Hom.   O God, O God, that ever I was borne,
This deede hath made me flaue to abiect fcorne.

Exeunt Omnes.

Enter the Clowne.

Clo.   O poore fhrimpe, how art thou falne away

for want of mouching? O Colen cries out moft
tirannically, the little gut hath no mercie, whats heere
vittailes?
O rare! O good!
Feede chops, drinke throate, good victailes makes
    good blood.

Enter Homes with a Halter about his necke.

But ftay, whofe heere? more Sheriffes, more
fearchers? O no, this is Homes that betraide his
honeft Maifter, How with a Halter about his necke?
I hope hee doth not meane to hang himfelfe? ile ftep
a fide.
    Ho. This is the place, where I betraide my
      Lord,
This is the place where oft I haue releeu'd :
And villaine I, betraide him to the Iawes of death,
But heere before I further will proceede
Heere will I burie this inticing gould,
Lye there damn'd fiend neuer ferue humaine more.
    Clo. This is rare, now in this moode if hee would
hang himfelfe twere excellent.
    Ho. Shall I aske mercie? no it is too late,
Heauen will not heare, and I am defperate.

He ftrangles himfelf.

    Clo. So, fo, a very good ending, would all falce
Seruants might drinke of the fame fauce.
Gold, you are firft mine, you muft helpe
To fhift my felfe into fome counterfeite fuite
Of apparel, and then to London :
If my olde Maifter be hanged, why fo :
If not, why rufticke and lufticke :
Yet before I goe, I doe not care if I throwe this Dog
in a Ditch : come away diffembler : this cannot chufe
but be a hundred pound it wayes fo heauy.
                    Exeunt with him.

Enter Queene Mary, Wincheſter, Norfolke, Pembroke,
Wyat, Arundell, Attendants.

Mary.   By Gods affiſtance, and the power of
    heauen,
After our Troubles we are ſafely ſet,
In our inheritance, for which we doe ſubſcribe
The praiſe and benefit to God, next thankes
To you my Lordes.   Now ſhall the ſanctuarie,
And the houſe of the moſte high be newly built.
The ancient honours due vnto the Church,
Buried within the Ruine Monaſtaries,
Shall lift their ſtately heads, and riſe againe
To aſtoniſh the deſtroyers wandring eyes.
Zeale ſhall be deckt in golde,
Religion not like a virgin rob'd of all her pompe,
But briefly ſhining in her Iemmes of ſtate,
Like a faire bride be offerd to the Lord.
To build large houſes, pull no churches downe,
Rather inrich the Temple with our crowne.
Better a poore Queene, then the Subiects poore.
   Win.   May it pleaſe your grace to giue releaſe
Vnto ſuch ancient Biſhops that haue loſt their
Honours in the church affaires.
   Ma.   We haue giuen order to the Duke of Nor-
folke to releaſe them.
   Aru.   Your ſacred Highneſſe will no doubt be
mindefull
Of the late Oath you tooke at Framingam.
   Ma.   O my Lord of Arundell, wee remember that,
But ſhall a ſubiect force his Prince to ſweare
Contrarie to her conſcience and the Law ?
Wee heere releaſe vnto our faithfull people,
one intire ſubſidie,
Due vnto the Crowne in our dead Brothers daies :
The Commonaltie ſhal not be ore-burdned
In our reigne, let them be liberall in Religion,
and wee will ſpare their treaſure to themſelues :

Better a poore Prince then the Nation poore,
The Subiects Treasure, is the Soueraignes store.
    Arun.   What is your Highnesse pleasure about the
Rebels?
    Mar.   The Queene-like Rebels,
Meane you not Queene Iane?
    Arun.   Guilford and Iane, with great Northumber-
land,
And hauty Suffolkes Duke.
    Ma.   The Duke of Suffolke is not yet appre-
    hended,
Therefore my Lords,
Some of you most deare to vs in loue,
Be carefull of that charge:
The rest weele leaue for tryall of the other prisoners.
    Wia.   The Lady Iane most mightie Soueraigne,
Alyde to you in blood:
For shes the Daughter of your Fathers Sister.
Mary the Queene of France: Charles Brandon's
    Wife
Your Neece, your next of blood, except your sister,
Deserues some pittie, so doth youthfull Guilford.
    Win.   Such pittie as the law alowes to Traitors.
    Norf.   They were misled by their ambitious
    Fathers.
    Win.   What Sonne to obey his Father proues a
    Traitor,
Must buy their disobedience with their death.
    Wia.   My Lord of Winchester still thirsts for
    blood.
    Mar.   Wiat no more, the law shall be their Iudge,
Mercie to meane offenders weele ostend,
Not vnto such that dares vsurpe our Crowne.
    Arun.   Count Egmond the Embassador from
    Spaine,
Attends your highnesse answere, brought those Letters
Sent from the Emperor in his Sonnes behalfe.
    Mar.   In the behalfe of louely Princely Philip,
Whose person wee haue shrined in our heart?

At the firſt ſight of his delightfull picture
That picture ſhould haue power to tingle Loue
In Royall breſts : the Dartes of loue are wordes,
Pictures, conceite, heele preuaile by any,
Your counſell Lords about this forraine buſineſſe.
 Arun. I ſay and it like your royall Maieſtie,
A royall treatie, and to be confirm'd,
And I alowe the match.
 Win. Alow it Lordes, we haue cauſe
To thanke our God, that ſuch a mightie Prince
As Philip is, Sonne to the Emperor,
Heire to wealthy Spaine, and many ſpacious
Kingdomes, will vouchſafe—
 Wia. Vouchſafe ! my Lord of Wincheſter, pray
what ?
 Win. To grace our mightie Soueraigne with his
honourable Title.
 Wia. To marrie with our Queene : meane you
not ſo ?
 Win. I doe, what then ?
 Wiat. O God ! is ſhee a beggar, a forſaken Maide,
that ſhe hath neede of grace from forraine princes ?
By Gods deare mother, O God pardon ſweare I,
Me thinkes ſhe is a faire and louely Prince,
Her onely beautie (were ſhe of meane birth)
Able to make the greateſt Potentate,
I the great Emperor of the mightie Cham,
That hath more Nations vnder his Commaund,
Then ſpaniſh Philip's like to inherrit townes,
To come and lay his Scepter at her feet,
And to intreate her to vouchſafe the grace
To take him and his Kingdome to her mercy.
 Win. Wyat you are too hot.
 Wiat. And you to proude, vouchſafe ? O baſe !
I hope ſheele not vouchſafe to take the Emperors
ſonne to her deare mercie.
 Mar. Proceede my Lord of Wincheſter I pray.
 Win. Then ſtill I ſay, we haue cauſe to thanke our
  God,

That fuch a mightie Prince will looke fo lowe,
As to refpect this Iland and our Queene.
   Wia. Pardon me Madam, hee refpect your Iland
more then your perfon ? thinke of that.
   Norf. Wiat, you wrong the affection of the
      Prince,
For he defires no fortreffes nor towers,
Nor to beare any office, rule or ftate,
Either by perfon or by Subftitute,
Nor yet himfelfe to be a Counfellor
In our affaires.
   Wiat. What neede hee (Noble Lords)
To afke the fruite, when he demaundes the tree ?
No Caftle, fortreffes, nor Towers of ftrength,
It bootes not, when the chiefeft Tower of all
The key that opens vnto all the Land,
I meane our Gratious Soueraigne muft be his,
But he will beare no office in the land,
And yet will mary with the Queene of all.
Nor be of counfell in the Realmes affaires,
And yet the Queene inclofed in his armes :
I doe not like this ftrange marriage.
The Fox is futtle, and his head once in,
The flender body eafily will follow.
I grant, he offers you in name of dowre,
The yearely fumme of threefcore thoufand Duccats.
Befides the feauenteene famous Prouinces,
And that the heire fucceding from your loynes,
Shall haue the Souereigne rule of both the Realmes.
What, fhall this mooue your Highneffe to the match ?
Spaine is too farre for England to inherit,
But England neare enough for Spaine to woe.
   Win. Has not the Kinges of England (good Sir
      Thomas)
Efpouf'd the Daughters of our Neighbour Kinges ?
   Wia. I graunt, your predeceffors oft haue fought
Their Queene from France, and fometimes to from
      Spaine.
But neuer could I heare that England yet

Has bin fo bafe, to feeke a King from either :
Tis policie deare Queene, no loue at all.
    Win.   Tis loue great Queene, no pollicie at all.
    Wiat.   Which of you all, dares iuftifie this match,
And not be toucht in confcience with an oath ?
Remember, O remember I befeech you,
King Henries laft will, and his act at Court,
1 meane that royall Court of Parliament,
That does prohibit Spaniards from the Land,
That Will and Act, to which you all are fworne,
And doe not damme your foules with periurie.
    Mory.   But that wee knowe thee Wyat to be
        true
Vnto the Crowne of England and to vs,
Thy ouer-boldneffe fhould bee payde with death.
But ceafe, for feare your liberall tongue offend,
With one confent my Lordes you like this match ?
    Omnes.   We doe great Soueraigne.
    Mary.   Call in Count Egmond Honorable Lords.

              Enter Egmond.

Wee haue determined of your Ambaffie,
And thus I plight, our loue to Philips heart,
Imbarke you ftraight, the winde blowes wondrous
        faire :
Till he fhall land in England, I am all care.
               Exeunt all but Sir Thomas Wyat.
    Wia.   And ere hee land in England, I will offer
My loyall breft for him to treade vpon.
O who fo forward Wyat as thy felfe,
To raife this troublefome Queene in this her Throane ?
Philip is a Spaniard, a proud Nation,
Whome naturally our Countriemen abhorre.
Affift me gratious heauens, and you fhall fee
What hate I beare vnto their Slauerie.
Ile into Kent, there mufter vp my friendes,
To faue this Countrie, and this Realme defend.
               Exit Sir Thomas Wyat.

Enter Guilford, Dudley, Iane, and Leftenant.

Guil. God morrow to the Patron of my woe.

Iane. God morrowe to my Lord, my louely
Dudley.
Why doe you looke fo fad my dearest Lord?

Guil. Nay why doth Iane, thus with a heauie eye,
And a deiected looke, falute the day?
Sorrow doth ill become thy filuer brow,
Sad griefe lyes dead, fo long as thou liues fayre,
In my Ianes ioy, I doe not care for care.

Iane. My lookes (my loue) is forted with my
heart,
The Sunne himfelfe, doth fcantly fhow his face
Out of this firme grate, you may perceiue the Tower
Hill
Thronged with ftore of people,
As if they gap'd for fome ftrange Noueltie.

Guil. Though fleepe doe fildome dwell in men
of care,
Yet I did this night fleepe, and this night dream't,
My Princely father great Northumberland
Was marryed to a ftately Bride :
And then me thought, iuft on his Bridall day,
A poyfoned draught did take his life away.

Iane. Let not fond vifions fo appale my Loue,
For dreames doe oftentimes contrarie prooue.

Guil. The nights are teadious, and the daies
are fad,
And fee you how the people ftand in heapes,
Each man fad, looking on his oppofed obiect,
As if a generall paffion poffeft them?
Their eyes doe feeme, as dropping as the Moone,
As if prepared for a Tragedie.
For neuer fwarmes of people there doe tread,
But to rob life, and to inrich the dead
And fhewe they wept.

Lef. My Lord they did fo, for I was there.

Gui. I pra'y refolue vs good Maifter Lieftenant

Who was it yonder, that tendered vp his life
To natures death?
   Lief.   Pardon mee my Lord, tis fellony to acquaint
you with death of any Prifoner, yet to refolue your
grace, it was your Father, great Northumberland, that
this day loft his head.
   Guil.   Peace reft his foule, his finnes be buried in
     his graue,
And not remembred in his Epitaph :
But who comes heere?
   Iane.   My Father Prifoner?

     Enter Suffolke garded foorth.

   Suff.   O Iane! now naught but feare thy Tytle &
     thy ftate,
Thou now muft leaue for a fmall graue.
Had I bin contented to a bin great, 1 had ftood,
But now my rfing is puld downe with blood.
Farwell, point me my houfe of prayers.
   Iane.   Is greefe fo fhort? twa's wont to be full of
     wordes, tis true,
But now Deathes leffon, bids a coulde adue.
Farwell, thus friendes on defperate iourneys parte,
Breaking of wordes with teares, that fwelles the heart.
                    Exit Suffolke.
   Lief.   It is the pleafure of the Queene that you
     part lodgings.
Till your Arrainement, which muft be to morrow.
   Iane.   Good Maifter Lieftenant let vs pray together.
   Lief.   Pardon me Madam I may not, they that owe
     you, fway me.
   Guil.   Intreate not Iane, though fhee our bodies
     part,
Our foules fhall meete.   Farwell my loue.
   Iane.   My Dudley, my owne heart.   *Exeunt Omnes.*

     Enter Wyat with Souldiers.

   Wiat.   Hold Drumme, ftand Gentlemen,

Giue the word along : ſtand, ſtand :
Maiſters, friendes, Souldiers, and therefore Gentle-
    men,
I know ſome of you weare warme purſſes
Linde with golde, to them I ſpeake not,
But to ſuch leane knaues that cannot put vp
Croſſes, thus I ſay, fight valiantly,
And by the Mary God, you that haue all
Your life time ſiluer lackt,
Shall now get Crownes, marry they muſt be crackt.
   Sol. No matter, weele change them for white
    money.
   Wiat. But it muſt needs be ſo, deare Countrie-
    men,
For Souldiers are the maiſters of wars mint,
Blowes are the ſtamps, they ſet vpon with bullets,
And broken pates are when the braines lyes ſpilt :
Theſe light crownes, that with blood are double
    guilt,
But thats not all, that your ſtout hearts ſhall earne,
Sticke to this glorious quarrell, and your names
Shall ſtand in Chronicles ranck'd euen with Kings :
You free your Countrie from baſe ſpaniſh thrall,
From Ignominious ſlauerie,
Who can diſgeſt a Spaniard, that's a true Engliſhman ?
   Sol. Would he might choake that diſgeſts him.
   Wiat. Hee that loues freedome and his Countrie,
    crie
A Wyat : he that will not, with my heart
Let him ſtand forth, ſhake handes, and weele depart.
   Sol. A Wyat, a Wyat, a Wyat.

Enter Norry ſounding a Trumpet.

   Har. Forbeare, or with the breath thy Trumpet
    ſpends,
This ſhall let foorth thy ſoule.
   Nor. I am a Herald,
And chalenge ſafetie by the lawe of armes.

Her. So ſhalt thou when thou art lawfully im-
ploide.

Wia. What loude knaues that?

Nor. No knaue Sir Thomas, I am a true man to
my Queene, to whome thou art a Traytor.

Sol. Knocke him downe.

Wiat. Knock him downe, fie no,
Weele handle him, he ſhall found before he goe.

Har. Hee comes from Norfolke and thoſe fawn-
ing Lords,
In Maries name, waying out life to them
That will with baſeneſſe buie it.
Ceaze on him as a pernitious enemie.

Wia. Sir George be ruld,
Since we profeſſe the Arte of Warre,
Let's not be hiſt at for our ignorance,
He ſhall paſſe and repaſſe, iuggle the beſt he can,
Leade him into the Citie. Norry ſet foorth
Set foorth thy braſen throate, and call all Rocheſter
About thee : doe thy office, fill their
Light heads with proclamations, doe,
Catch Fooles with Lime-twigs dipt with pardons.
But Sir George and good ſir Harry Iſley,
If this Gallant open his mouth too wide,
Powder the Varlet, piſtoll him, fire the Roofe that's
ore his mouth.
He craues the law of Armes, and he ſhall ha't,
Teach him our law, to cut's throate if he prate.
If lowder reach thy Proclamation,
The Lord haue mercie vppon thee.

Nor. Sir Thomas, I muſt doe my office.

Her. Come, weele doe ours too.

Wia. I, I, doe, blowe thy ſelfe hence.

               Exit. Harper, Iſeley, and Norry.
Whorſon prou'd Herrald, becauſe he can
giue armes, he thinkes to cut vs off by the elbowes
Maiſters and fellow Souldiers, ſay, will you leaue old
Tom Wiat?

Omnes. No, no, no.

Wia.   A March! tis Norfolkes Drum vpon my
   life.
I pra'y fee what Drum it is.

Within crie arme.

The word is giuen, arme, arme flies through the
   camp
As loude, though not fo full of dread as thunder:
For no mans cheekes looke pale, but euerie face,
Is lifted vp aboue his foremans head,
And euerie Souldier does on tip-toe ſtand,
ſhaking a drawne fword in his threatning hand.
   Wiat.   At whome, at whofe Drum?
   Rod.   At Norfolke, Norfolkes drum:
With him comes Arundell, you may beholde
The filken faces of their enfignes ſhowe,
Nothing but wrinckles ſtragling in the winde,
Norfolke rides formoſtly, his creſt well knowne,
Proud, as if all our heads were now his owne.
   Wiat.   Soft, he ſhall pay more for them.
Sir Robert Rodſton, bring our Mufcateers,
To flancke our Pikes, let all our archery,
Fall off in winges of ſhot a both fides of the van,
To gall the firſt Horfe of the enemie
That ſhall come fiercely on:
Our Canoneres, bid them to charge, charge my harts.
   Omnes.   Charge, charge.
   Wiat.   Saint George for England, Wiat for poore
      Kent,
Blood loſt in Countries quarrell, is nobly fpent.

Enter Ifely.

Ifely.   Bafe flaue, hard hearted fugitiue,
He that you fent with Norry, falfe Sir George
Is fled to Norfolke.
   Rod.   Sir George Harper fled?
   Wiat.   I nere thought better of a Counterfeite,
His name was Harper, was it not? let him goe,
Hencefoorth all Harpers for his fake ſhall ſtand,
But for plaine nine pence, throughout all the land.

They come, no man giue ground in thefe hot cafes,
Be Englifhmen and berd them to their faces.

Exeunt.

Enter Norfolke, Arundell, Bret and Souldiers.

Norf.   Yonder the Traitor marcheth with a fteele
   bowe
Bent on his Souereigne, and his kingdomes peace :
To waue him to vs with a flag of truce,
And tender him foft mercie,
Were to call our right in queftion,
Therefore put in act, your refolute intendments,
If rebellion be fuffered to take head,
She liues too long, treafon doth fwarme.
Therefore giue fignall to the fight.
   Bre.   Tis good, tis good, my Lord.
   Norf.   Where's Captaine Bret ?
   Br.   Heere my Lord.
   Norf.   To doe honour to you and thofe fiue hun-
   dred
Londoners that march after your colours,
You fhall charge the Traitor in the Vantgard
Whilft my felfe with noble Arundell
And ftout Jarningam, fecond you in the maine.
God and Saint George, this day fight on our fide,
While thus we tame a defperate Rebels pride.

Exit. all but Bret and fouldiers.

   Br.   Countrimen and friendes,
And you the mofte valiant fword and Buckler-Men of
London, the Duke of Norfolk in honour has pro-
moted you to the Vangard, and why to the Vangard ?
but becaufe he knowes you to be eager men, martiall
men, men of good ftomacks, verie hot fhots, verie
actious for valour, fuch as fcornes to fhrink for a wetting, who wil beare off any thing with head and
fhoulders.
   Omn.   Well forwards good commander forwards.
   Bre.   I am to leade you, and whether ? to fight, and

with whom? with Wyat, and what is Wyat? a moſt famous and arch traytor to nobody by this hand that I knowe.

Omn. Nay ſpeake out good captaine.

Bret. I ſay againe, is worthy Norfolke gone ?

Omn. I I, gon gon.

Bret. I ſay againe that Wyat for riſing thus in armes, with the Kentiſh men dangling thus at his taile, is worthy to be hanged like a iewell in the kingdomes eare. Say I well my lads?

Omn. Forwards, forwards.

Bret. And whoſoeuer cuts off his head ſhal haue for his labour.

Clown. What ſhall I haue? Ile do't.

Bre. The poxe, the plague, and all the diſeaſes the ſpitle-houſes and hoſpitalls can throw vpon him.

Clo. Ile not do't, thats flat.

Bre. And wherefore is Wyat vp ?

Clo, Becauſe he cannot keepe his bed.

Bre. No Wyat is vp to keepe the Spaniards downe, to keepe King *Phillip* out, who comming in will giue the land ſuch a *Phillip* twil make it reele againe.

Clo. A would it were come to that, we would, we would leaue off Phillips and fall to hot cockles.

Bre. Phillip is a Spaniard, and what is a Spaniard ?

Clo. A Spaniard is no Engliſhman that I know.

Bre. Right a Spaniard is a Camocho, a Callimanco, nay which is worſe a Dondego, and what is a Dondego?

Clo. A Dondego is a kind of Spaniſh ſtock fiſh or poore Iohn.

Bre. No, a Dondego is a deſperate Viliago, a very Caſtillian, God bleſſe vs. There came but one Dondego into England, and he made all Paules ſtinke againe, what ſhall a whole armie of Dondegoes doe my ſweete countriemen ?

Clo. Mary they wil make vs al ſmell abhominably, he comes not heere thats flat.

Bre.   A Spaniard is cald ſo becauſe he's a Spaniard, his yard is but a ſpan.

Clo.   That's the reaſon our Engliſhwomen loue
them not.

Bre.   Right, for he carries not the Engliſhmans
yard about him. If you deale with him, looke for
hard meaſure, if you giue an inch hee'le take an ell:
if he giue an ell, hele take an inch, therefore my fine
ſpruce dapper finicall fellowes, if you are now, as
you haue alwayes been counted pollitick Londoners to
flie to the ſtronger ſide, leaue Arundell, leaue Norfolke
and loue Bret.

Clo.   Weele fling our flat-caps at them.

Bre. Weare your owne neates leather ſhooes, ſcorne
Spaniſh leather : cry a figge for the Spaniards.   Saide
I well bollies ?

Omn.   I, I, I.

ı *Bret.*   Why then fiat, fiat.
And euerie man die at
His foote that cries not a *Wyat,* a *Wyat.*

Omnes.   A *Wyat,* a *Wyat,* a *Wyat.*

Enter Wyat.

Wiat.   Sweet muſicke, gallant fellow Londoners.

Clo.   Y faith we are the madcaps, we are the lick-
pennies.

Wiat.   You ſhall be all Lord Maiors at leaſt.

Exeunt Wyat, Bret, and Souldiers.

Alarum ſounds, and enter Wyat, Bret, Rodſton, Iſely,
and Souldiers againe.

Wyat.   Thoſe eight braſſe peeces ſhall do ſeruice
now
Againſt their maſters, Norfolk and Arundell,
They may thank their heeles
More then their hands for ſauing of their liues.
When ſouldiers turne ſurueyors, and meaſure lands,

God helpe poore farmers. Soldiers and friends let
    vs all
Play nimble bloudhounds and hunt them ſtep by
    ſtep.
We heare
The lawyers plead in armour ſtead of gownes,
If they fall out about the caſe they iarre,
Then they may cuffe each other from the barre.
Soft this is Ludgate, ſtand aloofe, Ile knock.

    He knocks : Enter Pembroke vpon the walles.

   Pem.   Who knockes ?
   Wyat.   A Wyat, a true friend,
Open your gates, you louing cittizens,
I bring you freedom from a forraine prince,
The queene has heard your ſuite, and tis her pleaſure
The cittie gates ſtand open to receiue vs.
   Pem.   Avuant thou traytor, thinkest thou by for-
    gerie
To enter London with rebellious armes ?
Know that theſe gates are bard againſt thy entrance,
And it ſhall coſt the liues
Of twenty thouſand true ſubiects to the Queene
Before a traytor enters.
   Omn.   Shoote him through.
   Wyat.   Stay, lets know him firſt.
   Clo.   Kill him, then lets know him afterwards.
   Pem.   Looke on my face, and bluſhing ſee with
    ſhame
Thy treaſons characterd.
   Bret.   Tis the Lord Pembroke.
   Wyat.   What haue wee to doe with the Lord Pem-
    broke ?
Wheres the Queenes Lieſtenant ?
   Pem.   I am lieſtenant of the Citty now.
   Wiat.   Are you Lord Maior ?
   Pem.   The greateſt Lord that breathes enters not
    heere

Without expreſſe commaund from my deare Queene.
   Wyat.   She commands by vs.
   Pem.   I do command thee in her Highneſſe name
To leaue the Citty gates, or by my honour,
A peece of ordinance ſhall be ſtreight diſchargd
To be thy deathesman and ſhoote thee to thy graue.
   Wyat.   Then heres no entrance.
   Pem.   No, none.   *Exit Pembroke.*
   Bret.   What ſhould we doe following Wiat any
     longer ?
   Wyot.   O London, London, thou perfidious towne,
Why haſt thou broke thy promiſe to thy friend ?
That for thy fake, and for thy generall fake,
Hath thruſt myſelf into the mouth of danger ?
March backe to Fleeteſtreete, if that Wiat dye,
London vniuſtly buy thy treacherie.
   Bret.   Would I could ſteale away from Wyat ! it
ſhould be the firſt thing that I would doe.
Here they all ſteale away from Wyat and leaue him alone.
   Wyat.   Wheres all my Souldiers ? what all gone,
And left my drum and colours without guard ?
O infellicitie of carefull men,
Yet will I fell my honor'd bloud as deere
As ere did faithfull ſubieċt to his prince.   *Exit Wyat.*

Enter Norfolke and Iſely.

   Iſl.   Pembroke reuolts, and flies to Wiats ſide.
   Norf.   Hees damb'd in hell that ſpeakes it.

Enter Harper.

   Iſl.   O my good Lord ! tis ſpread
That Pembroke and Count Arundel both are fled.

Enter Pembroke and Arundell.

   Pem.   Sfoot, who faid ſo ? what deuill dares ſtir my
     patience ?

Zwounds I was talking with a crue of vagabondes
That laggd at Wiat's taile ; and am I thus
Paid for my paines.
    Norf.	And there being miſt
Some villaine, finding you out of ſight, hath raiſ'd
This ſlander on you, but come my Lord.
    Pem.	Ile not fight.
    Norf.	Nay ſweete Earle.
    Pem.	Zounds fight and heare my name dif
      honoured ?
    Arun.	Wyat is marcht down Fleeteſtreete, after
      him.
    Pem.	Why do not you, and you, purſue him ?
    Norf.	If I ſtrike one blowe, may my hand fall off.
    Pem.	And if I doe, by this—
    Norf.	Come leaue your ſwearing, did not countries
      care
Vrge me to this quarrell, for my part,
I would not ſtrike a blow.
    Pem.	No more would I ;
Ile eate no wrongs, lets all die, and Ile dye.

          Enter Meſſenger.

    Meſſ.	Stand on your guard,
For this way Wyatt is perſude amaine.

*A great Noiſe, follow. Enter Wyat with his ſword
       drawne, being wounded.*

    Within.	Follow, follow.
    Nor.	Stand traytor ſtand, or thou ſhalt nere ſtand
      more.
    Wyat.	Lords, I yield :
An eaſie conqueſt tis to win the field
After alls loſt.   I am wounded, let me haue
A ſurgeon that I may goe found vnto my graue.
Tis not the name of Traytor
Pals me nor pluckes my weapon from my hand.

Vſe me how you can,
Though you ſay traytor, I am a gentleman.
Your dreadfull ſhaking me, which I defie,
Is a poore loſſe of life ; I wiſh to die,
Death frights my ſpirit no more then can my bed,
Nor will I change one haire, loſing this head.
    Pem.   Come, guard him, guard him.
    Wyat.   No matter where,
I hope for nothing, therefore nothing feare.
                        Exit Omnes.

Enter Wincheſter, Norfolk, Arundell, Pembroke, with
other Lords.

    Win.   My Lord of Norfolk, will it pleaſe you
    ſit
By you the noble Lord of Arundell.
Since it hath pleaſ'd her ſacred Maieſtie
To nominate vs heere Commiſſioners,
Let vs without all partiality
Be open-eard to what they can alleadge.
Wheres the Lieftenant of the Tower ?

Enter Lieftenant of the Tower.

    Lef.   Heere my good Lord.
    Win.   Fetch forth the priſoners.
Place them ſeuerally in chaires of ſtate.
Clarke of the Crowne, proceede as Law requires.

Enter Guilford and Iane.
    Cla.   Guilford Dudley, hold vp thy hand at the
bar.
    Guil.   Heere at the bar of death I hold it vp,
And would to God this hand heau'd to the lawe,
Might haue aduanct itſelf in better place,
For Englands good and for my ſoueraigns weale.
    Cla.   Iane Gray, Lady Iane Gray, hold vp thy
hand at the barre.

Ian.   A hand as pure from Treafons Innocence
As the white liuerie
Worne by the Angels in their Makers fight?
  Cla.   You are here indited by the names of Guil-
ford Dudley, Lord Dudley, Iane Gray, Lady Iane
Gray, of capitall and high treafon againft our moft
Soueraign Ladie the Queenes Maieftie.   That is to fay
that you Guilford Dudley and Lady Iane Gray, haue
by all poffible meanes, fought to procure vnto yourfelues the roialtie of the Crowne of England, to the
difinheriting of our now Soueraign Lady the Queenes
Maieftie, the true and lawfull iffue to that famous
King Henry the Eight, and haue manifeftly adorned
yourfelues with the States garland Imperiall, and
haue granted warrants, commiffions, and fuch like, for
leuying of men and Souldiers to be fent againft the
faid Maieftie : what anfwere you to this inditement,
guiltie or not guiltie?
  Guil.   Our anfwer fhall be feuerall like ourfelues.
Yet noble Earle we confeffe the inditement.
May we not make fome apologie vnto the court?
  Norf.   It is againft the order of the law,
Therefore directly pleade vnto the inditement,
And then you fhall be heard.
  Guil.   Againft the law?
Words vtterd then as good vnfpoken were,
For whatfoere you fay, you know your form,
And you will follow it vnto our deathes.
  Norf.   Speake are you guilty of thefe crimes or
no?
  Ian.   Ile anfwere firft, I am and I am not,
But fhould we ftand vnto the laft vnguiltie,
You haue large-confcience iurors to befmeare
The faireft browe with ftile of trecherie.
  Norf.   The Barrons of the land fhall be your iurie.
  Ian.   An honorable and worthy trial,
And God forbid fo many noblemen
Should be made guilty of our timeleffe deathes.

Arun. Youle anſwer to the inditement will you not ?

Guil. My Lord I will, I am——

Nor. What are you guilty or no ?

Guil. I ſay vnguilty ſtill, yet I am guilty.

Ian. Slander not thyſelf :
If there be any guilty, it was I,
I was proclaim'd Queene, I the Crowne ſhould
    weare.

Guel. Becauſe I was thy huſband I ſtand heere.

Ian. Our loues we ſought ourſelues, but not our
    pride,
And ſhall our fathers faults our liues diuide ?

Guil. It was my father that made thee diſtreſt.

Ian. O but for mine my Guilford had beene bleſt.

Guil. My Iane had beene as fortunate as faire.

Ian. My Guilford free from this foul-grieuing care.

Guil. If we be guiltie, tis no fault of ours,
And ſhall wee dye for whats not in our powres ?
We ſought no Kingdom, we deſir'd no crowne,
It was impoſ'd vpon vs by conſtraint,
Like golden fruit hung on a barraine tree,
And will you count ſuch forcement treacherie ?
Then make the ſiluer Thames as blacke as Styx,
Becauſe it was conſtraind to beare the barkes
Whoſe battering ordnance ſhould haue beene im-
    ployde
Againſt the hinderers of our roialtie.

Win. You talke of fenceleſſe things.

Guil. Do trees want fence,
That by the powre of Muſicke haue beene drawne
To dance a pleaſing meaſure ?
Weele come then neerer vnto liuing things.
Say wee vſurpt the Engliſh roialtie,
Was't not by your conſents ?
I tell you Lordes I haue your hands to ſhowe
Subſcrib'd to the commiſſion of my Father,
By which you did authorize him to wage armes.

If they were rebellious againſt your Soueraigne,
Who cride ſo loud as you God ſaue Queene Iane?
And come you now your Soueraign to arraigne?
Come downe, come down, heere at a Priſoners barre,
Better do ſo then iudge yourſelues amiſs :
For looke what ſentence on our heads you lay,
Vpon your own may light another day.
   Win. The Queene hath pardond them.
   Guil. And wee muſt die
For a leſſe fault.   O partiallitie !
   Ian. Patience, my Guilford, it was euer knowne,
They that ſinn'd leaſt the puniſhment haue borne.
   Guil. True, my faire Queene, of ſorrowe truely
     ſpeake,
Great men like great flies through Lawes cobwebs
     breake,
But the thinn'ſt frame the priſon of the weake.
   Nor. Now truſt me Arundel, it doth grieue me
     much
To ſit in judgment of theſe harmleſſe———
   Arun. I helpt to attach the Father, but the
     Sonne—
O through my bloud I feele compaſſion.
Run my Lords, weele be humble ſuitors to the Queene,
To ſaue theſe innocent creatures from their deaths.
   Norf. Lets break vp Court : if Norfolke long
     ſhould ſtay
In teares and paſſion I ſhould melt away.
   Win. Sit ſtill,
What, will you take compaſſion vpon ſuch?
They are hereticks.
   Ian. We are Chriſtians, leaue our conſcience to
     ourſelues,
We ſtand not heere about religious cauſes,
But are accuſ'd of capitall treaſon.
   Win. Then you confeſſe the inditement?
   Guil. Euen what you will :
Yet ſaue my Iane, although my bloud you ſpill.
   Ian. If I muſt die, ſaue princely Guilfords life.

Norf.   Who is not moou'd to fee this louing ftrife ?
Arun.   Pray pardon me, do what you will to-day,
And Ile approue it, though it be my death.
   Win.   Then heare the fpeedie fentence of your
    deaths :
You fhall be carried to the place from whence you
    came,
From thence vnto the place of execution,
Through London to be drawn on hurdles,
Where thou, Iane Gray, fhalt fuffer death by fire,
Thou Guilford Dudley, hang'd and quartered,
So Lord haue mercy vpon you.
   Guil.   Why this is well,
Since we muft die, that we muft die togither.
   Win.   Stay, and heare the mercie of the Queene,
Becaufe you are of noble parentage,
Although the crime of your offence be great,
Shee is only pleas'd that you fhall ——
   Both.   Will fhee pardon vs ?
   Win.   Only I fay that you fhal loofe your heades
Vpon the Tower Hill.   So conuay them hence,
Liefetenant ftrictly looke ynto your charge.
   Guil.   Our doomes are knowne, our liues haue
    plaid their part.
Farwell my Iane.
   Ian.   My Dudley, mine owne heart.
   Guil.   Faine would I take a ceremonious leaue,
But thats to dye a hundred thoufand deaths.
   Ian.   I cannot fpeake for teares.
   Left.   My Lord, come :
   Guil.   Great griefes fpeake louder
When the leaft are dumb'd.   *Exeunt.*

    Enter Sir Thomas Wyat in the Tower.

   Wia.   The fad afpect this Prifon doth affoord
Iumps with the meafure that my heart doth keepe,
And this inclofure heere of nought but ftone,
Yieldes far more comfort then the ftony hearts

Of the.n that wrong'd their country, and their friend :
Heere is no periur'd Counfellors to fweare
A facred oath, and then forfweare the famc,
No innovators heere doth harbor keepe,
A ftedfaft filence doth poffeffe the place,
In this the Tower is noble, being bafe.

Enter Lords to Wyat.

Norf.   Sir Thomas Wyat.
Wyat.   Thats my name indeede.
Win.   You fhould fay Traitor.
Wiat.   Traitor and Wyats name,
Differ as farre as Winchefter and honor.
   Win.   I am a Piller of the Mother Church.
   Wiat.   And what am I ?
   Win.   One that fubuerts the ftate.
   Wyat.   Infult not too much, ore th' vnfortunate,
I haue no Bifhoppes Rochet to declare my inno-
      cencie.
This is my croffe,
That caufeleffe I muft fuffer my heads loffe.
When that houre comes, wherein my blood is fpilt,
My croffe will looke as bright as yours twice guilt.
   Norf.   Here's for that purpofe.
   Wiat.   Is your grace fo fhort ?
Belike you come to make my death a fport.
   Win.   We come to bring you to your execution,
You muft be hang'd and quartered inftantly ;
At the parke Corner, is a gallous fet,
Whither make haft to tender natures debt.
   Wiat.   Then here's the end of Wyats rifing vp,
I to keepe Spaniards from the Land was fworne,
Right willingly I yeelde my felfe to death,
But forry fuch, fhould haue my place of birth.
Had London kept his word, Wyat had ftood,
But now King Phillip enters through my blood.
Exit Officers with Wyat.

Enter Lieftenant.

Lie. Heere my Lord.

Win. Fetch foorth your other Priſoners.

Lief. My Lord I will, heere lyes young Guilford, here the Lady Iane.

Norfol. Conduct them forth.

Fnter Young Guilford and the Lady Iane.

Guil. Good morrowe once more to my louelye Iane.

Iane. The laſt good morrow my ſweete loue to thee.

Guil. What were you reading ?

Iane. On a prayer booke.

Guil. Truſt me ſo was I, wee hade neede to pray,
For ſee, the Miniſters of death drawe neere.

Iane. To a prepared minde Death is a pleaſure,
I long in ſoule, till I haue ſpent my breath.

Guil. My Lord High Chancelor, you are welcome heather,
What come you to beholde our execution ?
And my Lord Arundell thrice welcome, you
Helpt to attache our Father, come you now,
To ſee the blacke concluſion of our Tragedie ?

Win. We come to doe our office.

Guil. So doe wee.
Our office is to die, yours to looke on :
We are beholding vnto ſuch beholders,
The time was Lords, when you did flock amaine,
To ſee her crownd, but now to kill my Iane,
The world like to a ſickell, bends it ſelfe,
Men runne their courſe of liues as in a maze,
Our office is to die, yours but to gaze.

Iane. Patience my Guilford.

Guil. Patience my louely Iane :
Patience has blancht thy ſoule as white as ſnow,
But who ſhall anſwere for thy death ? this know,

An innocent to die, what is it leffe,
But to adde Angels to heauens happineffe.
The guiltie dying, doe applaud the law,
But when the innocent creature ftoopes his neck
To an vnjuft doome; vpon the Iudge the checke.
Liues are like foules, requird of their negle&ctors,
Then ours of you, that fhould bee our prote&ctors.
    Win.   Raile not againft the law.
    Guilfor.   No, God forbidde, my Lord of Win-
      chefter,
It's made of lawe, and fhould I raile againft it ?
Twere againft you, if I forget not,
You reioyc'd to fee that fall of Cromwel,
Ioy you now at me ?
Oft dying men are fild with prophefies,
But ile not be a prophet of your il.
Yet knowe my Lordes, they that behold vs now,
May to the axe of Iuftice one day bowe,
And in that plot of ground where we muft die,
Sprinckle their bloodes, though I know no caufe why.
    Norf.   Speake you to me Lord Guilford ?
    Gui.   Norfolke no,
I fpeake to ——
    Norf.   To whome ?
    Gui.   Alaffe I doe not knowe which of vs two dies
      firft.
    Win.   The better part.
    Gui.   O rather kill the worft.
    Jane.   Tis I fweete loue, that firft muft kiffe the
      blocke.
    Guilf.   I am a man, men better brooke the fhocke
Of threatning death, Your fexe are euer weake.
The thoughts of death, a womans heart will breake.
    Jane.   But I am armde to die.
    Guilf.   Likelyer to liue :
Death to the vnwilling dooth his prefence giue ;
Hee dares not looke the bolde man in the face,
But on the fearefull layes his killing Mace.
    Winc.   It is the pleafure of the Queene, that the

Lady Jane muſt firſt ſuffer death.

Jane.   I thanke her Highneſſe,
That I ſhall firſt depart this hapleſſe world,
And not ſuruiue to ſee my deere loue dead.

Guilfo.   She dying firſt, I three times looſe my
head.

Enter the Headſman.

Headſm.   Forgiue me Lady I pra'y your death.

Guilf.   Ha? haſt thou the heart to kill a face ſo
faire.

Win.   It is her Headeſ-man.

Guil.   And demaundes a pardon,
Onely of her, for taking off her head?

Jane.   I gentle Guilford, and I pardon him.

Guil.   But ile not pardon him, thou art my wife.
And he ſhall aske me pardon for thy life.

Hea.   Pardon me my Lord.

Gui.   Riſe, doe not kneele.
Though thou ſubmit'ſt, thou haſt a lowring ſteele
Whoſe fatal declynation brings our death :
Good man of earth, make haſte to make vs earth.

Hedſ.   Pleaſeth the Lady Iane, ile helpe her off
with her night-Gowne.

Jane.   Thankes gentle friend,
But I haue other waiting women to attend mee.
Good Miſtris Ellin lend me a helping hand,
To ſtrip me of this worldly ornaments
Off with theſe robes, O teare them from my ſide,
Such ſilken couers are the guilt of pride.
Inſteede of gownes, my couerture be earth,
My worldly death or new Celeſtiall breath.
What is it off?

Lad.   Madam almoſte.

Jane.   Not yet, O God !
How hardly can we ſhake off this worldes Pomp,
That cleaues vnto vs like our bodies skinne ?
Yet thus O God ſhake off thy ſeruants ſinne.

Lady.   Here is a ſcarfe to blinde your eies.

Jane. From all the world, but from my Guilfords
    fight :
Before I faften this beneath my browe,
Let me behold him with a conftant looke.
   Gui. O doe not kill me with that pitious eie :
   Jane. Tis my laft farwell, take it patiently,
My deareft Guilford let vs kiffe and part. ·
Now blinde mine eyes, neuer to fee the skie,
Blindefolde thus leade me, to the blocke to die.
   Guil. Oh !   *He falles in a trance.*
   Norf. How fares my Lord ?
   Arun. Hee's falne into a trance.
   orf. Wake him not, vntill hee wake himfelfe,
O happie Guilford if thou die in this,
Thy foule will be the firft in heauenly bliffe.

     Enter the Headef-man with Janes head.

   Win. Heare comes the Headf-man with the head
    of Iane.
   Guil. Who fpake of Iane ? who namde my louely
    Iane ?
   Win. Behold her head.
   Gui. O I fhall faint againe !
Yet let me beare this fight vnto my graue.
My fweete Ianes head :
Looke Norfolke, Arundell, Winchefter,
Doe malefa&ctors, looke :
Thus when they die,
A ruddie lippe, a cleere reflecting eye,
Cheekes purer then the Maiden orient pearle,
That fprinkles bafhfulues through the cloudes
Her innocence, has giuen her this looke :
The like for me to fhow fo well being dead,
How willingly, would Guilford loofe his head.
   Win. My Lord, the time runs on.
   Guil. So does our death.
Heeres one has run fo faft fhee's out of breath,
But the time goes on,
And thy faire Ianes white foule, will be
3   K

In heauen before me
If I doe ſtay : ſtay gentle wife,
Thy Guilford followes thee,
Though on the earth we part, by aduerſe fate,
Our ſoules ſhall knock together at heauens gate.
The skie is calme, our deathes haue a faire day,
And we ſhall paſſe the ſmoother on our way.
My Lords farwell, I once farwel to all,
The Fathers pride has cauſde the Childrens fall.

                          Exit Guilford to Death.

Nor. Thus haue we ſeene her Highneſſe will per-
    form'd,
And now their heads and bodies ſhall bee ioynd
And buried in one graue, as fits their loues.
Thus much ile ſay in their behalfes now dead,
Their Fathers pride their liues haue feuered.

F I N I S.

THE

Roaring Girle.

OR,

Moll Cut-Purſe.

As it hath lately beene Acted on the Fortune-
ſtage by *the Prince his Players.*

Written by *T. Middleton* and *T. Dekkar.*

My caſe is altered, I muſt worke for my liuing.

Printed at *London* for *Thomas Archer*, and are to be ſold at his
ſhop in Popes head-pallace, neere the Royall
Exchange. 1611.

Prologus.

A Play (expected long) makes the Audience looke
   For wonders :—that each Scæne should be a booke,
Compos'd to all perfection ; each one comes
And brings a play in's head with him : vp he summes,
What he would of a Roaring Girle haue writ ;
If that he findes not here, he mewes at it.
Onely we intreate you thinke our Scæne
Cannot speake high (the subiect being but meane)
A Roaring Girle (whose notes till now neuer were)
Shall fill with laughter our vast Theater,
That's all which I dare promise : Tragick passion,
And such graue stuffe, is this day out of fashion.
I see attention sets wide ope her gates
Of hearing, and with couetous listning waites,
To know what Girle, this Roaring Girle should be.
(For of that Tribe are many.)   One is shee
That roares at midnight in deepe Tauerne bowles,
That beates the watch, and Constables controuls ;
Another roares i' th day time, sweares, stabbes, giues
      braues,
Yet sells her soule to the lust of fooles and slaues.
Both these are Suburbe-roarers.   Then there's (besides)
A ciuill Citty Roaring Girle, whose pride,
Feasting, and riding, shakes her husbands state,
And leaues him Roaring through an yron grate.

None of thefe Roaring Girles is ours : fhee flies
With wings more lofty.   Thus her character lyes,
Yet what neede characters ? when to giue a geffe,
Is better then the perfon to expreffe ;
But would you know who 'tis ? would you heare her
    name ?
Shee is cal'd madde Moll ; *her life, our acts proclaime.*

Dramatis Perſonæ.

Sir *Alexander Wentgraue*, and *Neatſ-foot* his man
Sir *Adam Appleton.*
Sir *Dauy Dapper.*
Sir *Bewteous Ganymed.*
Lord *Noland.*
Yong *Wentgraue.*
Iacke Dapper, and *Gull* his page.
Goſhawke.
Greenewit.
Laxton.

Tilt-yard.	
Openworke.	Ciues & Vxores.
Gallipot.	

Mol the Roaring Girle.
Trapdoore.
    Sir *Guy Fitz-allard.*
    Mary Fitz-allard his daughter.
Curtilax a Sergiant, and
Hanger his Yeoman.

Miniſtri.

The Roaring Girle.

Act 1. Scæ. 1.

Enter Mary Fitz-Allard *difguifed like a fempfter with
a cafe for bands, and* Neatfoot *a feruingman with
her, with a napkin on his fhoulder, and a trencher
in his hand as from table.*

Neatfoote.

He yong gentleman (our young maifter)
Sir *Alexanders* fonne, is it into his eares
(fweet Damfell) (embleme of fragility) you
defire to haue a meffage tranfported, or to
be tranfcendent.

Mary.   A priuate word or two Sir, nothing elfe.

Neat.   You fhall fruƈtifie in that which you come
for : your pleafure fhall be fatisfied to your full con-
tentation : I will (faireft tree of generation) watch
when our young maifter is ereƈted, (that is to fay vp)
and deliuer him to this your moft white hand.

Mary.   Thankes fir.

Neat.   And withall certifie him, that I haue culled

out for him (now his belly is replenifhed) a daintier
bit or modicome then any lay vpon his trencher at
dinner ——— hath he notion of your name, I befeech
your chaftitie.

Mary.   One Sir, of whom he befpake falling bands.

Neat.   Falling bands, it fhall fo be giuen him, ———
if you pleafe to venture your modefly in the hall,
amongft a curle-pated company of rude feruingmen,
and take fuch as they can fet before you, you fhall
be moft ferioufly, and ingenioufly welcome.

Mary.   I haue dyned indeed already fir.

Neat.   ——— Or will you vouchfafe to kiffe the lip
of a cup of rich *Orleans* in the buttry amongft our
waiting women.

Mary.   Not now in truth fir.

Neat.   Our yong Maifter fhall then haue a feeling
of your being here prefently it fhall fo be giuen him.

Exit Neatfoote.

Mary.   I humbly thanke you fir, but that my
     bofome
Is full of bitter forrowes, I could fmile,
To fee this formall Ape play Antick tricks :
But in my breaft a poyfoned arrow ftickes,
And fmiles cannot become me, Loue wouen fleightly
(Such as thy falfe heart makes) weares out as lightly,
But loue being truely bred ith the foule (like mine)
Bleeds euen to death, at the leaft wound it takes,
The more we quench this, the leffe it flakes :
O me !

Enter Sebaftian Wengraue *with* Neatfoote.

Seb.   A Sempfter fpeake with me, faift thou.

Neat.   Yes, fir, fhe's there, *viua voce*, to deliuer her
auricular confeffion.

Seb.   With me fweet heart. What ift ?

Mary.   I haue brought home your bands fir.

Seb.   Bands : *Neatfoote.*

Neat.   Sir.

Seb. Prithee look in, for all the Gentlemen are
vpon rifing.

Neat. Yes fir, a moft methodicall attendance fhall
be giuen.

Seb. And doft heare, if my father call for me, fay
I am bufy with a Sempfter.

Neat. Yes fir, hee fhall know it that you are bufied
with a needle woman.

Seb. In's eare good *Neat-foote.*

Neat. It fhall be fo giuen him.   *Exit Neat-foote.*

Seb. Bands, y'are miftaken fweete heart, I befpake
none, when, where, I prithee, what bands, let me fee
them.

Mary. Yes fir, a bond faft fealed, with folemne
    oathes,
Subfcribed vnto (as I thought) with your foule:
Deliuered as your deed in fight of heauen,
Is this bond canceld, haue you forgot me.

Seb. Ha ! life of my life : Sir *Guy Fitz-Allards*
    daughter,
What has transform'd my loue to this ftrange fhape ?
Stay : make all fure,—fo : now fpeake and be briefe,
Becaufe the wolfe's at dore that lyes in waite,
To prey vpon vs both albeit mine eyes
Are bleft by thine, yet this fo ftrange difguife
Holds me with feare and wonder.

Mary. Mines a loathed fight,
Why from it are you banifht elfe fo long.

Seb. I muft cut fhort my fpeech, in broken lan-
    guage,
Thus much fweete *Moll*, I muft thy company fhun,
I court another *Moll*, my thoughts muft run,
As a horfe runs, thats blind, round in a Mill,
Out euery ftep, yet keeping one path ftill.

Mary. Vmh : muft you fhun my company, in one
    knot
Haue both our hands byt'h hands of heauen bene
    tyed,
Now to be broke, I thought me once your Bride :

Our fathers did agree on the time when,
And muſt another bed-fellow fill my roome.
　　Seb.　Sweete maid, lets looſe no time, tis in heauens
　　　　booke
Set downe, that I muſt haue thee : an oath we tooke,
To keep our vowes, but when the knight your father
Was from mine parted, ſtormes began to ſit
Vpon my couetous fathers brow : which fell
From them on me, he reckond vp what gold
This marriage would draw from him, at which he
　　　　ſwore,
To looſe ſo much bloud, could not grieue him more.
He then diſwades me from thee, cal'd thee not faire,
And askt what is ſhee, but a beggars heire ?
He ſcorn'd thy dowry of (5000) Markes.
If ſuch a ſumme of mony could be found,
And I would match with thee, hee'd not vndoe it,
Prouided his bags might adde nothing to it,
But vow'd, if I tooke thee, nay more, did ſweare it,
Saue birth from him I nothing ſhould inherit.
　　Mary.　What followes then, my ſhip-wracke.
　　Seb.　Deareſt no :
Tho wildly in a laborinth I go,
My end is to meete thee : with a ſide winde
Muſt I now ſaile, elſe I no hauen can finde
But both muſt ſinke for euer.　There's a wench
Cal'd *Mol*, mad *Mol*, or merry *Mol*, a creature
So ſtrange in quality, a whole citty takes
Note of her name and perſon, all that affection
I owe to thee, on her in counterfet paſſion,
I ſpend to mad my father : he beleeues
I doate vpon this *Roaring Girle*, and grieues
As it becomes a father for a ſonne,
That could be ſo bewitcht : yet ile go on
This croked way, ſigh ſtill for her, faine dreames,
In which ile talke onely of her, theſe ſtreames
Shall, I hope, force my father to conſent
That heere I anchor rather then be rent
Vpon a rocke ſo dangerous, Art thou pleaſ'd,

Becaufe thou feeft we are way-laid, that I take
A path thats fafe, tho it be farre about.
  Mary.   My prayers with heauen guide thee.
  Seb.   Then I will on,
My father is at hand, kiffe and begon;
Howres fhall be watcht for meetings; I muft now
As men for feare, to a ftrange Idoll bow.
  Mary.   Farewell.
  Seb.   Ile guide thee forth, when next we meete,
A ftory of *Moll* fhall make our mirth more fweet.
Exeunt.

Enter Sir Alexander Wengraue, Sir Dauy Dapper, Sir
    Adam Appleton, Gofhake, Laxton, *and Gentle-*
    men.

  Omnes.   Thanks good Sir *Alexander* for our boun-
    teous cheere.
  Alex.   Fy, fy, in giuing thankes you pay to deare.
  S. Dap.   When bounty fpreades the table, faith
    t'were finne,
(at going of) if thankes fhould not ftep in.
  Alex.   No more of thankes, no more, I mary Sir,
Th' inner roome was too clofe, how do you like
This Parlour Gentlemen?
  Omnes.   Oh paffing well.
  Adam.   What a fweet breath the aire cafts heere,
    fo coole.
  Gofh.   I like the profpect beft.
  Lax.   See how tis furnifht.
  S. Dap.   A very faire fweete roome.
  Alex.   Sir *Dauy Dapper,*
The furniture that doth adorne this roome,
Coft many a faire gray groat ere it came here,
But good things are moft cheape, when th'are moft
    deere,
Nay when you looke into my galleries,
How brauely they are trim'd vp, you all fhall fweare
Yare highly pleafd to fee whats fet downe there :
Stories of men and women (mixt together

Faire ones with foule, like fun-fhine in wet wether)
Within one fquare a thoufand heads are laid
So clofe, that all of heads, the roome feemes made,
As many faces there (fill'd with blith lookes)
Shew like the promifing titles of new bookes,
(Writ merily) the Readers being their owne eyes,
Which feeme to moue and to giue plaudities,
And here and there (whilft with obfequious eares,
Throng'd heapes do liften) a cut purfe thrufts and
    leeres
With haukes eyes for his prey : I need not fhew him,
By a hanging villanous looke, your felues may know
    him,
The face is drawne fo rarely, Then fir below,
The very flowre (as twere) waues to and fro,
And like a floating Iland, feemes to moue,
Vpon a fea bound in with fhores aboue.

Enter Sebaftian and M. Greene-wit.

Omnes.   Thefe fights are excellent.
Alex.   I'le fhew you all,
Since we are met, make our parting Comicall.
    Seb.   This gentleman (my friend) will take his
    leaue Sir.
    Alex.   Ha, take his leaue (*Sebaftian*) who ?
    Seb.   This gentleman.
    Alex.   Your loue fir, has already giuen me fome
    time,
And if you pleafe to truft my age with more,
It fhall pay double intereft : Good fir ftay.
    Green.   I haue beene too bold.
    Alex.   Not fo fir.   A merry day
Mongft friends being fpent, is better then gold fau'd.
Some wine, fome wine.   Where be thefe knaues I
    keepe.

Enter three or foure Seruingmen, and Neatfoote.

Neat.   At your worfhipfull elbow, fir.

Alex. You are kiffing my maids, drinking, or faft
afleep.

Neat. Your worfhip has giuen it vs right.

Alex. You varlets ftirre,
Chaires, ftooles and cufhions: pre' thee fir *Dauy
Dapper,*
Make that chaire thine.

Sir Dap. Tis but an eafie gift,
And yet I thanke you for it fir, I'le take it.

Alex. A chaire for old fir *Adam Appleton.*

Neat. A backe friend to your worfhip.

Adam. Mary good *Neatfoot,*
I thanke thee for it: backe friends fometimes are
good.

Alex. Pray make that ftoole your pearch, good M.
Gofhawke.

Gofh. I ftoope to your lure fir.

Alex. Sonne *Sebaftian,*
Take Maifter *Greenewit* to you.

Seb. Sit deere friend.

Alex. Nay maifter *Laxton*—furnifh maifter *Laxton*
With what he wants (a ftone) a ftoole I would fay, a
ftoole.

Laxton. I had rather ftand fir. *Exeunt feruants.*

Alex. I know you had (good M. *Laxton.*) So,
fo——
Now heres a meffe of friends, and (gentlemen)
Becaufe times glaffe fhall not be running long,
I'le quicken it with a pretty tale.

Sir Dap. Good tales do well,
In thefe bad dayes, where vice does fo excell.

Adam. Begin fir *Alexander.*

Alex. Laft day I met
An aged man vpon whofe head was fcor'd,
A debt of iuft fo many yeares as thefe,
Which I owe to my graue, the man you all know.

Omnes. His name I pray you fir.

Alex. Nay you fhall pardon me,
But when he faw me (with a figh that brake,

Or feem'd to breake his heart-ftrings) thus he fpake :
Oh my good knight, faies he, (and then his eies
Were richer euen by that which made them poore,
They had fpent fo many teares they had no more.)
Oh fir (faies he) you know it, for you ha feene
Bleffings to raine vpon mine houfe and me :
Fortune (who flaues men) was my flaue : her wheele
Hath fpun me golden threads, for I thanke heauen,
I nere had but one caufe to curfe my ftarres,
I ask't him then, what that one caufe might be.
    Omnes.   So Sir.
    Alex.   He paus'd, and as we often fee,
A fea fo much becalm'd, there can be found
No wrinckle on his brow, his waues being drownd
In their owne rage : but when th' imperious wind,
Vfe ftrange inuifible tyranny to fhake
Both heauens and earths foundation at their noyfe :
The feas fwelling with wrath to part that fray
Rife vp, and are more wild, more mad, then they,
Euen fo this good old man was by my queftion
Stir'd vp to roughneffe, you might fee his gall
Flow euen in's eies : then grew he fantafticall.
    Sir Dap.   Fantafticall, ha, ha.
    Alex.   Yes, and talke odly.
    Adam.   Pray fir proceed,
How did this old man end ?
    Alex.   Mary fir thus.
He left his wild fit to read ore his cards,
Yet then (though age caft fnow on all his haires)
He ioy'd becaufe (faies he) the God of gold
Has beene to me no niggard : that difeafe
(Of which all old men ficken) Auarice
Neuer infeéted me.
    Lax.   He meanes not himfelfe i' me fure.
    Alex.   For like a lamp,
Fed with continuall oyle, I fpend and throw
My light to all that need it, yet haue ftill
Enough to ferue my felfe, oh but (quoth he)
Tho heauens dew fall, thus on this aged tree,

I haue a fonne thats like a wedge doth cleaue,
My very heart roote.
   S. Dap.   Had he fuch a fonne.
   Seb.   Now I do fmell a fox ftrongly.
   Alex.   Lets fee : no Maifter *Greene-wit* is not yet
So mellow in yeares as he ; but as like *Sebaftian*,
Iuft like my fonne *Sebaftian*,—fuch another.
   Seb.   How finely like a fencer my father fetches his
by-blowes to hit me, but if I beate you not at your
owne weapon of fubtilty.
   Alex.   This fonne (faith he) that fhould be
The columne and maine arch vnto my houfe,
The crutch vnto my age, becomes a whirlewind
Shaking the firme foundation.
   Adam.   'Tis fome prodigall.
   Seba.   Well fhot old *Adam Bell.*
   Alex.   No citty monfter neither, no prodigall,
But fparing, wary, ciuill, and (tho wiueleffe),
An excellent husband, and fuch a traueller,
He has more tongues in his head then fome haue
   teeth.
   S. Dap.   I haue but two in myne.
   Gofh.   So fparing and fo wary.
What then could vex his father fo.
   Alex.   Oh a woman.
   Seb.   A flefh fly, that can vex any man.
   Alex. A fcuruy woman,
On whom the paffionate old man fwore he doated :
A creature (faith he) nature hath brought forth
To mocke the fex of woman. . . It is a thing
One knowes not how to name, her birth began
Ere fhe was all made. 'Tis woman more then man,
Man more then woman, and (which to none can hap)
The Sunne giues her two fhadowes to one fhape,
Nay more, let this ftrange thing, walke, ftand or fit,
No blazing ftarre drawes more eyes after it.
   S. Dap.   A Monfter, tis fome Monfter.
   Alex.   Shee's a varlet.
   Seb.   Now. is my cue to briftle.
   3

L

Alex.   A naughty packe,
Seb.   Tis falſe.
Alex.   Ha boy.
Seb.   Tis falſe.
Alex.   Whats falſe, I ſay ſhee's nought.
Seb.   I ſay that tongue
That dares ſpeake ſo (but yours) ſtickes in the throate
Of a ranke villaine, ſet your ſelfe aſide. . . .
Alex.   So ſir what then.
Seb.   Any here elſe had lyed.
I thinke I ſhall fit you——aſide.
Alex.   Lye.
Seb.   Yes.
Sir Dap.   Doth this concerne him.
Alex.   Ah ſirra boy.
Is your bloud heated : boyles it : are you ſtung,
Ile pierce you deeper yet : oh my deere friends,
I am that wretched father, this that ſonne,
That ſees his ruine, yet headlong on doth run.
Adam.   Will you loue ſuch a poyſon.
S. Dap.   Fye, fye.
Seb.   Y'are all mad.
Alex.   Th'art ſicke at heart, yet feelſt it not : of all
    theſe,
What Gentleman (but thou) knowing his diſeaſe
Mortall, would ſhun the cure : oh Maiſter *Greenewit,*
Would you to ſuch an Idoll bow.
Greene.   Not I ſir.
Alex.   Heer's Maiſter *Laxton,* has he mind to a
    woman
As thou haſt.
Lax   No not I ſir.
Alex.   Sir I know it.
Lax.   There good parts are ſo rare, there bad ſo
    common,
I will haue nought to do with any woman.
Sir Dap.   Tis well done Maiſter *Laxton.*
Alex.   Oh thou cruell boy,
Thou wouldſt with luſt an old mans life deſtroy,

Becaufe thou feeft I'me halfe way in my graue,
Thou fhouelft duft vpon me : wod thou mighteft haue
Thy wifh, moft wicked, moft vnnaturall.
   Dap. Why fir, tis thought, fir *Guy Fitz-Allards*
     daughter
Shall wed your fonne *Sebaftian.*
   Alex. Sir *Dauy Dapper.*
I haue vpon my knees, wood this fond boy,
To take that vertuous maiden.
   Seb. Harke you a word fir.
You on your knees haue curft that vertuous maiden,
And me for louing her, yet do you now
Thus baffle me to my face : were not your knees
In fuch intreates, giue me *Fitz-Allards* daughter.
   Alex. Ile giue thee rats-bane rather.
   Seb. Well then you know
What difh I meane to feed vpon.
   Alex. Harke Gentlemen,
He fweares to haue this cut-purfe drab, to fpite my
     gall.
   Omnes. Maifter *Sebaftian.*
   Seb. I am deafe to you all.
Ime fo bewitcht, fo bound to my defires,
Teares, prayers, threats, nothing can quench out thofe
     fires
That burne within me.   *Exit Sebastian.*
   Alex. Her bloud fhall quench it then,
Loofe him not, oh difwade him Gentlemen.
   Sir Dap. He fhall be weand I warrant you.
   Alex. Before his eyes
Lay downe his fhame, my griefe, his miferies.
   Omnes. No more, no more, away.
                Exeunt all but fir Alexander.
   Alex. I wafh a *Negro,*
Loofing both paines and coft : but take thy flight,
Ile be moft neere thee, when I'me leaft in fight.
Wild Bucke ile hunt thee breathleffe, thou fhalt run
     on,
But I will turne thee when I'me not thought vpon.
                    L 2

Enter Ralph Trapdore.

Now firra what are you, leaue your Apes trickes and
    fpeake.

    Trap.   A letter from my Captaine to your Worfhip.

    Alex.   Oh, oh, now I remember tis to preferre
    thee into my feruice.

    Trap.   To be a fhifter vnder your Worfhips nofe of
a clean trencher, when ther's a good bit vpon't.

    Alex.   Troth honeft fellow . . humh . . ha . . .
    let me fee.

This knaue fhall be the axe to hew that downe
At which I ftumble, has a face that promifeth
Much of a villaine, I will grind his wit,
And if the edge proue fine make vfe of it.
Come hither firra, canft thou be fecret, ha.

    Trap.   As two crafty Atturneys plotting the vndo-
ing of their clyents.

    Alex.   Didft never, as thou haft walkt about this
    towne

Heare of a wench cal'd *Moll*, mad merry *Moll*.

    Trap.   *Moll* cutpurfe fir.

    Alex.   The fame, doft thou know her then.

    Trap.   Afwell as I know twill raine vpon *Simon* and
Iudes day next, I will fift all the tauernes ith citty,
and drinke halfe pots with all the Watermen ath
bankfide, but if you will fir Ile find her out.

    Alex.   That task is eafy, doot then, hold thy hand
    vp.

Whats this, ift burnt ?

    Trap.   No fir no, a little findgd with making fire
workes.

    Alex.   Ther's money, fpend it, that being fpent
fetch more.

    Trap.   Oh fir that all the poore fouldiers in *Eng-
land* had fuch a leader. For fetching no water Spaniell is like me.

    Alex.   This wench we fpeake of, ftraies fo from her
    kind

Nature repents fhe made her.   Tis a Mermaid
Has told my fonne to fhipwracke.
   Trap.   Ile cut her combe for you.
   Alex.   Ile tell out gold for thee then : hunt her
     forth,
Caft out a line hung full of filuer hookes
To catch her to thy company : deepe fpendings
May draw her thats moft chaft to a mans bofome.
   Trap.   The gingling of Golden bels, and a good
foole with a hobbyhorfe, wil draw all the whoores ith
towne to dance in a morris.
   Alex.   Or rather, for thats beft (they fay fometimes
Shee goes in breeches) follow her as her man.
   Trap.   And when her breeches are off, fhee fhall
follow me.
   Alex.   Beate all thy braines to ferue her.
   Trap. Zounds fir, as country wenches beate creame,
till butter comes.
   Alex.   Play thou the futtle fpider, weaue fine nets
To infnare her very life.
   Trap.   Her life.
   Alex   Yes fucke
Her heart-bloud if thou canft, twift thou but cords
To catch her, Ile finde law to hang her vp.
   Trap.   Spoke like a Worfhipfull bencher.
   Alex.   Trace all her fteps : at this fhee-foxes den
Watch what lambs enter : let me play the fheepeheard
To faue their throats from bleeding, and cut hers.
   Trap.   This is the goll fhall doot.
   Alex.   Be firme and gaine me
Euer thine owne.   This done I entertaine thee :
How is thy name.
   Trap.   My name fir is *Raph Trapdore*, honeft
Raph.
   Alex.   *Trapdore*, be like thy name, a dangerous
     ftep
For her to venture on, but vnto me.
   Trap.   As faft as your fole to your boote or fhooe fir.

Alex. Hence then, be little feene here as thou canft.

Ile ftill be at thine elbow.

Trap. The trapdores fet.

Moll if you budge y'are gon : this me fhall crowne,
A Roaring Boy, the Roaring Girle puts downe.

Alex. God a mercy, loofe no time. *Exeunt.*

The three fhops open in a ranke : the firft a Poticaries fhop, the next a Fether fhop : the third a Sempfters fhop : Miftreffe Gallipot in the firft, Miftreffe Tiltyard in the next, Maifter Openworke and his wife in the third, to them enters Laxton, Gofhawke and Greenewit.

Mi. Open. Gentlemen what ift you lacke. What ift you buy, fee fine bands and ruffes, fine lawnes, fine cambrickes, what ift you lacke Gentlemen, what ift you buy ?

Lax. Yonders the fhop.

Gofh. Is that fhee.

Lax. Peace.

Green. Shee that minces Tobacco.

Lax. I : fhees a Gentlewoman borne I can tell you, tho it be her hard fortune now to fhread Indian pot-hearbes.

Gofh. Oh fir tis many a good womans fortune, her husband turns bankrout, to begin with pipes and fet vp againe.

Lax. And indeed the rayfing of the woman is the lifting vp of the mans head at all times, if one florifh, tother will bud as faft I warrant ye.

Gofh. Come th'art familiarly acquainted there, I grope that.

Lax. And you grope no better ith dark you may chance lye ith ditch when y'are drunke.

Gofh. Go th'art a mifticall letcher.

Lax. I will not deny but my credit may take vp an ounce of pure fmoake.

Gofh. Make take vp an ell of pure fmock ; away go, tis the clofeft ftriker. Life I think he commits venery 40 foote deepe, no mans aware on't, I like a palpable fmockfter go to worke fo openly, with the tricks of art, that I'me as aparantly feen as a naked boy in a viall, & were it not for a guift of trechery that I haue in me to betray my friend when he puts moft truft in me (maffe yonder hee is too—) and by his iniurie to make good my acceffe to her, I fhould appeare as defeƈtiue in courting, as a Farmers fonne the firft day of his feather, that doth nothing at Court, but woe the hangings and glaffe windowes for a month together, and fome broken wayting woman for euer after. I find thofe imperfeƈtions in my venerie, that were't not for flatterie and falfhood, I fhould want difcourfe and impudence, and hee that wants impudence among women, is worthy to bee kickt out at beds feet.—He fhall not fee me yet.

Green. Troth this is finely fhred.

Lax. Oh women are the beft mincers.

Mifl. Gal. 'Thad bin a good phrafe for a Cookes wife fir.

Lax. But 'twill ferue generally, like the front of a newe Almanacke ; as thus : Calculated for the meridian of Cookes wiues, but generally for all Englifh-women.

Mifl. Gal. Nay you fhall ha'te fir, I haue fild it for you.

Shee puts it to the fire.

Lax. The pipe's in a good hand, and I wifh mine alwaies fo.

Gree. But not to be vs'd a that fafhion.

Lax. O pardon me fir, I vnderftand no french. I pray be couerd. Iacke a pipe of rich fmoake.

Gofh. Rich fmoake ; that's 6. pence a pipe ift ?

Green. To me fweet Lady.

Mift. Gal. Be not forgetful ; refpect my credit ; feem ftrange ; Art and Wit makes a foole of fufpition :—pray be warie.

Lax. Pufh, I warrant you :—come, how ift gallants ?

Green. Pure and excellent.

Lax. I thought 'twas good, you were growne fo filent ; you are like thofe that loue not to talke at victuals, tho they make a worfe noyfe i' the nofe then a common fidlers prentice, and difcourfe a whole Supper with fnuffling ;—I muft fpeake a word with you anone.

Mift. Gal. Make your way wifely then.

Gofh. Oh what elfe fir, hee's perfection it felfe, full of manners, But not an acre of ground belonging to 'em.

Greeen. I and full of forme, h'as ne're a good ftoole in's chamber.

Gofh. But aboue all religious : hee prayeth daily vpon elder brothers.

Green, And valiant aboue meafure ; h'as runne three ftreets from a Serieant.

Lax. Puh. Puh. *he blowes tobacco in their faces.*

Green. Gofh. Oh, puh, ho, ho.

Lax. So, fo.

Mift. Gal. What's the matter now fir ?

Lax. I proteft I'me in extreame want of money if you can fupply mee now with any meanes, you doe mee the greateft pleafure, next to the bountie of your loue, as euer poore gentleman tafted.

Mift. Gal. What's the fumme would pleafure ye fir ? Tho you deferue nothing leffe at my hands.

Lax. Why 'tis but for want of opportunitie thou know'ft ; I put her off with opportunitie ftill : by this light I hate her, but for meanes to keepe me in fafhion with gallants ; for what I take from her, I fpend vpon other wenches, beare her in hand ftill ; fhee has wit enough to rob her husband, and I waies enough to

confume the money : why how now ? what the chin-
cough ?

Gofh. Thou haft the cowardlieft tricke to come
before a mans face and ftrangle him ere hee be aware,
I could find in my heart to make a quarrell in
earneft.

Lax. Poxe and thou do'ft, thou know'ft I neuer
vfe to fight with my friends, thou'l but loofe thy labour
in't.

Iacke Dapper !

Enter I. Dapper, and his man Gull.

Greene. Mounfier Dapper, I diue downe to your
anckles.

I. Dap. Saue ye gentlemen all three in a peculiar
falute.

Gofh. He were ill to make a lawyer, hee difpatches
three at once.

Lax. So wel faid : but is this of the fame
Tobacco miftreffe *Gallipot ?*

M. Gal. The fame you had at firft fir.

Lax. I wifh it no better : this will ferue to drinke
at my chamber.

Gofh. Shall we tafte a pipe on't ?

Lax. Not of this by my troth Gentlemen, I haue
fworne before you.

Gofh. What not *Iacke dapper.*

Lax. Pardon me fweet *Iacke*, I'me forry I made
fuch a rafh oath, but foolifh oathes muft ftand : where
art going *Iacke.*

Iac. Dap. Faith to buy one fether.

Lax. One fether, the foole's peculiar ftill.

Iac. Dap. Gul.

Gul. Maifter.

Iac. Dap. Heer's three halfepence for your ordinary, boy, meete me an howre hence in Powles.

Gul. How three fingle halfepence ; life, this will
fcarce ferue a man in fauce, a halporth of muftard, a

halporth of oyle, and a halporth of viniger, whats
left then for the pickle herring: this ſhowes like ſmall
beere ith morning after a great ſurfet of wine ore
night, hee could ſpend his three pound laſt night in a
ſupper amongſt girles and braue baudy-houſe boyes, I
thought his pockets cackeld not for nothing, theſe are
the egs of there pound, Ile go ſup 'em vp preſently.

Exit Gul.

Lax. Eight, nine, ten Angels, good wench ifaith,
and one that loues darkeneſſe well, ſhe puts out a candle with the beſt tricks of any drugſters wife in England : but that which mads her I raile vpon oportu-
nity ſtill, and take no notice on't. The other night
ſhe would needs lead me into a roome with a candle
in her hand to ſhow me a naked picture, where no
ſooner entred but the candle was ſent of an arrant :
now I am intending to vnderſtand her, but like a
puny at the Innes of venery, cal'd for another light
innocently, thus reward I all her cunning with ſimple
miſtaking. I know ſhe coſens her husband to keepe
me, and Ile keepe her honeſt, as long as I can, to
make the poore man ſome part of amends, an honeſt
minde of a whooremaiſter, how thinke you amongſt
you, what a freſh pipe, draw in a third man.

Goſh. No your a horder, you ingroſe bith ounces.

At the Fether ſhop now.

Iac. Dap. Puh I like it not.
M. Tiltyard. What fether iſt you'ld haue ſir.
Theſe are moſt worne and moſt in faſhion,
Amongſt the Beuer gallants the ſtone Riders.
The priuate ſtages audience, the twelu peny ſtool
    Gentlemen,
I can enforme you tis the generall fether.
Iac. Dap. And therefore I miſlike it, tell me of
    generall.
Now a continuall *Simon* and *Iudes* raine
Beate all your fethers as flat downe as pancakes.

Shew me — — a —— fpangled fether.
 Mist. Tilt. Oh to go a feafting with,
You'd haue for a hinchboy, you fhall.

At the Sempsters fhop now.

 Maifl. Open. Maffe I had quite forgot,
His Honours footeman was here lafl night wife,
Ha you done with my Lords fhirt.
 Mifl. Open. Whats that to you fir,
I was this morning at his Honours lodging,
Ere fuch a fnaile as you crept out of your fhell.
 Maifl. Open. Oh 'twas well done good wife.
 Mi. Op. I hold it better fir, then if you had don't
  your felfe.
 Ma. Op. Nay fo fay I: but is the Counteffes
  fmocke almofl donne moufe.
 Mi. Op. Here lyes the cambricke fir, but wants I
  feare mee.
 Mi. Op. Ile refolue you of that prefently.
 Mi. Op. Haida, oh audacious groome,
Dare you prefume to noble womens linnen,
Keepe you your yard to meafure fheepeheards
  holland,
I mufl confine you I fee that.

At the Tobacco fhop now.

 Gofh. What fay you to this geere.
 Lax. I dare the arrants critticke in Tobacco
To lay one falt vpon't.

Enter Mol *in a freefe Ierkin and a blacke fauegard.*

 Gofh. Life yonders *Mol.*
 Lax. Mol which Mol.
 Gofh. honefl *Mol.*
 Lax. Prithee lets call her——*Mol.*
 All. *Mol, Mol,* pifl *Mol.*

Mol. How now, whats the matter.

Goſh. A pipe of good tobacco *Mol.*

Mol. I cannot ſtay.

Goſh. Nay *Mol* puh, prethee harke, but one word ifaith.

Mol. Well what iſt.

Green. Prithee come hither ſirra.

Lax. Hart I would giue but too much money to be nibling with that wench, life, ſh' as the Spirit of foure great pariſhes, and a voyce that will drowne all the Citty, methinkes a braue Captaine might get all his ſouldiers vpon her, and nere bee beholding to a company of mile-end milke ſops, if hee could come on, and come off quicke enough : Such a *Moll* were a maribone before an *Italian*, hee would cry *bona roba* till his ribs were nothing but bone. Ile lay hard ſiege to her, mony is that *Aqua fortis*, that eates into many a maidenhead, where the wals are fleſh and bloud. Ile euer pierce through with a golden auguer.

Goſh. Now thy iudgement *Moll*, iſt not good ?

Mol. Yes faith tis very good tobacco, how do you ſell an ounce, farewell. God b'y you Miſtreſſe *Gallipot.*

Goſh. Why, *Mol*, *Mol.*

Mol. I cannot ſtay now ifaith, I am going to buy a ſhag ruffe, the ſhop will be ſhut in preſently.

Goſh. Tis the maddeſt fantaſticalſt girle :— I neuer knew ſo much fleſh and ſo much nimbleneſſe put together.

Lax. Shee ſlips from one company to another, like a fat Eele between a Dutchmans fingers :—Ile watch my time for her.

Miſt. Gal. Some will not ſticke to ſay ſhees a man
And ſome both man and woman.

Lax. That were excellent, ſhe might firſt cuckold the husband and then make him do as much for the wife.

The Fether ſhop againe.

Moll. Saue you ; how does Miſtreſſe *Tiltyard ?*

1. Dap. Mol.

Mol. Iacke Dapper.

1. Dap. How doſt *Mol.*

Mol. Ile tel the by and by, I go but toth' next ſhop.

1. Dap. Thou ſhalt find me here this howre about a fether.

Mol. Nay and a fether hold you in play a whole houre, a goofe will laſt you all the daies of your life. Let me fee a good ſhag ruffe.

The Sempſter ſhop.

Maiſt. Open. Miſtreſſe *Mary* that ſhalt thou ifaith, and the beſt in the ſhop.

Miſt. Open. How now, greetings, loue tearmes with a pox betweene you, haue I found out one of your haunts, I fend you for hollands, and you're ith the low countries with a mifchiefe, I'me feru'd with good ware byth ſhift, that makes it lye dead fo long vpon my hands, I were as good ſhut vp ſhop, for when I open it I take nothing.

Maiſt. Open. Nay and you fall a ringing once the diuell cannot ſtop you, Ile out of the Belfry as faſt as I can—*Moll.*

Miſt. Open. Get you from my ſhop.

Mol. I come to buy.

Miſt. Open. Ile fell ye nothing, I warne yee my houfe and ſhop.

Mol. You goodly *Openworke*, you that prick out a
      poore liuing
And fowes many a bawdy skin-coate together,
Thou priuate pandreſſe betweene ſhirt and fmock,
I wiſh thee for a minute but a man :
Thou ſhouldſt neuer vfe more ſhapes, but as th'art
I pitty my reuenge, now my ſpleenes vp,

Enter a fellow with a long rapier by his fide.

I would not mocke it willingly—ha be thankfull.
Now I forgiue thee.

Mift. Open.   Mary hang thee, I never askt forgiue-
neffe in my life.

Mol.   You goodman fwinesface.

Fellow.   What wil you murder me.

Mol.   You remember flaue, how you abufd me
t'other night in a Tauerne.

Fel.   Not I by this light.

Mol.   No, but by candlelight you did, you haue
trickes to faue your oathes, referuations haue you, and
I haue referued fomewhat for you,—as you like that
call for more, you know the figne againe.

Fel.   Pox ant, had I brought any company along
with mee to haue borne witneffe on't, 'twold ne're
haue grieu'd me, but to be ftrucke and nobody by, tis
my ill fortune ftill, why tread vpon a worme they fay
twill turne taile, but indeed a Gentleman fhould haue
more manners.   *Exit fellow.*

Lax.   Gallantly performed ifath *Mol*, and manfully,
I loue thee for euer fort, bafe rogue, had he offerd but
the leaft counter-buffe, by this hand I was prepared for
him.

Mol.   You prepared for him, why fhould you be
prepared for him, was he any more then a man.

Lax.   No nor fo much by a yard and a handfull
London meafure.

Moll.   Why do you fpeake this then, doe you
thinke I cannot ride a ftone horfe, vnleffe one lead
him bith fnaffle.

Lax.   Yes and fit him brauely, I know thou canft
Mol, twas but an honeft miftake through loue, and Ile
make amends fort any way, prethee fweete plumpe
Mol, when fhall thou and I go out a towne together.

Mol.   Whether to Tyburne prethee.

Lax.   Maffe thats out a towne indeed, thou

hangſt ſo many ieſts vpon thy friends ſtil.   I meane
honeſtly to *Brainford, Staines*, or *Ware.*
   Mol.   What to do there.
   Lax.   Nothing but bee merry and lye together, I'le
hire a coach with foure horſes.
   Mol.   I thought 'twould bee a beaſtly iourney, you
may leaue out one wel, three horſes will ſerue, if I
play the iade my ſelfe.
   Lax.   Nay puſh th'art ſuch another kicking wench,
prethee be kind and lets meete.
   Mol.   Tis hard but we ſhall meete ſir.
   Lax.   Nay but appoint the place then, there's ten
Angels in faire gold *Mol*, you ſee I do not trifle with
you, do but ſay thou wilt meete me, and Ile haue a
coach ready for thee.
   Mol.   Why here's my hand Ile meete you ſir.
   Lax.   Oh good gold,—the place ſweete *Mol.*
   Mol.   It ſhal be your appointment.
   Lax.   Somewhat neere Holborne *Mol.*
   Mol.   In Graies-Inne fields then.
   Lax.   A match.
   Mol.   Ile meete you there.
   Lax.   The houre.
   Mol.   Three.
   Lax.   That will be time enough to ſup at *Braine-
ford.*

Fall from them to the other.

   Ma. Op.   I am of ſuch a nature ſir, I cannot
endure the houſe when ſhee ſcolds, ſh' has a tongue
will be hard further in a ſtill morning then Saint
Antlings-bell, ſhe railes vpon me for forraine wenching, that I being a freeman muſt needs keep a whore
ith ſubburbs, and ſeeke to impoueriſh the liberties,
when we fall out, I trouble you ſtill to make all whole
with my wife.
   Goſh.   No trouble at all, tis a pleaſure to mee to
ioyne things together.

Maiſt. Open. Go thy waies, I doe this but to try thy honeſty *Goſhawke.*

The Fether ſhop.

Iac. Dap. How lik'ſt thou this *Mol.*

Mol. Oh ſingularly, your fitted now for a bunch, he lookes for all the world with thoſe ſpangled fethers like a noblemans bedpoſt: The purity of your wench would I faine try, ſhee ſeemes like Kent vnconquered, and I beleeue as many wiles are, in her——oh the gallants of theſe times are ſhallow letchers, they put not their courtſhip home enough to a wench, tis im-poſſible to know what woman is throughly honeſt, becauſe ſhee's nerc thorougly try'd. I am of that cer-taine beleefe there are more queanes in this towne of their owne making, then of any mans prouoking, where lyes the ſlackneſſe then? many a poore ſoule would downe, and ther's nobody will puſh em:
Women are courted but nere ſoundly tri'd,
As many walke in ſpurs that neuer ride.

The Sempſters ſhop.

Miſt. Open. Oh abominable.

Goſh. Nay more I tell you in priuate, he keeps a whore ith ſubburbs.

Miſt. Open. O ſpittle dealing, I came to him a Gentlewoman borne. Ile ſhew you mine armes when you pleaſe ſir.

Goſh. I had rather ſee your legs, and begin that way.

Miſt. Openworke. Tis well knowne he tooke me from a Ladies ſeruice, where I was well beloued of the ſteward. I had my Lattine tongue, and a ſpice of the French before I came to him, and now doth he keepe a ſubberbian whoore vnder my noſtrils.

Goſh. There's waies enough to cry quite with him,
harke in thine eare.

Miſt. Open. Theres a friend worth a Million.

Mol. I'le try one ſpeare againſt your chaſtity
    Miſt. *Tiltyard*
Though it proue too ſhort by the burgh.

Trap. Maſſe here ſhe is.   *Enter Ralph Trapdore.*
I'me bound already to ſerue her, tho it be but a
ſluttiſh tricke. Bleſſe my hopefull yong Miſtreſſe with
long life and great limbs, ſend her the vpper hand of
al balifes, and their hungry adherents.

Mol. How now, what art thou?

Trap. A poore ebbing Gentleman, that would
gladly wait for the yong floud of your ſeruice.

Mol. My ſeruice! what ſhould moue you to offer
your ſeruice to me ſir?

Trap. The loue I beare to your heroicke ſpirit and
maſculine womanhood.

Mol. So ſir, put caſe we ſhould retaine you to vs,
what parts are there in you for a Gentlewomans
ſeruice.

Trap. Of two kinds right Worſhipfull : moueable,
and immoueable : moueable to runne of arrants, and
immoueable to ſtand when you haue occaſion to
vſe me.

Mol. What ſtrength haue you.

Trap. Strength Miſtreſſe *Mol*, I haue gon vp into
a ſteeple, and ſtaid the great bell as 'thas beene
ringing ; ſtopt a windmill going.

                  Mol *trips vp his heels he fals.*

Mol. And neuer ſtrucke downe your ſelfe.

Trap. Stood as vpright as I do at this preſent.

Mol. Come I pardon you for this, it ſhall bee no
diſgrace to you : I haue ſtrucke vp the heeles of the
high Germaines ſize ere now, —— what not ſtand.

Trap. I am of that nature where I loue, I'le bee
at my miſtreſſe foot to do her ſeruice.

Mol. Why well ſaid, but ſay your Miſtreſſe ſhould

receiue iniury, haue you the ſpirit of fighting in you,
durſt you ſecond her.
    Trap.   Life I haue kept a bridge my ſelfe, and
droue ſeuen at a time before me.
    Mol.   I.
    Trap.   But they were all Lincolneſhire bullockes
by my troth.   aſide.
    Mol.   Well, meete me in Graies-Inne fields, be-
tween three and foure this afternoone, and vpon
better conſideration weele retaine you.
    Trap.   I humbly thanke your good Miſtreſhip,
Ile crack your necke for this kindneſſe.
                              Exit Trapdore.

                    Mol meets Laxton.

    Lax.   Remember three.
    Moll.   Nay if I faile you hange me.
    Lax.   Good wench Ifaith.

                    then Openworke.

    Moll.   Whole this.
    Maiſt. Open.   Tis I *Moll.*
    Moll.   Prithee tend thy ſhop and preuent baſ-
tards.
    Maiſt. Open.   Wele haue a pint of the ſame wine
ifaith *Mol.*
                    The bel rings.
    Goſh.   Harke the bell rings, come Gentlemen.
Iacke Dapper, where ſhals all munch.
    Iac. Dap.   I am for Parkers ordinary.
    Lax.   Hee's a good gueſt to'm, hee deſerues his
        boord,
He drawes all the Gentlemen in a terme time
        thither,
Weele be your followers *Iacke,* lead the way,
Looke you by my faith the foole has fetherd his
        neſt well.   *Exeunt Gallants.*

Enter Maiſter Gallipot, *Maiſter* Tiltyard, *and ſeruants
with water Spaniels and a ducke.*

Maiſt. Tilt. Come ſhut vp your ſhops, where's
Maiſter Openworke.
Miſt. Gal. Nay aske not me *Maiſter Tiltyard.*
Maiſt. Tilt. Wher's his water dog, puh—piſt—hur
—hur—piſt.
Maiſt. Gal. Come wenches come, we're going all
to Hogſden.
Miſt. Gal. To Hogſden husband.
Maiſt. Gal. I to Hogſden pigsny.
Miſt. Gal. I'me not ready husband.
ſpits in the dogs mouth.
Maiſt. Gal. Faith thats well—hum—piſt—piſt
Come Miſtreſſe *Openworke* you are ſo long.
Miſt. Open. I haue no ioy of my life Maiſter
Gallipot.
Maiſt. Gal. Puſh, let your boy lead his water
Spaniel along, and weele ſhow you the braueſt ſport
at parlous pond, he trug, he trug, he trug, heres the
beſt ducke in England, except my wife, he, he, he,
fetch, fetch, fetch,
Come lets away
Of all the yeare this is the ſportfulſt day.

Enter Sebaſtian *ſolus.*

Seb. If a man haue a free will, where ſhould
    the vſe
More perfeſt ſhine then in his will to loue.

Enter Sir Alexander *and liſtens to him.*

All creatures haue their liberty in that,
Tho elſe kept vnder ſeruile yoke and feare,
The very bondſlaue has his freedome there,
Amongſt a world of creatures voyc'd and ſilent.
Muſt my deſires weare fetters —— yea are you

M 2

So neere, then I muſt breake with my hearts truth ;
Meete griefe at a backe way —— well : why ſuppoſe
The two leaud tongues of ſlander or of truth
Pronounce *Mol* loathſome : if before my loue
Shee appeare faire, what iniury haue I,
I haue the thing I like ? in all things elſe
Mine owne eye guides me, and I find 'em proſper,
Life what ſhould aile it now ?   I know that man
Nere truely loues, if he gaineſayt he lyes,
That winkes and marries with his fathers eyes.
Ile keepe myne owne wide open.

Enter Mol *and a porter with a viall on his backe.*

Alex.   Here's braue wilfulneſſe,
A made match, here ſhe comes, they met a purpoſe.
   Por.   Muſt I carry this great fiddle to your chamber
Miſtreſſe *Mary*.
   Mol.   Fiddle goodman hog-rubber, ſome of theſe
porters beare ſo much for others, they haue no time to
carry wit for themſelues.
   Por.   To your owne chamber Miſtreſle *Mary*.
   Moll.   Who'le heare an Aſſe ſpeake : whither elſe
goodman pagent-bearer : the're people of the worſt
memories.   *Exit Porter.*
   Seb.   Why 'twere too great a burthen loue, to haue
them carry things in their minds, and a' ther backes
together.
   Mol.   Pardon me ſir, I thought not you ſo neere.
   Alex.   So, ſo, ſo.
   Seb.   I would be neerer to thee, and in that
      faſhion,
That makes the beſt part of all creatures honeſt.
No otherwiſe I wiſh it.
   Mol.   Sir I am ſo poore to requite you, you muſt
looke for nothing but thankes of me, I haue no
humor to marry, I loue to lye aboth ſides ath bed
my ſelfe ; and againe ath' other ſide, a wife you know
ought to be obedient, but I feare me I am too head-

strong to obey, therefore Ile nere go about it, I loue
you fo well fir for your good will I'de be loath you
fhould repent your bargaine after, and therefore weele
nere come together at firft, I haue the head now of
my felfe, and am man enough for a woman, marriage
is but a chopping and changing, where a maiden loofes
one head, and has a worfe ith place.

Alex. The moft comfortableft anfwer from a Roaring Girle, that euer mine eares drunke in.

Seb. This were enough now to affright a foole for
euer from thee, when tis the muficke that I loue
thee for.

Alex. There's a boy fpoyles all againe.

Mol. Beleeue it fir I am not of that disdainefull
temper, but I could loue you faithfully.

Alex. A pox on you for that word. I like
you not now, Y'are a cunning roarer I fee that
already.

Mol. But fleepe vpon this once more fir, you may
chance fhift a minde to morrow, be not too hafty to
wrong your felfe, neuer while you liue fir take a wife
running, many haue run out at heeles that haue don't :
you fee fir I fpeake againft my felfe, and if euery
woman would deale with their futer fo honeftly, poore
yonger brothers would not bee fo often gul'd with
old cofoning widdowes, that turne ore all their
wealth in truft to fome kinfman, and make the
poore Gentleman worke hard for a penfion, fare you
well fir.

Seb. Nay prethee one word more.

Alex. How do I wrong this girle, fhe puts him
of ftill.

Moll. Thinke vpon this in cold bloud fir, you
make as much haft as if you were a going vpon a
fturgion voyage, take deliberation fir, neuer chufe a
wife as if you were going to *Virginia.*

Seb. And fo we parted, my too curfed fate.

Alex. She is but cunning, giues him longer
time in't.

Enter a Tailor.

Taylor. Miftreffe *Mol*, Miftreffe *Mol*: fo ho ho
fo ho.

Mol. There boy, there boy, what doft thou go
a hawking after me with a red clout on thy finger.

Taylor. I forgot to take meafure on you for your
new breeches.

Alex. Hoyda breeches, what will he marry a monfter with two trinckets, what age is this? if the wife
go in breeches, the man muft weare long coates like a
foole.

Mol. What fidlings heere, would not the old pat-
terne haue feru'd your turne.

Taylor. You change the fafhion, you fay you'le
haue the great Dutch flop Miftreffe *Mary.*

Mol. Why fir I fay fo ftill.

Taylor. Your breeches then will take vp a yard
more.

Mol. Well pray looke it be put in then.

Taylor. It fhall ftand round and full I warrant
you.

Mol. Pray make em eafy enough.

Taylor. I know my fault now, t'other was fomewhat ftiffe betweene the legges, Ile make thefe open
enough I warrant you.

Alex. Heer's good geere towards, I haue brought
vp my fonne to marry a Dutch flop, and a French
dublet, a codpice daughter.

Taylor. So, I haue gone as farre as I can go.

Mol. Why then farewell.

Taylor. If you go prefently to your chamber Miftreffe *Mary*, pray fend me the meafure of your thigh,
by fome honeft body.

Mol. Well fir, Ile fend it by a Porter prefently.

Exit Mol.

Taylor. So you had neede, it is a lufty one, both
of them would make any porters backe ake in England.
Exit Taylor.

Seb. I haue examined the beft part of man,
Reafon and iudgement, and in loue they tell me,
They leaue me vncontrould, he that is fwayd
By an vnfeeling bloud, paft heat of loue
His fpring time muft needes erre, his watch nere goes
   right
That fets his dyall by a rufty clocke.
   Alex. So, and which is that rufty clocke fir you.
   Seb. The clocke at Ludgate fir, it nere goes true.
   Alex. But thou goeft falfer: not thy fathers cares
Can keepe thee right, when that infenfible worke,
Obayes the workemans art, lets off the houre
And ftops againe when time is fatisfied,
But thou runft on, and iudgement, thy maine wheele,
Beats by all ftoppes, as if the worke would breake
Begunne with long paines for a minutes ruine,
Much like a fuffering man brought vp with care.
At laft bequeath'd to fhame and a fhort prayer.
   Seb. I taft you bitterer then I can deferue fir.
   Alex. Who has bewitch thee fonne, what diuell or
      drug,
Hath wrought vpon the weakneffe of thy bloud,
And betrayd all her hopes to ruinous folly?
Oh wake from drowfy and enchanted fhame,
Wherein thy foule fits with a golden dreame
Flatred and poyfoned, I am old my fonne,
Oh let me preuaile quickly, for I haue waightier bufi-
      neffe of mine owne
Then to chide thee : I muft not to my graue,
As a drunkard to his bed, whereon he lyes
Onely to fleepe, and neuer cares to rife,
Let me difpatch in time, come no more neere her.
   Seb. Not honeftly, not in the way of marriage.
   Alex. What fayft thou marriage, in what place,
the Seffions houfe, and who fhall giue the bride, pre-
the, an inditement.
   Seb. Sir now yee take part with the world to wrong
      her.

Alex.   Why, wouldſt thou faine marry to be pointed
    at,
Alas the numbers great, do not o're burden't,
Why as good marry a beacon on a hill,
Which all the country fixe their eyes vpon
As her thy folly doates on.   If thou longſt
To haue the ſtory of thy infamous fortunes,
Serue for diſcourſe in ordinaries and tauernes
Th'art in the way : or to confound thy name,
Keepe on, thou canſt not miſſe it : or to ſtrike
Thy wretched father to vntimely coldneſſe,
Keepe the left hand ſtill, it will bring thee to't.
Yet if no teares wrung from thy fathers eyes,
Nor ſighes that flye in ſparkles, from his ſorrowes,
Had power to alter what is wilfull in thee,
Me thinkes her very name ſhould fright thee from her,
And neuer trouble me.
    Seb.   Why is the name of *Mol* ſo fatall ſir.
    Alex.   Many one ſir, where ſuſpeċt is entred,
For ſeeke all *London* from one end to t'other,
More whoores of that name, then of any ten other.
    Seb.   Whats that to her ? let thoſe bluſh for them-
    ſelues.
Can any guilt in others condemne her ?
I'ue vowd to loue her : let all ſtormes oppoſe me,
That euer beate againſt the breſt of man,
Nothing but deaths blacke tempeſt ſhall diuide vs.
    Alex.   Oh folly that can dote on nought but
    ſhame.
    Seb.   Put caſe a wanton itch runs through one
    name
More then another, is that name the worſe,
Where honeſty ſits poſſeſt in't ? it ſhould rather
Appeare more excellent, and deſerue more praiſe.
When through foule miſts a brightneſſe it can raiſe.
Why there are of the diuels, honeſt Gentlemen,
And well deſcended, keepe an open houſe,
And ſome ath (good mans) that are arrant knaues.

He hates vnworthily, that by rote contemnes,
For the name neither faues, nor yet condemnes,
And for her honefty, 1 haue made fuch proofe an't,
In feuerall formes, fo neerely watcht her waies,
I will maintaine that ftrict, againft an army,
Excepting you my father : here's her worft,
Sh'has a bold fpirit that mingles with mankind,
But nothing elfe comes neere it : and oftentimes
Through her apparell fomewhat fhames her birth,
But fhe is loofe in nothing but in mirth,
Would all *Mols* were no worfe.

 Alex. This way I toyle in vaine and giue but ayme
To infamy and ruine : he will fall,
My bleffing cannot ftay him : all my ioyes
Stand at the brinke of a deuouring floud
And will be wilfully fwallowed : wilfully.
But why fo vaine, let all thefe teares be loft,
Ile purfue her to fhame, and fo al's croft.
Exit Sir Alexander.

 Seb. Hee is gon with fome ftrange purpofe, whofe
  effect
Will hurt me little if he fhoot fo wide,
To thinke I loue fo blindly : I but feed
His heart to this match, to draw on th'other.
Wherein my ioy fits with a full wifh crownd,
Onely his moode excepted which muft change.
By oppofite pollicies, courfes indirect,
Plaine dealing in this world takes no effect.
This madde girle I'le acquaint with my intent,
Get her affiftance, make my fortunes knowne,
Twixt louers hearts, fhee's a fit inftrument,
And has the art to help them to their owne,
By her aduife, for in that craft fhee's wife,
My loue and I may meete, fpite of all fpies.
Exit Sebaftian.

Enter Laxton *in Graies-Inne fields with the
Coachman.*

 Lax. Coachman.

Coach.   Heere fir.

Lax.   There's a tefter more, prethee driue thy coach to the hither end of Marybone parke, a fit place for *Mol* to get in.

Coach.   Marybone parke fir.

Lax.   I, its in our way thou knowft.

Coach.   It fhall be done fir.

Lax.   Coachman.

Coach.   A non fir.

Lax.   Are we fitted with good phrampell iades.

Coach.   The beft in Smithfield I warrant you fir.

Lax.   May we fafely take the vpper hand of any coacht veluet cappe or tuftaffety iacket, for they keepe a vilde fwaggering in coaches now a daies, the hye waies are ftopt with them.

Coach.   My life for yours and battle em to fir,— why they are the fame iades beleeue it fir, that haue drawne all your famous whores to *Ware.*

Lax.   Nay then they know their bufineffe, they neede no more inftructions.

Coach.   The're fo vfd to fuch iourneis fir, I neuer vfe whip to em ; for if they catch but the fent of a wench once, they runne like diuels.

Exit Coachman with his whip.

Lax.   Fine *Cerberus,* that rogue will haue the ftart of a thoufand ones, for whilft others trot a foot, heele ride prauncing to hell vpon a coach-horfe.

Stay, tis now about the houre of her appointment, but yet I fee her not, harke whats this, one, two, three,

The clocke ftriks three.

three by the clock at Sauoy, this is the houre, and Graies-Inne fields the place, fhee fwore fhe'ed meete mee : ha yonders two Innes a Court-men with one wench, but thats not fhee, they walke toward Iflington out of my way, I fee none yet dreft like her, I muft looke for a fhag ruffe, a freeze ierken, a fhort fword, and a fafeguard, or I get none : why *Mol* prethee make haſt, or the Coachman will curſſe vs anon.

Enter Mol *like a man.*

Mol. Oh heeres my Gentleman : if they would keepe their daies as well with their Mercers as their houres with their harlots, no bankrout would giue ſeuen ſcore pound for a ſeriants place, for would you know a catchpoole rightly deriued, the corruption of a Cittizen, is the generation of a ſeriant, how his eye hawkes for venery. Come are you ready ſir.

Lax. Ready, for what ſir.

Mol. Do you aske that now·ſir, why was this meeting pointed.

Lax. I thought you miſtooke me ſir,
You ſeeme to be ſome yong barriſter,
I haue no ſuite in law—all my land's ſold
I praiſe heauen for't : t'has rid me of much trouble.

Mol. Then I muſt wake you ſir, where ſtands the coach.

Lax. Whoſe this, *Mol* : honeſt *Mol.*

Mol. So young, and purblind, your an old wanton in your eyes I ſee that.

Lax. Th'art admirably ſuited for the three pigions at *Brainford*, Ile ſweare I knew thee not.

Mol. Ile ſweare you did not : but you ſhall know me now.

Lax. No not here, we ſhall be ſpyde efaith, the coach is better, come.

Mol. Stay.

Lax. What wilt thou vntruſſe a point *Mol.*

She puts of her cloake and drawes.

Mol. Yes, heere's the point that I vntruſſe, 'thas but one tag, 'twill ſerue tho to tye vp a rogues tongue.

Lax. How.

Mol. There's the gold with which you hir'd your
    hackney, here's her pace,
Shee rackes hard, and perhaps your bones will feele
    it,
Ten angels of mine own, I'ue put to thine, win em, &
    weare em.
Lax. Hold *Moll*, Miftreffe *Mary*.
Mol. Draw or Ile ferue an execution on thee
Shall lay thee vp till doomes day.
Lax. Draw vpon a woman, why what doft meane
Mol ?
Mol. To teach thy bafe thoughts manners : th'art
    one of thofe
That thinkes each woman thy fond flexable whore,
If fhe but caft a liberall eye vpon thee,
Turne backe her head, fhees thine, or amongft com-
    pany,
By chance drinke firft to thee : then fhee's quite gon,
There's no meanes to help her ; nay for a need,
Wilt fweare vnto thy credulous fellow letchers,
That th'art more in fauour with a Lady at firft
    fight
Then her monky all her life time,
How many of our fex, by fuch as thou
Haue their good thoughts paid with a blafted name
That neuer deferued loofly or did trip
In path of whooredome, beyond cup and lip.
But for the ftaine of confcience and of foule,
Better had women fall into the hands
Of an act filent, then a bragging nothing,
There's no mercy in't—what durft moue you fir,
To thinke me whoorifh ? a name which ·Ide teare
    out
From the hye Germaines throat, if it lay ledger
    there
To difpatch priuy flanders againft mee.
In thee I defye all men, their worft hates,
And their beft flatteries, all their golden witchcrafts,
With which they intangle the poore fpirits of fooles,

Diſtreſſed needlewomen and trade-fallne wiues.
Fiſh that muſt needs bite, or themſelues be bitten,
Such hungry things as theſe may ſoone be tooke
With a worme faſtned on a golden hooke.
Thoſe are the letchers food, his prey, he watches
For quarrelling wedlockes, and poore ſhifting ſiſters,
Tis the beſt fiſh he takes: but why good fiſherman,
Am I thought meate for you, that neuer yet
Had angling rod caſt towards me? cauſe you'le ſay
I'me giuen to ſport, I'me often mery, ieſt,
Had mirth no kindred in the world but luſt?
O ſhame take all her friends then: but how ere
Thou and the baſer world cenſure my life,
Ile ſend 'em word by thee, and write ſo much
Vpon thy breaſt, cauſe thou ſhalt bear't in mind,
Tell them 'twere baſe to yeeld, where I haue con-
    quer'd.
I ſcorne to proſtitute my ſelfe to a man,
I that can proſtitute a man to mee,
And ſo I greete thee.
    Lax.   Heare me.
    Mol.   Would the ſpirits of al my ſlanders, were
    claſpt in thine.
That I might vexe an army at one time.
    Lax.   I do repent me, hold.   *They fight.*
    Mol.   You'l die the better Chriſtian then.
    Lax.   I do confeſſe I haue wrong'd thee *Mol.*
    Mol.   Confeſſion is but poore amends for wrong,
Vnleſſe a rope would follow.
    Lax.   I aske thee pardon.
    Mol.   I'me your hir'd whoore ſir.
    Lax.   I yeeld both purſe and body.
    Mol.   Both are mine, and now at my diſpoſing.
    Lax.   Spare my life.
    Mol.   I ſcorne to ſtrike thee baſely.
    Lax.   Spoke like a noble girle i'faith.
Heart I thinke I fight with a familiar, or the Ghoſt of
a fencer. Sh'has wounded me gallantly, call you this
a letcherous viage? Here's bloud would haue ſeru'd

me this feuen yeare in broken heads and cut fingers,
& it now runs all out together, pox athe three pigions,
I would the coach were here now to carry mee to the
Chirurgions.   *Exit Laxton.*
    Mol.   If I could meete my enemies one by one
        thus,
I might make pretty fhift with 'em in time,
And make 'em know, fhee that has wit, and fpirit,
May fcorne to liue beholding to her body for meate,
Or for apparell like your common dame,
That makes fhame get her cloathes, to couer fhame.
Bafe is that minde, that kneels vnto her body,
As if a husband flood in awe on's wife,
My fpirit fhall be Miftriffe of this houfe,
As long as I haue time in't.   — — oh

Enter Trapdore.

Heere comes my man that would be : 'tis his houre.
Faith a good well fet fellow, if his fpirit
Be anfwerable to his vmbles ; he walkes fliffe,
But whether he will ftand to't ftifly, there's the point ;
Has a good calfe for't, and ye fhall haue many a
        woman
Choofe him fhee meanes to make her head, by his
        calfe ;
I do not know their trickes in't, faith he feemes
A man without ; I'le try what he is within.
    Tray.   Shee told me Graies-Inne fields twixt three
        & foure,
Ile fit her Miftrefhip with a peece of feruice,
I'me hir'd to rid the towne of one mad girle.
                          Shee iuftles him.
What a pox ailes you fir ?
    Mol.   He beginnes like a Gentleman.
    Trap.   Heart, is the field fo narrow, or your eye-
        fight :
Life he comes back againe.   *She comes towards him.*
    Mol.   Was this fpoke to me fir.
    Trap.   I cannot tell fir.

Mol.   Go y'are a coxcombe.

Trap.   Coxcombe.

Mol.   Y'are a flaue.

Trap.   I hope there's law for you fir.

Mol.   Ye, do you fee fir.   *Turne his hat.*

Trap.   Heart this is no good dealing, pray let me know what houfe your off.

Mol.   One of the Temple fir.   *Philips him.*

Trap.   Maffe fo me thinkes.

Mol.   And yet fometime I lye about chicke lane.

Trap.   I like you the worfe becaufe you fhift your lodging fo often, Ile not meddle with you for that tricke fir.

Mol.   A good fhift, but it fhall not ferue your turne.

Trap.   You'le giue me leaue to paffe about my bufineffe fir.

Mol.   Your bufineffe, Ile make you waite on mee before I ha done, and glad to ferue me too.

Trap.   How fir, ferue you, not if there were no more men in England.

Moll.   But if there no more women in England I hope you'd waite vpon your Miftreffe then,

Trap.   Miftreffe.

Mol.   Oh your a tri'd fpirit at a pufh fir,

Trap.   What would your Worfhip haue me do.

Mol.   You a fighter.

Trap.   No, I praife heauen, I had better grace & more maners.

Mol.   As how I pray fir.

Trap.   Life 'thad bene a beaftly part of me to haue drawne my weapons vpon my Miftreffe, all the world would a cry'd fhame of me for that.

Mol.   Why but you knew me not.

Trap.   Do not fay fo Miftreffe, I knew you by your wide ftraddle, as well as if I had bene in your belly.

Mol.   Well, we fhall try you further, ith meane time wee giue you intertainement.

Trap.   Thanke your good Miftrefhip.

Mol.   How many fuites haue you.

Trap.   No more fuites then backes Miftreffe.

Mol.   Well if you deferue, I caft of this, next weeke,
And you may creepe into't.

Trap.   Thanke your good Worfhip.

Mol.   Come follow me to S. *Thomas Apoftles*,
Ile put a liuery cloake vpon your backe, the firft thing
    I do.

Trap.   I follow my deere Miftreffe.   *Exeunt omnes.*

Enter Miftreffe Gallipot *as from fupper, her husband
after her.*

Maift. Gal.   What *Pru*, Nay fweete *Prudence.*

Mift. Gal.   What a pruing keepe you, I thinke the
baby would haue a teate it kyes fo, pray be not fo
fond of me, leaue your Citty humours, I'me vext
at you to fee how like a calfe you come bleating
after me.

Maift. Gal.   Nay hony *Pru* : how does your rifing
vp before all the table fhew? and flinging from my
friends fo vnciuily, fye *Pru*, fye, come.

Miftt. Gal.   Then vp and ride ifaith.

Maift. Gal.   Vp and ride, nay my pretty *Pru*, thats
farre from my thought, ducke : why moufe, thy minde
is nibbling at fomething, what ift, what lyes vpon thy
Stomach?

Mift. Gal.   Such an affe as you : hoyda, y'are beft
turne midwife, or Phyfition : y'are a Poticary already,
but I'me none of your drugs.

Maist. Gal.   Thou art a fweete drug, fweeteft *Pru*,
and the more thou art pounded, the more pretious.

Mift. Gal.   Muft you be prying into a womans
fecrets : fay ye?

Maift. Gal.   Womans fecrets.

Mift. Gal.   What? I cannot haue a qualme come
vpon mee but your teeth waters, till your nofe hang
ouer it.

Maift. Gal.   It is my loue deere wife.

Mift. Gal. Your loue? your loue is all words; giue mee deeds, I cannot abide a man thats too fond ouer me, fo cookifh; thou doft not know how to handle a woman in her kind.

Maift. Gal. No *Pru?* why I hope I haue handled ——

Mift. Gal. Handle a fooles head of your owne,— fih—fih.

Maift. Gal. Ha, ha, tis fuch a wafpe; it does mee good now to haue her fing me, little rogue.

Mift. Gal. Now fye how you vex me, I cannot abide thefe aperne husbands: fuch cotqueanes, you ouerdoe your things, they become you fcuruily.

Maift. Gal. Vpon my life fhe breeds, heauen knowes how I haue ftraind my felfe to pleafe her, night and day: I wonder why wee Cittizens fhould get children fo fretfull and vntoward in the breeding, their fathers being for the moft part as gentle as milch kine: fhall I leaue thee my *Pru.*

Mift. Gal. Fye, fye, fye.

Maift. Gal. Thou fhalt not bee vext no more, pretty kind rogue, take no cold fweete *Pru.*

Exit Maift. Gallipot.

Mift. Gal. As your wit has done: now Maifter *Laxton* fhew your head, what newes from you? would any husband fufpect that a woman crying, Buy any fcurui-graffe, fhould bring loue letters amongft her herbes to his wife, pretty tricke, fine conueyance? had iealoufy a thoufand eyes, a filly woman with fcuruy-graffe blinds them all;

Laxton with bayes

Crown I thy wit for this, it deferues praife.

This makes me affect thee more, this prooues thee wife,

Lacke what poore fhift is loue forc't to deuife?

(Toth' point.)

She reads the letter.

O Sweete Creature——(a fweete beginning) *pardon my long abfence, for thou fhalt fhortly be poffeffed with*

my prefence; though Demophon *was falfe to*
Phillis, *I will be to thee as* Pan-da-rus *was to*
Cref-fida : *tho* Eneus *made an affe of* Dido, *I will
dye to thee ere I do fo; o fweetefl creature make
much of me, for no man beneath the filuer moone
fhall make more of a woman then I do of thee, furnifh me therefore with thirty pounds, you mufl doe
doe it of neceffity for me; I languifh till I fee fome
comfort come from thee, protefling not to dye in thy
debt, but rather to liue fo, as hitherto I haue and
will.*

Thy true *Laxton* euer.

Alas poore Gentleman, troth I pitty him,
How fhall 1 raife this money ? thirty pound ?
Tis thirty fure, a 3 before an o,
I know his threes too well ; my childbed linnen ?
Shall I pawne that for him ? then if my marke
Be knowne I am vndone ; it may be thought
My husband's bankrout : which way fhall I turne ?
Laxton, what with my owne feares, and thy wants,
I'me like a needle twixt two adamants.

Enter Maifter Gallipot *haftily*.

Maifl. Gal.   Nay, nay, wife, the women are all vp,
ha, how, reading a letters ? I fmel a goofe, a couple of
capons, and a gammon of bacon from her mother out
of the country, I hold my life,—fteale,—fteale.
Mifl. Gal.   O befhrow your heart.
Maifl. Gal.   What letter's that ? I'le fee't.
She teares the letter.
Mifl. Gal.   Oh would thou had'ft no eyes to fee
the downefall of me and thy felfe : I'me for euer, for
euer I'me vndone.
Maifl. Gal.   What ailes my *Pru* ? what paper's
that thou tear'ft ?
Mifl. Gal.   Would I could teare
My very heart in peeces : for my foule
Lies on the racke of fhame, that tortures me

Beyond a womans fuffering.

   Maiſt. Gall. What meanes this?

   Miſt. Had you no other vengeance to throw
    downe,

But euen in heigth of all my ioyes?

   Maiſt. Gal. Deere woman.

   Miſt. Gal. When the full fea of pleafure and con·
    tent

Seem'd to flow ouer me.

   Maiſt. Gal. As thou defireſt to keepe mee out of
bedlam, tell what troubles thee, is not thy child at
nurfe falne ficke, or dead?

   Miſt. Gal. Oh no.

   Maiſt. Gal. Heauens bleffe me, are my barnes
    and houfes

Yonder at Hockly hole confum'd with fire,

I can build more, fweete *Pru.*

   Miſt. Gal. Tis worfe, tis worfe.

   Maiſt. Gal. My factor broke, or is the *Ionas*
    funcke.

   Miſt. Gal. Would all we had were fwallowed in
    the waues,

Rather then both fhould be the fcorne of flaues.

   Maiſt. Gal. I'me at my wits end.

   Miſt. Gal. Oh my deere husband,

Where once I thought my felfe a fixed ſtarre,

Plac't onely in the heauen of thine armes,

I feare now I fhall proue a wanderer,

Oh *Laxton, Laxton,* is it then my fate

To be by thee orethrowne?

   Maiſt. Gal. Defend me wifedome,

From falling into frenzie, on my knees.

Sweete *Pru,* fpeake, whats that *Laxton* who fo heauy
    lyes on thy bofome.

   Miſt. Gal. I fhall fure run mad.

   Maiſt. Gal. I fhall run mad for company then:
    fpeak to me,

I'me *Gallipot* thy husband, . . *Pru,*—why *Pru.*

Art ficke in confcience for fome villanous deed

Thou wert about to act, didſt meane to rob me,
Tuſh I forgiue thee, haſt thou on my bed
Thruſt my ſoft pillow vnder anothers head ?
Ile winke at all faults *Pru*, las thats no more,
Then what ſome neighbours neere thee, haue done
    before,
Sweete hony *Pru*, whats that *Laxton* ?
   Miſt. Gall. Oh.
   Maiſt. Gal. Out with him.
   Miſt. Gall. Oh hee's borne to be my vndoer,
This hand which thou calſt thine, to him was giuen,
To him was I made ſure ith ſight of heauen.
   Maiſt. Gal. I neuer heard this thunder.
   Miſt. Gall. Yes, yes, before
I was to thee contracted, to him I ſwore,
Since laſt I ſaw him twelue moneths three times told,
The Moone hath drawne through her light ſiluer
    bow,
For ore the ſeas hee went, and it was ſaid,
(But Rumor lyes) that he in France was dead.
But hee's aliue, oh hee's aliue, he ſent,
That letter to me, which in rage I rent,
Swearing with oathes moſt damnably to haue me,
Or teare me from this boſome, oh heauens ſaue me.
   Maiſt. Gal. My heart will breake,—ſham'd and
vndone for euer.
   Miſt. Gal. So blacke a day (poore wretch) went ore
thee neuer.
   Maiſt. Gal. If thou ſhouldſt wraſtle with him at the
    law,
Th'art ſure to fall, no odde ſlight, no preuention.
Ile tell him th'art with child.
   Miſt. Gal. Vmh.
   Maiſt. Gall. Or giue out one of my men was tane
a bed with thee.
   Miſt. Gal. Vmh, vmh.
   Maiſt. Gal. Before I looſe thee my deere *Pru*,
Ile driue it to that puſh.
   Miſt. Gal. Worſe, and worſe ſtill,

You embrace a mifchiefe, to preuent an ill.
    Maiſt. Gal. Ile buy thee of him, ſtop his mouth
      with Gold,
Think'ſt thou twill do.
    Maiſt. Gall. Oh me, heauens grant it would,
Yet now my fences are ſet more in tune,
He writ, as I remember in his letter,
That he in riding vp and downe had ſpent,
(Ere hee could finde me) thirty pounds, ſend that,
Stand not on thirty with him.
    Maiſt. Gal. Forty *Pru,*
Say thou the word tis done, wee venture liues
For wealth, but muſt do more to keepe our wiues,
Thirty or forty *Pru,*
    Miſt. Gal. Thirty good ſweete
Of an ill bargaine lets ſaue what we can,
Ile pay it him with my teares, he was a man
When firſt I knew him of a meeke ſpirit,
All goodneſſe is not yet dryd vp I hope.
    Maiſt. Gal. He ſhall haue thirty pound, let that
      ſtop all :
Loues ſweets taſt beſt, when we haue drunke downe
      Gall.

Enter Maiſter Tiltyard, *and his wife,* Maiſter Gof-
      hawke, *and* Miſtreſſe Openworke.

Gods ſo, our friends; come, come, ſmoth your
      cheeke ;
After a ſtorme the face of heauen looks ſleeke.
    Maiſt. Tilt. Did I not tell you theſe turtles were
      together ?
    Miſt. Tilt. How doſt thou ſirra ? why ſiſter *Galli-*
pot ?
    Miſt. Open. Lord how ſhee's chang'd ?
    Goſh. Is your wife ill ſir ?
    Maiſt. Gal. Yes indeed la ſir, very ill, very ill,
neuer worſe.

Miſt. Tilt.   How her head burnes, feele how her pulſes work.

Miſt. Open.   Siſter lie downe a little, that alwaies does mee good.

Miſt. Tilt.   In good ſadneſſe I finde beſt eaſe in
that too,
Has ſhee laid ſome hot thing to her Stomach ?

Miſt. Gal.   No, but I will lay ſomething anon.

Maiſt. Tilt.   Come, come fooles, you trouble her, ſhal's goe Maiſter *Goſhawke*?

Goſh.   Yes ſweete Maiſter *Tiltyard*, ſirra *Roſamond* I hold my life *Gallipot* hath vext his wife.

Miſt. Open.   Shee has a horrible high colour indeed.

Goſh.   Wee ſhall haue your face painted with the ſame red ſoone at night, when your husband comes from his rubbers in a falſe alley ; thou wilt not beleeue me that his bowles run with a wrong byas.

Miſt. Open.   It cannot ſinke into mee, that hee feedes vpon ſtale mutten abroad, hauing better and freſher at home.

Goſh.   What if I bring thee, where thou ſhalt ſee him ſtand at racke and manger?

Miſt. Open.   Ile ſaddle him in's kind, and ſpurre him till hee kicke againe.

Goſh.   Shall thou and I ride our iourney then.

Miſt. Open.   Heere's my hand.

Goſh.   No more ; come Maiſter *Tiltyard*, ſhall we leape into the ſtirrops with our women, and amble home ?

Maiſt. Tilt.   Yes, yes, come wife.

Miſt. Tilt.   Introth ſiſter, I hope you will do well for all this.

Miſt. Gal.   I hope I ſhall : farewell good ſiſter : ſweet Maiſter *Goſhawke*.

Maiſt. Gal.   Welcome brother, moſt kindlie welcome ſir.

Omnes.   Thankes ſir for our good cheere,
Exeunt all but Gallipot *and his wife.*

Maift. Gal.   It fhall be fo, becaufe a crafty knaue
Shall not out reach me, nor walke by my dore
With my wife arme in arme, as 'twere his whoore,
I'le giue him a golden coxcombe, thirty pound :
Tufh *Pru*, what's thirty pound? fweete ducke looke
    cheerely.
Mift. Gal.   Thou art worthy of my heart thou
bui'ft it deerely.

Enter Laxton *muffled.*

Lax.   Vds light the tide's againft me, a pox of
your Potticarifhp : oh for fome glifter to fet him going ;
'tis one of *Hercules* labours, to tread one of thefe
Cittie hennes, becaufe their cockes are ftil crowing
ouer them ; there's no turning tale here, I muft on.
Mift.   Gal.   Oh, husband fee he comes.
Maift. Gal.   Let me deale with him.
Lax.   Bleffe you fir.
Maift. Gal.   Be you bleft too fir if you come in
peace.
Lax.   Haue you any good pudding Tobacco fir ?
Mift. Gal.   Oh picke no quarrels gentle fir, my
    husband
Is not a man of weapon, as you are,
He knowes all, I haue opned all before him, concern-
    ing you.
Lax.   Zounes has fhe fhowne my letters.
Mift. Gal.   Suppofe my cafe were yours, what would
    you do,
At fuch a pinch, fuch batteries, fuch affaultes,
Of father, mother, kinred, to diffolue
The knot you tyed, and to be bound to him ?
How could you fhift this ftorme off ?
Lax.   If I know hang me.
Mift. Gal.   Befides a ftory of your death was
    read
Each minute to me.

Lax.   What a pox meanes this ridling ?
Maiſt. Gal.   Be wiſe ſir, let not you and I be toſt
On Lawiers pens ; they haue ſharpe nibs and draw
Mens very heart bloud from them ; what need you ſir
To beate the drumme of my wifes infamy,
And call your friends together ſir to prooue
Your precontract, when ſh'has confeſt it ?
Lax.   Vmh ſir, . . . has ſhe confeſt it ?
Maiſt. Gal.   Sh'has 'faith to me ſir, vpon your letter
   ſending.
Miſt. Gal.   I haue, I haue.
Lax.   If I let this yron coole call me ſlaue,
Do you heare, you dame *Prudence ?* think'ſt thou vile
   woman
I'le take theſe blowes and winke ?
Miſt. Gal.   Vpon my knees.
Lax.   Out impudence.
Maiſt. Gal.   Good ſir.
Lax.   You goatiſh ſlaues,
No wilde foule to cut vp but mine ?
Maiſt. Gal.   Alas ſir,
You make her fleſh to tremble, fright her not,
She ſhall do reaſon, and what's fit.
Lax.   I'le haue thee, wert thou more common
Then an hoſpitall, and more diſeaſed.—
Maiſt. Gal.   But one word good ſir.
Lax.   So ſir.
Maiſt. Gal.   I married her, haue line with her, and
   got
Two children on her body, thinke but on that ;
Haue you ſo beggarly an appetite
When I vpon a dainty diſh haue fed
To dine vpon my ſcraps, my leauings ? ha ſir ?
Do I come neere you now ſir ?
Lax.   Be Lady you touch me.
Maiſt. Gal.   Would not you ſcorne to weare my
   cloathes ſir ?
Lax.   Right ſir.

Maiſt. Gal. Then pray ſir weare not her, for ſhee's
    a garment
So fitting for my body, I'me loath
Another ſhould put it on, you will vndoe both.
Your letter (as ſhee ſaid) complained you had ſpent
In queſt of her, ſome thirty pound, I'le pay it ;
Shall that ſir ſtop this gap vp twixt you two ?
    Lax. Well if I ſwallow this wrong, let her thanke
    you :
The mony being paid ſir, I am gon :
Farewell, oh women happy's hee truſts none.
    Miſt. Gall. Diſpatch him hence ſweete husband.
    Maiſt. Gall. Yes deere wife : pray ſir come in, ere
    Maiſter *Laxton* part
Thou ſhalt in wine drinke to him.
                Exit Maiſter Gallipot *and his wife.*
    Miſt. Gal. With all my heart ; . . . how doſt thou
like my wit ?
    Lax. Rarely, that wile
By which the Serpent did the firſt woman beguile,
Did euer ſince, all womens boſomes fill ;
Y'are apple eaters all, deceiuers ſtill.   *Exit Laxton.*

    Enter Sir Alexander Wengrave : Sir Dauy Dap-
    per, Sir Adam Appleton, *at one dore, and* Trap-
    dore *at another doore.*

    Alex. Out with your tale Sir *Dauy*, to Sir *Adam.*
A knaue is in mine eie deepe in my debt.
    Sir Da. Nay : if hee be a knaue ſir, hold him
    faſt.
    Alex. Speake ſoftly, what egge is there hatching
now.
    Trap. A Ducks egge ſir, a ducke that has eaten a
frog, I haue crackt the ſhell, and ſome villany or other
will peep out preſently ; the ducke that ſits is the
bouncing Rampe (that Roaring Girle my Miſtreſſe)
the drake that muſt tread is your ſonne *Sebaſtian.*
    Alex. Be quicke.

Trap. As the tongue of an oifter wench.

Alex. And fee thy newes be true.

Trap. As a barbars euery fatterday night . . . mad
Mol.

Alex. Ah.

Trap. Muft be let in without knocking at your
backe gate.

Alex. So.

Trap. Your chamber will be made baudy.

Alex. Good.

Trap. Shee comes in a fhirt of male.

Alex. How fhirt of male ?

Trap. Yes fir or a male fhirt, that's to fay in mans
apparell.

Alex. To my fonne.

Trap. Clofe to your fonne: your fonne and her
Moone will be in coniunction, if all Alminacks lie not,
her blacke faueguard is turned into a deepe floppe,
the holes of her vpper body to button holes, her
waftcoate to a dublet, her placket to the ancient feate
of a codpice, and you fhall take 'em both with ftanding
collers.

Alex. Art fure of this ?

Trap. As euery throng is fure of a pick-pocket, as
fure as a whoore is of the clyents all *Michaelmas*
Tearme, and of the pox after the Tearme.

Alex. The time of their tilting ?

Trap. Three.

Alex. The day ?

Trap. This.

Alex. Away ply it, watch her.

Trap. As the diuell doth for the death of a baud,
I'le watch her, do you catch her.

Alex. Shee's faft : heere weaue thou the nets ;
harke.

Trap. They are made.

Alex. I told them thou didft owe mee money ;
hold it vp : maintain't.

Trap. Stifly ; as a Puritan does contention,

Foxe I owe thee not the value of a halfepenny
halter.

Alex. Thou fhalt be hang'd in't ere thou fcape fo.
Varlet I'le make thee looke through a grate.

Trap. Ile do't prefently, through a Tauerne grate,
drawer: pifh.   *Exit Trapdore.*

Adam. Has the knaue vext you fir?

Alex. Askt him my mony,
He fweares my fonne receiu'd it : oh that boy
Will nere leaue heaping forrowes on my heart,
Till he has broke it quite.

Adam. Is he ftill wild?

Alex. As is a ruffian Beare.

Adam. But he has left
His old haunt with that baggage.

Alex. Worfe ftill and worfe,
He laies on me his fhame, I on him my curfe.

S. Dauy. My fonne *Iacke Dapper* then fhall run
    with him,
All in one pafture.

Adam. Proues your fonne bad too fir?

S. Dauy. As villany can make him : your *Sebaf-
    tian*
Doates but on one drabb, mine on a thoufand,
A noyfe of fiddlers, Tobacco, wine and a whoore,
A Mercer that will let him take vp more,
Dyce, and a water fpaniell with a Ducke : oh,
Bring him a bed with thefe, when his purfe gingles,
Roaring boyes follow at's tale, fencers and ningles,
(Beafts *Adam* nere gaue name to) thefe horfe-leeches
    fucke
My fonne, he being drawne dry, they all liue on
    fmoake.

Alex. Tobacco?

S. Dauy. Right, but I haue in my braine
A windmill going that fhall grind to duft
The follies of my fonne, and make him wife,
Or a ftarke foole ; pray lend me your aduife.

Both. That fhall you good fir *Dauy.*

S. Dauy.   Heere's the fprindge
I ha fet to catch this woodcocke in : an action
In a falfe name (vnknowne to him) is entred
I'th Counter to arreft *Iacke Dapper.*
    Both.   Ha, ha, he.
    S. Dauy.   Thinke you the Counter cannot breake
        him ?
    Adam.   Breake him ?
Yes and breake's heart too if he lie there long.
    S. Dauy.   I'le make him fing a Counter tenor
        fure.
    Adam.   No way to tame him like it, there hee fhall
        learne
What mony is indeed, and how to fpend it.
    S. Dauy.   Hee's bridled there.
    Alex.   I, yet knowes not how to mend it,
Bedlam cures not more madmen in a yeare,
Then one of the Counters does, men pay more deere
There for there wit then any where ; a Counter
Why 'tis an vniuerfity, who not fees ?
As fchollers there, fo heere men take degrees,
And follow the fame ftudies (all alike.)
Schollers learne firft Logicke and Rhetoricke.
So does a prifoner ; with fine honied fpeech
At's firft comming in he doth perfwade, befeech,
He may be lodg'd with one that is not itchy ;
To lie in a cleane chamber, in fheets not lowfy,
But when he has no money, then does he try,
By fubtile Logicke, and quaint fophiftry,
To make the keepers truft him.
    Adam.   Say they do.
    Alex.   Then hee's a graduate.
    S. Dauy.   Say they truft him not.
    Alex.   Then is he held a frefhman and a fot
And neuer fhall commence, but being ftill bar'd
Be expulft from the Maifters fide, to th' twopenny
ward,
Or elfe i'th hole, beg plac't.
    Adam.   When then I pray proceeds a prifoner.

Alex.   When mony being the theame,
He can difpute with his hard creditors hearts,
And get out cleere, hee's then a Maifter of Arts ;
Sir *Dauy* fend your fonne to Woodftreet Colledge,
A Gentleman can no where get more knowledge.
    S. Dauy.   There Gallants ftudy hard.
    Alex.   True : to get mony.
    S. Dauy.   'lies bith' heeles i'faith, thankes, thankes,
I ha fent for a couple of beares fhall paw him.

    Enter Seriant Curtilax *and Yeoman* Hanger.

    Adam.   Who comes yonder ?
    S. Dauy.   They looke like puttocks, thefe fhould
        be they.
    Alex.   I know 'em, they are officers, fir wee'l leaue
        you.
    S. Dauy.   My good knights.
Leaue me, you fee I'me haunted now with fpirits.
    Both.   Fare you well fir.   *Exeunt Alex. and Adam*
    Curt.   This old muzzle chops fhould be he.
By the fellowes difcription : Saue you fi .
    S. Dauy.   Come hither you mad varlets, did not
my man tell you I watcht here for you.
    Curt.   One in a blew coate fir told vs, that in this
place an old Gentleman would watch for vs, a thing
contrary to our oath, for we are to watch for euery
wicked member in a Citty.
    S. Dauy.   You'l watch then for ten thoufand,
what's thy name honefty ?
    Curt.   Seriant *Curtilax* I fir.
    S. Dauy.   An excellent name for a Seriant,
        Curtilax.
Seriants indeed are weapons of the law,
When prodigall ruffians farre in debt are growne,
Should not you cut them ; Cittizens were orethrowne,
Thou dwel'ft hereby in Holborne *Curtilax.*
    Curt.   That's my circuit fir, I coniure moft in that
        circle.

S. Dauy. And what yong toward welp is this ?
Hang. Of the fame litter, his yeoman fir, my
name's *Hanger.*
S. Dauy. Yeoman *Hanger.*
One paire of fheeres fure cut out both your coates,
You haue two names moft dangerous to mens throates,
You two are villainous loades on Gentlemens backs,
Deere ware, this *Hanger* and this *Curtilax.*
Curt. We are as other men are fir, I cannot fee
but hee who makes a fhow of honefty and religion, if
his clawes can faften to his liking, he drawes bloud ;
all that liue in the world, are but great fifh and little
fifh, and feede vpon one another, fome eate vp whole
men, a Seriant cares but for the fhoulder of a man,
they call vs knaues and curres, but many times hee
that fets vs on, worries more lambes one yeare, then
we do in feuen.
S. Dauy. Spoke like a noble *Cerberus,* is the
action entred ?
Hang. His name is entred in the booke of vn-
beleeuers.
S. Dauy. What booke's that ?
Curt. The booke where all prifoners names ftand,
and not one amongft forty, when he comes in,
beleeues to come out in haft.
S. Da. Be as dogged to him as your office allowes
you to be.
Both. Oh fir.
S. Dauy. You know the vnthrift *Iacke Dapper.*
Curt. I, I, fir, that Gull ? afwell as I know my
yeoman.
S. Dauy. And you know his father too, *Sir Dauy
Dapper* ?
Curt. As damn'd a vfurer as euer was among
Iewes ; if hee were fure his fathers skinne would
yeeld him any money, he would when hee dyes flea it
off, and fell it to couer drummes for children at Bar-
tholmew faire.
S. Dauy. What toades are thefe to fpit poyfon on

a man to his face ? doe you fee (my honeſt raſcals ?)
yonder gray-hound is the dog he hunts with, out of
that Tauerne *Iacke Dapper* will ſally ſa, ſa : giue the
counter, on, ſet vpon him.

Both. Wee'l charge him vppo' th backe ſir.

S. Dauy. Take no baile, put mace enough into
his caudle, double your files, trauerſe your ground.

Both. Braue ſir.

S. Dauy. Cry arme, arme, arme.

Both. Thus ſir.

S. Dauy. There boy, there boy, away : looke to
your prey my trew Engliſh wolues, and ſo I vaniſh.

Exit S. Dauy.

Curt. Some warden of the Seriants begat this old
fellow, vpon my life, ſtand cloſe.

Hang. Shall the ambuſcado lie in one place ?

Curt. No nooke thou yonder.

Enter Mol *and* Trapdore.

Mol. Ralph.

Trap. What ſayes my braue Captaine male and
female ?

Mol. This Holborne is ſuch a wrangling ſtreete.

Trap. That's becauſe Lawiers walkes to and fro
in't.

Mol. Heere's ſuch iuſtling, as if euery one wee
met were drunke and reel'd.

Trap. Stand Miſtreſſe do you not ſmell carrion ?

Mol. Carryon ? no, yet I ſpy rauens.

Trap. Some poore winde-ſhaken gallant will anon
fall into ſore labour, and theſe men-midwiues muſt
bring him to bed i'the counter, there all thoſe that
are great with child with debts, lie in.

Mol. Stand vp.

Trap. Like your new maypoll.

Hang. Whiſt, whew.

Curt. Hump, no.

Mol. Peeping ? it ſhall go hard huntſmen, but I'le

fpoyle your game, they looke for all the world like two
infeſted malt-men comming muffled vp in their cloakes
in a froſty morning to London.

Trap.   A courfe, Captaine ; a beare comes to the
ſtake.

Enter Iacke Dapper and Gul.

Mol.   It fhould bee fo, for the dogges ſtruggle to bee
let loofe.

Hang.   Whew.

Curt.   Hemp.

Moll.   Harke *Trapdore,* follow your leader.

Iacke Dap.   Gul.

Gul.   Maiſter.

Iacke Dap.   Did'ſt euer fee fuch an affe as I am
boy ?

Gul.   No by my troth fir, to loofe all your mony,
yet haue falfe dice of your owne, why 'tis as I faw a
great fellow vfed t'other day, he had a faire fword
and buckler, and yet a butcher dry beate him with a
cudgell.

Both.   Honeſt Serieant fly, flie Maiſter *Dapper* you'l
be arreſted elfe.

Iacke Dap.   Run *Gul* and draw.

Gul.   Run Maiſter, *Gull* followes you.

Exit Dapper and Gull.

Curt.   I know you well enough, you'r but a whore
to hang vpon any man.

Mol.   Whores then are like Serieants, fo now hang
you, draw rogue, but ſtrike not : for a broken pate
they'l keepe their beds, and recouer twenty markes
damages.

Curt.   You fhall pay for this refcue, runne downe
fhoe-lane and meete him.

Trap.   Shu, is this a refcue Gentlemen or no ?

Mol.   Refcue ? a pox on 'em, *Trapdore* let's away,
I'me glad I haue done perfeſt one good worke to
    day,

If any Gentleman be in Scriueners bands,
Send but for *Mol*, fhe'll baile him by thefe hands.

Exeunt.

Enter Sir Alexander Wengraue *folus.*

Alex.   Vnhappy in the follies of a fonne,
Led againft iudgement, fence, obedience,
And all the powers of nobleneffe and wit ;

Enter Trapdore

Oh wretched father, now *Trapdore* will fhe come ?
   Trap.   In mans apparell fir, I am in her heart now,
And fhare in all her fecrets.
   Alex.   Peace, peace, peace.
Here take my Germane watch, hang't vp in fight,
That I may fee her hang in Englifh for't.
   Trap.   I warrant you for that now, next Seffions
      rids her fir,
This watch will bring her in better then a hundred
      conftables.
   Alex.   Good *Trapdore* faift thou fo, thou cheer'ft
      my heart
After a ftorme of forrow,— my gold chaine too,
Here take a hundred markes in yellow linkes.
   Trap.   That will do well to bring the watch to
      light fir.
And worth a thoufand of your Headborowes lan-
      thornes.
   Alex.   Place that a' the Court cubbart, let it lie
Full in the veiw of her theefe-whoorifh eie.
   Trap.   Shee cannot miffe it fir, I fee't fo plaine
That I could fteal't my felfe.
   Alex.   Perhaps thou fhalt too,
That or fomething as weighty ; what fhee leaues,
Thou fhalt come clofely in, and filch away,
And all the weight vpon her backe I'le lay.
   Trap.   You cannot affure that fir.
   Alex.   No, what lets it ?

3   ()

    Trap. Being a ſtout girle, perhaps ſhee'l deſire
      preſſing,
Then all the weight muſt ly vpon her belly.
    Alex. Belly or backe I care not ſo I'ue one.
    Trap. You'r of my minde for that ſir.
    Alex. Hang vp my ruffe band with the diamond
      at it,
It may be ſhee'l like that beſt.
    Trap. It's well for her, that ſhee muſt haue her
choice, hee thinkes nothing too good for her, if you
hold on this minde a little longer, it ſhall bee the firſt
worke I doe to turne theefe my ſelfe ; would do a
man good to be hang'd when he is ſo wel prouided for.
    Alex. So, well ſayd ; all hangs well, would ſhee
      hung ſo too,
The ſight would pleaſe me more, then all their
      gilſterings :
Oh that my myſteries to ſuch ſtreights ſhould runne,
That I muſt rob my ſelfe to bleſſe my ſonne. *Exeunt.*

    Enter Sebaſtian, *with* Mary Fitz-Allard *like a page,*
          and Mol.

    Seb. Thou haſt done me a kind office, without
      touch
Either of ſinne or ſhame, our loues are honeſt.
    Mol. I'de ſcorne to make ſuch ſhift to bring you
      together elſe.
    Seb. Now haue I time and opportunity
Without all feare to bid thee welcome loue.   *Kiſſe.*
    Mary. Neuer with more deſire and harder venture.
    Mol. How ſtrange this ſhewes one man to kiſſe
      another.
    Seb. I'de kiſſe ſuch men to chuſe *Moll,*
Me thinkes a womans lip taſts well in a dublet.
    Mol. Many an old madam has the better fortune
      then,
Whoſe breathes grew ſtale before the faſhion came,

If that will help 'em, as you thinke 'twill do,
They'l learne in time to plucke on the hofe too.
   Seb. The older they waxe *Moll*, troth I fpeake
      ferioufly,
As fome haue a conceit their drinke tafts better
In an outlandifh cup then in our owne,
So me thinkes euery kiffe fhe giues me now
In this ftrange forme, is worth a paire of two,
Here we are fafe, and furtheft from the eie
Of all fufpicion, this is my fathers chamber,
Vpon which floore he neuer fteps till night.
Here he miftrufts me not, nor I his comming,
At mine owne chamber he ftill pries vnto me,
My freedome is not there at mine owne finding,
Still checkt and curb'd, here he fhall miffe his purpofe.
   Mol. And what's your bufineffe now, you haue your
      mind fir ;
At your great fuite I promifd you to come,
I pittied her for names fake, that a *Moll*
Should be fo croft in loue, when there's fo many,
That owes nine layes a peece, and not fo little :
My taylor fitted her, how like you his worke ?
   Seb. So well, no Art can mend it, for this purpofe,
But to thy wit and helpe we're chiefe in debt,
And muft liue ftill beholding.
   Mol. Any honeft pitty
I'me willing to beftow vpon poore Ring-doues.
   Seb. I'le offer no worfe play.
   Mol. Nay and you fhould fir,
I fhould draw firft and prooue the quicker man.
   Seb. Hold, there fhall neede no weapon at this
      meeting,
But caufe thou fhalt not loofe thy fury idle,
Heere take this viall, runne vpon the guts,
And end thy quarrell finging.
   Mol. Like a fwan aboue bridge,
For looke you heer's the bridge, and heere am I.
   Seb. Hold on fweete *Mol.*
   Mary. I'ue heard her much commended fir, for

one that was nere taught.

Mol.   I'me much beholding to 'em, well fince you'l
needes put vs together fir, Ile play my part as wel as
I can : it fhall nere be faid I came into a Gentlemans
chamber, and let his inftrument hang by the walls.

Seb.   Why well faid *Mol* i'faith, it had bene a fhame
for that Gentleman then, that would haue let it hung
ftill, and nere offred thee it.

Mol.   There it fhould haue bene ftil then for *Mol*,
for though the world iudge impudently of mee, I nere
came into that chamber yet, where I tooke downe the
inftrument my felfe.

Seb.   Pifh let 'em prate abroad, th' art heere where
thou art knowne and lou'd, there be a thoufand clofe
dames that wil cal the viall an vnmannerly inftrument
for a woman, and therefore talke broadly of thee, when
you fhall haue them fit wider to a worfe quality.

Mol.   Pufh, I euer fall a fleepe and thinke not of
'em fir, and thus I dreame.

Seb.   Prithee let's heare thy dreame *Mol.*

Mol.   *I dreame there is a Miftreffe,*
          And fhe layes out the money,   The fong.
        Shee goes vnto her Sifters,
        Shee neuer comes at any.

                    Enter Sir *Alexander* behind them

Shee fayes fhee went to'th Burffe for patternes,
      You fhall finde her at Saint Katherns,
And comes home with neuer a penny.

Seb.   That's a free Miftreffe 'faith.

Alex.   I, I, I, like her that fings it, one of thine
own choofing.

Mol.   But fhall I dreame againe ?

        Here comes a wench will braue ye,
          Her courage was fo great,
        Shee lay with one o' the Nauy,
          Her husband lying i' the Fleet.

Yet oft with him fhe cauel'd,
I wonder what fhee ailes,
Her husbands fhip lay grauel'd,
When her's could hoyfe vp failes.
Yet fhee beganne like all my foes,
To call whoore firft: for fo do thofe,
A pox of all falfe tayles.

Seb.   Marry amen fay I.
Alex.   So fay I too.
Mol.   Hang vp the viall now fir: all this while I
was in a dreame, one fhall lie rudely then ; but being
awake, I keepe my legges together ; a watch, what's
a clocke here.
Alex.   Now, now, fhee's trapt.
Moll.   Betweene one and two ; nay then I care not:
a watch and a mufitian are coffen Germanes in one
thing, they muft both keepe time well, or there's no
goodneffe in 'em, the one elfe deferues to be dafht
againft a wall, and tother to haue his braines knockt
out with a fiddle cafe, what? a loofe chaine and a
dangling Diamond.
Here were a braue booty for an euening-theefe now,
There's many a younger brother would be glad
To looke twice in at a window for't,
And wriggle in and oute like an eele in a fandbag,
Oh if mens fecret youthfull faults fhould iudge 'em,
'Twould be the general'ft execution,
That ere was feene in England ; there would bee but
few left to fing the ballets, there would be fo much
worke : moft of our brokers would be chofen for hang-
men, a good day for them : they might renew their
wardrops of free coft then.
Seb.   This is the roaring wench muft do vs good.
Mary.   No poyfon fir but ferues vs for fome vfe,
Which is confirm'd in her.
Seb.   Peace, peace,
Foot I did here him fure, where ere he be.
Mol.   Who did you heare?

Seb.   My father,
'Twas like a fight of his, I muft be wary.
   Alex.   No wilt not be, am I alone fo wretched
That nothing takes? I'le put him to his plundge for't.
   Seb.   Life, heere he comes,—fir I befeech you
      take it,
Your way of teaching does fo much content me,
I'le make it foure pound, here's forty fhillings fir.
I thinke I name it right : helpe me good *Mol,*
Forty in hand.
   Mol.   Sir you fhall pardon me,
I haue more of the meaneft fcholler I can teach,
This paies me more, then you haue offred yet.
   Seb.   At the next quarter
When I receiue the meanes my father 'lowes me,
You fhall haue tother forty.
   Alex.   This were well now,
Wer't to a man, whofe forrowes had blind eies,
But mine behold his follies and vntruthes,
With two cleere glaffes—how now?
   Seb.   Sir.
   Alex.   What's he there?
   Seb.   You'r come in good time fir, I'ue a fuite to
      you,
I'de craue your prefent kindneffe.
   Alex.   What is he there?
   Seb.   A Gentleman, a mufitian fir, one of excellent
      fingring.
   Alex.   I, I thinke fo, I wonder how they fcapt her.
   Seb.   Has the moft delicate ftroake fir.
   Alex.   A ftroake indeed, I feele it at my heart.
   Seb.   Puts downe all your famous mufitians.
   Alex.   I, a whoore may put downe a hundred
      of 'em.
   Seb.   Forty fhillings is the agrement fir betweene vs,
Now fir, my prefent meanes, mounts but to halfe
      on't.
   Alex.   And he ftands vpon the whole.
   Seb.   I indeed does he fir.

Alex. And will doe ftill, hee'l nere be in other
taile.

Seb. Therefore I'de ftop his mouth fir, and I could.

Alex. Hum true, there is no other way indeed,
His folly hardens, fhame muft needs fucceed.
Now fir I vnderftand you profeffe mufique.

Mol. I am a poore feruant to that liberall fcience
fir.

Alex. Where is it you teach ?

Mol. Right againft Cliffords Inne.

Alex. Hum that's a fit place for it : you haue many
fcholers.

Mol. And fome of worth, whom I may call my
maifters.

Alex. I true, a company of whooremaifters ; you
teach to fing too ?

Mol. Marry do I fir.

Alex I thinke you'l finde an apt fcholler of my
fonne, efpecially for pricke-fong.

Mol. I haue much hope of him.

Alex. I am fory for't, I haue the leffe for that : you
can play any leffon.

Mol. At firft fight fir.

Alex. There's a thing called the witch, can you
play that ?

Mol. I would be fory any one fhould mend
me in't.

Alex. I, I beleeue thee, thou haft fo bewitcht my
fonne,
No care will mend the worke that thou haft done,
I haue bethought my felfe fince my art failes,
I'le make her pollicy the Art to trap her.
Here are foure Angels markt with holes in them
Fit for his crackt companions, gold he will giue her,
Thefe will I make induction to her ruine,
And rid fhame from my houfe, griefe from my heart.
Here fonne, in what you take content and pleafure,
Want fhall not curbe you, pay the Gentleman
His latter halfe in gold.

Seb.   I thanke you fir.

Alex.   Oh may the operation an't, end three,
In her, life : fhame, in him ; and griefe, in mee.

          Exit Alexander.

Seb.   Faith thou fhalt haue 'em 'tis my fathers
  guift,
Neuer was man beguild with better fhift.

Mol.   Hee that can take mee for a male mufitian,
I cannot choofe but make him my inftrument,
And play vpon him.   *Exeunt omnes.*

Enter Miftreffe Gallipot, *and Miftreffe* Openworke.

Mi. Gal.   Is then that bird of yours (Maifter *Gofhawke*) fo wild ?

Mift. Open.   A Gofhawke, a Puttocke ; all for prey,
he angles for fifh, but he loues flefh better.

Mift. Gal.   Is't poffible his fmoth face fhou'd haue
wrinckles in't, and we not fee them ?

Mift. Open.   Poffible ? why haue not many handfome legges in filke flockins villanous fplay feete for
all their great rofes ?

Mift. Gal.   Troth firra thou faift true.

Mift. Op.   Didft neuer fee an archer (as tho' aft
walkt by Bunhill) looke a fquint when he drew his
bow ?

Mift. Gal.   Yes, when his arrowes haue flin'e toward
Iflington, his eyes haue fhot cleane contrary towards
Pimlico.

Mift. Open.   For all the world fo does Maifter
Gofhawke double with me.

Mift. Gal.   Oh fie vpon him, if he double once he's
not for me.

Mift. Open.   Becaufe *Gofhawke* goes in a fhag-ruffe
band, with a face flicking vp in't, which fhowes like
an agget fet in a crampe ring, he thinkes I'me in loue
with him.

Mift. Gal.   'Las I thinke he takes his marke amiffe
in thee.

Mifl. Open. He has by often beating into me made mee beleeue that my husband kept a whore.

Mifl. Gal. Very good.

Mifl. Open. Swore to me that my husband this very morning went in a boate with a tilt ouer it, to the three pidgions at *Brainford*, and his puncke with him vnder his tilt.

Mifl. Gal. That were wholefome.

Mifl. Open. I beleeu'd it, fell a fwearing at him, curffing of harlots, made me ready to hoyfe vp faile, and be there as foone as hee.

Mifl. Gal. So fo.

Mifl. Open. And for that voyage *Gofhawke* comes hither incontinently, but firra this water-fpaniell diues after no ducke but me, his hope is hauing mee at *Braincford* to make mee cry quack.

Mifl. Gall. Art fure of it ?

Mifl. Open. Sure of it ? my poore innocent *Openworke* came in as I was poking my ruffe, prefently hit I him i'the teeth with the three pidgions : he forfwore all, I vp and opened all, and now ftands he (in a fhop hard by) like a musket on a reft, to hit *Gofhawke* i' the eie, when he comes to fetch me to the boate.

Mifl. Gal. Such another lame Gelding offered to carry mee through thicke and thinne, (*Laxton* firra) but I am ridd of him now.

Mifl. Open. Happy is the woman can bee ridde of 'em all ; 'las what are your whisking gallants to our husbands, weigh 'em rightly man for man.

Mifl. Gall. Troth meere fhallow things.

Mifl. Open. Idle fimple things, running heads, and yet let 'em run ouer vs neuer fo faft, we fhop-keepers (when all's done) are fure to haue 'em in our purfnets at length, and when they are in, Lord what fimple animalls they are.

Mifl. Open. Then they hang the head.

Mifl. Gal. Then they droupe.

Mifl. Open. Then they write letters.

Mifl. Gal. Then they cogge.

Mift. Open.   Then deale they vnder hand with vs,
aud wee muft ingle with our husbands a bed, and wee
muft fweare they are our cofens, and able to do vs a
pleafure at Court.

Mift. Gal.   And yet when wee haue done our beft,
al's but put into a riuen difh, wee are but frumpt at and
libell'd vpon.

Mift. Open.   Oh if it were the good Lords wil,
there were a law made, no Cittizen fhould truft any of
'em all.

Enter Gofhawke.

Mift. Gal.   Hufh firra, *Gofhawke* flutters.

Gofh.   How now, are you ready ?

Mift. Open.   Nay are you ready ? a little thing you
fee makes vs ready.

Gofh.   Vs ? why, muft fhee make one i'the voiage ?

Mift. Open.   Oh by any meanes, doe I know how
my husband will handle mee ?

Gofh.   'Foot, how fhall I find water, to keepe thefe
two mils going ?   Well fince you'l needs bee clapt vnder hatches, if I fayle not with you both till all fplit,
hang mee vp at the maine yard, & duck mee ; it's
but lickering them both foundly, & then you fhall
fee their corke heeles flie vp high, like two fwannes
when their tayles are aboue water, and their long
neckes vnder water, diuing to catch gudgions : come,
come, oares ftand ready, the tyde's with vs, on with
thofe falfe faces, blow winds and thou fhalt take thy
husband, cafting out his net to catch frefh *Salmon* at
Brainford.

Mift. Gal.   I beleeue you'l eate of a coddes head
of your owne dreffing, before you reach halfe way
thither.

Gofh.   So, fo, follow clofe, pin as you go.

Enter Laxton muffled.

Lax.   Do you heare ?

Miſt. Gal.   Yes, I thanke my eares.
Lax.   I muſt haue a bout with your Potticariſhip.
Miſt. Gal.   At what weapon ?
Lax.   1 muſt ſpeake with you.
Miſt. Gal.   No.
Lax.   No? you ſhall.
Miſt. Gal.   Shall ? away ſouſt Sturgion, halfe fiſh, halfe fleſh.
Lax.   'Faith gib, are you ſpitting, I'le cut your tayle puſ-cat for this.
Miſt. Gal.   'Las poore *Laxton,* I thinke thy tayle's cut already : your worſt ;
Lax.   If I do not, —— . . . .   *Exit Laxton.*
Goſh.   Come, ha' you done ?

Enter Maiſter Openworke.

Sfoote *Roſamond,* your husband.
  Maiſt. Open.   How now ? ſweete Maiſt. *Goſhawke,* none more welcome,
I haue wanted your embracements : when friends meete,
The muſique of the ſpheares ſounds not more ſweete,
Then does their conferenc : who is this ? *Roſamond* :
Wife : how now ſiſter ?
  Goſh.   Silence if you loue mee.
  Maiſt. Open.   Why maſkt ?
  Miſt. Open.   Does a maske grieue you ſir ?
  Maiſt. Open.   It does.
  Miſt. Open.   Then y'are beſt get you a mumming.
  Goſh.   S'foote you'l ſpoyle all.
  Miſt. Gall.   May not wee couer our bare faces with maskes
As well as you couer your bald heads with hats ?
  Ma. Op.   No maskes, why, th'are theeues to beauty, that rob eies
Of admiration in which true loue lies,
Why are maskes worne ? why good ? or why deſired ?
Vnleſſe by their gay couers wits are fiered

To read the vild'ſt lookes ; many bad faces,
(Becauſe rich gemmes are treaſured vp in caſes)
Paſſe by their priuiledge currant, but as caues
Dambe miſers Gold, ſo maskes are beauties graues,
Men nere meete women with ſuch muffled eies,
But they curſe her, that firſt did maskes deuiſe,
And ſweare it was ſome beldame.　Come off with't.
　　Miſt. Open.　I will not.
　　Maiſt. Open.　Good faces maskt are Iewels kept by
　　　ſpirits.
Hide none but bad ones, for they poyſon mens ſights,
Show then as ſhop-keepers do their broidred ſtuffe,
(By owle light) fine wares cannot be open enough,
Prithee (ſweete Roſe) come ſtrike this ſayle.
　　Miſt. Open.　Saile ?
　　Maiſt. Op.　Ha ? yes wife ſtrike ſaile, for ſtormes
are in thine eyes :
　　Miſt. Open.　Th'are here ſir in my browes if any
riſe.
　　Maiſt. Open.　Ha browes ? (what ſayes ſhe friend)
　　　pray tel me why
Your two flagges were aduaunſt ; the Comedy,
Come what's the Comedy ?
　　Miſt. Open.　Weſtward hoe.
　　Maiſt. Open.　How ?
　　Miſt. Open.　'Tis Weſtward hoe ſhee ſaies.
　　Goſh.　Are you both madde ?
　　Miſt. Open.　Is't Market day at *Braineford*, and
your ware not ſent vp yet ?
　　Maiſt. Open.　What market day ? what ware ?
　　Miſt. Open.　A py with three pidgions in't, 'tis
drawne and ſtaies your cutting vp.
　　Goſh.　As you regard my credit.
　　Maiſt. Open.　Art madde ?
　　Miſt. Open.　Yes letcherous goate ; Baboone.
　　Maiſt. Open.　Baboone ? then toſſe me in a blanc-
ket.
　　Miſt. Open.　Do I it well ?
　　Miſt. Gall.　Rarely.

Goſh. Belike ſir ſhee's not well ; beſt leaue her.

Maiſt. Open. No,
I'le ſtand the ſtorme now how fierce ſo ere it blow.

Miſt. Open. Did I for this looſe all my friends ? refuſe
Rich hopes, and golden fortunes, to be made
A ſtale to a common whore ?

Maiſt. Open. This does amaze mee.

Miſt. Open. Oh God, oh God, feede at reuerſion now ?
A Strumpets leauing ?

Maiſt. Open. Roſamond.

Goſh. I ſweate, wo'ld I lay in cold harbour.

Miſt. Open. Thou haſt ſtruck ten thouſand daggers
through my heart.

Maiſt. Open. Not I by heauen ſweete wife.

Miſt. Open. Go diuel go ; that which thou ſwear'ſt
by, damnes thee.

Goſh. S'heart will you vndo mee ?

Miſt. Open. Why ſtay you heere ? the ſtarre, by which you ſaile,
Shines yonder aboue *Chelſy* ; you looſe your ſhore
If this moone light you : ſeeke out your light whore.

Maiſt. Open. Ha ?

Miſt. Gal. Puſh ; your Weſterne pug.

Goſh. Zounds now hell roares.

Miſt. Open. With whom you tilted in a paire of oares,
This very morning.

Maiſt. Open. Oares ?

Miſt. Open. At *Brainford* ſir.

Maiſt. Open. Racke not my patience : Maiſter
Goſhawke, ſome ſlaue has buzzed this into her, has he
not ? I run a tilt in *Brainford* with a woman ? 'tis a
lie : What old baud tels thee this ? S'death 'tis a lie.

Miſt. Open. 'Tis one to thy face ſhall iuſtify all
that I ſpeake.

Maiſt. Open. Vd' ſoule do but name that raſcall.

Miſt. Open. No ſir I will not.

Gofh. Keepe thee there girle :—then !

Mifl. Open. Sifter know you this varlet ?

Mifl. Gall. Yes.

Maifl. Open. Sweare true,

Is there a rogue fo low damn'd ? a fecond *Iudas* ? a
common hangman ? cutting a mans throate ? does it
to his face ? bite mee behinde my backe ? a cur dog ?
fweare if you know this hell-hound.

Mifl. Gall. In truth I do.

Maifl. Open. His name ?

Mifl. Gall. Not for the world ;

To haue you to ftab him.

Gofh. Oh braue girles : worth Gold.

Maifl. Open. A word honeft maifter *Gofhawke.*

Draw out his fword.

Gofh. What do you meane fir ?

Maifl. Open. Keepe off, and if the diuell can giue
a name to this new fury, holla it through my eare, or
wrap it vp in fome hid charaƈter : I'le ride to *Oxford,*
and watch out mine eies, but I'le heare the brazen
head fpeak : or elfe fhew me but one haire of his head
or beard, that I may fample it ; if the fiend I meet (in
myne owne houfe) I'le kill him :—the ftreete.

Or at the Church dore :—there—(caufe he feekes to
  vnty
The knot God faftens) he deferues moft to dy.

Mifl. Open. My husband titles him.

Maifl. Open. Maifter *Gofhawke,* pray fir
Sweare to me, that you know him or know him not,
Who makes me at *Brainford* to take vp a peticote
  befides my wiues.

Gofh. By heauen that man I know not.

Mifl. Open. Come, come, you lie.

Gofh. Will you not haue all out ?
By heauen I know no man beneath the moone
Should do you wrong, but if I had his name,
I'de print it in text letters.

Mifl. Open. Print thine owne then,
Did'ft not thou fweare to me he kept his whoore ?

Mifl. Gal. And that in finfull *Brainford* they
    would commit
That which our lips did water at fir,—ha ?
  Mifl. Open. Thou fpider, that haft wouen thy cun-
    ning web
In mine owne houfe t' infnare me : haft not thou
Suck't nourifhment euen vnderneath this roofe,
And turned it all to poyfon ? fpitting it,
On thy friends face (my husband ?) he as t'were
    fleeping :
Onely to leaue him vgly to mine eies,
That they might glance on thee.
  Mifl. Gal. Speake, are thefe lies ?
  Gofh. Mine own fhame me confounds :
  Mifl. Open. No more, hee's ftung ;
Who'd thinke that in one body there could dwell
Deformitie and beauty, (heauen and hell)
Goodneffe I fee is but outfide, wee all fet,
In rings of Gold, ftones that be counterfet :
I thought you none.
  Gofh. Pardon mee.
  Maifl. Open. Truth I doe.
This blemifh growes in nature not in you,
For mans creation fticke euen moles in fcorne
On faireft cheeks, wife nothing is perfect borne.
  Mifl. Open. I thought you had bene borne perfect.
  Maifl. Open. What's this whole world but a gilt
    rotten pill ?
For at the heart lies the old chore ftill.
I'le tell you Maifter *Gofhawke*, I in your eie
I haue feene wanton fire, and then to try
The foundneffe of my iudgement, I told you
I kept a whoore, made you beleeue t'was true,
Onely to feele how your pulfe beat, but find,
The world can hardly yeeld a perfect friend.
Come, come, a tricke of youth, and 'tis forgiuen,
This rub put by, our loue fhall runne more euen.
  Mifl. Open. You'l deale vpon mens wiues no
    more ?

Goſh.   No :—you teach me a tricke for that.
Miſt. Open.   Troth do not, they'l o're-reach thee.
Mai. Open.   Make my houfe yours ſir ſtill.
Goſh.   No.
Maiſt. Open.   I ſay you ſhall :
Seeing (thus befieg'd) it holds out, 'twill neuer fall.

Enter Maiſter Gallipot, *and* Greenewit *like a Somner,*
Laxton *muffled a loofe off.*

Omnes.   How now ?
Maiſt. Gall.   With mee ſir ?
Greene.   You ſir ? I haue gon ſnaffling vp and
downe by your dore this houre to watch for you.
Miſt. Gall.   What's the matter husband ?
Greene.   — I haue caught a cold in my head ſir,
by fitting vp late in the rofe tauerne, but I hope you
vnderſtand my ſpeech.
Maiſt. Gal.   So ſir.
Greene.   I cite you by the name of *Hippocrates
Gallipot,* and you by the name of *Prudence Gallipot,*
to appeare vpon *Craſtino,* doe you fee, *Craſtina
ſanĉti Dunſtani* (this *Eaſter* Tearme) in Bow Church.
Maiſt. Gal.   Where ſir ? what faies he ?
Greene.   Bow : Bow Church, to anſwere to a libel
of precontraĉt on the part and behalfe of the ſaid
Prudence and another ; y'are beſt ſir take a coppy of
the citation, 'tis but tweluepence.
Omnes.   A Citation ?
Maiſt. Gal.   You pocky-nofed rafcall, what ſlaue
fees you to this?
Lax.   Slaue ? I ha nothing to do with you, doe
you heare ſir ?   '
Goſh.   *Laxton* iſt not ?—what fagary is this ?
Maiſt. Gal.   Truſt me I thought ſir this ſtorme
long ago had bene full laid, when (if you be remembred) I paid you the laſt fifteene pound, befides the
thirty you had firſt,—for then you ſwore.
Lax.   Tuſh, tuſh ſir, oathes,

Truth yet I'me loth to vexe you, . . tell you what ;
Make vp the mony I had an hundred pound,
And take your belly full of her.
   Maifl. Gal.   An hundred pound ?
   Mifl. Gal. What a 100 pound ? he gets none :
what a 100 pound ?
   Maifl. Gal. Sweet *Pru* be calme, the Gentleman
     offers thus,
If I will make the monyes that are pafl
A 100 pound, he will difcharge all courts,
And giue his bond neuer to vexe us more.
   Mifl. Gal. A 100 pound ? 'Las ; take fir but three-
     fcore,
Do you feeke my vndoing ?
   Lax. I'le not bate one fixpence, . . . I'le mall
you puffe for fpitting.
   Mifl. Gal. Do thy worfl,
Will fourefcore flop thy mouth ?
   Lax. No.
   Mifl. Gal. Y'are a flaue,
Thou Cheate, I'le now teare mony from thy throat,
Husband lay hold on yonder tauny-coate.
   Greene. Nay Gentlemen, feeing your woemen are
fo hote, I mufl loofe my haire in their company
I fee.
   Mifl. Ope. His haire fheds off, and yet he fpeaks
not fo much in the nofe as he did before.
   Gofh. He has had the better Chirurgion, Maifler
Greenewit, is your wit fo raw as to play no better a
part then a Somners ?
   Maifl. Gal. I pray who playes a knacke to know an
honefl man in this company ?
   Mifl. Gall. Deere husband, pardon me, I did dif-
     femble,
Told thee I was his precontracted wife,
When letters came from him for thirty pound,
I had no fhift but that.
   Maifl. Gal. A very cleane fhift : but able to make
mee lowfy, On.
   3   P

Mist. Gal. Husband, I pluck'd (when he had tempted
mee to thinke well of him) Get fethers from thy
wings, to make him flie more lofty.

Maist. Gall. A' the top of you wife : on.

Mist. Gal. He hauing wasted them, comes now for
     more,
Vsing me as a ruffian doth his whore,
Whofe finne keepes him in breath : by heauen I vow,
Thy bed he neuer wrong'd, more then he does now.

Maist. Gal. My bed? ha, ha, like enough, a
fhop-boord will ferue to haue a cuckolds coate cut out
vpon : of that wee'l talke hereafter : y'are a villaine :

Lax. Heare mee but fpeake fir, you fhall finde mee
     none.

Omnes. Pray fir, be patient and heare him.

Maist. Gal. I am muzzled for biting fir, vfe me
how you will.

Lax. The firft howre that your wife was in my
     eye,
My felfe with other Gentlemen fitting by,
(In your fhop) tafting fmoake, and fpeech being vfed,
That men who haue faireft wiues are moft abufed,
And hardly fcapt the horne, your wife maintain'd
That onely fuch fpots in Citty dames were ftain'd,
Iuftly, but by mens flanders : for her owne part,
Shee vow'd that you had fo much of her heart ;
No man by all his wit, by any wile,
Neuer fo fine fpunne, fhould your felfe beguile,
Of what in her was yours.

Maist. Gal. Yet *Pru* 'tis well :
Play out your game at Irifh fir : Who winnes ?

Mist. Open. The triall is when fhee comes to bearing :

Lax. I fcorn'd one woman, thus, fhould braue all
     men,
And (which more vext me) a fhee-citizen.
Therefore I laid fiege to her, out fhe held,
Gaue many a braue repulfe, and me compel'd

With fhame to found retrait to my hot luft,
Then feeing all bafe defires rak'd vp in duft,
And that to tempt her modeft eares, I fwore
Nere to prfumne againe : fhe faid, her eie
Would euer giue me welcome honeftly,
And (fince I was a Gentleman) if it runne low,
Shee would my ftate relieue, not to o'rethrow
Your owne and hers : did fo ; then feeing I wrought
Vpon her meekeneffe, mee fhe fet at nought,
And yet to try if I could turne that tide,
You fee what ftreame I ftroue with, but fir I fweare
By heauen, and by thofe hopes men lay vp there,
I neither haue, nor had a bafe intent
To wrong your bed, what's done, is incriment :
Your Gold I pay backe with this intereft,
When I had moft power to do't I wrong'd you leaft.
   Maift. Gal. If this no gullery be fir,
   Omnes. No, no, on my life.
   Maift. Gal. Then fir I am beholden (not to you
     wife)
But Maifter *Laxton* to your want of doing ill,
Which it feemes you haue not Gentlemen,
Tarry and dine here all.
   Maift. Open. Brother, we haue a ieft,
As good as yours to furnifh out a feaft.
   Maift. Gal. Wee'l crowne our table with it : wife
     brag no more
Of holding out : who moft brags is moft whore.
                Exeunt omnes.

   Enter Iacke Dapper, Moll, *Sir* Beautious Ganymed,
        and Sir Thomas Long.

   Iacke Dap. But prethee Maifter Captaine *Iacke* be
plaine and perfpicuous with mee ; was it your *Megge* of
Weftminfters courage, that refcued mee from the Poul-
try puttockes indeed.
   Mol. The valour of my wit I enfure you fir fetcht

you off brauely, when you werre i'the forlorne hope among thofe defperates, Sir *Bewtious Ganymed* here, and fir *Thomas Long* heard that cuckoe (my man *Trapdore*) fing the note of your ranfome from captiuity.

Sir Bewt.   Vds fo *Mol,* where's that *Trapdore?*

Mol.   Hang'd I thinke by this time, a Iuftice in this towne, (that fpeakes nothing but make a *Mittimus* a way with him to Newgate) vfed that rogue like a fire-worke to run vpon a line betwixt him and me.

Omnes.   how, how?

Mol.   Marry to lay traines of villany to blow vp my life ; I fmelt the powder, fpy'd what linftocke gaue fire to fhoote againft the poore Captaine of the Gallifoyft, & away flid I my man, like a fhouell-board fhilling, hee ftroutes vp and downe the fuburbes I thinke : and eates vp whores : feedes vpon a bauds garbadg.

T. Long.   Sirra *Iacke Dapper.*

Iac. Dap.   What fai'ft *Tom Long?*

T. Long.   Thou hadft a fweet fac't boy haile fellow with thee to your little *Gull* : how is he fpent?

Iack Dap.   Troth I whiftled the poore little buzzard of a my fift, becaufe when hee wayted vpon mee at the ordinaries, the gallants hit me i' the teeth ftill, and faid I lookt like a painted Aldermans tomb, and the boy at my elbow like a deaths head.   Sirra *Iacke, Mol.*

Mol.   What faies my little *Dapper?*

Sir Bewt.   Come, come, walke and talke, walke and talke.

Iack Dap.   Mol and I'le be i' the midft.

Mol.   Thefe Knights fhall haue fquiers places belike then : well *Dapper* what fay you?

Iack. Dap.   Sirra Captaine mad *Mary,* the gull my owne father (*Dapper*) *Sir Dauy*) laid thefe London boote-halers the catch poles in ambufh to fet vpon mee.

Omnes.   Your father? away *Iacke.*

Iack. Dap. By the taffels of this handkercher 'tis true, and what was his warlicke ftratageme thinke you ? hee thought becaufe a wicker cage tames a nightingale, a lowfy prifon could make an affe of mee.

Omnes. A nafty plot.

Iack. Dap. I : as though a Counter, which is a parke, in which all the wilde beafts of the Citty run head by head could tame mee.

Enter the Lord Noland.

Mol. Yonder comes my Lord *Noland.*

Omnes. Saue you my Lord.

L. Nol. Well met Gentlemen all, good *Sir Bew-tious Ganymed,* Sir *Thomas Long ?* and how does Maifter *Dapper ?*

Iack. Dap. Thankes my Lord.

Mol. No Tobacco my Lord ?

L. Nol. No faith *Iacke.*

Iack. Dap. My Lord *Noland* will you goe to Pim-lico with vs ? wee are making a boone voyage to that nappy land of fpice-cakes.

L. Nol. Heeres fuch a merry ging, I could find in my heart to faile to the worlds end with fuch com-pany, come Gentlemen let's on.

Iack Dap. Here's moft amorous weather my Lord.

Omnes. Amorous weather.   *They walke.*

Iac. Dap. Is not amorous a good word ?

Enter Trapdore *like a poore Souldier with a patch
o're one eie, and* Teare-Cat *with him, all
tatters.*

Trap. Shall we fet vpon the infantry, thefe troopes of foot ? Zounds yonder comes *Mol* my whoorifh Maifter and Miftreffe, wo'ld I had her kidneys be-tweene my teeth.

Tear-Cat. I had rather haue a cow heele.

Trap. Zounds I am fo patcht vp, fhe cannot difcouer me : wee'l on.

T. Cat. Alla corago then.

Trap. Good your Honours, and Worfhips, enlarge
the eares of commiferation, and let the found of a
hoarfe military organ-pipe, penetrate your pittiful
bowels to extract out of them fo many fmall drops of
filuer, as may giue a hard ftrawbed lodging to a couple
of maim'd fouldiers.

Iacke Dap. Where are you maim'd ?

T. Cat. In both our neather limbs.

Mol. Come, come, *Dapper*, lets giue 'em fomething, las poore men, what mony haue you ? by my
troth I loue a fouldier with my foule.

Sir Bewt. Stay, ftay, where haue you feru'd ?

T. Long. In any part of the Low countries ?

Trap. Not in the Low countries, if it pleafe your
manhood, but in *Hungarie* againft the *Turke* at the
fiedge of *Belgrad*.

L. Nol. Who feru'd there with you firra ?

Trap. Many *Hungarians*, *Moldauians*, *Valachians*,
and *Tranfiluanians*, with fome *Sclauonians*, and
retyring home fir, the *Venetian* Gallies tooke vs
prifoners, yet free'd vs, and fuffered vs to beg vp and
downe the country.

Iack. Dap. You haue ambled all ouer *Italy* then.

Trap. Oh fir, from *Venice* to *Roma*, *Vecchio*, *Bono-
nia*, *Romania*, *Bolonia*, *Modena*, *Piacenza*, and *Tuf-
cana*, with all her Cities, as *Piftoia*, *Valteria*, *Mounte-
pulchena*, *Arrezzo*, with the *Siennois*, and diuerfe
others.

Mol. Meere rogues, put fpurres to 'em once more.

Iack. Dap. Thou look'ft like a ftrange creature, a
    fat butter-box, yet fpeak'ft Englifh,
What art thou ?

T. Cat. **Ick mine Here. Ick bin den
ruffling Teare-Cat,**

𝕯𝖊𝖓 𝖇𝖗𝖆𝖚𝖊 𝕾𝖔𝖑𝖉𝖆𝖉𝖔, 𝕴𝖈𝖐 𝖇𝖎𝖓 𝖉𝖔𝖗𝖎𝖈𝖐 𝖆𝖑𝖑
    𝕯𝖚𝖙𝖈𝖍𝖑𝖆𝖓𝖙.
𝕲𝖚𝖊𝖗𝖊𝖘𝖊𝖓: 𝕯𝖊𝖗 𝕾𝖍𝖊𝖑𝖑𝖚𝖒 𝖉𝖆𝖘 𝖒𝖊𝖊𝖗𝖊 𝕴𝖓𝖊
    𝕭𝖊𝖆𝖘𝖆
𝕴𝖓𝖊 𝖜𝖔𝖊𝖗𝖙 𝖌𝖆𝖊𝖇.
𝕴𝖈𝖐 𝖘𝖑𝖆𝖆𝖌 𝖇𝖒 𝖘𝖙𝖗𝖔𝖆𝖐𝖊𝖘 𝖔𝖓 𝖙𝖔𝖒 𝕮𝖔𝖕.
𝕭𝖆𝖘𝖙𝖎𝖈𝖐 𝕯𝖊𝖓 𝖍𝖚𝖓𝖉𝖗𝖊𝖉 𝖙𝖔𝖚𝖟𝖚𝖓 𝕯𝖎𝖚𝖊𝖑𝖑
    𝖍𝖆𝖑𝖑𝖊,
𝕱𝖗𝖔𝖑𝖑𝖎𝖈𝖐 𝖒𝖎𝖓𝖊 𝕳𝖊𝖗𝖊.

Sir Bewt. Here, here, let's be rid of their iob-
bering.

Moll. Not a croſſe, *Sir Bewtious*, you baſe rogues,
I haue taken meaſure of you, better then a taylor can,
ind I'le fit you, as you (monſter with one eie) haue
itted mee.

Trap. Your Worſhip will not abuſe a fouldier.

Moll. Souldier? thou deſeru'ſt to bee hang'd vp
by that tongue which diſhonours ſo noble a·profeſſion,
fouldier you skeldering varlet? hold, ſtand, there ſhould
be a trapdore here abouts.   *Pull off his patch.*

Trap. The balles of theſe glaſiers of mine (mine
eyes) ſhall be ſhot vp and downe in any hot peece of
ſeruice for my inuincible Miſtreſſe.

Iacke Dap. I did not thinke there had bene ſuch
knauery in blacke patches as now I ſee.

Mol. Oh ſir he hath bene brought vp in the Ile of
dogges, and can both fawne like a Spaniell, and bite
like a Maſtiue, as hee finds occaſion.

L. Nol. What are you ſirra? a bird of this feather
too.

T. Cat. A man beaten from the wars ſir.

T. Long. I thinke ſo, for you neuer ſtood to fight.

Iac. Dap. What's thy name fellow fouldier?

T. Cat. I am cal'd by thoſe that haue ſeen my
valour, *Tear-Cat.*

Omnes.　Teare-Cat ?

Moll.　A meere whip-Iacke, and that is in the Commonwealth of rogues, a flaue, that can talke of fea-fight, name all your chiefe Pirats, difcouer more countries to you, then either the Dutch, Spanifh, French, or Englifh euer found out, yet indeed all his feruice is by land, and that is to rob a Faire, or fome fuch venturous exploit; *Teare-Cat,* foot firra I haue your name now I remember me in my booke of horners, hornes for the thumbe, you know how.

T. Cat.　No indeed Captaine *Mol* (for I know you by fight) I am no fuch nipping Chriftian, but a maunderer vpon the pad I confeffe, and meeting with honeft *Trapdore* here, whom you had cafhierd from bearing armes, out at elbowes vnder your colours, I inftructed him in the rudements of roguery, and by my map made him faile ouer any Country you can name, fo that now he can maunder better then my-felfe.

Iack. Dap.　So then *Trapdore* thou art turn'd fouldier now.

Trap.　Alas fir, now there's no warres, 'tis the fafeft courfe of life I could take.

Mol.　I hope then you can cant, for by your cudgels, you firra are an vpright man.

Trap.　As any walkes the hygh way I affure you.

Mol.　And *Teare-Cat* what are you ? a wilde rogue, an angler, or a ruffler ?

T. Cat.　Brother to this vpright man, flefh and bloud, ruffling *Teare-Cat* is my name, and a ruffler is my ftile, my title, my profeffion.

Mol.　Sirra where's your Doxy, halt not with mee.

Omnes.　Doxy *Mol*, what's that ?

Mol.　His wench.

Trap.　My doxy I haue by the *Salomon* a doxy, that carries a kitchin mort in her flat at her backe, befides my dell and my dainty wilde del, with all whom I'le tumble this next darkmans in the ftrommel,

and drinke ben baufe, and eate a fat gruntling cheate,
a cackling cheate, and a quacking cheate.

Iack. Dap. Here's old cheating.

Trap. My doxy ftayes for me in a boufing ken,
braue Captaine.

Mol. Hee fayes his wench ftaies for him in an ale-
houfe : you are no pure rogues.

T. Cat. Pure rogues ? no, wee fcorne to be pure
rogues, but if you come to our lib ken, or our ftalling
ken, you fhall finde neither him nor mee, a quire
cuffin.

Mol. So, fir, no churle of you.

T. Cat. No, but a ben caue, a braue caue, a gentry
cuffin.

L. Nol. Call you this canting ?

Iack. Dap. Zounds, I'le giue a fchoolemaifter halfe
a crowne a week, and teach mee this pedlers French.

Trap. Do but ftrowle fir, halfe a harueft with vs
fir, and you fhall gabble your belly-full.

Mol. Come you rogue cant with me.

T. Long. Well fayd *Mol,* cant with her firra, and
you fhall haue mony, elfe not a penny.

Trap. I'le haue a bout if fhe pleafe.

Mol. Come on firra.

Trap. Ben mort, fhall you and I heaue a booth,
mill a ken or nip a bung, and then wee'l couch a
hogfhead vnder the Ruffemans, and there you fhall
wap with me, & Ile niggle with you.

Mol. Out you damn'd impudent rafcall.

Trap. Cut benar whiddes, and hold your fambles
and your ftampes.

L. Nol. Nay, nay, *Mol,* why art thou angry ? what
was his gibberifh ?

Mol. Marry this my Lord fayes hee ; Ben mort
(good wench) fhal you and I heaue a booth, mill a
ken, or nip a bung ? fhall you and I rob a houfe, or
cut a purfe ?

Omnes. Very Good.

Mol.   And then wee'l couch a hogfhead vnder the
        Ruffemans :
And then wee'l lie vnder a hedge.

Trap.   That was my defire Captaine, as 'tis fit a
fouldier fhould lie.

Mol.   And there you fhall wap with mee, and I'le
niggle with you, and that's all.

Sir Bewt.   Nay, nay *Mol* what's that wap ?

Iack. Dap.   Nay teach mee what niggling is, I'de
faine bee niggling.

Mol.   Wapping and niggling is all one, the rogue
my man can tell you.

Trap.   'Tis fadoodling : if it pleafe you.

Sir Bewt.   This is excellent, one fit more good *Moll.*

Mol.   Come you rogue fing with me.

A gage of ben Rom-boufe
In a boufing ken of Rom-vile.

T. Cat.   Is Benar then a Cafter,
Pecke, pennam, lay or popler,
Which we mill in deufe a vile.
Oh I wud lib all the lightmans.   *The fong.*
Oh I woud lib all the darkemans,
By the follamon vnder the Ruffemans.
By the follamon in the Hartmans.

T. Cat.   And fcoure the Quire cramp ring,
And couch till a pallyard docked my dell,
So my boufy nab might skew rome boufe
    well
Auaft to the pad, let vs bing,
Auaft to the pad, let vs bing.

Omnes.   Fine knaues i'faith.

Iack Dap.   The grating of ten new cart-wheeles,
and the gruntling of fiue hundred hogs comming from
Rumford market, cannot make a worfe noyfe then
this canting language does in my eares ; pray my
Lord *Noland*, let's giue thefe fouldiers their pay.

Sir Bewt.   Agreed, and let them march.

L. Nor.   Heere *Mol.*

Mol.   Now I fee that you are ftal'd to the rogue,
and are not afhamed of your profeffions, looke you:
my Lord *Noland* heere and thefe Gentlemen, beftowes
vpon you two, two boordes and a halfe, that's two
fhillings fixe pence.

Trap.   Thankes to your Lordfhip.

T. Cat.   Thankes heroicall Captaine.

Mol.   Away.

Trap.   Wee fhall cut ben whiddes of your Maiflers
and Miftrefhip, wherefoeuer we come.

Moll.   You'l maintaine firra the old Iuftices plot to
his face.

Trap.   Elfe trine me on the cheats: hang me.

Mol.   Be fure you meete mee there.

Trap.   Without any more maundring I'le doo't,
follow braue *Tear-Cat.*

T. Cat.   *I præ, fequor*, let us go moufe.

Exeunt they two manet the reft.

L. Nol.   Mol what was in that canting fong?

Mol.   Troth my Lord, onely a praife of good
drinke, the onely milke which thefe wilde beafts loue
to fucke, and thus it was:

A rich cup of wine, oh it is iuyce Diuine,

More wholefome for the head, then meate, drinke, or
    bread,

To fill my drunken pate, with that, I'de fit vp late,

By the heeles wou'd I lie, vnder a lowfy hedge die,

Let a flaue haue a pull at my whore, fo I be full

Of that precious liquor; And a parcell of fuch ftuffe
    my Lord

Not worth the opening.

*Enter a Cutpurfe very gallant, with foure or fiue men
    after him, one with a wand.*

L. Nol.   What gallant comes yonder?

T. Long.   Maffe I thinke I know him, 'tis one of
Cumberland.

1. *Cut.*   Shall we venture to fhuffle in amongft yon heap of Gallants, and ftrike?

2. *Cut.*   'Tis a queftion whether there bee any filuer fhels amongft them, for all their fattin out-fides.

Omnes.   Let's try?

Mol.   Pox on him, a gallant? fhaddow mee, I know him: 'tis one that cumbers the land indeed; if hee fwimme neere to the fhore of any of your pockets, looke to your purfes.

Omnes.   Is't poffible?

Mol.   This braue fellow is no better then a foyft.

Omnes.   Foyft, what's that?

Mol.   A diuer with two fingers, a picke-pocket; all his traine ftudy the figging law, that's to fay, cutting of purfes and foyfting; one of them is a nip, I tooke him once i' the twopenny gallery at the Fortune; then there's a cloyer, or fnap, that dogges any new brother in that trade, and fnappes will haue halfe in any booty; Hee with the wand is both a ftale, whofe office is, to face a man i' the ftreetes, whil'ft fhels are drawne by an other, and then with his blacke coniuring rod in his hand, he by the nimbleneffe of his eye and iugling fticke, will in cheaping a peece of plate at a goldfmithes ftall, make foure or fiue ringes mount from the top of his *caduceus,* and as if it were at leape-frog, they skip into his hand prefently.

2. *Cut.*   Zounds wee are fmoakt.

Omnes.   Ha?

2. *Cut.*   Wee are boyl'd, pox on her; fee *Moll* the roaring drabbe.

1. *Cut.*   All the difeafes of fixteene hofpitals boyle her: away.

Mol.   Bleffe you fir.

1. *Cut.*   And you good fir.

Mol.   Do'ft not ken mee man?

1. *Cut.*   No truft mee fir.

Mol.   Heart, there's a Knight to whom I'me bound for many fauours, loft his purfe at the laft new play

i' the Swanne, feuen Angels in't, make it good you'r
beft ; do you fee ? no more.

1. *Cut.* A Sinagogue fhall be cal'd Miftreffe *Mary*,
difgrace mee not · *pacus palabros*, I will coniure for
you, farewell :

Mol. Did not I tell you my Lord ?

L. Nol. I wonder how thou cam'ft to the knowledge of thefe nafty villaines.

T. Long. And why doe the foule mouthes of the
world call thee *Mol* cutpurffe ? a name, me thinkes,
damn'd and odious.

Mol. Dare any ftep forth to my face and fay,
I haue tane thee doing fo *Mol* ? I muft confeffe,
In younger dayes, when I was apt to ftray,
I haue fat amongft fuch adders ; feene their ftings,
As any here might, and in full play-houfes
Watcht their quicke-diuing hands, to bring to fhame
Such rogues, and in that ftreame met an ill name :
When next my Lord you fpie any one of thofe,
So hee bee in his Art a fcholler, queftion him,
Tempt him with gold to open the large booke
Of his clofe villanies ; and you your felfe fhall cant
Better then poore *Mol* can, and know more lawes
Of cheaters, lifters, nips, foyfts, puggards, curbers,
Withall the diuels blacke guard, then it is fit
Should be difcouered to a noble wit.
I know they haue their orders, offices,
Circuits and circles, vnto which they are bound,
To raife their owne damnation in.

Iack Dap. How do'ft thou know it ?

Moll. As you do, I fhew it you, they to me fhow
  it.
Suppofe my Lord you were in *Venice*.

L. Nol. Well.

Mol. If fome Italian pander there would tell
All the clofe trickes of curtizans ; would not you
Hearken to fuch a fellow ?

L. Nol. Yes.

Mol. And here,

Being come from *Venice*, to a friend moſt deare
That were to trauell thither, you would proclaime
Your knowledge in thoſe villanies, to ſaue
Your friend from their quicke danger : muſt you have
A blacke ill name, becauſe ill things you know,
Good troth my Lord, I am made *Mol* cut-purſe ſo.
How many are whores, in ſmall ruffes and ſtill lookes ?
How many chaſt, whoſe names fill ſlanders bookes ?
Were all men cuckolds, whom gallants in their
    ſcornes
Cal ſo, we ſhould not walke for goring hornes,
Perhaps for my madde going ſome reproue mee,
I pleaſe my ſelfe, and care not elſe who loues mee.
    Omnes.   A braue minde *Mol* i'faith.
    T. Long. Come my Lord, ſhal's to the Ordinary ?
    L. Nol. I, 'tis noone ſure.
    Mol. Good my Lord, let not my name condemne
me to you or to the world : A fencer I hope may be
cal'd a coward, is he ſo for that ? If all that haue ill
names in London, were to be whipt, and to pay but
tweluepence a peece to the beadle, I would rather
haue his office, then a Conſtables.
    Iack. Dap. So would I Captaine *Moll*: 'twere a
ſweete tickling office i'faith.   *Exeunt.*

    Enter Sir Alexander Wengraue, Goſhawke *and*
          Greenewit, *and others.*

    Alex. My ſonne marry a theeſe, that impudent
    girle,
Whom all the world ſticke their worſt eyes vpon ?
    Greene. How will your care preuent it ?
    Goſh. 'Tis impoſſible.
They marry cloſe, thei'r gone, but none knows whe-
    ther.
    Alex. Oh Gentlemen, when ha's a fathers heart-
    ſtrings

          Enter a ſeruant.
Held out ſo long from breaking : now what newes ſir ?

Seruant. They were met vppo'th the water an houre
  fince, fir.
Putting in towards the Sluce.
  Alex. The Sluce? come Gentlemen,
'Tis *Lambith* workes againft vs.
  Greene. And that *Lambith,* ioynes more mad
matches, then your fixe wet townes, twixt that and
Windfor-bridge, where fares lye foaking.
  Alex. Delay no time fweete Gentlemen : to Blacke
  Fryars,
Wee'l take a paire of Oares and make after 'em.

Enter Trapdore.

  Trap. Your fonne, and that bold mafculine rampe
  my miftreffe,
Are landed now at Tower.
  Alex. Hoyda, at Tower?
  Trap. I heard it now reported.
  Alex. Which way Gentlemen fhall I beftow my
  care?
I'me drawne in peeces betwixt deceipt and fhame.

Enter fir Fitz-Allard.

  Fitz-Alla. Sir *Alexander,*
You'r well met, and moft rightly ferued,
My daughter was a fcorne to you.
  Alex. Say not fo fir.
  Fitz.All. A very abiect, fhee poore Gentlewoman,
Your houfe had bene difhonoured. Giue you
  ioy fir,
Of your fons Gaskoyne-Bride, you'l be a Grandfather
  fhortly
To a fine crew of roaring fonnes and daughters,
'Twill helpe to ftocke the fuburbes pafling well fir.
  Alex. O play not with the miferies of my heart,
Wounds fhould be dreft and heal'd, not vext, or left
Wide open, to the anguifh of the patient,

And fcornefull aire let in : rather let pitty
And aduife charitably helpe to refrefh 'em.
   Fitz-All.   Who'd place his charity fo vnworthily.
Like one that giues almes to a curfing beggar,
Had I but found one fparke of goodneffe in you
Toward my deferuing child, which then grew fond
Of your fonnes vertues, I had eafed you now.
But I perceiue both fire of youth and goodneffe,
Are rak'd vp in the afhes of your age,
Elfe no fuch fhame fhould haue come neere your
    houfe,
Nor fuch ignoble forrowe touch your heart.
   Alex.   If not for worth, for pitties fake affift mee.
   Greene.   You vrge a thing paft fenfe, how can he
    helpe you ?
All his affiftance is as fraile as ours,
Full as vncertaine, where's the place that holds 'em ?
One brings vs water-newes ; then comes an other
With a full charg'd mouth, like a culuerins voyce,
And he reports the Tower ; whofe founds are trueft ?
   Gofh.   In vaine you flatter him fir *Alexander.*
   Fitz-All.   I flatter him, Gentlemen you wrong mee
grofly.
   Green.   Hee doe's it well i'faith.
   Fitz-All.   Both newes are falfe,
Of Tower or water : they tooke no fuch way yet.
   Alex.   Oh ftrange : heare you this Gentlemen, yet
    more plundges ?
   Fitz-Alla.   Th'are neerer then you thinke for yet
more clofe, then if they were further off.
   Alex.   How am I loft in thefe diftractions ?
   Fitz-Alla.   For your fpeeches Gentlemen,
In taxing me for rafhneffe ; fore you all,
I will engage my ftate to halfe his wealth,
Nay to his fonnes reuenewes, which are leffe,
And yet nothing at all, till they come from him ;
That I could (if my will ftucke to my power)
Preuent this mariage yet, nay banifh her
For euer from his thoughts, much more his armes.

Alex. Slacke not this goodneſſe, though you heap
    vpon me
Mountaines of malice and reuenge hereafter :
I'de willingly reſigne vp halfe my ſtate to him,
So he would marry the meaneſt drudge I hire.
    Greene. Hee talkes impoſſibilities, and you beleeue
'em.
    Fitz-Alla. I talke no more, then I know how to
    finiſh,
My fortunes elſe are his that dares ſtake with me,
The poore young Gentleman I loue and pitty :
And to keepe ſhame from him, (becauſe the ſpring
Of his affection was my daughters firſt,
Till his frowne blaſted all,) do but eſtate him
In thoſe poſſeſſions, which your loue and care
Once pointed out for him, that he may haue roome,
To entertaine fortunes of noble birth,
Where now his deſperate wants caſts him vpon her :
And if I do not for his owne ſake chiefly,
Rid him of this diſeaſe, that now growes on him,
I'le forfeit my whole ſtate, before theſe Gentlemen.
    Greene. Troth but you ſhall not vndertake ſuch
    matches,
Wee'l perſwade ſo much with you.
    Alex. Heere's my ring,
He will beleeue this token : fore theſe Gentlemen,
I will confirme it fully : all thoſe lands,
My firſt loue lotted him, he ſhall ſtraight poſſeſſe
In that refuſall.
    Fitz-All. If I change it not, change mee into a
    beggar.
    Green. Are you mad ſir ?
    Fitz-All. 'Tis done.
    Goſh. Will you vndoe your ſelfe by doing,
And ſhewe a prodigall tricke in your old daies ?
    Alex. 'Tis a match Gentlemen.
    Fitz-All. I, I, ſir I.
I aske no fauour ; truſt to you for none,

My hope refts in the goodneffe of your fon.
Exit Fitz-Allard.
Greene.   Hee holds it vp well yet.
Gofh.   Of an old knight i'faith.
Alex.   Curft be the time, I laid his firft loue
  barren,
Wilfully barren, that before this houre
Had fprung forth fruites, of comfort and of honour ;
He lou'd a vertuous Gentlewoman.

Enter Moll.

Gofh.   Life, heere's *Mol.*
Green.   Iack.
Gofh.   How doft thou *Iacke* ?
Mol.   How doft thou Gallant ?
Alex.   Impudence, where's my fonne ?
Mol.   Weakeneffe, go looke him.
Alex.   Is this your wedding gowne ?
Mol.   The man talkes monthly :
Hot broth and a darke chamber for the knight,
I fee hee'l be ftarke mad at our next meeting.
Exit Moll.
Gofh.   Why fir, take comfort now, there's no fuch
  matter,
No Prieft will marry her, fir, for a woman,
Whiles that fhape's on, and it was neuer knowne,
Two men were married and conioyn'd in one :
Your fonne hath made fome fhift to loue another.
Alex.   What ere' fhe be, fhe has my bleffing with
  her,
May they be rich, and fruitfull, and receiue
Like comfort to their iffue, as I take in them,
Ha's pleas'd me now, marrying not this,
Through a whole world he could not chufe amiffe.
Green.   Glad y'are fo penitent, for your former
  finne fir.
Gofh.   Say he fhould take a wench with her fmocke-
  dowry,

No portion with her, but her lips and armes ?
   Alex. Why ? who thriue better fir ? they haue moft
     blefling,
Though other haue more wealth, and leaft repent,
Many that want moft, know the moft content.
   Greene. Say he fhould marry a kind youthfull fin-
     ner.
   Alex. Age will quench that, any offence but theft
     and drunkennefle,
Nothing but death can wipe away.
There finnes are greene, euen when there heads are
     gray,
Nay I difpaire not now, my heart's cheer'd Gentle-
     men,
No face can come vnfortunately to me,
Now fir, your newes ?

Enter a feruant.

   Seruant. Your fonne with his faire Bride is neere
     at hand.
   Alex. Faire may their fortunes be.
   Green. Now you'r refolu'd fir, it was neuer fhe.
   Alex. I finde it in the muficke of my heart.

Enter Mol *maskt, in* Sebaftians *hand, and* Fitz-
Allard.

See where they come.
   Gofh. A proper lufty prefence fir.
   Alex. Now has he pleas'd me right, I alwaies coun-
     feld him
To choofe a goodly perfonable creature,
Iuft of her pitch was my firft wife his mother.
   Seb. Before I dare difcouer my offence,
I kneele for pardon.
   Alex. My heart gaue it thee, before thy tongue
     could aske it,
Rife, thou haft rais'd my ioy to greater height

Q 2

Then to that feat where griefe deiected it,
Both welcome to my loue, and care for euer,
Hide not mine happineffe too long, al's pardoned,
Here are our friends, falute her, Gentlemen.

They vnmaske her.

Omnes.   Heart, who this *Mol* ?
   Alex.   O my reuiuing fhame, is't I muft liue,
To be ftrucke blind, be it the worke of forrow,
Before age take't in hand.
   Fitz-All.   Darkeneffe and death.
Haue you deceau'd mee thus ? did I engage
My whole eftate for this.
   Alex.   You askt no fauour,
And you fhall finde as little, fince my comforts,
Play falfe with me, I'le be as cruell to thee
As griefe to fathers hearts.
   Mol.   Why what's the matter with you ?
Leffe   too   much   joy,   fhould   make   your   age   for-
      getfull,
Are you too well, too happy ?
   Alex.   With a vengeance.
   Mol.   Me   thinkes   you   fhould   be   proud   of   fuch   a
      daughter,
As good a man, as your fonne.
   Alex.   O monftrous impudence.
   Mol.   You had no note before, an vnmarkt Knight,
Now all the towne will take regard on you,
And all your enemies feare you for my fake,
You may pafle where you lift, through crowdes moft
      thicke,
And come of brauely with your purffe vnpickt,
You do not know the benefits I bring with mee,
No   cheate   dares   worke   vpon   you,   with   thumbe   or
      knife,
While y'aue a roaring girle to your fonnes wife.
   Alex.   A diuell rampant.
   Fitz-Alla.   Haue you fo much charity,

Yet to releaſe mee of my laſt raſh bargaine ?
And I'le giue in your pledge.
   Alex. No ſir, I ſtand to't, I'le worke vpon aduan-
    tage,
As all miſchiefes do vpon mee.
   Fitz-All. Content, beare witneſſe all then
His are the lands, and ſo contention ends.
Here comes your ſonnes Bride, twixt two noble
    friends.

      Enter the Lord Noland, *and Sir* Bewtious Gany-
      med, *with* Mary Fitz-Allard *betweene them, the*
      Cittizens and their wiues with them.

   Mol. Now are you gull'd as you would be, thanke
    me for't,
I'de a fore-finger in't.
   Seb. Forgiue mee father,
Though there before your eyes my ſorrow fain'd,
This ſtill was ſhee, for whom true loue complain'd.
   Alex. Bleſſings eternall, and the ioyes of Angels,
Beginne your peace heere, to be ſign'd in heauen,
How ſhort my ſleepe of ſorrow ſeemes now to me,
To this eternity of boundleſſe comforts,
That finds no want but vtterance, and expreſſion.
My Lord your office heere appeares ſo honourably :
So full of ancient goodneſſe, grace, and worthineſſe,
I neuer tooke more ioy in ſight of man,
Then in your comfortable preſence now.
   L. Nol. Nor I more delight in doing grace to
    vertue,
Then in this worthy Gentlewoman, your ſonnes Bride,
Noble *Fitz-Allards* daughter, to whoſe honour
And modeſt fame, I am a ſeruant vow'd,
So is this Knight.
   Alex. Your loues make my ioyes proud,
Bring foorth thoſe deeds of land, my care layd ready,
And which, old knight, thy nobleneſſe may challenge,
Ioyn'd with thy daughters vertues, whom I priſe now,

As deerely as that flefh, I call myne owne.
Forgiue me worthy Gentlewoman, 'twas my blindnefle
When I reiected thee, I faw thee not,
Sorrow and wilfull rafhnefle grew like filmes
Ouer the eyes of iudgement, now fo cleere
I fee the brightnefle of thy worth appeare.
    Mary.   Duty and loue may I deferue in thofe,
And all my wifhes haue a perfect clofe.
    Alex.   That tongue can neuer erre, the found's fo
      fweete,
Here honeft fonne, receiue into thy hands,
The keyes of wealth, poffeffion of thofe lands,
Which my firft care prouided, thei'r thine owne,
Heauen giue thee a bleffing with 'em, the beft ioyes,
That can in worldly fhapes to man betide,
Are fertill lands, and a faire fruitfull Bride,
Of which I hope thou'rt fped.
    Seb.   I hope fo too fir.
    Mol.   Father and fonne, I ha' done you fimple
feruice here.
    Seb.   For which thou fhalt not part *Moll* vnre-
      quited.
    Alex.   Thou art a madd girle, and yet I cannot
now condemne thee.
    Mol.   Condemne mee? troth and you fhould fir,
I'de make you feeke out one to hang in my roome,
I'de giue you the flip at Gallowes, and cozen the
      people.
Heard you this ieft my Lord?
    L. Nol.   What is it *Iacke*?
    Mol.   He was in feare his fonne would marry
      mee,
But neuer dreamt that I would nere agree.
    L. Nol.   Why? thou had'ft a fuiter once *Iacke*,
      when wilt marry?
    Mol.   Who I my Lord, I'le tell you when ifaith,
      When you fhall heare,
        Gallants voyd from Serieants feare,
        Honefty and truth vnflandred,

Woman man'd, but neuer pandred,
Cheates booted, but not coacht,
Veſſels older e're they'r broacht.
If my minde be then not varied,
Next day following, I'le be married.
L. Nol.   This ſounds like domeſ-day.
Mol.   Then were marriage beſt,
For if I ſhould repent, I were ſoone at reſt.
Alex.   Introth tho' art a good wench, I'me ſorry
   now,
The opinion was ſo hard, I conceiu'd of thee.
Some wrongs I'ue done thee.

Enter Trapdore.

Trap.   Is the winde there now ?
'Tis time for mee to kneele and confeſſe firſt,
For feare it come too late, and my braines feele it,
Vpon my pawes, I aske you pardon miſtreſſe.
Mol.   Pardon ? for what ſir ? what ha's your rogue-
   ſhip done now ?
Trap.   I haue bene from time to time hir'd to con-
   found you, by this old Gentleman.
Mol.   How ?
Trap.   Pray forgiue him,
But may I counſell you, you ſhould neuer doo't.
Many a ſnare to entrapp your Worſhips life,
Haue I laid priuily, chaines, watches, Iewels,
And when hee ſaw nothing could mount you vp,
Foure hollow-hearted Angels he then gaue you,
By which he meant to trap you, I to ſaue you.
Alex.   To all which ſhame and griefe in me cry
   guilty,
Forgiue mee now, I caſt the worlds eyes from mee,
And looke vpon thee freely with mine owne :
I ſee the moſt of many wrongs before thee,
Caſt from the iawes of enuy and her people,
And nothing foule but that, Il'e neuer more
Condemne by common voyce, for that's the whore,

That deceiues mans opinion ; mockes his truſt,
Cozens his loue, and makes his heart vniuſt.
   Mol. Here be the Angels Gentlemen, they were
      giuen me
As a Muſitian, I purſue no pitty,
Follow the law, and you can cucke mee, ſpare not
Hang vp my vyall by me, and I care not.
   Alex. So farre I'me ſorry, I'le thrice double 'em
To make thy wrongs amends,
Come worthy friends my honourable Lord,
Sir *Bewteous Ganymed*, and Noble *Fitz-Allard*,
And you kind Gentlewoman, whoſe ſparkling pre-
      fence,
Are glories ſet in mariage, beames of ſociety,
For all your loues giue luſter to my ioyes,
The happineſſe of this day ſhall be remembred,
At the returne of euery ſmiling ſpring :
In my time now 'tis borne, and may no ſadneſſe
Sit on the browes of men vpon that day,
But as I am, ſo all goe pleas'd away.

Epilogus.

A Painter hauing drawne with curious Art
    The picture of a woman (euery part,
Limb'd to the life) hung out the peece to fell :
People (who pafs'd along) veiwing it well,
Gaue feuerall verdicts on it : fome difpraifed
The haire, fome fayd the brows too high were
    raifed,
Some hit her o're the lippes, miflik'd their colour,
Some wifht her nofe were fhorter ; fome, the eyes
    fuller,
Others fayd rofes on her cheekes fhould grow,
Swearing they lookt too pale, others cry'd no,
The workeman ftill as fault was found, did mend
    it,
In hope to pleafe all ; (but this worke being ended)
And hung open at ftall, it was fo vile,
So monftrous and fo vgly all men did fmile
At the poore Painters folly.   Such wee doubt
Is this our Comedy.   Some perhaps do floute
The plot, faying ; 'tis too thinne, too weake, too
    meane,
Some for the perfon will reuile the Scœne.
And wonder, that a creature of her being
Should bee the fubiect of a Poet, feeing
In the worlds eie, none weighes fo light : others
    looke
For all thofe bafe trickes publifh'd in a booke,

(Foule as his braines they flow'd from) ot Cut-
    purſe,
Of Nips and Foyſts, naſtie, obſcœne diſcourſes,
As full of lies, as emptie of worth or wit,
For any honeſt eare or eye vnfit.
And thus,
If we to euery braine (that's humerous)
Should faſhion Sceanes, we (with the Painter)
    ſhall
In ſtriuing to pleaſe all, pleaſe none at all.
Yet for ſuch faults, as either the writers wit,
Or negligence of the Actors do commit,
Both craue your pardons : if what both haue
    done,
Cannot full pay your expectation,
The *Roring Girle* her ſelfe ſome few dayes hence,
Shall on this Stage, giue larger recompence.
Which Mirth that you may ſhare in, her ſelfe does
    woe you,
And craues this ſigne, your hands to becken her
    to you.

FINIS.

London Triumphing,

OR,

The Solemne, Magnificent, and Me-
morable Receiuing of that worthy Gentle-
man, Sir IOHN SWINERTON Knight, into
the Citty of LONDON, after his Returne from
taking the Oath of Maioralty at Weſtminſter,
on the Morrow next after *Simon* and
Iudes day, being the 29. of
October. 1612.

All the Showes, Pageants, Chariots of Triumph, with
other Deuices, (both on the Water and Land)
here fully expreſſed.

By *Thomas Dekker.*

LONDON,

Printed for *Nicholas Okes,* and are to be ſold by *Iohn*
Wright dwelling at Chriſt Church-gate. 1612.

To the Deſeruer of all thoſe Honors,

Which the Cuſtomary Rites of this Day,

And the generall Loue of this City beſtow vpon
him, Sir Iohn Swinerton, Knight, Lord
Maior of the renowmed City
of London.

Onor (*this day*) *takes you by the* Hand, *and giues you* welcomes *into your* New Office *of* Pretorſhip. A Dignity worthie the Cities beſtowing, and *moſt worthy your* Re-ceiuing. *You haue it with* the Harts *of many people,* Voices, *and* Held-vp hands : *they know it is a* Roabe *fit for you, and therefore haue clothed you in it.* May *the* Laſt-day *of your wearing the* ſame, *yeeld to your Selfe as much Ioy, as to* Others *does this* Firſt-day *of your putting it on. I ſwimme (for my owne part) not onely in the Maine Full-ſea of the* General praiſe *and* Hopes *of you. But powre out alſo (for my particular) ſuch a ſtreame as my* Prayers *can render, for a ſucceſſe anſwerable to the* On-ſet : *for it is no* Field, *unleſſe it be Crowned with victory.*

I preſent (Sir) *vnto you, theſe labours of my Pen, as the firſt and neweſt* Congratulatory Offrings *tendred into your hands, which albeit I ſhould not (of my ſelfe) deſerue to ſee accepted, I know notwithſtanding you will*

*giue to them a generous and gratefull entertainement, in
regard of that* Noble Fellowſhip *and* Society, (*of which
you* Yeſterday *were a* Brother, *and* This Day *a* Father)
who moſt freely haue beſtowed theſe their Loues *vpon
you. The* Colours *of this* Peece *are mine owne*; *the*
Coſt theirs: *to which nothing was wanting, that could
be had, and euery thing had that was required. To
their* Laſting memory *I ſet downe* This; *And to your
Noble* Diſpoſition, *this I* Dedicate. *My wiſhes being
(as euer they haue bene) to meete with any* Obieƈt,
whoſe reflexion may preſent to your Eyes, *that* Loue
and Duty, *In which*

I ſtand Bounden

To your Lordſhip.

Thomas Dekker.

Troia Noua Triumphans.

London Triumphing.

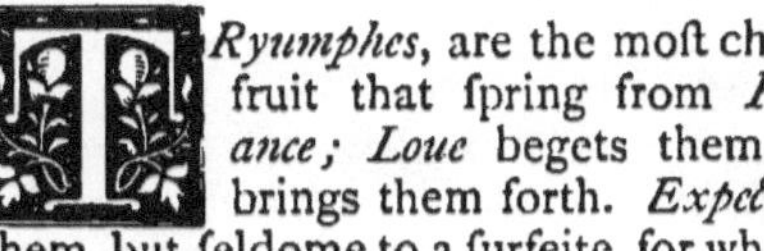

Ryumphes, are the moſt choice and daintieſt fruit that ſpring from *Peace* and *Abundance; Loue* begets them ; and *Much Coſt* brings them forth. *Expectation* feeds vpon them, but ſeldome to a ſurfeite, for when ſhe is moſt full, her longing wants ſomething to be ſatisfied. So inticing a ſhape they carry, that *Princes* themſelues take pleaſure to behold them ; they with delight ; common people with admiration. They are now and then the *Rich* and *Glorious Fires* of *Bounty, State,* and *Magnificence,* giuing light and beauty to the *Courts* of *Kings*: And now and then, it is but a debt payd to *Time* and *Cuſtome* : and out of that dept come *Theſe. Ryot* hauing no hand in laying out the *Expences,* and yet no hand in plucking backe what is held decent to be beſtowed. A *ſumptuous Thriftineſſe* in theſe *Ciuil Ceremonies* managing *All.* For it were not laudable, in a City (ſo rarely gouerned and tempered) ſuperfluouſly to *exceed* ; As contrariwiſe it is much honor to her (when the *Day* of *ſpending* comes) not to be *ſparing* in any thing. For the *Chaires* of *Magiſtrates* ought to be adorned, and to ſhine like the Chariot which caries the *Sunne* ; And *Beames* (if it were poſſible) muſt be thought to be ſhot from the *One* as from the *Other* : As well to dazle and amaze the common *Eye,* as to make it learne that there is fome *Excellent,* and *Extra-ordinary Arme* from heauen thruft downe to exalt a *Superior* man, that thereby the *Gazer* may be drawne to more obedience and admiration.

In a happy houre therefore did your Lordfhip take vpon you this infeperable burden (of *Honor and Cares*) becaufe your felfe being *Generous* of mind, haue met with men, and with a *Company* equall to your felfe in *Spirit.* And vpon as fortunate a *Tree* haue they ingrafted their *Bounty*; the fruites whereof fhoot forth and ripen, are gathered, and tafte fweetly, in the mouthes not onely of this *Citty*, but alfo of our beft-to-be-beloued friends, the *Nobleft ftrangers.* Vpon whom, though none but our *Soueraigne King* can beftow *Royall welcomes*; yet fhall it be a *Memoriall* of an *Exemplary Loue* and *Duty* (in thofe who are at the *Coft* of thefe *Triumphs*) to haue *added* fome *Heightning* more to them then was intended at firft, of purpofe to do honor to their Prince and Countrey. And I make no doubt, but *many worthy Companies* in this City could gladly be content to be partners in the *Difburfements*, fo they might be fharers in the *Glory.* For to haue bene leaden-winged now, what infamy could be greater? When all the ftreames of *Nobility* and *Gentry*, run with the *Tide* hither. When all *Eares* lye liftning for no newes but of *Feafts* and *Triumphs*: All *Eyes* ftill open to behold them: And all harts and hands to applaud them : When the heape of our *Soueraignes Kingdomes*, are drawne in *Little* : and to be feene within the Walles of this *City.* Then to haue tied *Bounty* in too ftraight a girdle : *Proh fcelus infandum !* No ; fhe hath worne her garments loofe, her lippes haue bene free in Welcomes, her purfe open, and her hands liberall. If you thinke I fet a flattering glaffe before you, do but fo much as lanch into the *Riuer*, and there the *Thames* it felfe fhall fhew you *all the Honors*, which this day hath beftowed vpon her : And that done, ftep againe vpon the *Land*, and *Fame* will with her owne *Trumpet* proclaime

what I fpeake ; And her I hope you cannot deny to
beleeue, hauing at leaft twenty thoufand eyes about
her, to witneffe whether fhe be a *True-tong'd Fame* or
a *Lying.*

By this time the Lord Maior hath taken his oath, is
feated in his barge againe ; a lowd thundring peale of
Chambers giue him a *Fare-well* as he paffes by. And fee !
how quickly we are in ken of land, as fuddenly therefore
let vs leap on fhore, and there obferue what honorable entertainement the Citty affoords to their new
Prætor, and what ioyfull falutations to her noble
Vifitants.

The firft Triumph on the Land.

THE Lord *Maior,* and *Companyes* being landed,
the firft *Deuice* which is prefented to him on the
fhore, ftands ready to recciue him at the end of
Pauls-Chayne, (on the fouth fide the Church) and this
it is.

A *Sea-Chariot* artificially made, proper for a God of
the fea to fit in ; fhippes dancing round about it,
with *Dolphins* and other great *Fifhes* playing or lying
at the foot of the fame, is drawne by two *Sea-horfes.*

Neptune.

In this Chariot fits *Neptune,* his head circled with a
Coronet of filuer *Scollup-fhels,* ftucke with branches of
Corrall, and hung thicke with ropes of pearle ; becaufe fuch things as thefe are the treafures of the
Deepe, and are found in the fhels of fifhes. In his
hand he holds a filuer *Trident,* or *Three-forked Mace,*
by which fome Writers will haue fignified the three
Naturall qualities proper to *Waters* ; as thofe of
fountaines to bee of a delitious tafte, and Chriftalline
colour : thofe of the Sea to bee faltifh and unplea-
fant, and the colour fullen, and greenifh : And laftly,
thofe of ftanding Lakes, neither fweet nor bitter, nor

cleere, nor cloudy, butal together vnwholefome for the tafte, and loathfome to the eye.   His roabe and mantle with other ornaments are correfpondent to the quality of his perfon ; Buskins of pearle and cockle-fhels being worne vpon his legges.   At the lower part of this Chariot fit *Mer-maids*, who for their excellency in beauty, aboue any other creatures belonging to the fea, are preferred to bee ftill in the eye of *Neptune.*

At *Neptunes* foot fits *Luna* (the *Moone*) who beeing gouernefle of the fea, and all petty Flouds, as from whofe influence they receiue their ebbings and flow-ings, challenges to herfelfe this honour, to haue rule and command of thofe Horfes that draw the Chariot, and therefore fhe holds their reynes in her hands.

She is atlred in light roabes fitting her ftate and condition, with a filuer *Crefcent* on her head, exprefsing both her power and property.

The whole Chariot figuring in it felfe that vaft com-paffe which the fea makes about the body of the earth : whofe *Globicall Rotundity* is *Hieroglifically* reprefented by the wheele of the Chariot.

Before this *Chariot* ride foure *Trytons*, who are feyned by poets to bee Trumpeters to *Neptune*, and for that caufe make way before him, holding ftrange Trumpets in their hands, which they found as they paffe along, their habits being Antike, and Sea-like, and fitting vpon foure feuerall fifhes, *viz.* two *Dolphins*, and two *Mer-maids*, which are not (after the old procreation), begotten of painted cloath, and browne paper, but are liuing beafts, fo queintly difguifed like the natural fifhes, of purpofe to auoyd the trouble and peftering of Porters, who with much noyfe and little comlineffe are euery yeare moft vnneceffarily imployed.

The time being ripe when the fcope of this *Deuice* is to be deliuered, *Neptunes* breath goeth forth in thefe following *Speeches*.

Neptunes Speeches.

Whence breaks this warlike thunder of lowd drummes,
(Clarions *and* Trumpets) *whofe fhrill eccho comes*
Vp to our Watery Court, *and calles from thence*
Vs *and our* Trytons ?   *As if violence*
Weere to our Siluer-footed Sifter *done*
(Of Flouds *the* Queene) *bright* Thamefis, *who does*
    runne
Twice euery day to our bofome, and there hides   Ebbe
**Her wealth, whofe* Streame *in liquid* Chriftall   &
    glides   Flow.
Guarded with troopes of Swannes ? *what does beget*
Thefe Thronges ? *this* Confluence ? *why do voyces*
    beate
The Ayre *with acclamations of applaufe,*
Good wifhes, Loue, *and* Praifes ? *what is't drawes*
All Faces *this way ?   This way* Rumor *flyes,*
Clapping her infinite wings, whofe noyfe the Skyes
From earth receiue, with Muficall *rebounding,*
And ftrike the Seas *with repercufsiue founding.*
Oh ! now I fee the caufe : vanifh vaine feares,
***Ifis *no danger feeles : for her head weares*   Thamefis.
Crowns *of* Rich Triumphes, *which* This day *puts on,*
And in Thy Honor *all thefe* Rites *are done.*
Whofe Name *when* Neptune *heard, t'was a ftrange*
    Spell,
Thus farre-vp into th' Land to make him fwell
Beyond his Bownds, *and with his* Sea-troops *wait*
Thy wifh't arriuall *to* congratulate.
Goe therefore on, goe boldly : thou muft faile
In rough Seas (*now*) *of* Rule : *and euery* Gale
Will not perhaps befriend thee :   But (*how blacke*
So ere the Skyes *looke*) *dread not* Thou *a* Wracke,
For when Integrity *and* Innocence *fit*
Steering the Helme, *no* Rocke *the* Ship *can fplit.*
Nor care the Whales (*neuer fo great*) *their* Iawes
Should ftretch to fwallow thee : Euery good mans
    caufe

Is in all ſtormes his Pilot: He that's found
To himſelfe (in Conſcience) nere can run a-ground.
Which that thou mayſt do, neuer looke on't ſtill :
For (*Spite of* Fowle guſts) *calmer* Windes *ſhall fill*
Thy Sayles *at laſt-　And ſee* ! *they home have brought*
A Ship *which* Bacchus (*God of* Wines) *hath fraught*
With richeſt Iuice of Grapes, which thy Friends *ſhall*
Drinke off in Healths *to this* Great Feſtiuall.
If any at Thy Happineſſe *repine*
They gnaw but their Owne hearts, *and touch not*
　　Thine.
Let Bats *and* Skreech-Owles *murmure at bright* Day,
Whiles Prayers *of* Good-men *Guid* Thee *on the way.*
Sownd, old Oceanus Trumpeters, *and lead on.*

The *Trytons* then ſownding, according to his command, *Neptune* in his *Chariot* paſſeth along before the
Lord Maior. The foure *Windes* (habilimented to
their quality, and hauing both *Faces* and *Limbes* pro-
portionable to their bluſtring and boiſterous condition) driue forward that *Ship* of which *Neptune*
ſpake. And this concludes this firſt *Triumph* on the
Land.

Theſe two Shewes paſſe on vntill they come into
Pauls-Church-yard, where ſtandes another *Chariot*;
the former *Chariot* of *Neptune,* with the *Ship,* beeing
conveyd into *Cheap-ſide,* this other then takes the
place ; And this is the *Deuice.*

The ſecond Land-Triumph.

It is the *Throne* of *Vertue,* gloriouſly adorned &
beautified with all things that are fit to expreſſe the
Seat of ſo noble and diuine a *Perſon.*

Vpon the height, and moſt eminent place (as
worthieſt to be exalted) ſits *Arete* (*Vertue*) herſelfe ;
her temples ſhining with a *Diadem* of ſtarres, to ſhew
that her *Deſcent* is onely from heauen : her roabes are
rich, her mantle white (figuring *Innocency*) and pow-

dred with ſtarres of gold, as an *Embleme* that ſhe puts vpon *Men*, the garments of eternity.

Beneath *Her*, in diſtinct places, ſit the *Seauen liberall Sciences*, viz. *Grammer, Rhetoricke, Logicke, Muſicke, Arithmetike, Geometry, Aſtronomy*.

Hauing thoſe roomes alotted them, as being *Mothers* to all *Trades, Profeſsions, Myſteries* and *Societies*, and the readieſt guide to *Vertue*. Their habits are *Light Roabes*, and *Looſe* (for *Knowledge* ſhould be free.) On their heads they weare garlands of *Roſes*, mixt with other flowers, whoſe ſweet *Smels* are arguments of their cleere and vnſpotted thoughts, not corrupted with uice. Euery one carrying in her hand, a *Symbole*, or *Badge* of that *Learning* which ſhe profeſſeth.

At the backe of this *Chariot* ſit foure *Cupids*, to ſignifie that vertue is moſt honored when ſhe is followed by *Loue*.

This *Throne*, or *Chariot*, is drawne by foure *Horſes*, vpon the two formoſt ride *Time* and *Mercury* : the firſt, the *Begetter* and *Bringer forth* of all things in the world, the ſecond, the *God* of *Wiſedome* and *Eloquence*. On the other two *Horſes* ride *Deſire* and *Induſtry* ; it beeing intimated hereby, that *Tyme* giues wings to *Wiſedome*, and ſharpens it, *Wiſedome* ſets *Deſire* a burning, to attaine to *Vertue*, and that *Burning Deſire* begets *Induſtry* (earneſtly to purſue her.) And all theſe (together) make men in *Loue* with *Arts, Trades, Sciences*, and *Knowledge*, which are the onely ſtaires and aſcenſions to the *Throne of Vertue*, and the onely glory and vpholdings of Cities. *Time* hath his wings, *Glaſſe*, and *Sythe*, which cuts downe *All*.

Mercury hath his *Caduceus*, or *Charming Rod*, his fethered *Hat*, his *Wings*, and other properties fitting his condition, *Deſire* caries a burning heart in her hand.

Induſtry is in the ſhape of an old *Country-man*, bearing on his ſhoulder a *Spade*, as the *Embleme* of *Labour*.

Before this *Chariot*, or *Throne* (as *Guardians* and

Protectors to *Vertue*, to *Arts*, and to the reſt ; and as
Aſsiſtants to *Him* who is *Chiefe* within the *Citty* for
that yeare) are mounted vpon horſebacke twelue *Perſons* (two by two) repreſenting the twelue ſuperior
Companyes, euery one carrying vpon his left arme a
faire *Shield* with the armes in it of one of the twelue
Companies, and in his right hand a launce with a light
ſtreamer or pendant on the top of it, and euery horſe
led and attended by a *Footman.*

The Lord *Maior* beeing approached to this *Throne,*
Vertue thus ſalutes him.

The Speech of ARETE *(Vertue).*

HAile (*worthy* Pretor) *ſlay, and do* Me *grace,*
    (*Who ſtill haue cald thee* Patron) *In this place*
To take from me heap'd welcomes, who combine
Theſe peoples hearts in one, *to make them* thine.
Bright Vertues *name thou know'ſt and heau'nly birth,*
And therefore (ſpying thee) downe ſhe leapd to earth
Whence vicious men *had driuen her* : *On her* throne
The Liberall Arts *waite* : *from whoſe* breſts *do runne*
The milke *of* Knowledge : *on which,* Sciences *feed,*
Trades *and* Profeſſions : *And by* Them, *the* ſeed
Of Ciuill, Popular Gouernment, *is ſowne* ;
Which ſpringing vp, loe ! to what heigth *tis growne*
In Thee *and* *Theſe *is ſeene.   And (to maintaine*
                                     The Aldermen.
This Greatneſſe) Twelue *ſtrong* Pillars *it ſuſtaine* ;
Vpon whoſe Capitals, *Twelue Societies *ſtand,*
                                  The twelue Companies.
Graue *and* well-ordred) *bearing chiefe Command*
Within this City, *and (with* Loue) *thus reare*
·*Thy* fame, *in* free election, *for this* yeare.
All arm'd, *to knit their* Nerues (*in* One) with Thine,
To guard this new Troy : *And, (that* She *may ſhine*
In Thee, *as* Thou *in* Her) *no* Miſers *kay*
Has bard the Gold *vp* ; Light *flies from the* Day
Not of more free gift, than from them their Coſt :
For whats now ſpar'd, *that only they count* Loſt.

As then their Ioynd-hands *lift* Thee *to thy* Seate.
(*Changing thereby thy* Name *for* one *More* *Great),
                                        Lord Maior.
And as this City, *with her* Loud, Full Voice,
(*Drowning all* fpite *that murmures at the* Choice,
If at leaft fuch *there be*) *does* Thee *preferre,*
So art thou bound to loue, both Them *and* Her.
For know, *thou art not like a* Pinnacle, *plac'd*
Onely to ftand aloft, and to be grac'd
With wondring eyes, or to haue caps and knees
Heape worfhip on thee : *for* that Man *does leeze*
Himfelfe and his Renowne, *whofe* growth *being* Hye
In the weale publicke like the Cypres tree)
Is neither good to Build-with, *nor beare* Fruit ;
Thou muft be now, Stirring, *and* Refolute.
To be what thou art Sworne, (a waking Eye)
Afarre off (*like a* Beacon) *to defcry*
What ftormes are comming, and (*being come*) *muft then*
Shelter with fpread armes, the poor'ft Citizen.
Sit Plenty *at thy* Table, *at thy* Gate
Bounty, *and* Hofpitality : *hee's moft* Ingrate
Into whofe lap the Publick-weale *hauing pow'r'd*
Her Golden fhewers, from Her *his wealth fhould hoord.*
Be like thofe Antient Spirits, *that* (*long agon*)
Could thinke no Good deed *fooner than twas* Don ;
Others *to pleafure.*   Hold *it* Thou *more* Glory,
Than to be pleas'd Thy Selfe.   *And be not fory*
If Any *ftriue* (*in beft things*) *to* exceed *thee,*
But glad, to helpe thy Wrongers, *if they need thee.*
Nor feare the flings of Euny, *nor the Threates*
Of her invenomd Arrowes, which at the Seates
Of thofe Who Beft Rule *euermore are fhot,*
But the Aire *blowes off their fethers, and they hit not,*
Come therefore on, nor dread her, nor her Sprites,
The poyfon fhe fpits vp, on her owne Head lights.
On, on, away.

This Chariot or Throne of Vertue is then fet forward, and followes that of *Neptune,* this taking place

iuſt before the Lord Maior : And this concludes the ſecond Triumphant ſhew.

The third Deuice.

THe Third Deuice is a Forlorne Caſtle, built cloſe to the little Conduit in Cheap-ſide, by which, as the Throne of *Vertue* comes neerer and neerer, there appeare aboue (on the battlements) *Enuy*, as chiefe Commandreſſe of that infernall Place, and euery part of it guarded with perſons repreſenting all thoſe that are fellowes and followers of *Enuy* : as *Ignorance, Sloth, Oppreſsion, Diſdaine,* &c. *Enuy* herſelfe being attired like a *Fury*, her haire full of ſnakes, her countenance pallid, meagre and leane, her body naked, in her hand a knot of ſnakes, crawling and writhen about her arme.

The reſt of her litter are in as vgly ſhapes as the dam, euery one of them beeing arm'd with black bowes, & arrows ready to bee ſhot at *Vertue*. At the gates of this Fort of Furies, ſtand *Ryot* and *Calumny*, in the ſhapes of Gyants, with clubs, who offer to keep back the Chariot of *Vertue*, and to ſtop her paſſage. All the reſt likewiſe on the battlements offering to diſcharge their blacke Artillery at her : but ſhe onely holding vp her bright ſhield, dazzles them, and confounds them ; they all on a ſudden ſhrinking in their heads, vntill the Chariot be paſt, and then all of them appearing againe : their arrowes, which they ſhoote vp into the aire, breake there out in fire-works, as hauing no power to do wrong to ſo ſacred a Deity as *Vertue*.

This caue of Monſters ſtands fixed to the Conduit, in which *Enuie* onely breathes out her poyſon to this purpoſe.

The ſpeech of Enuy.

Enuy. ADDers ſhoote, hyſſe ſpeckled ſnakes ;
Sloth craule up, ſee *Oppreſſion* wakes ;
(Baine to learning.) *Ignorance,*

 Shake thy Affes eares, *Difdaine*, aduance
 Thy head *Luciferan* : *Ryot* fplit
 Thy ribbes with curfes : *Calumny* fpit
 Thy rancke-rotten gall vp. See, See, See,
 That witch, whofe bottomleffe Sorcery
 Makes fooles runne mad for her, that Hag
 For whom your Dam pines, hangs out her flag
 Our Den to ramfacke : *Vertue*, that whoore ;
 See, fee, how braue fhee's, I am poore.
Vertue. On, on, the beames of Vertue are fo bright,
 They dazzle *Enuy*, on : the Hag's put to flight.
Enuy. Snakes, from your virulent fpawne ingender
 Dragons, that may peece-meale rend her :
 Adders, fhoote your ftings like quils
 Of Porcupines (Stiffe) ; hot Aetnean hils,
 Vomit fulphure to confound her,
 Fiends and Furies (that dwell vndei)
 Lift hell gates from their hindges : come
 You cloven-footed broode of Barrathrum,
 Stop, ftay her, fright her with your fhreckes,
 And put frefh bloud in *Enuies* cheekes.
Vertue. On, on, the beames of *Vertue* are fo bright,
 They dazle Enuy : the Hag's put to flight.
Omnes. Shoote, fhoote, &c. *All that are with Enuy.*

Either during this fpeech, or elfe when it is done,
certain Rockets flye vp into the aire ; the Throne of
Vertue paffing on ftill, neuer ftaying, but fpeaking ftill
thofe her two laft lines, albeit, fhee bee out of the
hearing of *Enuy* : and the other of *Enuies* Faction
crying ftill, fhoote, fhoote, but feeing they preuaile not,
all retire in, and are not feene till the Throne comes
backe againe.

And this concludes this Triumphant affault of *Enuy*:
her conqueft is to come.

The fourth Deuice.

THis Throne of *Vertue* paffeth along vntill it comes
 to the Croffe in *Cheape*, where the prefentation of

another Triumph attends to welcome the *Lord Maior*
in his paſſage ; the Chariot of *Vertue* is drawne then
along, this other that followes taking her place, the
Deuice bearing this Argument.

Vertue hauing by helpe of her followers, conducted the *Lord Maior* ſafely, euen, as it were,
through the iawes of *Enuy* and all her Monſters : the
next, and higheſt honour ſhee can bring him to, is to
make him ariue at the houſe of *Fame,* and that is
this Pageant.   In the vpper ſeat ſits *Fame* crowned
in rich attire, a Trumpet in her hand, &c.   In other
ſeuerall places ſit Kings, Princes, and Noble perſons,
who haue bene free of the *Marchant-tailors* : A per-
ticular roome being reſerued for one that repreſents
the perſon of *Henry* the now *Prince of Wales.*

The onely ſpeaker heere is Fame herſelfe, whoſe
wordes found out theſe glad welcomes.

The ſpeech of Fame.

WElcome to *Fames* high Temple : here fix faſt
      Thy footing ; for the wayes which thou haſt paſt
Will be forgot and worne out ; and no Tract
Of ſteps obſeru'd, but what thou *now* ſhalt Act.
The booke is ſhut of thy precedent deedes,
And *Fame* vnclaſpes another, where ſhee reades
(Aloud) the Chronickle of a dangerous yeare,
For Each Eye will looke through thee, and Each Eare
Way-lay thy wordes and workes.   Th' haſt yet but
       gon
About a Pyramid's foote ; the top's not won,
That's glaſſe ; who ſlides there, fals, and once falne
       downe,
Neuer more riſes : no art cures renowne,
The wound being ſent to th' heart.   'Tis kept from
       thence
By a ſtrong armor, *Vertues* influence ;
She guides thee, follow her.   In this Court of *Fame*
None elſe but *Vertue* can enrole thy name.

Erect thou then a ferious eye, and looke
What worthies fill vp *Fames* voluminous booke,
That now (thine owne name read there) none may
    blot
Thy leafe with foule inke, nor thy margent quoate
With any act of thine, which may difgrace
This Cittie's choice, thy felfe, or this thy place :
Or that which may difhonour the high Merits
Of thy renown'd fociety : roiall fpirits
Of Princes holding it a grace to weare
That crimfon badge, which thefe about them beare,
Yea, Kings themfelues 'mongft you haue fellowes
    bene,
Stil'd by the name of a free-citizen :
For inftance, fee, feuen Englifh Kings there plac'd,
Cloth'd in your liuery, the firft feat being grac'd
By fecond *Richard* : next him *Bullingbrooke* :
                           Henry the 4.
Then that Fift (thundring) *Henry*, who all France
    fhook :
By him, his fonne (fixth *Henry*) by his fide
Fourth *Edward*, who the *Rofes* did diuide :
Richard the third next him : and then that King
Who made both *Rofes* in one branch to fpring :
A fprig of which branch (higheft now but one)
Is *Henry Prince of Wales*, followed by none :
Who of this brotherhood, laft and beft fteps forth,
Honouring your Hall : to heighten more your worth.
I can a regifter fhow of feuenteene more
(Princes and Dukes all) : entombed long before,
Yet kept aliue by Fame ; Earles thirty-one,
And Barons fixty-fix that path haue gone :
Of Vifcounts onely one your order tooke :
Turne ouer one leafe more in our vaft booke,
And you may reade the names of prelates there,
Of which one Arch-bifhop your cloth did weare.
And Byfhops twenty-foure : of Abbots feuen
As many Priors, to make the number euen :
Of forty Church-men, I one fub-prior adde,

You from all thefe, thefe from you honour had.
Women of high bloud likewife laid afide
Their greater ftate fo to be dignified :
Of which a *Queene* the firft was, then a paire
Of Dukes' wiues : and, to leaue the roll more faire,
Fiue Counteffes and two Ladies are the laft,
Whofe birth and beauties haue your order gracd.
But I too long fpin out this thrid of gold ;
Here breakes it off.   Fame hath them all en-rold
On a large file (with Others), And their ftory
The world fhall reade, to adde vnto thy glory,
Which I am loath to darken : thoufand eyes
Yet aking till they enjoy thee : win then that prife
Which Vertue holds vp for thee, And (that done),
Fame fhall the end crowne, as fhe hath begun.
Set forward.

Thofe Princes and Dukes (befides Kings nominated before) are thefe.

John Duke of Lancafter.
Edmund Duke of Yorke.
The Duke of Glofter.
The Duke of Surrey.
} In the time of Richard the Second.

Humfry Duke of Glofter.
Richard Duke of Yorke.
} In the time of Henry the Fifth.

George D. of Clarence.
{ In the time of Edward the Fourth.

Duke of Suffolke.
Iohn D. of Norfolke.
George D. of Bedford.
} In the time of Richard the Third.

Edward D. of Buckingham, In the time of Henry the 7. with others, whofe Rol is too long here to be opened.

The Queene fpoken of, was Anne, wife to Richard the 2.   Dukes wiues thefe, viz :—

The Dutcheffe of Glofter. In the time of Richard the 2.

Elionor Dutcheffe of Glofter. In the time of H. the 5.

Now for Prelates I reckon onely thefe,
The Prior of Saint Bartholmewes.
And his Sub-Prior.
The Prior of Elfinge-fpittle.
Thomas Arundell, Arch-bifhop of Canterbury.
Henry Bewfort, Bifhop of Winton.
The Abbot of Barmondfey.
The Abbot of Towrchill.
Philip Morgan, Bifhop of Worfter.
The Abbot of Tower-hill.
The Prior of Saint Mary Ouery.
The Prior of Saint Trinity in Cree-Church.
The Abbot and Prior of Weftminfter.
Kemp Bifhop of London.
W. Wainfleete, B. of Winchefter.
George Neuill, Bifhop of Winchefter, and Chauncelor
    of England.
Iohn May, Abbot of Chertfay.
Laurence, Bifhop of Durham.
Iohn Ruffell, Bifhop of Rochefter.

If I fhould lengthen this number, it were but to
trouble you with a large index of names onely, which
I am loath to do, knowing your expectation is to be
otherwife feafted.

The fpeech of *Fame* therefore being ended, as 'tis
fet downe before, this Temple of her's takes place next
before the *Lord Maior*, thofe of *Neptune* and *Vertue*
marching in precedent order. And as this Temple is
carryed along, a fong is heard, the muficke being
queintly conueyed in a priuate roome, and not a perfon difcouered.

THE SONG.

H*Onor*, eldeft child of *Fame*,
Thou farre older then thy name,

Waken with my fong, and fee
One of thine, here waiting thee.
                    Sleepe not now,
                    But thy brow,
Chac't with Oliues, Oke, and Baies
And an age of happy dayes
                    Vpward bring,
                    Whilſt we fing
In a Chorus altogether,
Welcome, welcome, welcome hither.

Longing round about him ſtay,
Eyes, to make another day,
Able with their vertuous light,
Vtterly to baniſh night.
                    All agree,
                    This is hee,
Full of bounty, honour, ſtore,
And a world of goodneſſe more
                    Yet to ſpring
                    Whilſt we fing
In a Chorus altogether,
Welcome, welcome, welcome hither.

Enuy, angry with the dead,
Far from this place hide thy head ;
And *Opinion*, that nere knew
What was either good or true ;
                    Fly, I fay,
                    For this day
Shall faire *Juſtice*, *Truth*, and *Right*,
And ſuch happy ſonnes of *Light*,
                    To us bring,
                    Whilſt we fing
In a Chorus altogether,
Welcome, welcome, welcome hither.

Goe on nobly, may thy name,
Be as old and good as fame,
Euer be remembred here,
Whilſt a bleſſing, or a teare
        Is in ſtore,
        With the pore,
So ſhall *Swinerton* nere dye,
But his vertues vpward flye,
        And ſtill ſpring,
        Whilſt we ſing,
In a Chorus ceaſing neuer,
He is liuing, liuing euer.

And this concludes this fourth *Triumph*, till his lord-
ſhips returne from the *Guild-hall.*

In returning backe from the *Guild-hall*, to performe
the ceremoniall cuſtomes in *Pauls Church*, theſe
ſhewes march in the ſame order as before ; and comming with the Throne of *Vertue*, *Enuy* and her crue
are as buſie again, *Enuie* uttering ſome three or foure
lines at the end of her ſpeech onely : As thus :

Enuy.   Fiends and furies, that dwell vnder,
          Lift hell-gates from their hindges : come,
       You clouen-footed brood of *Barathrum*,
       Stop, ſtony her, fright her with your ſhreekes,
       And put freſh blood in *Enuyes* cheekes.
Vertue.   On, on, the beames of *Vertue* are ſo bright,
       They dazzle *Enuy* ; on, the Hag's put to
       flight.

This done, or as it is in doing, thoſe twelue that
ride armed diſcharge their piſtols, at which *Enuy* and
the reſt vaniſh, and are ſeene no more.

When the *Lord Maior* is (with all the reſt of their
Triumphs), brought home, *Juſtice* (for a fare-well) is
mounted on ſome couenient ſcaffold cloſe to his entrance at his gate, who thus ſalutes him :—

The *fpeech* of *Juftice.*

MY this-dayes·fworne-proteſtor, welcome home,
    If Iuſtice fpeake not now, be ſhe euer dumbe :
The world giues out ſhee's blinde ; but men ſhall fee
Her light is cleere, by influence drawne from thee.
For one-yeare therefore, at thefe gates ſhee'll ſit,
To guid thee in and out : thou ſhalt commit
(If ſhee ſtand by thee) not one touch of wrong :
And though I know thy wifdome built up ſtrong,
Yet men (like great ſhips) being in ſtorms, moſt
    neere
To danger, when vp their ſailes they beare.
And ſince all Magiſtrates tread ſtill on yce,
From mine owne fchoole I read thee this aduice :
    Do good for no mans fake (now) but thine owne,
Take leaue of friends and foes, both muſt be knowne
But by one face : the rich and poore muſt lye
In one euen fcale : all ſuiters, in thine eye,
Welcome alike ; euen hee that feemes moſt bafe,
Looke not vpon his clothes, but on his cafe.
Let not *Oppreſſion* waſh his hands i' th' teares
Of widowes, or of orphans : widowes prayers
Can pluck downe thunder, and poore orphans cries
Are lawrels held in fire ; the violence flyes
Vp to Heauen-gates, and there the wrong does tell,
Whilſt *Innocence* leaues behind it a fweet fmell.
Thy Confcience muſt be like that fcarlet dye ;
One fowle fpot ſtaines it all : and the quick eye
Of this prying world, will make that fpot thy fcorne.
That Collar (which about thy necke is worne)
Of Golden Eſſes, bids thee fo to knit
Mens hearts in loue, and make a chayne of it.
That fword is feldome drawne, by which is meant,
It ſhould ſtrike feldom : neuer th' innocent.
'Tis held before thee by anothers hand,
But the point vpwards (heauen muſt that command)
Snatch it not then in wrath ; it muſt be giuen,
But to cut none, till warranted by Heauen.

The head, the politicke body muſt aduance
For which thou haſt the cap of maintenance,
And ſince the moſt iuſt magiſtrate often erres,
Thou guarded art about with officers,
Who knowing the pathes of others that are gone,
Should teach thee what to do, what leaue vndone.
Nights candles lighted are, and burne amaine,
Cut therefore here off thy officious traine,
Which *Loue* and *Cuſtome* lend thee ; all delight
Crowne both this day and Citty : a good night
To thee, and theſe graue ſenators, to whom
My laſt fare-wels in theſe glad wiſhes come,
That thou and they, (whoſe ſtrength the City beares),
May be as old in goodneſſe as in yeares.

The Title-page of this Booke makes promiſe of all the ſhewes by water, as of theſe on the land ; but *Apollo* hauing no hand in them, I ſuffer them to dye by that which fed them ; that is to ſay, powder and ſmoake. Their thunder (according to the old gally-foyſt-faſhion), was too lowd for any of the *Nine Muſes* to be bidden to it. I had deviz'd *one* altogether muſi-call, but *Time's* glaſſe could ſpare no ſand, nor lend convenient howres for the performance of it. Night cuts off the glory of this day, and ſo conſequently of theſe triumphes, whoſe brightneſſe beeing ecclipſed, my labours can yeeld no longer ſhadow. They are ended, but my loue and duty to your Lordſhip ſhall neuer.

——— *Non diſplicuiſſe meretur,*
Feſtinat (*Prætor*) *Qui placuiſſe tibi.*

F I N I S.

IF

IT BE NOT GOOD,

The Diuel is in it.

A

Nevv Play,

AS IT HATH BIN

lately Acted, vvith great
applaufe, by the Queenes Maiefties
Seruants : At the Red Bull.

Written by THOMAS DEKKER.

Flectere fi nequeo Superos, Acheronta mouebo.

LONDON,

Printed for *I. T.* And are to be fold by *Edward Marchant*,
at his fhop againft the Croffe in *Pauls*
Church-yarde. 1612.

TO MY LOVING,

AND LOVED FRIENDS

and fellowes, the Queenes

Maiesties seruants.

*Nowledge* and *Reward* dwell far a-sunder. *Greatnes* lay once betweene them. But (in his stead) *Couet-ousnes* now. And ill neighbour, a bad *Benefactor*, no pay maister to *Poets*. By *This Hard-Houskeeping*, (or rather, *Shutting* vp of *Liberalities Doores*,) *Merit* goes a *Begging*, & *Learning* starues. *Bookes*, had wont to haue *Patrons*, and (now,) *Patrons* haue *Bookes*. The *Snufft* hat is *Lighted*, consumes *That* which *Feeds* it. A *Signe*, the *World* hath an ill *Eare*, when no *Musick* is good, vnles it *Strikes-vp* for *Nothing*. *I* haue *Sung* so, but wil no more. *A Hue*-and *Cry* follow, his *Wit*, that sleeps, when sweete *Tunes* are sounding. But tis now the *Fashion*. *Lords*, look wel : *Knights*, *Thank* well ; *Gentlemen*, promise well ; *Citizens*, *Take* well ; *Gulles*, *Sweare* well : but *None*, *Giue well*, I leaue therefore All, for *You :* And All (that *This* can be) to *You*. Not in hope to*Haue ;* but in *Recognition* of *What I Haue* (as I think) *Already* (your *Loues*.)

Acknowledgement is part of payment sometimes, but it neither is, nor shall be (betweene you and me) a *Cancelling*. I haue cast mine eye vpon many, but find none more fit, none more worthy, to *Patronize this*, than *you*, who haue *Protected it*. Your *Cost*, *Counsell*, and *Labour*, had bin ill spent, if a *Second* should by my hand snatch from you *This Glory*. No : When *Fortune* (in her blinde pride) set her foote vpon *This imperfect Building*, (as scorn-ing the *Foundation* and *Workmanship* :) you, gently raizd it vp (on the fame *Columnes,*) the *Frontiſpice* onely a little more *Gar-niſhed:* To you therefore deferuedly, *Whole Frame* is the confe-crated: For I durſt fweare, if *Wiſhes* and *Curſes* could haue become *Witches,* the necke of this *Harmles Diuell* had long a goe bin broken.

But I am glad that *Ignorance* (fo infolent for being flattered) is now ſtript naked, and her deformities difcouered: And more glad, that *Enuie* fits maddingly gnawing her owne *Snakes,* whofe *Stinges* fhe had armed to ſtrike *Others.* *Feede* let her fo ſtill. So, ſtill let the *Other* be laughed at. Whilſt I (*pittying* the *One,* and not *Dreading* the *Other,*) fend thefe *my Wiſhes* flying into your *Bofomes;* That the *God* of *Poets,* may neuer peſter your *Stage* with a *Cherilus,* nor a *Suffenus,* (*Males, Eminent* in nothing but in Long *Eares,* in *Kicking* and in *Braging* out *Calumnies*) vpon whofe *Cruppers* may be aptly pind, *That Morrall* of poore *Ocnus* making *Ropes* in *Hell,* whil'ſt an Affe ſtands by, and (as he twiſts) bites them in funder. But if *His Verſifying Deity,* fends you *Any, I wiſh* they may be fuch, as are worthy to fit, *At the Table of the Sun.* None els.

I wifh a *Faire* and *Fortunate Day* to your *Next New-Play* for the *Makers-fake* and your *Owne,*) becaufe fuch *Braue Triumphes* of *Poefie,* and *Elaborate Induſtry,* which my *Worthy Friends Mufe* hath there fet forth, deferue a *Theater* full of very *Mufes* themfelues to be *Spectators.* To that *Faire Day* I wifh a *Full, Free,* and *Knowing Auditor.* And to that *Full Audience, One Honeſt Doore-keeper.* So, *Fare-well.*

Yours. Tho: Dekker.

Prologue.

WOuld t'were a Cuftome that at all New-playes
   The Makers fat o'th *Stage,* either with *Bayes*
To haue their *Workes Crownd,* or beate in with
   Hiffing,
Pied and bold *Ideotes,* durft not then fit *Kifsing*
A *Mufes* cheeke : *Shame* would bafe *Changelings* weane,
From *Sucking* the mellifluous *Hypocrene :*
Who write as blinde-men fhoote, (by *Hap,* not *Ayme,*)
So, Fooles by lucky *Throwing,.* oft win the Game.
Phœbus has many Baftards, *True Sonnes* fewe,
I meane of thofe, whofe quicke cleare eyes can viewe
Poefies pure *Effence,* It being fo diuine
That the *Suns Fires,* (euen when they brighteft fhine)
Or *Lightning,* when moft fubtillie *Ioue* does fpend it,
May as foone be approchd, weyed, touchd, or com-
   prehended.
   But tis with *Poets* now, as tis with Nations,
   Thil-fauourdft *Vices,* are the braueft *Fafhions.*
A Play whofe *Rudenes, Indians* would abhorre,
Ift fill a houfe with Fifhwiues, *Rare, They All Roare.*
It is not Praife is fought for (Now) but *Pence,*
Tho dropd, from Greafie-apron *Audience.*
Clapd may he bee with *Thunder,* that plucks *Bayes,*
With fuch *Foule Hands,* & with *Squint-Eyes* does
   gaze
On *Pallas Shield* ; not caring (fo hee *Gaines,*
A Cramd *Third-Day,* what *Filth* drops from his *Braines.*
Let *Thofe* that loue *Pans pipe,* daunce ftill to *Pan,*
They fhall but get *long Eares* by it : Giue me *That*
   Man,

Who when the *Plague* of an Impoſtumd *Braynes*
(*Breaking* out) infeċts a *Theater*, and hotly raignes,
Killing the *Hearers* hearts, that the vaſt roomes
Stand empty, like ſo many Dead-mens toombes,
Can call the *Baniſhd* Auditor home, And tye
His Eare (with golden chaines) to his Melody :
Can draw with *Adamantine Pen* (euen creatures
Forg'de out of th'*Hammer*, on tiptoe, to *Reach* vp,
And (from *Rare ſilence*) clap their *Brawny hands*,
T' *Applaud*, what their *charmd* ſoule ſcarce vnder-
    ſtands.
That Man giue mee ; whoſe Breſt fill'd by the *Muſes*,
With Raptures, Into a ſecond, them infuſes :
Can giue an Aċtor, Sorrow, Rage, Ioy, Paſſion,
Whilſt hee againe (by ſelfe-ſame Agitation)
Commands the *Hearers*, ſometimes drawing out
    Teares,
Then ſmiles, and fills them both with *Hopes* & *Feares*.
That Man giue mee : And to bee ſuch-a-*One*,
Our *Poet* (this day) ſtriues, or to bee *None* :
Lend not (*Him*) hands for *Pittie*, but for *Merit*,
If he *Pleaſe*, hee's *Crownd*, if *Not*, his *Fate* muſt beare
    it.

IF THIS BE NOT

A GOOD PLAY, THE

DIVELL IS IN IT.

Plu.   H A !
Cha.   So.
Plu. What fo.
Cha. Ile be thy flaue no longer.
Plu. What flaue ?
Cha. Hels drudge, her Gally-flaue. I ha' wore
My flefh toth' bones, bones marrowles, at the *Oare*
Tugging to waft to' thy Stygian empire, Soules,
Which (but for *Charon*) neuer had come in Sholes,
Yet (fwarmde they nere fo) them on fhore I fet,
Hell gets by *Charon*, what does *Charon* get ?
  Plu. His Fare.
  Cha. Scuruy fare, ile firfl cry garlick.
  Plu. Doe :
And make hel flinck, as that does hither.
  Cha. If I doe

Some like that fmell, my boate to fhore ile pull ;
Not worke a ftroake more.
    Plu. How ?
    Cha. Not touch a Scull.
    Plu. Why ?
    Cha. I ha' no doings : Graues-end-barge has
      more,
And caries as good as any are in hell ;
I feare th' infernall riuers are frozen or'e
So few by water come : els the whores that dwell
Next dore to hell, goe about : befides, tis thought,
That men to find hell, now, new waies haue fought,
As Spaniards did to the Indies. *Pluto,* mend
My wages, or row thy felfe.
    Plu. Vgly, grumbling flaue,
Haue I not raifde thy price ? yet ftill do'ft craue ?
Such bold braue beggers (heard off ner'e before,
Are thy fares now, they teach thee to beg more.
Thy fare was (firft) a halfe-peny, then the foules gaue
    thee
A peny, then three-halfe-pence, we fhall haue thee
(As market-folkes on darth,) fo damned deere,
Men will not come to hell, crying out th'are heere
Worfe racke then th'are in tauernes : why doeft howle
    for mony ?
    Cha. For mony : Ile haue ij.d. for each foule
I ferry ouer ; I'me old, craz'd, Stiffe, and lam'de,
That foule thats not worth ij.d. wou'ld twere damb'd.
    Plu. Thou fhalt not.
    Cha. I will haue it, or lye ftill,
If *Charon* fill hell, hell fhall *Charon* fill :
For Ghofts now come not thronging to my boate,
But drop by one and one in ; none of note
Are fares now : I had wont braue fellowes to ply,
Who, (hack't and mangled) did in battailes dye.
But now thefe gallants which doe walke hells
    Rowndes,
Are fuller of difeafes, than of woundes.
If wounded any take my boate, they roare,

Being ſtabd, either drunke, or ſlaine about ſome
    whore.
Thats all the fight now.
    Prod. Charon.   *Within.*
    Plu. Get thee gon :
That call'd for.
    Prod : *Charon.*
    Cha. Ball not. Ile come anon.
Hagges of hell gnaw thee with their fowle furd-
    gummes.
    Plu. *Pluto,* no wonder if ſo few hither comes ?
    Cha. Why :
Gingerly : See See,
One of thine owne promooters, (with hawkes eyes,
That ſhould for prey be watching) here ſnoring lyes.
    Plu. With a miſchife ! cabind ! a fury.
    Char. Ile Ferret out more.

       Ruffman comes vp, Furie Enters.

    Cha. Another : looke : dancing a bawde on's
knee.

       Enter Shackle-foule comes vp.

    Shack. I doe enquire if rich bawdes Carted bee
On earth as well as poore ones : I ſleepe not *Pluto.*
    Plu. Twiſt ſtronger-knotted whips, Ile wake you
    (ſlaues !)
    Cha. Two of thy Summers dead-drunke here too.
    Lur. Thou lyeſt.
Charon.

    Lurchall and another Spirit comes vp.

    Cha. I come : If I muſt worke, let theſe
Thy Prentices, plye their occupation,
T'vphold hells Kingdome, more muſt worke then one.
                               Exit.
    Plu. Ha ; Are there whipping-poſts for ſuch as
    dwell

In Idlenes on Earth, and yet ſhall Hell
(As if wee tooke bribes here too,) let ſuch paſſe !
Ile haue you tawde : Is not the world as t'was ?
Once mother of Rapes, Inceſts, and Sodomies,
Atheiſme, and Blaſphemies, plump Boyes indeed.
That ſuck'd (our Dams breſt) is ſhee now barren ?
    Ha !
Is there a dearth of villaines ?
    Omn.   More now then euer ?
    Plu.   Is there ſuch penurie of man-kinde Hell-
    houndes ?
You can lye ſnoring.
    Ruff.   Each Land is full of Rake-hells.
    Shac.   But ſholes of Sharkes eate vp the Fiſh at
    Sea.
    Lur.   Braue pitchy villaines there.
    Plu.   Yet you playing here.
    Omn.   No, No ; moſt awefull *Pluto.*
    Plu.   Were you good Hell-hounds, euery day
    ſhould bee
A *Symon*-and-*Iude,* to crowne our bord with Feaſts
A blacke-eyde ſoules each minute : were you honeſt
    diuels
Each officer in hell ſhould haue at leaſt,
A brace of whores to his break-faſt : aboue vs dwell,
Diuells brauer and more ſubtill then in Hell.
    Omn.   Weele fill thy pallace with them.
    Plu.   Ile trye that : goe :
Rufman, take inſtantly a Courtiers ſhape
Of any country : chooſe thine owne diſguize
And returne ſwiftly.
    Ruf.   Yes.   *Exit.*
    Plu.   *Shackle-foule* weare thou
A Friers graue habit.
    Shac.   Well.   *Exit.*
    Plu.   *Grumſhall* walke thou
In trebble-ruffes like a Merchant.
    Lur.   So : tis don.   *Exit.*
    Plu.   The barres of our latigious Courts had wont

To crack with thronging pleaders, whofe lowde din
Shooke the infernall hell, as if 't had bin
An earth-quake burfting from the deepe Abiffe,
Or els *Ioues* thunder, throwne at the head of Dis
(The God of gold,) for hiding it below,
Thereby to tempt churles hither. Nor did we know
What a Vacation ment : continuall terme
Fattend hels Lawyers, and fhall fo againe.

Enter *Rufman*, *Shackle-foule* and *Lurchall.*

Ruf.　Here.
Shac.　Here.
Lur.　Command vs.
Plu.　Fly into the world :
As y'are in fhapes transformde be fo in name,
For men are out-fides onely : be you the fame ;
Hye thee to *Naples*, (*Rufman*), thou fhalt finde
A Prince there (newly crownde,) aptly inclinde
To any bendings ; leaft his youthfull browes
Reach at Stars only, wey down his loftieft boughes
With leaden plomets, poifon his beft thoughts with
　　taft
Of things moft fenfuall ; if the heart once waft
The body feeles confumption ; good or bad kings
Breede Subiects like them : cleere ftreames flow from
　　cleere fprings.
Turne therefore *Naples* to a puddle : with a ciuill
Much promifing face, and well oylde play the court
　　diuell.
　Ruff.　Ile doo't in brauery : if as deepe as hell,
Thy large eares heare a Land curfe me, my part's
　　playd well.
　Plu.　Fly *Shackle-foule*.
　Shac.　Whither ?
　Plu.　To the Friery,
Beft-famde in *Naples* for ftrict orders : throw
What nets thou feeft can catch them : Amongft
　　'em fow

Seedes of contention, or what euer fin
They moft abhor, fweate thou to bring that in.
   Shac.   A wolfe in lambe skin leapes into the rout,
Bell, booke, or candle cannot curfe me out ;
Ile curfe fafter than they.
   Plu.   Doe : *Grumball.*
   Lur.   Here.
   Plu.   Be thou a cittie-diuell, make thy hands
Of Harpyes clawes, which being on courtiers lands
Once faftend, ne're let loofe, the Merchant play,
And on the Burfe, fee thou thy flag difplay.
Of politicke banck-ruptifme : traine vp as many
To fight vnder it, as thou canft, for now's not any
That breake, (theile breake their necks firft) if, befide
Thou canft not through the whole citie meete with
      pride,
Riot, lechery, enuy, Auarice, and fuch ftuffe,
Bring 'em all in coach'd, the gates are wide enough.
The fpirit of gold inftruct thee : hence all.
   Omn.   Fly.
   Plu.   Stay, leaft you fhould want helpers at your
      calling
Any diuels fhall come, (Starch hound, Tobacco
      fpawling,
Vpfhotten, Suckland, Glitterbacke, or any
Whom you fhall neede to imploy, but call not many,
The'rs but few good in hell.   And ftay, remember
We all meete to heare how you profper.
   Omn.   Where ?
   Plu.   The Tree
Blafted with Goblins, that about whofe roote
5. Mandrakes growe, i'th Groue by *Naples* there,
Meete there.
   Omn.   Wee fhall.
   Plu.   Our bleffings with you beare.
   Ruff.   Dread King of Ghofts, weele plye our thrift
      fo well,
Thou fhalt be forc'd to enlarge thy Iayle of Hell.
   Plu.   Be quicke th'at beft, let fawcy mortals know,

How ere they fleepe, there's one wakes here below.
Exeunt.

> ¶ *Enter* Alphonfo (*King of Naples*) *Crownde,
> wearing Robes Imperiall, Swordes of State,
> Maces, &c., being borne before him, by* Octavio
> Aftolfo, (2. vnckles) Narcifo, Iouinelli, Brifco,
> (*Counts with others, Counte* Spendola *meeting
> them.*

Spen. One of thofe gallant Troupes went forth to
   meete
Your admirde Miftreffe (*Erminhild* the faire)
Hath left your Conuoy with her on the way.
   K. And brings glad newes of her being here (this
      day)
Let Canons tell in Thunder her Arriuall,
Flourifh When fhee's at hand our felfe will meete her.
   Omn. On.

Hee takes his Seate ; All kneele.

   K. Pray rife ; vntill about our browes were
      throwne,
Thefe fparkling beames, fuch adoration
Was not beftowde on vs : whom does the knee
Thus louely worfhip? this Idoll, (Gold) or mee?
Indeed t'is the worlds *Saynt*, if that you adore,
Goe, pray to your coffers. None to vs fhall bow,
Giue God your knees.
   Oct. Whofe owne voice does allow
That Subiects fhould to thofe who are *Supreme*,
Bend, as to God, (all Kings being like to him)
   Aft. Thou wonder of thy time, Ile pay no more
To thee of dutie than has bene before
And euer fhall be payd to thofe fit Hye.
   K. Pray mocke not mee with fuch Idolatry,
Kings, Gods are, (I confeffe) but Gods of clay,
Brittle as you are, you as good as they,

Onely in weight they differ, (this poore dram)
Yet all but flefh and bloud ; And fuch I am.
If fuch, pray let mee eate, drinke, fpeake, and walke,
Not look'd cleane through, with fuperftitious eyes,
(Not ftar'de at like a Comete.)   As you goe
Or fpeake, or feede (vn wondered at) let mee fo.
   Oɛt.   Not Kings of Ceremonie.
   K.   Vncle what then ?
Still are they Kings.
   Oɛt.   But fhew like common men.
   K.   Good vncle know, no Sunne in this our
     Spheare,
Shall rule but Wee, let others fhine as cleare,
In goodnes, None in greatnes fhall.
   Afl.   Bleft raigne !
The Golden worlde is molding new againe.
   K.   All that I craue is this, and tis not newe,
Pay vnto *Cæfar* onely *Cæfars* due.
   Oɛt.   We owe thee loyall hearts, and thofe weele
     pay,
Each minute (Mirrour of Kings.)
   Iou.   Marke, the olde Lords promife their hearts,
     but no money.
   Oɛt.   Here are the names of bold confpirators,
(Yong *Catilines,* and farre more defperate)
Who in your Fathers dayes kindled the fires
Of hote Rebellion.
   K.   Which are now burnt out.
   Oɛt.   Who knowes that ? embers in dead Afhes
     lye.
King, Set thy hand to this let Traytors dye.
   Afl.   Tis fit you fhould doe fo.
   Oɛt.   Sound Pollicie.
   K.   Men many things hold fit, that are not good,
A yong Beginner and fet vp in blood !
(Butchers can doe no more.)   Shall Recordes fay
Being Crownde, he playd the Tyran the firft day,
How fhould that Chronicler be curf'd ? your paper.
When fuch a fatall booke comes in my fight,

Ile with *Vefpafian* wifh I could not write,
Their bond is canceld. I forgiue the debt,
See that at liberty, they all be fet.
 Omn. A Princely Act.
 Oct. If wifely tis well done.
 Spen. That raigne muft boft, which mercy has
  begun.
 K. Beare witnes all, what pace the Chariot
  wheeles
Of our new guilded Soueraigntie fhall run.
 Ruf. A mayne gallop I hope.
 K. And here I vow to end as tis begun.
 Aft. Heauen fill thee full of dayes, but (being all
  told)
Ending no worfe, their fumme weele write in gold.
 Oct. The courfe youle take deere Lord.
 K. This : pray obferue it.
 Iou. Call you this Coronation day ? would I were
ith ftreetes where the conduites run claret wine, there's
fome good fellowfhip.
 Oct. Peace.
 K. Each weeke within the yeere fhall be a booke
Which each day ile reade o're : I well may doe't,
The booke being but fix leaues (fix dayes,) the
  feuenth
Be his that owes it ; Sacred is that and hye ;
And who prophanes one houre in that, fhall dye.
 Spen. How manie wilbe left aliue then this day
  fortnight ?
 Oct. Firft, beate all Tauernes downe then, Soules
  are loft
(Being drownde in Surfets) on that feuenth day moft.
Stay (beft of Kings) mine owne hand fhall fet downe
What lawes thou mad'ft firft day thou wor'ft a
  Crowne.
Begin, begin thy weeke.
 K. Write Monday.
 Oct. So fo,-Monday.

3   T

Iou.   They fay Monday's Shooemakers holliday,
   Ile fall to that trade.
Oct.   I haue writ it downe my liege.
Iou.   Peace, harken to your leffon.
K.   That day, from morne till night, Ile execute
The office of a Iudge, and wey out lawes
With euen fcales.
Iou.   Thats more than grocers doe.
K.   The poore and rich mans caufe
Ile poize alike : It fhall be my chiefe care
That bribes and wrangling be pitch'd o're the barre.
Iou.   We fhall haue old breaking of neckes then.
K.   Downe with that firft.
Oct.   O for a pen of gold !
Youle haue no bribes.
K.   None.
Oct.   Yet terme-time all the yeere !
A good ftrong law-fuite cannot now coft deere.
K.   Haue you done ?
Oct.   I'me at bribes, and wrangling done pre-
   fently.
Nar.   We muft all turne pettifoggers, and in ftead
of gilt rapiers, hang buckram bags at our girdles.
Iou.   All my clients, fhalbe women.
Spen.   Why ?
Iou.   Becaufe they are eafieft fetched ouer : there's
fomething to be gotten out of them.
Oct.   Thy monday's taske is done : whats next ?
Iou.   Sunday if the weeke goes backward.
King.   Tuefdayes wee'le fit to heare the poore-
   man's cryes,
Orphans and widowes : our owne princely eyes
Shall their petitions reade : our progreffe then
Shal be to hofpitalls which good minded men
Haue built to pious vfe, for lame, ficke, and poore
Weele fee whats giuen, what fpent, and what flowes
   or'e
Churles (with Gods mony) fhall not feaft, fwill wine,

And fat their rancke gutts whileſt poore wretches
    pine.
  Iou. This is a braue world for beggers, if it hold.
  Oct. Poore wretches pine, So are they left : tot'h
    next.
  Kin. Wedneſdaies weele ſpend—
  Iou. In fiſh dinners.
  Kin. In th' affaires
Of farren ſtates, treate with embaſſadors,
Heare them and giue them anſweres. Thurſday, for
    warres.
  Iou. That's well : better be together by th' eares,
then to goe halting to hoſpitalls.
  Kin. Our Neapolitane youths (that day) ſhall try
Their skill in armes, poore ſcorned Soldiers
Shall not be ſuffer'd beg here (as in ſome landes)
Nor ſtoope ſlaue-like to Captaines proud commands,
Starue, and lie naſtie, when the ſelfe-ſame pay,
The Souldier fights for, keepes the Leaders gay.
Nor ſhall he through ice and fire make gray his
    head,
Weare out new Moones, onely to earne his bread,
Wade vp to'th beard in torrents ; and be drownd
All ſaue the head ; march hard to meete a wound
I'th very face, and euen his heart-ſtrings cracke,
To win a towne, yet not to cloath his backe :
And the blacke ſtorme of troubles being gon,
Shund like a creditor, not looked vpon,
But as court-pallats (when bright day drawes nye)
Rold vp in ſome darke corner is throwne by.
Vncle write that.
  Oct. Faſt as my pen can trot.
  Spen. What a number of tottred roagues wilbe
turn'd into braue fellowes a this new change of the
moone.
  Iou. The brauer they are, the ſooner are mercers
vndon.
  Oct. Souldiers are downe too.
  Kin. Downe with Learning next.

For friday fhalbe fpent it'h reuerend Schooles,
Where weele fift branne from floure, (hiffe babling
     fooles,
But crowne the deepe-braind difputant) none fhall
     hold
Three or four Church-liuings (got by *Symonious*
     gold)
In them to fat himfelfe as in a ftye,
When greater Schollers languifh in beggery :
And in thin thred-bare caflacks weare out their age,
And bury their worth in fome by vicorage :
This weele fee mended.

Enter Iouenella.

Iou.   Tyth pigges youl'e fmoake for this.
Kin.   So fet it downe.
Oct.   Schollers languifh in beggery—So :
Thy fridaies law is writ ; for Satterday, what ?
King.   I mary fir, All our cares now for that.
Well to begin, and not end fo were bafe,
The winning of the gole crownes each mans race.

Narciffo ftepping in before in the Scene, Enters here.

Nar.   Sir, theres a ftranger newly ariu'de your
     court,
And much importunes to behold your Highnes.
Kin.   What is he ?
Nar.   Of goodly prefence.
Kin.   Let him fee vs.

Rufman brought in by all.

Ruff.   The powers that guide me, guard thee, I
     haue heard thy name
In regions far hence, where it does refound
Lowder than here at home ; to touch this ground
I ha paff'd through countries, into which none here

Would willingly faile I thinke, and with me bring,
My loue and feruice, which to your grace I tender.
    Kin.   What are you, and whence come you ?
    Ruff.   From *Heluetia.*
    Spen.   What hell fayes hee ?
    Iou.   Peace you fhall know hot hell time enough.
    Ruff.   I am an Heluetian borne, the houfe from
which I am defcended, ancient and well knowne to
many princes : Bohor is my name.
    Iou.   Zounds ! Bohor ! has ftruck two of my teeth
        out with hls name ;
    Ruff.   A Shalcan Tartar being my grandfather
Men call me *Shalkan Bohor.* About the world
My trauailes make a girdle (perfect round :)
So that, what wonders Kings on earth euer found
I know, and what I know, Is yours.
    K.   Braue Heluetian,
We giue you thankes and welcome : your arriuall
Is faire and to our wifh, of all thofe dayes.
Which Time fets downe, to number vp a weeke,
Euery day haue we tasked ; faue only one,
How in thefe courts of Kings (through which you
        haue gon,)
Doe Princes waft their howres ?
    Ruff.   How but in that,
For which they are borne Kings ? (Pleafure :) euery
        man's ayme,
Is to hit pleafure : onely tis changde in name,
Thats all the difference ; Are Kings Tirants ? Blood
Is then their pleafure : thirft they after warres !
Ambition tickles them : that for which man moft
        cares,
Good or bad, tis his pleafure, and to gaine it,
His foule muft compaffe it, tho hell reftraine it :
To this marke all mens thoughts, Creation drew,
That all might ftriue for a thing, thats got by fewe :
Who are thofe few but Kings ? and tis fit they
Should haue it, becaufe true pleafure does foone de-
        cay.

K.   How like you his counfell?
Omn.   Rarely.
Oct.   What ruffians this?
K.   Bohor tha'ft warm'd our yong blood; Al cares
    of ftate,
Shall that day fleepe, to our felfe weele Saterday
    haue,
Pleafure (the flaue of Kings fhall then be our flaue,
Lords let there be a proclamation drawne,
What man foeuer (ftrange or natiue borne,)
Can feaft our fpleene, and heigthen our delight,
He fhall haue gold and be our fauorite.
Tilts, turneys, mafques, playes, dauncing, drinking
    deepe
Tho ere noone all *Naples* lye dead-drunke a fleepe.
    Oct.   How King?
    Kin.   Weele haue it fo vncle.
    Omn.   Downe with that too.
    Iou.   Print Satterday in great text letters.
    Oct.   Well, well, it fhall.
Our fwan turnes crow, poifond with one drop of
    gall.
    Kin.   Ile haue this proclamation forthwith drawne.
    Nar.   And publifh al the daies.
    Prif.   And Satterday.
    Iou.   Efpecially that at large if you can in red, like
a Dominicall letter.
    Kin.   Goe fee it don.
    Iou.   My taske.   *Exit.*
    Kin.   Why figh you? Of fix dayes wo'd you not
fpare me one?
    Oct.   Thine owne lawes from thine owne mouth,
    weele proclaime,
If thine owne words thou e'atft, bee't thine owne
    fhame.

Enter Iouinelli haftily.

Iou.   Your long expected happines is arriu'd,

The princeffe of Calabria.

Kin. Thou crown'ft me agen :
Deere vncle, honored Lords, with our whole court
Honor her hither ; I am rapd with Ioy,
And loft till I behold her : fetch me my loue.

Oct. I feare deepe whirlepooles tho it run fmooth
aboue.

Ki. To our worthy friend your welcomes.

Exit Oct. & Aft.

Iou. But pray Sir tell vs, meane you that we
indeed

Shall haue but one playing day through the whole
weeke ?

Kin. All *Iouinelli,* weele be Iouiall all.

Brif. Till Satterday came, we liu'de in terrible
feare.

Thanke *Bohor,* who your dead fpirits vp did reare.

Kin. Had I (as firft I did begin) gon on,
I like a Schoole-boy fhould haue worne my crowne,
As if I had borrowed it.

Ruff. Had bin moft vile.

Kin. Ile be a Sea, (boundles.)

Spen. Thou art a funne,
And let no bafe cloudes muffle thee.

Kin. Braue Kings all !
Crowne, Scepter, Court, Cittie, Country, are at your
call.

Iou. There fpake young *Ioue* indeede.

Prif. The tyde now turnes.

Nar. And now weele fwim.

Kin. And laugh, tho the whole world mournes.

Florifh. Omn : Tantara, hey. Trumpets.

Erminghild *brought in.*

Enter Octavio *and* Aftolphe, *vfhering* Erminhild,
attended by Ladies and others.

Nar. Call vp your luftieft fpirits : the Lady's
come.

 K. O my earthly bliſſe ! embraces ! kiſſes ! how
  ſweete
Are you to parted Louers when they meete ?
That entertainement which the Duke your Father,
Lent royellie (late to mee,) I now can pay
At a Kings charge : to our *Neapolitane* Court,
None (brighteſt *Erminhild* can come longd for
More then your ſelfe.) You haue ſtolne vpon vs
  (Ladie)
 Erm. You haue good Law againſt me, (playing
  the thiefe)
Your Grace may keepe mee priſoner.
 K. In theſe Armes ;
From whence not *Ioue* ſhall raunſome thee ; We
  Twaine
Will wed, and bed, and get a Prince ſhall raigne
In *Naples* brauely, when wee both lye dead :
Till then, Pleaſures wings, to their full bredth be
  ſpread.   *Exeunt.*

Enter Scumbroth, *ringing a Bell* ; Alphege, *a Fryer*
& Shackle-ſoule, *in a Friers weede, with cloth to lay.*

 Scum. A mangier, a mangier, a mangier, I muſt
needs haue a mangie voice, when I doe nothing but
ball for a company of hungry Scabs ; a mangier.
 Alph. You muſt be nimble *Ruſh.*
 Sha. As a drawer in a new Tauern, firſt day the
buſh is hung vp.
 Scum. A mangier, a manger, a mangier. *Exit.*
 Alp. So : the Lord Priors napkin here, there the
Sub-priors : his knife and caſe of pick-toothes thus :
as for the couent, let them licke their fingers in ſtead
of wiping, and ſuck their teeth in ſteede of picking.
 Shac. What other dutie Sir, muſt I call mine ?
 Alp. As you are nouice, you are to ſay grace de-
murely, waite on the Priors Trencher ſoberly, ſteale
away a mouthfull cunningly, and munch it vp in a
corner hungerly. Ply your office, *Ruſh.* *Exit*

Shack. Thankes good Frier Alphege : yes, Shackle-
    foule will play
The taske hee's fet to : Diuels neuer idle lye :
Frier *Ruſh* ! ha, ha : y'haue now an excellent quire,
To fing in hell, the Diuell and the Frier.

*Enter Prior, Subprior, Alphege, Hillary, Ruſh,
    and other Friers. All ſit : diſhes brought in
    before.*

Pri. Where's *Ruſh,* our *Iunior Nouice* ?
Ru. Here Lord Prior.
Pri. Stand foorth, and render thankes.
Ru. Hum, hum :
For our bread, wine, ale and beere,
For the piping hot meates heere :
For brothes of fundrie taſts and fort,
For beefe, veale, mutton, lamb, and porke.
Greene-fawce with calfes head and bacon,
Pig and goofe, and cramd-vp capon.
For paſt raiz'd ſtiffe with curious art,
Pye, cuſtard, florentine and tart.
Bak'd rumpes, fried kidneys, and lam-ſtones,
Fat fweete-breads, lufcious maribones,
Artichoke, and oyſter-pyes,
Butterd Crab, prawnes, lobſters thighes,
Thankes be giuen for fleſh and fiſhes,
With this choice of tempting diſhes :
To which proface : with blythe lookes fit yee,
Ruſh bids this Couent, much good do't yee.
  Pri. How dar'ſt thou mock vs thou ill nurtur'd
flaue ?
  Sub. Contemn'ſt thou our order and religious
fare ?
  Shac. He has fpoken treafon to all our ſtomaches.
  Omn. Downe with the villaine.
  Sub. Mifchiefe on vs waites
If wee feede fo vile a wretch.
  Pri. Thruſt him out at gates.

Shac.   I doe coniure you by my hallowed beades
To heare me fpeake.
  Pri.   Canft thou excufe thy felfe ?
  Shac.   Alas (my Lord) I thought it had bin here
As in the neighbouring Churches, where the poor'ft
    Vicar
Is filled vp to the chin with choice of meates,
Yet feekes new wayes to whet dull appetite,
As there with holy fpels mens foules they cherifh,
So with delitious fare, they themfelues nourifh.
Nor want they argument for fweete belly-cheere
To proue it lawfull.
  Sub.   Moft prophane and fearefull.
  Shac.   But fince your order (pious and reuerend)
Tyed to religious fafts, fpends the fad day
Wholy in meager contemplation,
I abfolution beg on both my knees,
For what my tongue offended in : las ! poore *Rufh*
(See't by his cheekes) eates little : I can feede
On rootes, and drinke the water of the Spring
Out of mine owne cup : make an Anatomy
Of my moft finfull carcas : then pardon mee.
  Pri.   Thy ignorance is thy pardon, wee beleeue
    thee.
  Shac.   *Gratias reuerende domine Prior.*
  Pri.   But do our brethren in parts more remote,
Feede fo delitious faift thou?
  Shac.   *Rufh* cannot lye.
  Sub.   Thou falfely doeft accufe thofe holy men.
  Pri.   How can it ftand with their profeffion ?
  Sub.   Thou faift (vile yongman) they haue argu-
    ments
To proue it lawfull gluttonoufly to feede.
  Omn.   *Rufh,* anfwere the Sub-prior.
  Shac.   *Audite fratres,* they doe not onely proue it
lawfull, but make it palpable, that hee who eates not
good meate is damde.
  Sub.   *Benedicite.*
  Scu.   What fhall become of all vs then?

Pri. Thou art diſtracted, whence canſt thou force argument ?

Shac. From ſillie reaſon, would you heare me ſpeake ?

Pri. Speake freely and be bold, liſten.

Omn. Hum, hum, hum.

Shac. He that eats not good meate is dambd : *Sic Diſputo.*

If he that feedes well hath a good ſoule, then *è Contra.*

No, he that feedes ill, hath a bad and a poore ſoule.

Scu. Thats wee.

Shac. And ſo conſequently is dambd, for who regards poore ſoules ? and if they be not regarded they are caſt foorth, and if caſt foorth, then they are dambde.

Sub. I deny your minor, he that feedes well hath a good ſoule.

Shac. *Sic probo* : the ſoule followes the temperature of the body, hee that feedes well hath a good temperature of body, *Ergo,* he that feedes well hath a good ſoule.

Pri. A ful and edyfying argument.

Omn. Hum, hum, hum.

Sub. I deny that the ſoule followes the temperature of the body.

Shac. *Anima ſequitur temperaturam Corporib,* It is a principle, *&* *contra principia non eſt diſputandum.* All wee.

Pri. Its moſt apparent.

Scu. O moſt learned *Ruſh* !

Sub. A ſhallow Sophiſter, heare me farder.

Pri. Subprior, weele heare the reſt diſputed at our leiſure : you take too much vpon you.

Scu. Shall I take this vpon me my Lord ?

Pri. Hence with this traſh, we haue too long forborne to taſt heauens bleſſings fully, which to our dutie had more enabled vs, *Ruſh* thart ſome Angel.

Sub. Rather ſome diuell ſent to bewitch our ſoules.

Pri. Sub-prior no more.

Sub. I muſt ſpeake, heare me brethren,
Shall we (bound by ſolemne oathes) t' abiure the
　　world,
And all her ſorceries : to whom night and day
Are as one hower of prayer ? whoſe temperance makes
　　vs
Endure what ful-fild bellie Gods admire ;
Shall we (by zealous patrons) tyde to obſerue
Dirges and *Requiems* for their peacefull ſoules,
In glottonous riot bury ſacred almes ;
Turne Sanctimonious zeale and Charitie
To loathſome ſurfet ? and thoſe well-got goods
Our benefactors ſau'd, by their owne faſts
And moderate liuing, ſhall we feede vpon
Ful-gorging vs till we vomit ? fore-fend it heauen ?
By all the Saints, by him firſt taught our order
What temperance was, here ſhall poore *Clement* feede,
Till his ore-wearied life, takes her laſt leaue
Of this all tempting world where all ſinnes breede.

Pri. Howes this ? are you become our confeſſor ?
Beſt thruſt vs out at gates, locke vp the Cloiſter,
And cal in whom you like : be you the Prior.
Speake are you agreed, *Ruſh* be our maiſter-cooke ?

Scu. You haue my voice.

Alp. And mine.

Pri. Doe you all conſent ?

Omn. Yes, all.

Sub. Firſt ſend this fiend to baniſhment.

Pri. We haue moſt voices on our ſide.

Sub. You may ;
Las ! moſt men couet ſtill the broadeſt way.

Pri. Giue *Ruſh* his charge then, *Scumb* : you muſt
　　reſigne.

Scu. With a good maw, I ſhal haue a fatter office
to be his ſcullion.

Shac. Worthy Lord Prior, heare me yet,
I muſt not my profeſſion let,
To *Scumbroath,* what I know ile teach,

To make caudels, Iellies, leach,
Sirrup of violets, and of rofes,
Cowflip fallads, and kick chofes,
Preferue the apricock, and cherry,
Damfin peare-plom, rafpis berry;
Potates ike if you fhall lack,
To corroborate the back:
A hundred more fhall *Ruſh* deuice,
And yet to early mattins rife,
Our ladies office, fing at prime,
At euen-fong, and at compline time.
Chant Anthems, Aniuerfaries, Dirges,
And the dolefull *de profundis.*
    Pri. Thou fhalt not change thy order: Sirra,
      cooke,
From *Ruſh* take leffons againſt night, for fare
Abundance and delitious.
    Scu. I fhall be greedy to learne of him fir, fince
your lordfhip is turnde, our very Iack and his fpits
fhall turne too.   *Exit.*

Enter 2. Pilgrimes.

    Pri. What men are thefe?
    Sub. Welcome good holy father.
    Both. Thankes reuerend maifter.
    1. *Pil.* Bleft fir, according to the Churches rite
We (Pilgrimes, to Ierufalem bound) this night
Defire repofe, and pious charitie
In your moft holy Couent.
    Pri. You are moft welcome.
Alphege, goe lead 'em in.
    Shac: By no meanes.
    Pri. Why.
    Shac. Tis mortall fin.
    Sub. O black impietie!
    Pri: How? fin to feed religious votaries!
    Shac: Rather to nourifh idle vagabonds: ·
The Cleargy of other lands, haue with much pietie

And thrift deftroyde thofe drones, that lazily
Liue eating vp the labours of the bee.
A churchman there cares but to feede the foule,
He makes that charge his office.   Alfmifdeeds ! alas !
They through the Lawyers hands are fitt'ft to paffe.
   Sub.   Can you heare this Diuell ?
   Shac.   Befides my reuerend Lord,
Thefe manderers here as fpies, and foone beare word
To Princes eares of what they heare and fee.
   Pri.   Ha *Rufh* ! thou fpeak'ft right.
   Sub.   Dambd iniquitie !
   Pri.   Hence with thofe runnagates.
   Omn.   Come, hence.
   Pri.   Spurne 'em away.
   Sub.   Oh had mine eyes drop'd out cre feene this
     day.
Stay comfortles poore foules, my pittying teares
Shall fpeake what my tongue dares not, here holy men,
You nere fhall fay when next we meete againe,
Frier *Clement* to the hungrie grutch'd his meate,
Or to the weary pilgrim lodging, this makes you eate,
And when you haue relieu'd your fainting limbes,
Commend   me   in   your   prayers,   and   midft   your
     hymmes
Thus wifh, that he who did your Iorney furder,
May neuer liue, to breake his holy order.
   Pri.   Old fuperftitious dotard ; beate hence thefe
     beggers.
   1. *Pil.*   Many old mans curfes will on his foule be
     fpent,
Who thus defaces, Charities monument :   *Exeunt.*
   Shac.   I told you they were curs, that ceafe to
barke, no longer then you feede them.
   Pri.   Frier, thou fpeak'ft right :
Make haft with fare delitious, weele crowne the night.

Exeunt.   Manet Shackle-foule.

   Shac.   Ha ha, laugh Lucifer, dance grim fiends of
     hell,

Of foules thou iudge iuft, but moft terrible,
I muft exact a double pay from thee,
Nere hadft thou Iorney man deferude fuch fee,
Let me caft vp my reckonings, what I ha won
In this firft voiage : Charity ! fhees vndon :
Fat gluttony broke her back : next her ftep'd in
Contention (who fhakes Churches) now the fweete fin
(Sallow lechery,) fhould march after : Auarice,
Murder, and all finnes els, hell can deuice,
Ile broach : the head's in, draw the body after,
Begin thy feaft in full cuppes, end in flaughter.
That damnedft fury : oh, but Frier *Clement's* free !
True : ha'ft no fnare t' intrap him ? let me fee.
Hees old, choake him with gold ; hold on thy
     Reuells,
Pluto makes Shackle-foule prefident of Diuels.   *Exit.*

          Enter K. Octauio, Narciffo, Iouinelli, Spendola.

     K.   What pictar's that (Vncle *Octauio* ?)
     Oct.   The picture of thy ftate, (drawne by thy
          felfe,)
This is that booke of ftatutes, were enacted
In the high Parliament of thy roiall thoughts
Where wifedome was the fpeaker.   And becaufe
Thy fubiects fhall not be abufde by lawes
Wrap'd vp in caracters, crabbed and vnknowne,
Thefe thine owne language fpeake.
     K.   Hang 'em vp vncle.
     Oct.   What fayes the King ?
     Iou.   You muft hang vp the lawes.
     Oct.   Like cob-webbe in fowle roomes, through
          which great flies
Breake through, the leffe being caught bith wing,
     there dies.
No no, thy lawes ile fix full in thy fight,
                    Hangs a table vp.
(Like fea-markes,) that if this great fhip of fway
And kingly ventures, loofe her conftant way.

I'th bottomles gulph of ſtate, (beaten by the ſtormes
Of youthfull follie, raging in monſtrous formes)
Shee may be ſau'de from ſinking and from wrack,
(Steerd by this compaſſe, for the points of it
Shall guide her ſo, on rockes ſhe cannot ſplit.

   Kin.   You are our carefull pilat.   In this voiage
Of Gouernment, be you our Admirall.
Wiſedome and Age being props, realmes ſeldome fall.

Enter Briſco.

   Oct.   Oraculous is thy voice.
   Kin.   How now count *Briſco* ?
Me thinkes I read a comedy in thy lookes.
   Nar.   Has met ſome merry painter, hees drawne
     ſo liuely.
   Omn.   Come count your newes.
   Brif.   I ſhall beſtow them freely :
The phyſicke of your proclamation workes :
Your guilded pills (roll'd vp in promiſes
Of princely fauours to his wit, who higheſt
Can raiſe your pleaſures) ſlip ſo ſmoothly downe
Your Subieċts throates, that all (vpon a ſudden)
Are looſely giuen.
   Kin.   How ? looſely giuen ? why count ?
   Br.   Name but what ſport, your Highnes would
     haue Aċted
I'me prologue toot; your court muſt haue more gates
To let in ruſling Saterday : without (now) waites
Muſicke in ſome ten languages : each one ſweares
(By *Orpheus* fiddle-caſe) they will tickle your eares
If they can doo't with ſcraping.
   Bri.   Theres ſeuen ſcore Noiſe at leaſt of engliſh
fidlers.
   Io.   7. ſcore ! they are able to eate vp a citie in
very ſcraps.
   Bri.   Very baſe-viall men moſt of 'em : beſides
whole ſwarmes of welſh harpes, Iriſh bag-pipes, Iewes
trompes, and french kitts.

All thefe made I together play :
But their dambd catter-wralling, frighted me away.
    Oct.   Thefe fports to pleafe
A Princes eyes ?
    Bri.   How like you then of thefe ?
The cittie-waterbearers (trimly dight)
With yellow oaker-tankerds (pind vpright)
Like brooches in their hatts ; In their frefh loues
A may-game bring, All, wearing dog-skin gloues.
Made not to fhrinke it'h wetting.
    Kin.   Bid thefe poore men drinke well, and fo be
      gon.
    Bri.   What will you haue then ?
Will you fee the Turners fhew, brauely preparde
With colours, drumes, and gunnes (with ruft halfe
      mar'de
Bearing that, of which they long haue bin depriu'de.
    Kin.   What ift ?
    Bri.   Their daring Giant, (newly reui'de)
    Omn.   For *Ioues* fake lets fee that.
    Oct.   O fie (Prince) fie !
In thy court painted monfters, they come not here,
Ride forth, thou fhalt meete Giants euery where.
Me thinkes (yong Lords) your foules being new re-
      finde
With beames of honor, fhould not be declin'de
To fports fo low and vulgar : but fince the King
Of birdes (the Eagle) letts you fpred a wing
So neere his owne, you fhould put vp fuch game
As fits an Eagle, and purfue the fame.
And not like rauens, kites, or painted Iayes
Soare high, yet light on dunghills, for ftinking preyes.
    Iou.   Old Lord you raue.
    Nar.   What fports wood you deuife ?
    Oct.   Moft fit for Kings.   Were I (before his eyes)
To prefent obiects, they fhould all be rare,
Of Romane triumps, laden w'th the fpoiles of warre :
Or Lions, and wilde-Boares kill'd by actiue force :
Or fea-fights : or land-battailes on foote, or horfe :
    s   u

Such fights as thefe, kindle in Kings braue fire,
And meeting fpirits that dare mount, mount 'em
    higher,
Where apifh paftimes lay our foules downe flat,
Groueling on earth, bafe and effemminate.
    Bri.   I haue bowles of this bias too, for your
      Lordfhips alley.
    King.   Trundle 'em out before him.
    Bri.   The wodden-leg Souldier,
Waites to prefent you with his fhow of warre.
    Oct.   I mary my liege.
    Bri.   The Scholler has his deuice, the Mariner his.
    Oct.   Thefe are Kings fports indeed.
    Bri.   Will you fee thefe ?
    Kin.   Faith be it fo ; becaufe weele now rather
      pleafe
Our vncle than our felfe, pray fetch in thefe.
The reft cafhere.
    Spen.   Send the fidlers merily home.
    Bri.   And yet pa 'em fcuruily ! tis impoffible.
    Iou.   And bid the water-bearers clenfe the citie
Ther's many a foule thing in it.
    Oct.   Marfhall 'em in.
    Bri.   Ile fetch thefe worthy fpirits in my felfe.
No, no, weele ayde you fir.
    Iou.   March : and giue vs roome.   *Exeunt.*
    Ki.   Sdeath ! if thefe doting gray-beards might
      haue their wills,
We neuer fhall haue ours : let vs croffe them
As they croffe vs.
    Omn.   How, how !
    Kin.   Euery deuice
Their Ningles bring in, abufe with fcuruie ieft,
Beet nee're fo good.
    Omn.   Agreed.
    Nar : If *Ninies* bring away the Neft.
    Ki.   Teach *Iouinelli* and *Brifco* when to giue fire.
Dromes and trompets founding.

Enter Octauio, Iouinelli, Brifco, Rufman, the Souldier,
Scholler, Mariner.

Sol. I am a Souldier.
Iou : We know that by your legges.
Sol. Does my ſtump grieue you ?
Bri. Not if you beſtir your ſtumps nimbly ſir.
Nar. What hot ſhot's this ?
Sol. A Souldier ſir : thats all :
Thats more than ſir I thinke you dare be.   Zounds !
baffuld for my limbes loſt in ſeruice ! your noble
     father
Has clapd this buff-ierkin, when this Stump of wood
Has vp tot'h knee ſtucke three howres in french blood :
When ſuch as you, with your Spangled roſes, that day
Brauely beſtird their heeles, and ran away :
Ile ſtand toot, I.
Spen. With one leg.
Sol : Yes : with one.
Oct. Yong Lords, thus to ſcorne Souldiers, tis ill
     don.
Kin. Vncle, heres no man ſcornes 'em ; muſt we
     be brau'de
By a ſtaring fellow, for a little fighting ? goe.
Sol. Fighting ! I cannot halt I, but ſpeake plaine,
No King on earth baffalls me, ide baffall againe,
Th' whole race of great turkes, had iẹm ith field : I ha
     brought
With me a hundred Souldiers, (old Seruitors)
Poore as my ſelfe in clothes ; picke out fiue hundred
Of ſuch ſilke-ſtocken men, if they beate vs, hang vs,
S'bloud if we toſſe not them, hang's agen : a fort
We ha built without, and mand it, this was the ſport
A Souldier wood ha giuen thee : my one hundred
Had taught thee all the rules i'th Schoole of warre.
Kin. All this ile read without mayme, wound or
     ſcarre.
Sold. What ſay you to an Engine, that at once
Shall ſpoile ſome thirtie men ?

Iou.   Thirtie men : nothing.

Sold.   If nothing ! haſt thou bin beate for this ?
    farewell.

Iou.   I can fetch twenty ſcriueners haue don more
With a bare goofe-quill.

Sold.   Maiſt thou but liue, to need a Souldiers
    arme,
That laught to fee him bleed.   *Exit.*

Bri.   You haue loſt the day ſir, for your Souldiers
    fly.

Kin.   Fly to the diuell let 'em.

Iou.   Your leaders before.

Spen.   You fight all vnder one cullors ? doe you
    not ?

Scho.   Sir :
Thefe pleaſures to the King which I prefer,
Flow from *Ioues* braine.

Nar.   Heyda ! heres one has beaten out *Ioues*
    braines.

Spen.   Wud I had thee hung vp at our maine kit.

Sch :   No Sir *Ioues* braine, (*Minerua* queene of
    wit)
If all the *Muſes* and the Arts can fit
With their high Tunes, ſuch choice and Princely eares,
Apollo (Father to them all)—appeares——

Iou.   *Apollo* was an Affe ; he let a wench whom he
lou'de to be turnd into a Bay-tree, and now ſhees glad
for a peny to ſtick Ale-houfe-windowes, and wynde
dead coarſes.

Bri.   Let *Apollo* goe and lye with his owne
Daughters.

K.   Are you a Scholler Syr ?

Iou.   A fchool-maſter as I take it, and comes to
prefent a verie prettie fhow of his fchollers in broken
Latin.

Oct.   Can wee be dumb and fee this ?

Sch.   O haples Learning !
Flie and complaine, to Heauen (where thou wert
    borne)

That thou (whome Kings once nurſde,) art now their
　ſcorne.　　　　　　　　　　　　　　　　　*Exit.*
　Nar.　How blowes the winde Syr ?
　Scaf.　Wynde ! is *Nore-Nore-West.*
　Nar.　To hoyſe your ſayles vp too, I thinke tis
　beſt.
　Sea.　A blacke Guſt is comming : vp a-low-there
hey : A young-man vp toth Top-maſt-head, and looke-
out : ſtand to your Sayles : ſtand to your Top-ſailes :
let goe your Harriars, let goe, amaine louere amaine,
quicke, quick, Good fellowes.
　Omn.　Hees mad.
　Sea.　Whoes at Helme ? beare vp hard : and hard
vp : and thou beeſt a man beare vp ; Star-borde, Port-
agein : off with your Drablers, and your Banners ;
out with your Courſes : Ho,—I ſpie two Shippes
yonder, that yaw too and agen, they haue both ſprung
a Leake, I thinke the Diuell is ſucking Tabaccho,
heeres ſuch a Miſt : out with your boate, and you
Besmen, cut-downe Maſte-bith borde ; beare vp,
Ime a Blunt-fellow you ſee, All I ſay is this,
You that ſcorne Sea-men, ſhall a Sea-man miſſe. *Exit.*
　Oct.　Now by my life I haue patient ſtood too long.
To ſee rich merit and loue, payde with baſe wrong :
Learning ! and Armes ! and Traffique ! the triple wall
That fortifies a Kingdome, race em downe All !
This Seaman, (hee that deareſt earnes his bread)
Had rigd and mann'd 4. Gallies brauely furniſht,
With Souldiers, Rowers, and Fire-workes for a Sea-
　fight.
　K.　You are full of Squibs too, pray goe fire em all.
　Oct.　Muſt I bee then caſhierde too ? mary and
　ſhall.
To ſaue thy ſinking Honour, Ile ſend hence
Theſe men with thankes, with praiſe, and recompence.
　　　　　　　　　　　　　　　　　　　　Exit.
　Omn.　Pray doe.
　K :　Braue *Shalcan-Bohor*, all this while
Our eye has followed yours, and ſeene it ſmile,

(As twere in fcorne) of what thefe men could doe,
Which made vs flight them off ; to ingroffe you
(Our beft and richeft prize :) ith Courts of Kings
Through which you ha paffd, you ha feene wonders,
    fhew em.
   Ruff. I fhall at opportune howers. If your Grace
Arride the toyes, they bragd of (Fire-workes,
And fuch light ftuffes) Sit fearelefse without danger
Of murdring fhot, which villaines might difcharge
In (idle counterfet Sea-fights) you fhall fee
At opening of this hand, a thoufand Balles
Of wilde-Fire, flying round about the Aire—there.

Fire-workes on Lines.

  Omn. Rare, Rare.
  K. Tis excellent, Sdeath from whence flew they ?
  Bri. Hell, I thinke.
  Iou. Hell ! Nay, if any that are in Hell, skip vp
euer fo nye Heauen, as thefe Diuells that fpit fire did,
Ile drinke nothing but Gun-pouder.
  Ruff. Ha, ha, a trifle this. Your Scholler there,
Come with his Arts and Mufes fhallow, leaden braine,
Your fwaggering Souldier, lead a tottered traine
Of ruffianly Boore-hallers : I noted all
Thefe feafts for Kings : ith garden of varietie
The vaft world ! you are ftaru'de midft your fatietie,
Plucke no one Apple from the golden Tree,
But fhake the fruite of euery pleafure downe.
  K. Thanks *Bohor* ; why elfe weares a King his
    Crowne ?
Shalcan, all *Naples* fhall not buy thee from mee.
  Ruff. Nor you and thefe from me.
  K. Aske what thou wilt haue
But to ftay here.
  Ruff. Loe, this is all I craue.
  K. Thou haft our faft embraces.
  Ruff. Swift as mans thought,
Various delights fhall bee each minute borne,

And dye as faſt that freſh may riſe ; we ſcorne
To ſerue vp one diſh twice ; bee't nere ſo rare,
Will you that gainſt to morrow I prepare
A Feaſt of ſtrange Mirth for you ?
    K.   Deare *Bohor* doe.
    Ruff.   I ſhall ; Nor doe I thus your loue purſue,
With ſeruile hopes of Golde, I neede it not :
If out the jawes of Hell Golde may bee got
Blacke Artes are mine to doo't ; and what delights
Thoſe worke bee yours.
    K.   Thou art gratious in our ſight.   *Exeunt.*

¶ *A Table is ſet out by young fellowes like Merchants*
    men, Bookes of Accounts vpon it, ſmall Deskes to
    write vpon, they ſit downe to write Tickets, Lurchall
    with them.

    1.   Come fellow *Lurchall* write.
    Lur.   Fuh, Stay not for mee,
I ſhall out-goe you all.
    2.   I hold 5. Crownes,
We all leaue you behinde vs.
    Lur.   Don ; but I
Muſt not leaue you behinde mee ; what paines a poore
      Diuell
Takes to get into a Merchant ? hees ſo ciuill,
One of Hell muſt not know him, with more eaſe
A Diuell may win ten Gallants, then one of theſe,
Yet a Merchants wife, before theſe ten is wonne
To entertaine her Diuell, if Pride be one.
But *Lurchall,* now tha'rt in, and for yeares bound,
To play the Merchant, play him right : th'aſt found
A Maſter, who more villenie has by hart,
Then thou by rote ; See him but play his owne part,
And thou doeſt Hell good ſeruice ; *Barteruile,*
Theres in thy name a Harueſt makes mee ſmile.
    Bart.   *Lurchall* :—within.
    Omn.   My maſter calls.
    Lur.   I.

Enter Barteruile.
Men too and fro bring in Bags, & haue Bills.   Exit.

Bart :   Oh, art there ?
This day twixt one and two a Gallants bound
To pay 400. Crownes to free his Landes
Faſt morgag'de to mee, *Lurchall,* get thee vp hye
Into my Turret, where thou mayeſt eſpie
All commers euery way ; if by thy gueſſe,
Thou feeſt the Gull make hither.
   Lur.   So Syr.
   Bart.   That, his Hower
Lye gaſping, at the laſt Minutes ; let him beate at
      dore,
Within lle beate his heart out.
   Lur.   Ile let him ſtand.
   Bart.   Do, take my *Watch,* go faſter. All his Land
Is ſumd with theſe two Figures, (2. and 1.)
At paſt one, (his,) ſtrike but two, tis mine owne.
   Lur.   Ile turne the wheeles : and ſpin the howers
      vp faſter.
   Bart.   The Citie-clockes then ſtrike, and kill thy
      Maſter.
Would all the Citie Sextons, at my coſt
Were drunke this day 4 howres.
   Lur : Troth ſo wud I,
And wee their Iackes ath Clocke-houſe.
   Bar.   Wee'de ſtrike merily.
Fly vp to'th top ath houſe,
   Lur. There ſir, Ile ſit,
And croake like a Rauen, to damb thee in hels pit.
                                             Exit.

Barteruile ſet amongſt his men reading a long ſcroll.

Bar.   How goes this moneth ?
Omn.   Much ſhorter than the laſt.
Bar.   Weddings this moneth 12. thouſand : not
   worth the ſcoring,

But thinke ther's little marying, we ha fo much
   whoring.
Grynding milles fo much vfde ; about the citie
Such grinding, yet no more mony ; fuites in law,
Full brought to an end this moneth, no more but
   ten :
This law will begger vs : had I the bags againe,
I bought this combrous office with, the King
Should make his beft of't : hee that did farm't before
Had it for leffe than I, yet receiude more.
How much remaines of the falt tribute due ?
   1. Scr. 7000. Crownes.
   Bar. Thats well : a fauorie fumme :
Thefe our Italian tributes, were well deuifde,
Me thinkes tis fit a fubiect fhould not eate
But that his Prince from euery difh of meate
Should receiue nourifhment : for (being the head)
Why fhould he pine, when all the body is fed ?
Befides, it makes vs more to awe a King,
When at each bit we are forc'd to thinke on him.

Enter a Brauo with mony.

   1. Scr. What payment's this ?
   Bra. The penfion of the Stewes, you neede not
vntye it, I brought it but now from the fealers office :
ther's not a peece there, but has a hole in't, becaufe
men may knowe where twas had, and where it will be
taken againe : bleffe your worfhip ? Stew-mony fir,
Stew-Prune cafh fir.
   Bar. They are fure, tho not the foundeft pay-
   maifters,
Read whats the fumme.
   1. Scr. But bare 200. crownes.
   Bra. They are bare crownes indeede fir, and they
came from Animals and vermin that are more bare :
wee that are clarkes of thefe flefh-markets haue a great
deale of rotten mutton lying vpon our hands, and
finde this to bee a fore payment.

Bar.   Well, well, the world will mend.

Bra.   So our furgeons tell 'em euery day; but the
pox of mendment I fee.

Bar.   Doe not your gallants come off roundly
then ?

Bra.   Yes fir, their haire comes off faft enough, we
turne away crack't french crownes euery day.   I haue
a fuite to your worfhip in behalfe of all our dealers
in fmall wares, our free-whores fir, you know my meaning.

Bar.   If your whores are knowne, whats thy
fuite ?

Bra.   I fhould haue brought a petition from 'em,
but that tis put off fir, till clenfing-weeke, that they
may all be able to fet to their hands, or elfe a whores
marke.

Bar.   Well, well, whats their requeft ?

Bra.   Marry fir, that all the fhee-tobacco-fhops,
that creepe vp daily in euery hole about the Citie,
may bee put to filence.

Bar.   Why pray thee honeft fellow ?

Bra.   I thanke your good worfhip, I had not fuch
a fweete bit giuen me this 7 yeeres, honeft fellow ;
marry fir Ile open to you your fuppliants cafes :   they
that had wont to fpend a crowne about a fmocke, haue
now their delight dog-cheape, but for fpending one
quarter of that mony in fmoake : befides fir, they are not
contented to robbe vs of our cuftomes only, but wnen
their pipes are fowle with fpitting and driueling in
thofe forefaide fhops, they haue no place to burne
'em in, but our houfes.

Bar.   Draw their petition, and weele fee all
cur'de.

Bra. Let a froft come firft fir : I thanke your venerable worfhip ; the pox gnaw out fo many fmall guts
as haue payde thee crownes.   *Exit.*

Enter Lurchall running.

Lur.   The tyd's againft you fir, the crownes are
come.

Bar. How goes my watch ?

Lur. As moſt watches vſe to goe ſir, ſleepily, heauily.

Bar. Not reach'd to one yet ; wert thou to be hangd,
The hower had gallop'd.

Lur. I ſpurd it all that I could.

Bar. S'death keep his howre, heauen helpe poore Citizens,
If Gentlemen grow thus warie : let him in.

Exit Lurchall.

Barren now, that haſt in craft ſo fruitfull bin.
Your buſineſſe ſir to me.

Enter with 2. Gentlemen.

1. *Gent.* Doe you not know me ſir ?

Bar. No in good truth ſir.

1. *Gent.* To know you I am bold ſir,
You haue lands of mine in morgage, this is my day,
And heres your crownes.

Bar. Signior *Innocentio* ;
My memorie had quite loſt you, pray ſit both,
A bowle of wine here.

1. *Gent.* Sir it ſhall not neede :
Pleaſe you to fetch my euidence, whil'ſt we tell.

Bar. What needes this forward ſpring ? faith two moneths hence
Had bin to me as welcome.

1. *Gent.* Sir I thanke you.

2. *Gent.* Your hower drawes on Signior *Inno-centio,*

Bar. Goe beate a drumme ith garret, that no tongues
Of clockes be heard but mine.

Lur. Little paſt one.

Bar. Winde, winde.

Lur. Thus wind'ſt thou to damnation.

2. *Gent.*   Ile part with none fir, pardon me, till I
    fee
Your writings : will you fetch the euidence fir.
    Bar.   What euidence fir, haue I of yours ?
    1. *Gent.*   My friend fir,-whofe mony hee lends me
to redeeme my morgage.
    Bar.   Which you would haue for your fecuritie.
    2. *Gent.*   Tis fo fir?
    Bar.   No fir *Innocentio,*
To morrow on your bare word will I lend you 30.
crownes more : I loue you fir, and wifh you beware
whofe hands you fall into : the worlds a ferpent.
    2. *Gent.*   This does but fpend the hower fir, will
you take your mony ?
    Bar.   With all my heart.
    1. *Gent.*   Let me fee my writings then.
    Bar.   Haue you fuch couenant from mee ?   I re-
member none.
    1. *Gent.*   Your confcience is fufficient couenant fir.
    Bar.   Ha ! whats that confcience ?   I know no
    law-termes I,
Talke to me as to Citizen.
    2. *Gent.*   Weele dally no longer;
We knew what fnake would fting vs, and therefore
    brought
Our medicine gainft his venome : youle keepe the
    writings,
And weele ith Court of confcience tender your
    crownes,
Whither this writ does fummon you.
    Lur.   A fox, and ore-taken ?
    Bar.   Serue writs vpon me, yet keepe my mony
    too ?
Dull flaue haft thou no braine ?
    Lur.   Braine ! trye this.
    Bar.   Peace.
    2. *Gent.*   Will you as fits a Chriftian giue vs in
What is our right, and take your crownes fir yet ?

Bar. Tis good to try mens patience, fetch me
    downe *Exit Lur.*
Thofe writings on my pillow, there they ha flept
Thefe two howers for you: muft not friends ieft?
    ha !
Both. Yes fir: let your men tell, iuft 400.
    crownes.
Bar. Befides the vfe.
1. *Gent.* The vfe is there too.
Bar. Hold:
Ile take it without telling, put it vp.
Both. Not till we fee the writings.

Enter Lurchall.

Bar. Dare you touch it ?
Both. Dare ! yes fir, and dare ftab him to the
    heart,
Offers to take it from vs :
Bar. Who ftabs firft? *Flings mony amongft it.*
Now touch it if you dare : ther's gold of mine,
And if they lay one finger on't, cry theeues,
They come to rob me, touch it if you dare :
    1. *Gen.* Dambde wretch, thou wilt goe quicke to
    hell I feare.
Bar. No fir, the diuell fhall fetch me when I goe.
Lur. That all my errand.
2. *Gent.* We are cheated both.
Bar. Proceede, in your chancery fuite, I haue be-
    gun your bill.
Humbly complayning.
    1. *Gent.* Of thee villaine Ile complaine
That fels thy foule for mony, diuels on earth dwell,
And men are no where, all this world is hell.
    Exeunt.
Bar. I kiffe thy forhead, my wittie *Oedipus*
That canft vnfold fuch riddels :

One ringes. Exit. 1. *Seruant.*

Lur. Sir, I am bound

To doe you all feruice, till I you all confound.

    1. *Ser.* Maifter Siluerpen the procter fir, fends word, if you come not in to morrow and perfonally depofe your payment of the 200. crownes, youle be non-fuited.

    Bar. That is a law-draught goes downe coldly.

    Lur. Why fir? Tis but your fwearing the mony is payde.

    Bar. If oathes had back-dores to come in at, without danger of damnation, to catch a mans foule bith back, fwearing were braue.

    1. *Ser.* What anfwere fhall I giue the Proctors man?

    Lur. Tell him my maifter fhall come in and fweare.

Exit and Enters.

    Bar. Doe, tell him: on thee Ile build: now all my feare
Is for apparance at the Chancellors Court.
No trick to faue that?

    Lur. I haue a braue one fort.

Exit. 1. *for wine : bring't in.*

Bring in a pottle of wine : will Carlo here my fellow,
Depofe a truth if he fee it, to helpe his maifter?

    Bar. What thou not honeft Carlo?

    2. *Ser.* Yes fir.

    1. *Ser.* Here's the wine.   *Enter with wine.*

    Lur. Set this to your head anon fir, when tis there
Away you, and to morrow thou mai'ft fweare
Before the Chancelor, and fweare true, if hee
Were in that cafe thou leftft him, twere in vaine
To hope he could liue, till thou camft back againe.

    Bar. All Knights a'th Poft learne this trick : the fits vpon me now.

Lur.   Take a good draught, twill helpe you fir : It
   gulpes,
Hees almoft breathles Carolo, away.
   Car.   I am gon.   *Exit.*
   Lur.   Hees gon, hees gon fir.
   Bar.   One gulpe more had choaked me ;
This wine had wafhed my feares off, th'aft giuen mee
   power
To make me doate vpon thee.   Carolos gon.
   Lur.   Yes and will fweare his heart out, to your
   good.
Sweare let him ; bee thy felfe and hee dambde too.
   Bar.   So I may get by it.   In my bofome fleepe
(My doue, my loue,) profper but thou and I.
   Lur.   And let all els finck.
   Bvr.   Let 'em : fo I kiffe gold,
The yongmans whore, the faint of him thats old.
                              Exeunt.

*Enter Prior, Alphege, Hillary, and Friers with
   pruning kniues, fpades, &c., met by Subprior,
   and Shackle-foule.*

   Sub.   Whither (mad-men) run you ?
   Omn.   To our Vines.
   Sub.   Your Vines ?
(The tree of fin and fhame ?) this Serpent here,
Has with that liquorifh poifon, fo fet on fire,
The braines of *Nicodeme* and *Siluefter*,
That they in drunken rage haue ftabd each other.
   Pri.   Stabd !
   Shac.   Yes, they bleede a little, but haue no
   harme,
Their yong blood with the grapes Iuice being made
   warme,
They brawld and ftruck, but I kept off the blowes,
Yet the Subprior faies from me their quarrell rofe.
   Sub.   It did.
   Shac.   In very deede (for I not fweare)

It did not fir : to me you malice beare,
As if that all fuch mifchife don, were mine,
But caufe your felfe fhall fee how I repine
To fee vice profper, pardon me good Lord Prior,
If I a tell-tale be of what mine eyes
Beheld with water in them : fin will rife
In holy fircles I fee fometimes.
    Pri.   What fin ?
    Sub.   What haft thou feene ?
    Shac.   Wud prefent I had not beene,
But till I had vtter it, my clogd confcience beares
A man vpon a woman.
    Omn.   Ha !
    Shac.   I fpeak't in teares :
Scumbroth our cooke, and a female I beheld
Kiffing in our orchard : on her lippes he dwelld
I thinke fome halfe howre.
    Sub.   Shame to our reuerend order !
A woman in our couent !   Sin black as murder.
    Pri.   Our   cooke   fhalbe   feuerely   punifhed :   a
       woman,
A tempter here.
    Omn.   Abhominable !
Rufh, thoul't rebuke fin.
    Shac.   Though my Lord I'me bad, I'me not giuen
       that way.
    Pri.   Let vs fome plagues inuent to lay on this
       lecherous knaue.
    Shac.   Some light punifhment
(Good my Lord Prior) fuppofe twere your owne fault,
Whip as you would be whipd, the beft's naught.
    Sub.   He fhalbe punifht, and then loofe his place.
    Pri.   That fir fhall be as we will : to our Vines :
       away.
    Sub.   For fhame giue or'e, dare you prophane this
       day
That is to holy vfes confecrate ?
    Pri.   Why ? what day is this ?
    Omn.   Lambert the marter.

Pri.   No matter,
To vex thee deeper, this whole day weele fpend,
Onely about our Vines.
  Sub.   You vex not me,
But heauen : what warrants you to this ?
  Pri.   Our will.
  Sub.   Thou haft thy will, thy wifh thou ne're fhalt
    haue,
In fight of heauen who fees and punifhes
Mens blacke impieties ; And in fight of thefe
(Sharers in thy full fin :) And in his fight,
T' expreffe whofe vilenes, there's no epithite.
  Pri.   No matter what he faics Rufh.
  Shac.   I'me knowne what I am.
  Sub.   To thee I prophecie, (vitious old man to
    thee,
Who er'ft with lift-vp-hands, and downe-bowed knee,
Seemeft to' haue had worke in heauen : now (full of
    fpite,
Onely to eate a liquorifh appetite ;
Digft our religious wales vp, planting there
Luxurious fruits to pamper belly-cheere :
(For all thy paines to dreffe it,) of this Vine
Thy luftfull lips fhall neuer taft the wine.
  Pri.   Diftracted foole, in ftead of my iuft anger,
Thou onely haft my pittie : thou prophecie ?
  Omn.   Ha, ha.
  Sub.   Laugh on, but fince nor prayers preuaile nor
    teares,
Ile powre my griefe into my Princes eares.   *Exit.*
  Shac.   Heele goe and complaine to the King.
  Pri.   Let him complaine,
Kings cannot Subiects of their foode reftraine.
Away.

Exeunt : Manet Shackle-foule.

  Shac.   Ingender fin with fin ; that wines rich
    heate

3

May bring forth Luſt, Luſt murder may beget,
But here ſtrike ſaile, this barke awhile hale in,
And lanch into the deepe, a brighter ſin :
Ho, *Glitterbacke*, aſcend, to ſhackle-ſoule,
To ſhackle-ſoule aſcend, ho *Glitterbacke*;
Thou richeſt ſpirit, thruſt vp thy golden head
From hell thus hie : when ? art impriſoned
In miſers cheſts ſo faſt thou canſt not come ?
Or fearſt thou theeues, or cutpurſes ? here be
    ſome
Can ſaue thee from their fingers : when ? Ariſe ;
And dazle th' approching night with thy gliſtring
    eyes.
    Glitt. Here.

A golden Head aſcends.

    Shac. How thou ſweatſt with comming ? Saue me
    thoſe drops
(Golds pure *Elixar*) ſtilling from thy lockes :
Shake from thy browes and hayre that golden
    ſhowre,
So : get home : quicke : (to hell) leaſt hell grow
    poore,
If Rich mens pawes once faſten thee, and beware
It'h way thou meetſt no Lawyers : theile pull thee
    bare,
Hence : downe.
    Glitt. Ime gon.

Deſcendit.

    Shac. Coole night will call Frier *Clement* forth
    anon :
Angels, be you his ſtrong temptation :
Wines luſtfull fires him warme not : At this ſpring,
(Scornde by the reſt for him,) ſpred thy gilt wing,
Full in his eye ; As he drinks water downe,
In ſtreames of *Auarice*, let his weake ſoule droune.
Exit.

Enter the King, Narcifco, Brifco, Spendola, Jouinelli, Rufman, followed by Aftolfo.

Aft. I doe befeech your Highnes, yet turne backe
And comfort the fad Lady, whofe faire eyes
Are worne away with weeping.

Iou. If her eyes be worne away, what fhould a man
doe with a blind wife? kill her with flyes?

Kin. I cannot abide a woman thats fond of me.

Spen. Nor I.

Nar. I would loue a woman but as I loue a walnut,
to cracke it, and peele it, eate the meate, and then
throw away the Shell.

Iou. Or as noble-men vfe their great horfes, when
they are paft feruice : fell 'em to brewers and make
'em drey-horfes : So vfe a woman.

Aft. So fo.

Ruf. The Indians are warme without clothes, and
a man is beft at eafe without a woman : or if your
Highnes muft needs haue one, haue
Factors to buy the faireft, doate not any,
But like the turke, regard none, yet keepe many.

Kin. You heare the Iuries verdit.

Aft. Whofe foreman's the diuell?
Thefe counfell thee to thy deftruction.

Kin. Deftruction? why? the heauen can abide but
    one fun,
I hope we on earth may loue many mens daughters :
Tell *Erminhilda* fo : fend her home to the duke her
    father :
And tell him too, becaufe the difeafe of mariage
Brings the ftone with it, I hate a woman ; I loue not
To be cut : inclofde grounds are too rancke.

Ruf. Beft feeding on the Commons then,
Will you not mary this chaft Lady then?

Kin. No fir, and will you now my reafon haue?
A womans is an infatiate graue
Wherein hee's dambd that lyes buried.

Omn. On, on, away.

Ruf.   Braue battailes! fight you, but ile win the
day.   *Exeunt.*

Manet Aſtolpho.   Enter Octauio and Ermynhilda.

Erm.   I heard the ſtorie, tell't not or'e againe,
Twere crueltie to wound men, being halfe ſlaine.
  Oct.   Tis crueltie too much, and too much ſhame
That one of your high birth, youth, beautie, name,
And vertues ſhining bright, ſhould hence be ſent
(Like ſome offender into baniſhment)
Abuſde by a King, and his luxurious traine,
Of paraſites, knaues, & fooles, (a kingdomes bane,)
For them, by him not carde for; you came not ſo,
But as his bride, his Queene, and bedfellow.
  Erm.   And yet am neither, from my fathers court
Came I (being ſude by Princes too) for this?
To ſee him, his ſubiects ſcorne, and my ſelfe his?
Once thought I that his loue had bin (as fate)
Vnmoueable; and iſt now turn'd to hate?
Yes, yes, hees wauering as the running ſtreame,
And far more ydle than a mad-mans dreame.
  Aſt.   Send to the duke your father, let him inforce
Your plighted mariage.
  Erm.   Worſe than a diuorce.
No: to his eyes ſince hatefull I am growne,
Ile leaue his Court and him, and dye vnknowne.
                                                    Exit.

  Aſt.   All runnes I ſee to ruine.
  Oct.   If he perſue,
Theſe godles courſes, beſt we leaue him too,
That land to it ſelfe muſt a quick downefall bring,
Whoſe King has loſt all, but the name of King.
                                                    Exeunt.

Enter Subprior with an earthen pot, and a lanthorne;
Scumbroath with him with a peice.

Sub.   Get thee to bed thou fooliſh man and ſleepe.

Scu.   How? Sleepe? no fir no, I am turnd a tyrant
   and cannot fleepe :
I ftand centinell perdu, and fomebody dyes if I fleepe,
I am poffeft with the diuell and cannot fleepe.
   Sub.   What diuell poffeffes thee ?
   Scu.   The fencers diuell, a fighting diuell; Rufh
has committed a murder vpon my body, and his carcas fhall anfwere it ; the cock of my reuenge is vp.
   Sub.   Murder ! what murder ?
   Scu.   He has taken away my good name, which is
flat manflaughter, and halfe hangd me, which is as
much as murder, he told the Lord Prior and you that
I was kiffing a wench : Its a lye, I giue him the lye,
and he fhall fight with me at fingle piftall againft my
caliuer, do I looke like a whore-monger ? when haue
you feene a wencher thus hiary as I am : Rufh thou
dieft for this treafon againft my members concupifcen-
tiallitie.
   Sub.   Thou wut not kill him, wut thou ?
   Scu.   No, but Ile make him know what tis to boile
a cooke in's owne greafe.
   I am fcalding hot, I am chargd with furie, I carie
a heart-burning within me.   I kiffe a whore ?   I fhall
haue boyes cry out to me, now who kift Mary ?   No
Rufh, *Scumbroth* fhall giue thee fuger pellets to eate, I
will not be danc'de vpon.
   Sub.   Let me perfwade thy peace of minde to
   night,
Get thee to reft, if Rufh haue thee belide,
Reioyce, by wrongs to haue thy patience tride.
He fhall forgiuenes aske thee.
   Scu.   Let me but haue one blow ats head with my
cleauer Ith kitchin, and I freely forgiue him, or let me
bownce at him.
   Sub.   Thefe bloudie thoughts will dam thee into
hell.
   Scu.   Doe you thinke fo ? what becomes of our
roaring boyes then that ftab healths one to another,
doe you thinke they will be dambd vp too ?

Sub. I thinke fo, for I know it, deere fonne to
    prayer,
Two finnes befet thee, murder, and defpaire,
I charge thee meete me at my cell anon,
To faue thee will I fpend my orifon.
In name of heauen I charge.thee to be gon.

Scu. Well fir, the cold water of your counfell has
laid the heate of my furie : he had met with his
match, but I wil fhoote off my anger, I will be gon,
and why ? Looke you, becaufe the moone is vp and
makes hornes at one of vs ; As the noblemans coach
is drawne by foure horfes, the knights by two, & the
cuckold by three, euen fo am I drawne away with
none at all. *Vale, Bonos Noches* : I am poffeft ftill :
It buzzes, here. *Vale.*   *Exit.*

Sub. Bleft ftar of light, ftucke there to illuminate
This world darkned or'e with fin : thou watcheft late,
To guide mans comming home, fhewing thereby
Heauens care of vs, feeing how we tread awry.
We haue two great lights for midnight and for noon,
Becaufe blacke deeds at no time fhould be don.
All haile to thee (now my beft guide) be giuen,
What   needs   earths   candle,   hauing   the   lamp   of
    heauen ?
Now *Benedicite ?* where am I ?

Enter Rufh.

Rufh. O whether am I going ? which way came I ?
Ah wellada, I come to fill my pot,
With water not with thee ; thou art mif-begot.
Elfe wouldft thou not lye there ; what Orphans blood
Haft thou fuckt out, to make this golden flood ?
None drinke this well but I, how is it than
Thou thus way-lay'ft me, (theefe to the foule of man ?
Would fome poore wretch (by lofle of law vndone)
 Had thee : goe doe him good : me canft thou none.
My wholefome cup is poyfond, it flowes or'e
With mans damnation (gold,) drinke there no more.

Shac. Not taſt what all men thirſt for ? old and
  ſo braue,
When mony aſſaults, one combat more Ile haue. ;

Enter Scumbroth.

Scu. So, ho, ho, father, Subprior.
Sub. Whoes there ? what art thou callſt me ?
Scu. One that feedes the hungry, the cooke ſir,
  Scumbroth.
Sub. Come hither, I haue for thee a golden
  prize.
Shac. Ha ha : heele take it.
Villaines and fooles will ha gold, (tho got from hell,)
But they who doe ſo, (as thou ſhalt) pay for't well.

Exit.

Scu. But ſtay, father Subprior, before we goe one
ſtep farder, what doe you thinke I haue done ſince I
went from you ?
Sub. No hurt I hope, ſay haſt thou ?
Scu. Hurt ? If I did hurt in that, how much
harme doe Almanake makers, whol ye coldly quiuering
at it all the yeare long ? I did doe nothing but ſtand
ſtaring at the man in the moone.
Sub. And what good thoughts bred that within
thee ?
Scu. This : I thought to my ſelfe, what a happy
fellow that man in the moone was, to ſee ſo many
fooles and knaues here below, and yet neuer to be
troubled with 'em, nor meddle with 'em.
Sub. Hees happy that meddles not with this world
indeed.
Scu. If that man in the moone ſhould write a
prognoſtication, oh he ſhould not neede to tell aſtro-
nomicall lyes to fill his booke, nor talke in gibriſh no
man vnderſtands, of *Quartiles, Aſpects, Stations, Re-
trogradations, Peragrations* ; *Centricall, Eccentricall,
Coſmicall, Acronicall,* and ſuch *Palynodicall, Solar,
Lunar, Lunaticall* vaulting ouer the railes of heauen,

that no Chriſtian dare looke vpon their tricks, for feare his wit breake his necke.

Sub.   Thou putſt into a Sea, thou canſt not found, Ignorance ſtill is foe to Arts profound.
Come hither man, come hither.

Scu.   Arts profound, Arts make men as very aſſes as women doe, I haue no Art, and yet I knowe this Moone that ſhines to night, ſees more than you or I doe, for all your ſpectacles.

Sub.   True, tis the eye of heauen.

Scu.   Which of the eyes? tis but the left eye: and the Sun is the right: and yet the left ſometimes ſees more than the right, and the right as much as the left, there's paxoniſme for you father, globicall paxoniſme.

Sub.   I vnderſtand thee not.

Scu.   No, why heres the oyſter opend, I ſay the Sun ſees much knauery in a yere, & and the Moone more in a quarter: the Moone ſees men caryed by a quarelling watch to priſon, and the Sun ſees the conſtable and the booke-keeper ſhare ſees · the next morning.

Sub.   Thats not well.

Scu.   Yes, but they ſweare tis well: the Moone ſees baſtards come bawling into the world, & the Sun ſees 'em ſhifted and ſhuftled in doſſers, away to nurſe, & thats the cauſe we haue ſo many doſſer-heads: the Moone ſees old curmudgeons come reeling from Tauerns with ſipping of halfe pintes of Sacke, and the Sun ſees the ſame churles the next day, ſoberly cutting any mans throate for a pennie.

Sub.   Enough of this: come hither: looke what here lyes.

Scu.   What here lyes: mary, father Subprior, the diuell and ſome Vſurers mony haue bin here at their lecherie, and ſee what goodly children they haue begot: if you will ile keepe the baſtards at nurſe.

Sub.   I am content that halfe this gold be thine,
(If it bee ask'd for neuer, for tis not mine,)
So thou wilt promiſe tother halfe to giue

To fuch as I appoint.

Scu. By this gold I will lay it out brauely, as you appoint me.

Sub. Looke not to profper ; if thou dealſt amiſſe ;
Good workes are keyes opening the gates of bliſſe,
That golden key, thou in that heape maiſt find ;
If with it thou relieue the lame, fick, blind,
And hungry.

Scu. I will doe it I proteſt.

Sub. One halfe beſtow'd fo, take thy felfe the reſt.
So fare thee well. *Exit.*

Scu. Farewell good father,—foole : Ile giue the blinde a dog to lead 'em, the lame ſhall to the whipping-poſt, the fick ſhall dye in a cage, and the hungry leap at a cruſt : I feede roagues, the pox ſhall : the world is changde : a begger yeſterday, and full of gold to day : an aſſe to day, and a prow'd fcab to morrow.

Glit. Stay : ſtand. *Golden head aſcends.*

Scu. Stand : cannot a Gentleman grow rich, but he muſt keepe knaues about him ?

Glit. That gold is none of thine.

Scu. But all the craft in that great head of yours cannot get it out of my fangers. Zounds who the diuel art thou ?

Glit. A ſpirit ſent vp from hell to make thee rich,

Scu. Thanke hell for it : hell makes worfe fooles rich in a yeere.

Glit. That gold I laide there for thee.

Scu. When doe you lay againe, that I may haue more of thefe egges ?

Glit. Spend thofe I charge thee firſt.

Scu. Yes, Head.

Glit. And brauely I charge thee.

Scu. What neede you be at fuch charges, Ile doe't : but ſhall the poore be a pennie the better for me, as the old fellow charged me, yea, or no ?

Glit. No.

Shac. No. *Within.*

Scu. Whofe that ?
Glit. Tis thine owne Genius cryes vnto thee no.
Scu. My Genius, I am a cooke, my Genius then belike is a fcullion ; but when this is fpent, can my Genius tell mee whither I fhall haue more.
Shac. More.
Glit. More.
1. More. } *within.*
2. More. } *In a big voice.*
Scu. Becaufe my Genius keepes company with a great man, Ile take all their wordes ; and his bond.
Glit. When thou haft fpent all that : I charge thee come
To the blacke tree, that ftands in Naples groue,
Clymbe boldly to the top, and keepe faft hold,
For there ile rayne on thee a fhowre of gold,
If what thou feeft there, thou to any tell,
Diuels fhall teare thee.
Shac. Away.
Omn. Away.
Scu. Farewell.   *Exit.*

Enter Shacklefoule laughing.

Shac. Ha, ha ! downe downe bright fpirit, thou wut bee mift anon, hell mynt ftands ydle.
Glit. Loofe not that foole.
Shac. Be gon.
Glit. Haue care to meete at next infernall court : The day drawes nye.   *Goes downe.*
Shac. I thanke thee for this fpirit.   *Exit.*

*Enter K. Rufman, Narciffo, Spendola, Brifco,
            Iouinelli.*

K. You that complaine gainft *Barteruile,* (re-
      ceiuer
Of all our tribute-monies) fpeak your wrongs ;
Nay you haue deaft d our eares too much already,

Hee does confeſſe your crownes (payde and re-
  ceiude)
But to giue backe your writings ther's no clauſe,
If them youle win, fight it out by our lawes.
  Bar. I humbly thanke your highnes. A gratious
    doome.
  1. *Gent.* One day to try this plea, to hel thowlt
    come.   *Ex.* 2.
  K. Toth' next, we ha buſineſſe of our owne, toth'
    next :
O *Barteruile* ! for theſe 200. crownes.
  Bar. I payde 'em to that man.
  Bar. Now afore the King
And his Lords here, thou lieſt : th'aſt payde me
  none.
  K. Your chollers ſirra too hye.
  Far. Tho my collar ſtand
So hye, it ſcarce beares vp this falling band.
Thou ſay'ſt thowlt ſweare th'aſt payd it : vds nailes
  ſweare ſo,
And the fowle ſeende goe with't : 200. crownes ?
I ha loſt as much at loggets : ſweare but to reuel,
And ſpend't in hel, gallop thee and that toth'
  diuel.
  Far. Man wherefore doeſt not ſweare ?
  K. Reach me a booke.
  Bar. Let me before I ſweare, on my notes look,
Ile tell you the very day ; pray hold my ſtaffe,
Till I draw out my falſe eyes.
  Far. Draw thy heart out an't wut : thou maiſt wel
ſay thy falſe eyes.
  Bar. The day : Auguſt, 14.
  Far. Thats now, be dambd, and ſo away.
  Bar. On this day (Auguſt, 14.) I ſweare I payde
Into theſe handes, 200. crownes in gold.
  Far. Zounds nor in ſiluer : by this booke I had
    none.
  K. One of you two is periuriouſly forſworne.
  Far. He, he, as I am true Chriſtian man.

Iou.   He fweares,
To your owne hands he payde them.
   Bar.   Elfe let that eye,
Which fees me play falfe, fcourge my periury
With fearefull ftripes.
   Far.   O iuftice ! falne downe dead !
                    Lurchall & Rufman about him.
Wud I had loft all, tho I had bin cozened,
Rather than thou thy foule.
   Omn.   He bleedes at mouth.
   Far.   See his ftaffe (beating the earth, for heauen
      loues truth
Is burft in fhiuers, and that gold he fwore
Was pay'd to me, lyes fcattred on the flore.
   Ruff.   He comes againe, the diuell will not receiue
      him.
   K.   Take him away, weele punifh him for this
      cryme.
   Ruff.   Beg his office : you a Courtier ?
   Spen.   I haue a fuite to your highnes.
   K.   What ift count *Spendola ?*
   Lur.   Maifter, looke vp man,
In this black trance had thy foule flyen away,
I had wrought hard and made a holliday.
   Ruff.   Loofe not a minute (pue-fellow) leaue him
      not yet,
I haue whales here too, lye playing in the net.   *Exit.*
   Far.   Ile take this gold at venture, (fweete yong
      King,)
For all this hel-hound owes me.
   K.   Doe, and be gone.
   Far.   I am pay'd : the diuels turn'd puritane I
      feare,
He hates (me thinkes) to heare his own child fweare.
                                        Exit.

   K.   The office of this periurde *Barteruile,*
I frankly giue away, diuiding it
To the Count *Spendola,* and our worthy friend
Braue *Bohor* here ; farme it to whom you pleafe.

Both.   We thanke your Highnes.
Spen.   Who bids moſt, he buyes it.
K.   If to his life, the diuel giues longer leaſe,
To build more worke for hel ; goe fee, & from him
Exaᶜt a ſtriᶜt account of what he owes vs.
Ruff.   That ſtriᶜt account ile take.   *Exit.*
K.   Show him no fauour.

Enter Oᶜtauio with petitions.

Oᶜt.   If now thou art a iuſt King, keepe thy word,
With thy poore ſubieᶜts.
K.   How now vncle ? why.
Oᶜt.   This is thy day to heare the poore mans
    crye :
And yonders crying enough, at thy Court gates ;
Fiue hundred white heads, and ſcarce 10. good hats,
Yet haberdaſhers too, of all trades ſome,
Crying out they are vndon.
Omn.   Vndon, by whom ?
Oᶜt.   Mary, looke : by ſuch as you are, who goe
    gay,
Weare't out, booke downe more, ſet to their hands but
    neuer pay ;
Neuer in deare yeares was there ſuch complayning
Of poore ſtaru'd feruants, or (when plagues are raign-
    ing)
Mourne orphans ſo and widdowes, as thoſe doe
That owe theſe ſorrowfull papers.
K.   Pray how can I
To their complainings adde a remedy ?
Oᶜt.   Ile tell thee how : are any here in debt
To Merchants, Mercers, Taylors ? let 'em iet
In their owne fattins, pay for what they ha tane,
And theſe will goe leſſe braue, tother leſſe complaine.
Omn.   Ha ha !
Oᶜt.   The mightie wrongs the weake, the rich the
    poore,
This man ſhould haue his owne, could he greaze more

His too-fat lawyer ; that wretch for's coat does fue,
But his coat's gon, and his skin flead off too,
If his purfe bee ore-match'd : thefe groffe impure
And ranck difeafes, long vnto thy cure,
Thy word's in pawn fort, thefe are the poores cryes,
How wilt thou ftop their throates ?
  K. With halters.
  Omn. Hang 'em.
  Oct. Hang 'em ! any halters here ! ift fo fet
   down ?
This law-booke fpeakes not fo, yet tis thine own.
  K. Still brauing me with this ? burne it.
  Oct. Yes doe.
If you burne all the weeke, burne faterday too :
Doe one good dayes-deed firft, read poore mens
   plaints.
  K. Hels plagues confound 'em : in their heads and
   thine.
Vex me no more.
  Oct. I warrant thee ile faue mine. *Meetes the Sub.*
Holy Saint pardon me, (las good father, my braine
So wilde is I forgot thee, but ile to him againe,
Tis but an old mans head off. King take it, ile
   fpeake whileft this ftands on my fhoulders.
  K. But that you are——
  Oct. An honeft man, thoud'ft haue this, ô I
   befeeke
Thy attention to this Reuerend fub-Prior,
Who plaines againft diforders of this Houfe ;
Where once Deuotion dwelt and Charitie,
Ther's Drunkenneffe now, Gluttonie, and Lecherie,
Tell thou the Tale.
  Sub. Bad Storie foone is tolde ;
Becaufe tis foule, that Leafe does all infolde,
Their finnes grow hye, and fearefull, and ftrike at
   Heauen,
Punifh them *THOV*, whofe power from thence is giuen.
  K. Your Friers fo luftie !

Iou.   All the Barbers in *Naples* tell newes of that
Priorie.

Brif.   I would your Grace would let me purge this
houfe of her infection ; beftowe the Liuings of it on
mee, ile fweeten it in one Moneth.

Iou.   Heele lay it in Lauender.

K.   The Couent, the Demeafnes, Immunities,
Rents, Cuftomes, Chartres, what to this houfe of
Baall foeuer is belonging—*Brifco* tis thine.

Oct.   Wut rob the Church too, (Now th'aft nothing
left fcarce for thy felfe ?)

Sub.   O heauen for-fend fuch theft !

K.   Beftowe it at thy pleafure.

Oct.   Woe to thofe dayes,
When to raife Vpftarts, the poore *CHVRCH* decayes.

Sub.   Call backe thy gift (ô King) and ere thefe
eyes
Behold vnhallowed hands to Tyrannize
Where many a good man has his Orifons faid,
And many a *Requiem* bene fung out for the Dead,
(Till I am thruft out by Death) ô let mee haue
My dwelling there, there let me dig my Graue,
With mine owne Nayles, (fhut vp from worldly Light,
Betweene two walls,) and dye an *Anchoryte*.

K.   I referre you to your Patron there.

Brif.   Thats I :
Shew mee firft where your Abbey-gold fleeps, then goe
dye.

Sub : I feare *RELIGIONS* Fall : Alacke I fee
This world's a Cittie built by the moft Hie,
But kept by man, (*GODS*) greateft enemie.   *Exit.*

Oct.   Let ill-Newes flye together, thou art full of
teares,
But I more full of woes, of cares, of feares.   *Exit.*

Enter Aftolphe.

K.   S'death fhall wee haue yet faire weather ?

Iou.   Heeres one ftorme more.

Aſt. *Calabrias* Duke demaunds of you a Daughter.
K. Let me but lye with's wife, Ile giue him a
Sonne.
Aſt. Hee ſends for *Erminghild.*
K. Deliuer her.
Aſt. Shees not to be found.
K. Ya're an olde Foole,
To aske for that which is not.
Aſt. Thus hee ſayes,
Denie her and looke for warres.
K. So goe your wayes.
Aſt. I'me quickly gone. *Exit.*

Enter Ruffman and Barteruile.

K. With Sacke ile ſweare you are,
This was ſhort and ſweete,—Seemes then we ſhal ha
warres,
Bohor, the Drumme muſt ſcolde, the Canon thunder :
Fighting about a wench.
Omn. Tuſh, thats no wonder.
K. Who bayld him out of Hell ? dambd periurde
caytiffe !
Out of mine eye.
Ruff. I neuer begd before,
Pardon his crime (I intreate) and backe reſtore
Both your hye fauour to him, and his place.
Bar. Let me want life, rather then want your
Grace.
Spen. Doe you thinke Ile looſe the Kings gift ?
Bar. Ile ſend you Golde.
Spen. That ſtops my mouth, pray let him ſtill Sir
hold,
This Office of *Receiuer,* I reſigne
That part which I haue in it.
Ruff. And I all mine.
K. Sirra, thanke theſe Lords.
Bar. I ſhall their loues deſerue.
K. *Barteruile,* wee haue warres, Ile haue thee

lcnd mee fome 30000. Chicquines at leaft.
   Bar.   Take all my Golde.
   K.   Wel, get you home with your bags fir, weele make bold.
   Bart.   Your Maieftie fhall haue what bags you will,
Bags onely, but Ile keepe my money ftill.   *Exit.*

Enter Octauio and Astolphe.

   K.   Now *Shalcan*, fome newe Spirit.
   Ruff.   A thoufand wenches
Stark-nak'd, to play at Leap-frog.
   Omn.   O rare fight !
   Iou.   Your vncle.
   K.   Sdeath, ftill haunted with this gray fprite.
   Oct.   You need no Taylors now, but Armorers,
Theres a deere reckoning for you all to pay,
About a Ladie ; the *Calabrian* Duke
Is on a March : the Lightning flafhes now,
Youle heare the cracke anone.   Before the ftarre
To call whome vp, the wakefull Cocke doth fing
Bee twice more feene abroad ; At your Citie gates
The Diuells purfeuant will beate (the Canon)
Will thefe briske leaders (ftucke with Eftridge-
     feathers)
Goe braue your enemie now, and beate him backe ?
Saue thee, thy Kingdome, and themfelues from
     wracke ?
   K.   Dotard, I fcorne to take prefcription
From any breath to which ours is fupreame,
Stood Diuels with fire-works on your battlements,
A thoufand Armed *Ioues* at your proude walls
Hurling forked Thunder, and the gates rambd vp
With piles of Citizens heads, our fpring-tyde pleafures
No aduerfe windes, no *Torrent* fhall refift :
Midft flames weele dance, and dye a *Neronift.*   *Exit.*
   Omn.   Fight you, yare good for nothing elfe.
                          Exeunt.

3   Y

Ast.   They mocke vs.

Oct.   All ſtarke mad : let vs be wiſe,
And flye from buildings falling to'th ſurer ſide,
If wee can his ſafety, if not, (our owne prouide.)

Exeunt.

Enter Barteruile like a Turke ;—Lurchall.

Bar.   Thou hadſt like t'ha ſent mee ſwearing into
          Hell,
Ile weaue my Nettes my ſelfe, how doeſt thou like
          mee ?
Is not this habite *Turke*-Merchant-like ?

Lur.   A meere *Turke* ſir, none can take you for
          leſſe.

Bar.   King borrow 30000. Chequines of mee !
          ha, ha !

Lur.   But pray ſir, what iſt turnes you into a
          Turke ?

Bar.   That, for which manie their Religion,
Moſt men their Faith, all chaunge their honeſtie,
Profite, (that guilded god) *Commoditie.*
Hee that would grow damnd-Rich, yet liue ſecure,
Muſt keepe a caſe of Faces, ſometimes demure.
Sometimes a grum-ſurly ſir, now play the Iewe,
Then the Preciſian ; Not a man weele viewe.
But varies ſo.   My ſelfe, (of baſhfull nature)
Am thus ſupplyed by Arte.

Lur.   Mine owne deere creature.
But ſir, your Aymes, and endes in this.

Bar.   Mary theſe————
A hundred thouſand-Florens fill my Coffers,
Some of it is mine owne, and ſome the Kings,
Some taken vp at vſe of ſundry Merchants,
To pay at ſix ſix monthes, on mine owne band,)
Sue that, Ile keepe the monies in my hand.

Lur.   Youle breake ſir.

Bar.   Not mine owne necke, but their backes ;
To get their monies, *Bartaruile* muſt die,
Make will, name an executer, which am I.

Lur. Rare !

Bar. Giuen out his kinfman, lately imployed him
in Turky.

Lur. What will hence befall ?

Bar. Like an executer will I cozen all.
Make creditors Orphans, and widowes fpend thofe
    teares
They fau'de from their late husbands burialls ;
They get not ij.d. it'h pound.

Lur. Theile tell the King.

Bar. The King ? ha ha : the King is going this
    way ;
He meanes to borrow,
(If the warres holds) my gold : yes : when to morrow.
All debts of mine, on him fhall be conferd,
I ha breifes and tickets which from time to time
Shew what large fummes his minions ha fetcht from
    me,
His tribute mony has payd it, that's no matter,
The world bites thefe dead, whom aliue they flatter.
And fo muft I ; then giue it out I left
A compleate ftate, but the Kings death bereft
Me of thofe fummes he owde.

Lur. Say the King preuailes.

Bar. With that wind muft I likewife fhift my
    failes :
And where the fox gets nothing, will turne Ape,
Make legges, crouch, kiffe my paw, prefent fome ftale
Deuice of vertues triumph to expreffe
How much I ioy him fafe, wifh nothing leffe.

Lur. But how can you excufe your turning Turke ?

Bar. Eafieft of all : Ile fweare, this faude my
    life,
Purfued by kennells of barking creditors :
For my much loue to him, and thus being forcde
To walke obfcure, my credit fell to wracke,
Want of returne made all my factors breake,
In parts remote ; to recompence which loffe,

And that with fafetie I may giue direction
To my difturbd ftate, craue I the Kings protection.
   Lur.   Protection ! whats that ?
   Bar.   A merchant, and yet know'ft not
What a protection is ? Ile tell thee.
   Lur.   Pray fir, for I neuer broke with any man.
   Bar.   It is a buckler of a large fayre compaffe
Quilted within with Fox-skinnes : In the midft
A pike fticks out, (fometimes of two yeeres long,
And fometimes longer.)   And this pike keepes off
Serieants and Bailiffs, Actions, and Arrefts :
Tis a ftrong charme gainft all the noifome fmels
Of Counters, Iaylors, garnifhes, and fuch hels ;
By this, a debtor craizde, fo luftic growes,
He may walke by, and play with his creditors nofe.
Vnder this buckler, here ile lye and fence.
   Lur.   You haue out-reacht me.
   Bar.   Ile out-reache the diuell :
But I tempt danger : goe thou and fetch fome Frier
As if (at point of death,) I did defire,
(No, *Barteruile* did defire (to make confeffion :
If any creditors beate, or raile at dore,
Vpftarts this Turke and anfweres them.
   Lur.   Why fetch I a Frier ?
   Bar.   I haue a reaching plot in that (boy) haften,
That we may fmile in our fecurer port :
Seeing others fea-toft : why tis but a fport
For him thats fafe, to fee the proud waues fwallow
Whole fleetes of wretched foules : it needes muft
    follow,
Nature fent man into the world, (alone,)
Without all company, but to care for one,
And that ile doe.
   Lur.   True Citie doctrine fir.
   Bar.   Away, thy haft, our richeft loue fhall
    earne.
   Lur.   I came to teach, but now (me thinkes) muft
    learne.   *Exeunt.*

Enter Scumbroth like a begger.

Scu. What faies the prodigall child in the painted cloth ? when all his mony was fpent and gon, they turnd him out vnneceffary; then did hee weepe and wift not what to don, for he was in's hofe and doublet verily, the beft is, there are but two batches of people moulded in this world, thats to fay Gentlemen and Beggers; or Beggers and Gentlemen, or Gentleman-like Beggers, or Beggerlike Gentle-men ; I rancke with one of thefe I am fure, tag and rag one with another : Am I one of thofe whom Fortune fauours ? No, no, if Fortune fauourd me, I fhould be full, but Fortune fauours no body but Garlicke, nor Garlike neither now, yet fhe has ftrong reafon to loue it; for tho Garlicke made her fmell abhominably in the noftrills of the gallants, yet fhe had fmelt and ftuncke worfe but for garlike : One filthy fent takes away another. She once fmilde vpon me like a lambe, when fhee gaue me gold, but now fhe roares vpon me like a Lion. Stay : what faid head ? Spend this brauely, and thou fhalt haue more : can any prodigall new-come vpftart fpend it more brauely ? and now to get more, I muft goe into the groue of *Naples* thats here, and get into a blacke tree, heares a blacke tree too, but art thou he ?

Glitt. He.——*within.*

Scu. Ha ha, where art thou my fweete great head ?

Glitt. Head.

Scu. O at the head, thats to fay at the top : how fhall I get vp ? for tis hard when a man is downe in this world to get vp, I fhall neuer climbe hie.

Glitt. Hye.

Scu. I will hie me then, but I am as heauy as a fow of lead.

Glitt. Leade.

Scu. Yes, I will lead (big Head) whatfoeuer followes, Many a gallant for gold, has climbde higher on a
    gallowes.

The ſtorme euen as Head nodded) is comming :
Cooke, licke thy fingers, now or neuer.
   Glitt.   Now or neuer.

   Rayne, Thunder and lightning : Enter Lucifer and
                        Diuels.

   Omn.   Oooh.
   Luc.   This is the tree.
   Scu.   On which would you were all hang'd, ſo *I*
were off it ; and ſafe at home.
   Luc.   And this (I am ſure tis this) the horrid
     groue
Where witches broodes ingender, (our place of meet-
     ing).
   Scu.   Doe witches ingender here : zounds I ſhall
bee the diuels bawde whileſt he goes to his lecherie.
   Luc.   And this the hideous black infernall howre :
Ha ! no appearance yet ? if their leaſt minute
Our vaſſailes breake, ſinck ſhall theſe trees to hell.
   Scu.   Alas !
   Luc.   This groue ile turne into a brimſtone lake
Which ſhall be euer-burning.
   Scu.   The beſt is, if I be a match in the diuels
tinderbox, I can ſtinck no worſe than I doe alreadie.
   Luc.   Not yet come ?   Oooh !

   Enter Shacklefoule, Rufman and Lurchall, at ſeuerall
            dores with other diuels.

   Omn.   Oooh, oooh.   *embrace.*
   Scu.   Sure theſe are no Chriſtian Diuels, they ſo
loue one another.
   Luc.   Stand forth.

     Sits vnder the tree all about him.

   Scu.   Frier *Ruſh* amongſt 'em !
   Luc.   And here vnlade you of that pretious freight
For which you went, (mens ſoules ;) what voyage is
     made ?

Omn.   No fauing voyage, but a damning.
Luc.   Good.
Scu.   I thought the diuell was turnde Merchant,
theres fo many Pirates at Sea.
Ruff.   Ith Court of Naples haue I profpred well,
And braue foules fhall I fhortly fhip to hell.
In fenfuall ftreames, Courtier and King I ha crownde,
From whence warre is flowing, whofe tyde fhall all
     confound.
Scu.   Are there gentlemen diuels too? this is one
of thofe, who ftudies the black Art, thats to fay, drinkes
Tobacco.
Luc.   Are all then good ith Citie?
Lur.   No Lucifer.
Scu.   No nor fcarce ith fuburbes.
Lur.   Great Prince of diuels, Thy hefts I haue
     obayde,
I am bartring for one foule, able to lade
An Argocy ; if Citie-oathes, if periuries,
Cheatings, or gnawing mens foules by vfuries,
If all the villanies (that a Citty can,)
Are able to get thee a fonne, I ha found that man.
Luc.   Serue him vp,——*flands vp.*
Scu.   Alas, now now.
Lur.   Damnation giues his foule but one turne
     more,
Caufe he fhall be enough.
Scu.   Its no meruaile if markets be deere, when the
Citie is bound to find the diuell roaft-meate.
Luc.   Has *Rufh* lyen ydle?
Shac.   Ydle? no *Lucifer.*
Scu.   All the world is turnd diuell. *Rufh* is one
too.
Sha.   Ydle? I haue your nimbleft diuell bin,
In twentie fhapes begetting fin.
Scu.   One was to get me thruft out of the priory.
Sha.   I am fifhing for a whole fchoale of Friers.
Al are gluttoning or muttoning, ftabbing or fwelling,

Ther's onely one Lambe ſcapes my killing,
But I will haue him : then theres a cooke——
    Scu.   Whoſe arſe makes buttons.
    Sha.   Of whom I ſome reuenge haue tooke.
    Scu.   The diuell choake you fort.
    Sha.   He mickle ſcath has done me,
And the knaue thinkes to out-run me.
    Scu.   Not too faſt.
    Luc.   Kick his guilty ſoule hither.
    Sha.   Ile driue him to deſpaire,
And make him hang himſelfe.
    Scu.   For hanging I ſtand faire.
    Luc.   Goe, ply your workes, our Seſſions are at
      hand.
    Fire.   We fly to execute thy dread command.
                          Exeunt 3.
    Scu.   Would I could flye into a bench-hole.
    Luc.   But what haue you don ? nothing.
    1. *Diu.*   We haue all like bees
Wrought in that Hyue of ſoule (the buſie world :)
Some ha lyen in cheeſmongers ſhops, paring leaden
      waites.
    Scu.   Wud I were there but with a paring of
cheeſe.
    1. *Diu.*   For one halfe ounce, we had a chandlers
      ſoule.
    Scu.   If he melted tallow, hee ſmelt ſweetly as I doe.
    1. *Diu.*   Walke round hels ſhambles, thou ſhalt ſee
      there ſticks
Some 4. butchers ſoules, puft queintly vp with pricks.
    Scu.   4. Sweete-breads I hold my life, that diuels an
aſſe.
    1. *Diu.*   Taylors ore-reachers, for to this tis
      growne,
They ſcorne thy hell, hauing better of their owne:
    Scu.   They fear not ſattin nor all his workes.
    1. *Diu.*   I haue with this fiſt beate vpon rich-mens
      hearts,

To make 'em harder : and thefe two thumbes thruſt,
(In open Churches) into braue dames eares.
Damning vp attention ; whilſt the loofe eye peeres
For faſhions of gowne-wings, laces, purles, ruffes,
Fals, cals, tires, wires, caps, hats, and mufs, and pufs.
For fo the face be fmug, and carkas gay,
Thats all their pride.
   Luc.   Twill be a feſtiuall day
When thofe fweete Duckes comes to vs : loofe 'em
     not : goe :
More foules you pay to hell, the leffe you owe.
This Ewe-tree blaſt with your hot-fcorching breath,
A marke, (toth' witch who next fits here) of death.
   Omn.   Ooooh.——*Fireworkes : Scumbroath falls.*

Exeunt Omn.

   Scu.   Call you this, rayning downe of gold? I am
wet toth' skinne in the ſhowre, but tis with fweating
for feare : had I now had the confcience that fome
Vintners and Inholders haue? here might I haue
gotten the diuell and all. But two finnes haue vndone
me, prodigalitie, and couetoufneffe ; and three Pees
haue pepperd me,
     The Punck, the Pot, and Pipe of fmoake
     Out of my pocket my gold did foake.
I cannot fweare now, zounds I am gallant : but I can
fweare as many of the ragged Regiment doe, zounds I
haue bin a gallant. But I am now downe, deiected,
and debaſh'd, and can better drawe out a thirdendale
gallant, thats to fay, a gallant that wants of his true
meafure, than any tapſter can draw him out of his
fcores : thus he fets vp, and thus hee's pulld downe ;
thus is he raifed, and thus declinde :   *Singulariter,*
Nominatiuo, Hic Gallantus, a Gallant.
Genetiuo, Hugious, braue.
Datiuo Huic, If he gets once a lick,
Accufatiuo Hunc, Of a taffaty Punck.
Accufatiuo Hanc, His cheekes will growe lanck,
Hunc, Hanc, & Hoc, With lifting vp her fmock.

Vocatiuo, ô | Hees gon if he cryes ſo.
Ablatiuo, ab hoc, Away with him, he has the pock.
Pluraliter, Nominatiuo, Hi. gallanti, If the pox he can
    defie.
Genetiuo, Horum, Yet hees a begger in coram.
Datiuo, His : His gilt rapier he does miſſe.
Accuſatiuo Hos, Without his cloake he goes.
Accuſatiuo Has, To the Counter he muſt paſſe.
Hos, has, & Hæc, With two Catchpols at his back.
Vocatiuo, ô | A hole he deſirde, and to th' hole he
    muſt goe.
Ablatiuo, ab His, Thus many a Gallant declined is.
                                             Exit.

Enter Erminhild to the Subprior.

  Sub.   What art thou ?
  Er.   Daughter to the Calabrian Duke.
The haples troth-plight wife to your ſad King.
  Sub.   Alack ! what notes are theſe I heare you
      ſing ?
Pardon me madam :
O Lady ! want of you has bred much woe ;
Calamitie does euery where ore-flow,
All long of your ſtrange abſence.
                          Drummes afar off marching.
  Er.   I confeſſe,
Loaden with your Kings contempt, and loath to beare
Shame to my country, who from thence came
      freighted
With many glorious honours, I preferd
An obſcure life before a publick ſhame ;
O then (good father) be it not my blame
If my ſuppoſde death, on the King haue throwne,
Dangers, which from himſelfe are meerely gr;owne.
  Sub.   What (princely Mayden) would you wiſh me
      doe ?
  Er.   I doe coniure you ſir, by all the bonds
Tye you to pious Acts, you would make way
To my incenſed father ; giue him theſe lines,

This Ring, pledge of that bleffing he deliuerd me
At our laft parting : adde vnto thefe, if euer
His daughters memory to him were deare,
To wound the Prince let his rafh hand forbeare :
Since through each wound he giues him, I am flaine,
If the fad king you meete, venture to tell him
That more for him, than he for me, I bide,
And am his fubiect ftil, tho not his bride.
   Sub.   This fhall I doe, how fhall we meete againe ?
   Er.   Feares follow me fo, I know not where nor
     when.
   Sub.   Hearke how the found of horror beates the
     Ayre,
Your fathers vp in Armes and does prepare
Sharpe vengeance, for this citie, woe is me : truft
     you
To me, who nere made much of woman yet,
Reft here fweete maide, till an old Frier beget
What ioyes he can to comfort thee ? Is *Clement*
     growne
A womans man now? No, I am not mine owne,
Where your command may fway me : Much more in
     this,
Where heauen (through vertues triall) makes you his.
Exit.

A table is fet out with a candle burning, a deaths head,
    a cloke and a croffe ; Subprior *fits reading* :
    Enter Shackle-foule, leading in an Italian Zany,
    fiue or 6. Curtizans, euery one holding a Iewell.

   Shac.   Thats he, & theres your golden hire to
     charme him ;
Your fees ile treble, let but lufts flame be felt ;
The Alpine-fnow at the fun's beames does melt,
So let your beauties thaw his frozen Age,   *Mufick.*
Firft t'act an old Lecher, then a diuell on hells black
     Stage :

Strike, ftrike your filver ftrings : braue fet of whores ?
At your ftriking vp, diuells dance, and all hell roares.

Zany and Curtizans fall into a fhort dance.

    Sub. What found offends mine eare ? Soule of
      temptation ?
Enchanters I defie yee, get you gon ;
Ime blind to your enticements, from this I learne,
At how deere rate the careles world does earne,
That thing calld pleafure : how many foules doe
      fall ?
(Sold for a little guilt to daube this wall ?)
Hence with your witchcrafts, the fight of this driues
      hence
All thoughts befieging our voluptuous fence.
    Shac. Another baite, at this he will not bite.

*The Zany finges : Subprior holds his head downe
as faft afleepe.*

    Zany. Will you haue a daintie girle ? here tis :
Currall lippes, teeth of pearle : here tis :
Cherry cheekes, fofteft flefh ; that's fhee,
Breath like *May*, fweete and frefh ; fhee fhee.
Be fhe white, blacke, or browne,
Pleafure your bed fhall crowne,
      Chofe her then, vfe her then,
      Women are made for men.
        Prettie, prettie waft :
        Sweete to be embracde :
      Prettie leg, ô prettie foote,
      To beauties tree the roote,
      This is fhe fhall doo'te,
Or fhe fhall doo't, or fhe fhall doo't, fhe fhall doo't,
    fhe fhall doo't.
      Kiffe, kiffe, play, play, come and dally,
      Tumble, tumble, tumble, in beauties valley.

Shac. His foule is chaind in pleafures, bind it
   faft,
If he breake your charmes, the ftrongeft fpell comes
   laft.   *Exit.*

All wake him.

Sub. Hence diuells incarnate, tis not the forcerie
Of your deceitfull tunes, fhuts vp mine eye,
Mine eares are likewife ftop'd, hence, hence I fay.
   Omn. Ha ha, a man of yce, a clod of clay.
                               Exeunt.

Enter Shackle-foule, or fome fpirit in a frightfull fhape.

Sub. Are all thy incantations fpent now ? art
   come againe ?
Bafe workmanfhip of heauen, what other traine,
Were all hells frightfull horrors ftucke in thy looke,
Thou canft not fhake me.
   Shac. I can.
   Sub. Thou lieft, thou fhalt not.
   Shac. I bring thee tydings of thy death this
   night.
   Sub. How doeft thou know that houre of my laft
   fight ?
Falfe herald, Minifter of defpaire and lyes.
   Shac. I know to how many minutes thy daies
   muft rife.
   Sub. Who giues thee the number.
   Shac. All things to vs are knowne,
What euer haue bin, are or fhalbe don.
   Sub. Ile pofe thee prefently, whats this thou fiend
Which now I haue turnd too, doe but tell me that
And Ile belieue thee.
   Shac. I fcorne to be thy flaue.
   Sub. Downe, downe, and fincke into thy damned
   caue :
Looke here, doeft fly thou hell-hound ! I dare thee
   ftand,

Or'e thee by thefe holy fpells haue I ftrong com-
 mand,
Thy battries are too weake : by good mens prayers,
The continence of faints, (by which as ftayres,
They afcend to heauen) by Virgins chaftitie ;
By Martirs cround deaths, which recorded lye
In filuer leaues, aboue : I charge thee downe,
Howle where tha'rt bound in flauerie, till the laft
 dome.   *Exit.*
 Shac.   Stormes, thunder, lightning, rip vp the earths
 wombe.
 Sub.   Eternall power, thankes on my humbled
 knee,
Thou ftill to conftant brefts giu'ft victory.
 Shac.   No way to conquer thee ? Ile giue thee ore :
Ne're fifhd I fo, (yet loft a foule) before.   *Exit.*

*Allarums.   Enter King, Rufman, Spendola, Brifco,
 with drawne weapons.   Iouinelli here.*

 Kin.   Blacke horrors, mifchiefe, ruine and con-
 fufion
affright vs, follow vs.
 Ruf.   Dare them to the face,
And you fright them.
 Spen.   No fafetie but to fly.
 Kin.   Whither *Spendola,* whither ? better ftay, and
 die.

Enter Narcifco : King, Allarums afar of.

 Omn.   What hope ? what newes ?
 Kin.   Is my vncle fled ?
 Nar.   Hee is gon :—And fights againft you.
 Kin.   Follow him damnation,
That leaues his Prince fo in diftreffe, in miferie ;
O bane of Kings ! (thou inchanting flatterie,)
Thy venome now I feele, eating my heart,
More mortall than an Indians poifned dart.

Ruf. Yar'e too deiected, gather head and fight it
out.

Kin. The head's here, where are hands to lay
about ?

Enter Iouinelli.

Iou. Where is the King ?
Kin. The man that title mockes
Is here, (thou fad-vifage man) are any hirde to kill
me,
Or betray me ? let 'em come :
Griefes growing extreame, death is a gentle doome.
Iou. Prepare then for the worft.
Kin. I am armd fort : fhew it.
Iou. Thy kingdome is a weake fhip, bruizd, fplit,
finking,
Nor haft thou any pilot to waft vs o're
Out of this foule Sea, to fome calmer fhore.
Thy peoples hearts are turnd to rocks of flint,
The Scholler, Souldier, and the Mariner,
Whom (as themfelues fay) once thou trodft vpon,
Now ferue as wheeles of thy deftruction.
Flying fwiftly backward, the kingly Lions quaild,
What fhall the weaker heardes doe, if he fall ?
Spen. Lets fly.
Omn. Zounds whither ?
Brif. So we may be fafe ——
Iou. But where ?
Spen. At *Barteruile* : the churle's to me beholden,
His houfe fo ftands, we may enter without feare.
Omn. Beet fo, to *Barteruile.*
Spen. What will your Highnes doe ?
Kin. Die *Spendola*, a miferable King,
None here can hinder vs of that.
Spen. How ? die ? —— ha you any ftomach to
death firs ?
Omn. Not I.
Spen. Nor I.

Troth's, tho you grow defperate, weele grow wife.

    Omn.   Farewell fir, weele faue one.   *Exeunt.*

    King.   Oh my cruelft enemies !
Stabs *Brutus* at me too ?

    Ruf.   Now mine owne or neuer.

    Kin.   Why art not thou gon ?

    Ruf.   I, Ile fticke to you euer :
I am no Courtier fir of fortunes making.

    Kin.   Thou art no wife man to preferre thy loue
To me, before thy life, pray thee leaue me.

    Ruf.   Not I.

    K.   I fhall not hate the world fo really
As elfe I would, O had the ancient race
Of men (who had long leafes of their liues)
Bin wretched as we are, no recompence
Could the Gods haue giuen them for their being here,
But now more pittifull wife nature growes,
Who cuts of mans yeeres to cut off his woes.

    Ruff.   True fir, & teaches him a thoufand waies
To leade him out this horrid giddy maze.

    K.   I apprehend thee, a fmall daggers point,
Opens the vaines to cure our plurizy.

    Ruff.   Than to be made your foes-flaue, better dye.

    K.   A hundred thoufand deaths, than like a
     captiue
Be chaind to grace prowd *Cæfars* Chariot wheele.

    Ruff.   Much leffe a pettie Dukes.

    K.   Fetch me deare friend,
An armed Piftoll, and mouth it at my breft :
Ile make away my felfe, and all my forrowes
Are made away.

    Ruff.   The beft and nobler fpirits
Haue done the like.

    K.   Your braueft men at Armes
Haue done the like.

    Ruff.   Philofophers haue don it.

    K.   Great peeres haue don it.

    Ruff.   Kings haue done the like.

    K.   And *I* will doe it.

Ruff.   Nay it ſhall nere be ſaid,
I liu'd a minute after you : here, here.
    K.   I embrace thee nobleſt friend.
    Ruff.   Lets faile together.
    K.   Content braue *Bohor* : oh ! but whither ?
    whither ?
    Ruff.   From hell, (this world,) from fiends, (in
    ſhapes of men.)
    K.   No : into hel, from men to be dambd black
    with fiends.
Me thinkes I ſee hell iawne to ſwallow vs.
    Ruff.   Fuh, this is but the ſwimming of your
    braine,
By looking downe-wards with a timerous eye.
    K.   My ſoule was ſunck too low, to looke more
    hye,
Forgiuenes heauen.———   *Allarums.*
    Ruff.   The whippes of furies laſh mee : the foe
    comes on.
    K.   And we will meete him, dare confuſion,
And the worlds mixed poiſons, there is a hand
That fights for Kings, and vnder that weele ſtand.

    Allarum ſtill a farre off : Enter a Frier running.

    Ruff.   Whither runnes this Frier ?
    Fri.   To faue my wretched life,
From th' inſolent ſoldier, threatning the Cities ſpoile.
    K.   Of what houſe art thou ?
    Fri.   Of father Clements Order,
The Capachines Subprior : a quick meſſenger fetched
me to be rich Barteruiles confeſſor, who lyes a dying.
    K.   A dying !
    Fri.   He does, but I
Haue come thus far, with ſo much ieopardy,
That could I ſafely get the keys ſhore,
Nor the priory would I ſee more.
For charities ſake, direct me, and defend me.
    K.   To helpe deſtreſſed men, religion bindes me,
    s   z

Shouldſt thou in this hot broiles, be met abroad,
It will be iudgde you leaue your Priory,
Carying gold and ſiluer with you.
    Fri.   Las I haue none.
    K.   But Frier if you be thus taken, your life is
      gon,
Here, here, caſt off thy habit, better that lye
Ith Streetes, than thou poore wretch ; weare mine, &
      away
Strike downe that lane.
    Fri.   Thankes maiſter, for your liues ile pray.
Exit.

    K.   This *Bohor* ſhall diſguiſe me, whither wilt thou
      fly ?
    Ruff.   Ile ſhift I warrant : haſt thou toth' Priory.
    K.   If we nere meete againe, (beſt friend) farewell.
    Ruff.   Not meete, yes, I hope, you muſt not thus
      cheate hel.
    K.   I will not truſt this fellow : toth' Priory, no :
Barteruiles Confeſſor : if to betray
Thou findſt the churle apt, leaue him, if not, there
      ſtay,
The downefall of that Prince, is quick and ſteepe
Who has no heart to leaue, nor power to keepe. *Exit.*

    Enter Barteruile and Lurchall, with the Courtiers.

    Lur.   Make the doore ſure the houſe is round
      beſet.
    Omn.   Beſet !
    Bar.   Put vp : feare nothing : Armies ſhould they
      enter,
Cannot here find you.
    Omn.   How ſhall we eſcape ?
    Bar.   Send for your truncks and iewels, ile ſhip
you this night meane time, this vnknowne way, leads
to a cellar, where a world cannot fetch you forth : In,
In, if danger purſue you, in a dry-fat ile packe you
hence.

Omn.   Zounds into the dungeon?
Bar.   So to Sardini :   *Exeunt.*
Your cloakes and your gilt rapiers, downe, downe,
    downe.
   K.   How foone meetes Babels-pride, confufion ?
   Lur.   What neft of birds are thefe new-kild with
     feare ?
   Bar.   Fowle cannot laft long fweete, therefore kept
     there   (*Serieants.*
In my cold cellar ; ftay, houfe befet ? what fees ?
   Lur.   Such as ftrike dead the heart, yet giue no
     blowes.
   Bar.   This   .   footra for 'em : proclamations
     Lurchall,
6000. Crownes are his, can thefe betray,
Soone earnd, weele fhare, fetch the Calabrian hither,
They are here fay : dam 'em.
   Lur.   You fhall be dambd together.   *Exit.*

           Enter King as a Frier.

   K.   Wher's that deuote ficke man defires to take
Leaue off this world? *Deus hic* to all now here.
   Bar.   Now Domine Frier ; what I to you con-
     feffe
You are bound by oath to keepe.
   K.   I auer no lefle.
   Bar.   Keepe then this clofe, I am no Turke, not I,
But *Barteruile* difguifde in pollicy.
   K.   Are you the Sick man ?
   Bar.   Sick of a difeafe,
Bad as a plague to Citizens, I muft breake,
Play a banckrowts part) I haue monie of the kings,
Of merchants, Ile keepe all, thefe are Citie-fprings ;
Here lyes Serieants Leaguer : about my doores :
My houfe to me is an hofpitall, they the fores
Which run vpon me vily, (peepe I but out,)
To raize this Dunkirke feige, thus caft I about.
   K.   Lets heare, pray how ?

                          z 2

Bar.   Thus, thus fweete Domine Frier,
Ile be like you, a Capuchine : So, by your Prior,
Sub-prior, and couent, I may be fetcht hence,
Spite of all Showlder-clappers violence.
Tho the King fhould lay hands on me, I wud not
    tary.
   K.   You neede not.
   Bar.   You are my guard, my Sanctuary.
   K.   But what your leuel in this, when this is don ?
   Bar.   Alas ! what leuell but pure deuotion ?
   K.   The Diuell you haue.
   Bar.   When I dye there, take All :
Will you goe to your prior and tell this ?
   K.   Yes I fhall.   *A March afar.*
   Bar.   Ile fend him an earneſt peny (a 100. Crownes)
As the firſt ſtone my charitie builds vpon.
What drom's this ? come, difpatch Frier, and be gon.
                                  Exit.

   K.   Out of this hell thou meaneſt : yes ile fly
    from thee
As from the Diuels hangman : thowl't elfe betray
    mee.
World ! to what creſt of villanie art thou growne ?
When (of good men) whole kingdomes fcarce breede
    One.   *Exit.*
   Lur.   Heres the Duke of *Calabria* ſir if you haue
made mee tell a lye, theile fend me of a voiage to the
yland of Hogs and Diuels, (the *Barmudas,*) the Duke
    ſir.
   Bar.   His grace is welcome, las ! I had more
    neede
To haue Phiſitions and Apothecaries,
Than fighters at my gates : *Lurchall* why come they ?
   Cala.   Deliuer vp thofe monſters in thy houfe,
That haue deuourd a Kingdome and the King.
Tis death to thee, and him, if thou detainſt 'em.
   Bar.   I detaine 'em, here, here, here.
   Aſt.   Reward if thou deliuerſt them.

Bar. Ime paſt rewarding in this world, I looke
onely for good mens prayers, theres the key *Lurchall.*
   Cal. Vnbind him : ſtay why did thy houſe receiue
them ?
   Bar. Full ſore againſt my will : the bed I riſe
from
Count I my death-bed ; for (each minute) I looke
When Angells (heauens good porters) will let me in,
Yet (like my betters) I'me heauy laden with ſin.
And being thus ſicke, and at laſt gaſpe, I ſent
For my neerſt cozen, my executor,
Who ſeeing braue fellowes beating at my gates,
Tooke 'em for honeſt men, let 'em in ſimply,
And vndertooke this night, to ha ſhipd 'em hence ;
My faithfull Seruant telling me this, (In zeale,
To you and my country) I bid him, All reueale.
   Cal. Thaſt plaid a Subiects part in't.
   Bar. Heele lead you to them.
   Cal. My Lord, take force and ſeize 'em, nere ſtand
vpon
More trialls ; giue 'em ſpeedie execution.
   Aſt. Come fellow.—
          Exeunt Aſt : and *Lurchall cum Militibus.*
   Bar. Your grace has don with me ?
   Calab. Goe, looke to thy health :
The crownes the proclamation promiſed,
Shall to thy man be payd.
   Bar. Thankes to your Grace :
Las what I did in this, was for no hire.
   Cal. Ha ha, the rent of a cellar neuer was ſo
deere.
On beate the drum.   *Exit.*

As they goe off ; Enter Octauio with Ruſman and a
guard.

   Octa. Are the reſt tane ?
   Cal. Yes.
   Oct. The graund-Pyrat's here.

Heres the Diuells bellowes, kindled all thofe fires,
Which now are burning: This is the Snake, whofe
    fting
(Being kept warme in the bofome of a King)
Struck him to'th-heart: This hee, who by the force
Of his damb'd Arguments, was the firft-diuorce,
Of the Kings Loue, this is *Bohor.*

Cal. This that Serpent,
Y'haue all (like Traytors) wrought a Princes fall,
And all fhall tafte one death.

Oct. Sirra, wheres the King?

Ruff. Warrant mee life, ile bring you to the place
where you fhall take him.

Oct. Wult thou betray him Slaue?

Ruff. Yes.

Cal. Thou fhalt haue life.

Ruff. And you the King fhall haue.

Oct. And the Gallowes fhall haue thee, elfe hang
    me.

Away.   *Exeunt.*

Enter Scumbroth.

Scum. Alas, wheres the fub-Prior?

Sub. Here; what aileft thou?

Scu. Can you picke nothing out of my face?
Is there not a Deaths-head ftanding on my fhoulders?

Sub. Why, what's the matter?

Scu. The Lord Pryor is calld away.

Sub. Whither, by whome?

Scu. By the Great-head, I thinke he couzened mee,
Hee is gone to the blacke-fquibbe-tree, to *Iudas Okes,*
fet by the Diuell, I tolde you then, I faw Frier *Rufh*
fpit fire amongft other Hel-cats, and yee woud not
belieue me. Now I tell you, that the Pryor is choackt;
will his choaking goe downe your throate?

Sub. How choackt?

Scum. Yes, choackt: that of which men die ore-
night, and are well the next morning, wine has kild
the Lorde Pryor: he woud in a brauerie tafte the

liquor of our Vines, becaufe you threatned he fhould
neuer licke his lippes after.   And the Kernell of a
grape ftopt his winde-pipe, for want of a skowring-
fticke.

Sub.   Art thou fure hee is dead ?

Seum.   How dead, becaufe I wud be fure, I cut
his throate of purpofe, to take out the Kernell.

Sub.   Moft fearefull and prodigious, whither runft
thou ?

Scum.   To fee more throates cut, and Execution
certaine Gallants is this morning.   And I came running to fee them, who like a whore fpoyles euery
good thing that comes into his hand.
The hang-man, I leaue you to the Gallowes.

*Enter Barteruile like a Frier, brought in by the Sub-
    prior, the King, Shackle-foule, and Lurchall, with
    others.*

Rufh.   Welcome deare brother : now your heede
    muft be
Not to looke backe at this worlds vanitie,
Riches and pleafures ; you haue laide afide
That Garment, and muft now be mortifide.

Bar.   I am mortifide, I warrant you.

K.   So is the Diuell.

Pri.   Your Gold and filuer, you muft fee no more.

Bar.   O Fye ! giue it euery farthing to the poore,
When I haue fent for't hither.

Lur.   That will be neuer.

Rufh.   Your money fhalbe fpent in pious fort.

Bart.   I know that : Let my foule be the better
    for't,
Thats all I craue for, after I am dead.

Pri.   Many a *Requiem* for it fhall be faid.

Omn.   What Drum is this ?

Shack.   Fryers ftand vpon your Guard.
The Priorie is befet with Armed-men,
Of which fome Troupes are entred.

> *Kin.*   I am betrayd.
> *Bar.*   *Lurchall* I feele my wezand pipe cut.
> *Lur.*   I warrant you.

*Enter Calabria, Octauio, Aftolfo, Rufman led by
two holding piftalls, Souldiers, drums,
and Cullors.*

> *Cal.*   Guard the Abbey gates, let not a Frier goe
>   forth :
You haue a King amongft you, which is he ?
> *Omn.*   A King !
> *Sub.*   I know of none here.
> *Cal.*   Villaines you lie :
> *Oct.*   This caitife does delude you, tortur him.
> *Cal.*   Hang him, and thefe vp or'e the Abbey walls,
Our wrath fhall fmite like thunder where it falls.
> *Bar.*   I fhall like a dog, die without mony, *Lurchall.*
> *Lur.*   I warrant you.
> *Kin.*   Tyran, that royall hart thou huntft, is here,
Stand from me all, you haue betrayd me all,
And ile truft none of you, if the Lion muft fall,
Fall fhall he like a Lion ; thinkft thou (bafe Lord)
Becaufe the glorious Sun behind blacke cloudes
Has a while hid his beames, hees darkned for euer ?
Ecclipfd neuer more to fhine, yes, and to throw
Fires from his fparkling eyes, thee to confound,
Touch not that noble friend of mine, (It feemes,
For my fake markd for danger,) let your arrowes
(Dipd in rancke poyfon) be fhot all at me,
Since all is loft, die nobly, and loofe life too :
O vncle ! muft the firft dart fly from you ?
> *Oct.*   Into thy bofome fly I.
> *Kin.*   To betray me ?
> *Oct.*   To fight for thee till I can fight no more :
Hadft thou poffeft this Kingly fpirit before,
We ne're had left thee : what makes Iudas here ?
> *Aft.*   Heres he that to the Duke thy life betraide.
> *K.*   *Bohor* !

Oct.   I, *Bohor.*
Ruff.   I told him where you were.
Oct.   I tell thee tha'rt a traitor & ile haue
Thy head off, or thou mine.
Ruff.   Head?
Oct.   Thart a ſlaue?
Thou ſceſt Duke what to truſt too.
Bar.   I haue confeſt, and ſhal be hangd, the King?
Cal.   Our faire game come to this? our ſwordes
    I ſee
Muſt from your hearts-blood let out al my wronges,
A murdred daughter for iuſt vengeance cryes,
Whom to appeaſe, your liues weele ſacrafize :
Beate the drom.
K.   Thunder mock thunder, beate ours.
Sub.   O let theſe fires be quenchd out with my
    teares.
If waters cannot, (Duke) I bind thy rage
With this ſtrong charme, and this read ore that ſpell,
And let thy hard breſt grow more flexible.   *Exit.*
K.   Wheres *Iouinelli*, and that baſtard crue
Of my falſe friendes?
Oct.   Beheaded.
K.   They haue their due.
Cal.   The ring I gaue her, and her hand : old
    man, ——
Wheres the old Frier deliuerd theſe?
Omn.   Hees gon.
Cal.   Make after him, tis ſome deluſion.

Enter Subprior and Erminhild.

Erm.   Tis no deluſion (father) am I the ground
Of this your quarrell, which muſt both confound
If you goe on : your battailes thus ile part,
The firſt blow giuen, ſhall run cleane through my
    heart.
K.   Oh noble conſtant maid, forgiue my wrongs,
The warmth of heauen to a pyning ſpring

Cannot fuch comfort giue as thy glad prefence
Does to my bofome.

    Octa.   Will you fight or no ?

    Cal.   Twere madnes to wifh ftormes when faire
      windes blow :

Will you your faith yet keepe ?

    Kin.   Inuiolate.

    Cal.   Then here end all my warres.

    King.   And all my hate.

Haft all thefe Friers vp to the Abbey walles,
And with fhrill voyces, this our peace proclaime,
Stay holy father : *Bohor*, See you this don.   *Exeunt.*

    Ruf.   Vengeance, I haue now loft more than I
      haue won.

    Bar.   I fhall goe fcot-free *Lurchall.*

    Lur.   Paffing well ?

    Bar.   They doe not fmell me, yet my felfe I fmell.
                                 Exeunt.

    Oct.   Why fends your Highnes, thus thefe Friers to
      play

Your heralds parts in publifhing this peace ?

    Kin.   There's in't a riddle (vncle) which by
      none

But by thefe Friers onely, can be don.————

Enter Friers aboue.

So : are you mounted ? Sing now.

    Omn.   Sing.

    Kin.   Yes fing,

Like Swannes before your deathes : there you all
      fhall dye.

Giue fire to this moft damned priory.

    Sub.   Alacke for pitty !

    Kin.   Father, but for thee,

Thunder from heauen had (long ere this) to duft
Grinded thefe hellifh buildings : that hand was iuft,
Which ftruke your vitious Prior, fo is our doome,
That Synagogue of diuells, let fire confume.

Bar.   But meanes the King that I fhall burne here
too ?

Kin.   Thou ?   the grand villaine, giue him a villaines due.

Bar.   I am no Frier, fee I'me poore *Barteruile.*

Omn.   How ? *Barteruile* ?

Kin.   He lyes the flaue's a Turke.

Bar.   A Chriftian by this hand,   Your officer.

Kin.   The cittie canker, the courts cozener,

A diuell in fhape of man.

Bar.   Halfe that I haue

I freely giue, fo you my life will faue.

Ile lend your Hyghnes 30000. chequines.

K.   Ten Kingdomes cannot buy thee ; were there
10. hels

Thart damd in all.   S'death ! fire that houfe of diuels.

3. *Diu.*   Doe : lets not want light to fet forth our
Reuels.

Ruff.   King, little doeft thou know, whom (all this
while)

Thy court, this Couent, and this *Barteruile*,

Haue entertaind : of hell, 3. Spirits we are.

Omn.   How ?

Ruff.   Sent to catch foules for *Pluto*, our Prince
and maifter.

Omn.   Defend vs heauens.

Ruff.   Thy felfe haft burft thofe bandes

In which I once held thee : thefe are in our handes.

Bar.   If you be right Serieants, for mony youle
let mee goe. 5000. Crownes ile giue but to goe
home.

All. 3.   No.

Bar.   Ile put in 4. brokers to be my baile : I hope
theile be taken.

Ruff.   Yes as thou art, (to hell,) you dog leaue
howling.

This pile of greene young diuels, needes no fire

Of mortals kindling to confume, thefe frames,

You fhall with vs to hell ride, all in flames.
   Shac.   Catch.
   All. 3. Come.
   Ru.   Let euery fpirit his owne prize beare.
   All.   They are fo heauy with fin, theile foone be
    there.
   Ruff.   Away then and be dambd, wud you all were
    here.
   Omn.   Oooh.—*Sinck downe, aboue flames.*
   K.   Immortall thankes for our deliuerance :
Race to the ground thofe wals : no ftone fhall ftand,
To tell fuch place was euer in our land,
What welth can there be found, giue to the poore,
Another houfe weele build and thee reftore,
To former virginitie : weepe not for thefe ruines,
Thou fhalt from vs haue honours. Here we begin
Our reigne anew, which golden threds fhall fpin,
Iuftice fhall henceforth fit vpon our throne,
And vertue be your Kings companion.
Warre here refignes his black and horrid ftage
To fportfull Hymen, God of Mariage.   *(Exeunt.*

> *The play ending, as they goe off, from vnder the
> ground in feuerall places, rife vp fpirits, to
> them enter, leaping in great ioy, Rufman, Shac-
> kle-foule, and Lurchall, difcouering behind a
> curten, Rauillac, Guy Faulx, Barteruile, a
> Prodigall, ftanding in their torments.*

   Omn. *Spir.* Ha, ha, ha.
   Omn. *Dam.* Torments in-vtterable ! oh ! dambd
    for nothing ?
   Rauil.   Terrors incomprehenfible.
   Fau.   Back : y'are blowne vp elfe.
   Bar. Whooh : hot, hot, hot,—drinck,—I am heart-
burnt.
   Prod.   One drop, a bit.

Faul. Now, now, now.

Bar. I am perbold, I am ſtewd, I am ſod in a kettle of brimſtone pottage . . . . it ſcaldes, . . it ſcaldes, . . it ſcaldes, . . it ſcaldes . . whooh.

Diu. Ha ha ha.

Prod. But one halfe crom, a little little drop, a bit.

Faul. Towers, towers, towers, towers, pinnacles & towers, battlements and pynnacles, ſteeples, abbeys, churches and old chimneys.

Bar. Zounds drinke, ſhall I choake in mine Inne ? drinck.

Omn. Drinck, drinck, oh ! one drop, one drop, to coole vs.

Ruff. So many tapſters in hell, and none fill drinck here :

Omn. Ball no more, you ſhall be liquord.

Excunt.

Rau. Why art thou dambd toth' horrors of one
    hell,
Yet feelſt ten thouſand.

Fau. Wherefore is thy ſoule
Made ſenſible of tortures which (each minute)
Kill thee ten thouſand times, yet canſt not dye ?

Bar. Some ſacke.

Prod. Why for a few ſinnes that are long hence
    paſt,
Muſt I feele torments that ſhall euer laſt ?
Euer, euer.

Bar. Let the ſacke be mulld.

Rau. Why is the diuell,
(If man be borne good) ſuffred to make him euill ?

Bar. Man is an aſſe, if he ſit broyling thus ith glaſſe houſe without drinke : two links of my chaine for a threehalfepeny bottle of mother conſciences Ale : drinke.

Omn. One drop of puddle water to coole vs.

> *Enter Shacklefoule with a burning torch, and a*
> *long knife, Lurchall with a handfull of Snakes,*
> *A third fpirit with a ladle full of molten gold.*
> *All three make a ſtand, laughing.*

Omn.   Leaue howling and be dambd.
Shac.   Heres drinke for thee royall villaine.

Stabs Rauillac.

Rau.   Oh !
Shac.   Iſt not good !
For bloud th'aſt thirſted, and thy drinke is bloud.
Strikes it ſo cold to thy heart ? heres that ſhall warme
       thee.   (*Agen.*
Rau.   Damnation, furies, fire-brandes.—

Hand burn't off.

Omn.   Ha, ha, ha,
Prod.   One drop of moiſture, but one crum.
Lur.   Art hungry, eate this adder : dry ? Sucke
   this Snake.
Prod.   Sucke and be dambd thy felfe : Ile ſtarue
   firſt.
Away.
Bar.   Is not this all waters ? Ruby water, ſome
Ruby water, Or els a bottle of poſterne water to ſaue
charges, or els a Thimble-full of lymon water, to coole
my ſtomatch.
Spir.   The ruby is ſwilld vp all, heres lymon,
downe with't.
Bar.   Foh, the great diuell or els ſome Aquauite
woman has made water, It ſcalds me.
Omn.   Oooh.
Diu.   Ha ha ha——*Curtaines are drawne ouer them.*

Enter Rufman.

Ruf.   Hell grinnes to heare this roaring : wheres
this black child of faddomles perdition ? rareſt diuell

That euer hould in *Barathrum* ? here, (deere pupill)
Of a new damnations ſtamp, Saucer-eyde *Lucifer*,
Has drunke to thee this deepe infernall boule off,
Wut pledge his vglines ?
　Fau.　Reach it mee.
　Ruf.　Choake with it.
　Omn.　Ha ha ha.
　Fau.　Giue fire, blow all the world vp.
　Ruf.　Bounce : tis don : Ha ha ha.——

Fires the barrell-tops.

　Fau.　I ſhalbe grinded into duſt; It falls : I am
　　mad.
　Omn.　I am mad, I am mad.——　　　　*Within.*
　All 4.　Ha ha ha.
　Others.　Ho ho ho.——　　　*Spirits from below.*

*Enter Pluto, attended by Minos, Æacus, and Rhada-
　　manth, and 3. Furies.*

　Plu.　Fetch whippes of poyſoned ſteele, ſtrung
　　with glowing wires,
And laſh theſe ſaucie hell-hounds : ducke their ſoules,
Nine times to'th bottome of our brimſtone lakes,
From whence vp pull them by their ſindged hayre,
Then hang 'em in ropes of yce nine times frozen o're :
Are they ſcarce hot in hell, and muſt they roare ?
What holliday's this ? that heres ſuch grinning, ha !
Is hell a dancing Schoole ? yare in extreames,
Snoring, or els horne-mad ? who are ſet on ſhore,
On this vaſt land of horror, that it reſounds,
With laughter ſtead of ſhrikes, who are come to our
　　bounds ?
Ha !
　Ruf.　Dread Lord of this lower tortary, to thy
　　Iayle
Haue we thy buſie Catch-polls (priſoners) brought
Soules, for whoſe comming all hell long hath ſought.

Plu.   Their names : Is *Ward* and *Dantziker* then
   come ?
Omn.   Yes : *Dantziker* is come.
Plu.   Wheres the dutch Schellum ? wheres hells
   factor ! ha ?
Ruf.   *Charon* has bound him for a thoufand yeeres,
To tug ats oare ; he fcourd the Seas fo well,
Charon will make him ferriman of hell.
   Plut.   Where's Ward ?
   Rufh.   The Merchants are not pilld nor pulld
   enough,
They are yet but fhauen, when they are fleade, hee'le
   come.
And bring to hell fat booties of rich theeues,
A crew of fwearers and drinkers the beft that liues.
   Omn.   Ward is not ripe for damming yet.
   Plu.   Who is it then ?
Cutlar the Serieant : ha ! he come.
   Ruf.   Yes *Pluto* :
Cutlar has bin here long, fent in by a carman,
But his fterne lookes the feindes did fo difpleafe,
Bound hand and foote, he houles in little eafe,
Hauing onely mace to comfort him : he does yell,
And raue, becaufe he cannot reft in hell.
   Shac.   Tis not for him, that we this holliday hold.
   Plut.   The baude of Shorditch, Is that hellcat
   come ?
   Ruf.   No : but fha's bin a long time lanching
   forth,
In a Rofa-folis-barke.
   Plu.   Diuells ! who is it then ?
Mall Cutpurfe is fhe come ?
   Omn.   Our cofen come ? No.
   Shac.   Tis not yet fit Mall Cutpurfe here fhould
   houle,
Shee has bin too late a fore-tormented foule.
   Plu.   Where is our daughter ? ha ? Is fhee ydle ?
   Omn.   No.
Shee was beating hemp in bridewell to choke theeues,

Therefore to fpare this fhee-ramp fhe befeeches,
Till like her felfe all women weare the breeches.

    Lur.   Mall Cutpurfe plyes her taske and cannot
      come.
    Plu.   For whom then is this wilde Shroue-tuefday
      kept?
    Ruf.   See King of gloomie fhades what foules
      refort,
To this thy moft iuft, and leaft-fying court.
    Plu.   Stay, fince our Iayle is with braue fellowes
      ftorde,
Bid *Charon* that no more yet come aboard.
Seeing our Iudges of hell here likewife are
Sit : call a Seffions : fet the foules to a barre.
Minos (the iuft :) *Rhadamanth* (the temperate)
And *Æacus* (the feuere,) each take his ftate.
    Min.   Not an officer here?
    Omn.   A Fury.
    3. *Iud.*   Make an Oyes?
    Fury.   Oyes! All manner of foules, if they loue
their owne quietnes, keepe out of hell, vnleffe they
haue horrible bufineffe at this infernall feffions, vpon
paine of being damnably plagude for their luftines.
Back there, let thofe fhackeld rake-hels fhew their
faces.
    Omn.   Roome here, we muft come into the court
within.
    Plu.   What damned fiends are thofe dare make
this noife?
    Shac.   A Iury of Brokers impanelde, and deepely
fworne, to paffe on all the villaines in hell.
    Rhad.   *Euill-Confcience* be their keeper.
    Fury.   Looke to the Iury : *Euill-Confcience* looke
      to the Brokers.
    Plu.   Now proceede.
    Æac.   Stay, let the King of Ghofts haue firft a
      vew
Of thofe who are doom'd to paines horrid, but new.
Then produce thofe who came to your prifon vntryed.

   3   A A

Fur.   Peace there.

Omn.   Heres one, hels tortures does deride.——
Rauillac.

Rau.   Arraigne me, rend me peece-meale, ile confeſſe nothing.

Ruff.   Peace, thou ſhalt ball thy throate out.

Rau.   Merciles hangmen ! to tiranize ouer ſo braue
a Roman ſpirit.

Plu.   Ho, ho, what country diuell is this ?

Rau.   Thine owne.

Ruff.   A french.
The eagereſt bloodhound that ere came from thence ;
Is there a King to be murdred, whileſt he does ſtand
Coloſſus-like, ſupporting a wholc land,
And when by his fall that Land moſt feares a wracke,
Send forth this diuell ; his name is *Rauillac.*

Rau.   *Rauillac* : I am *Rauillac*, that laughes at tortures, ſpurnes at death, defies all mercy : Iybbets,
racks, fires, pincers, ſcalding oyle, wilde-horſes, I ſpit
in the face of all.

Fur.   Peace.

Rau.   No : were my tongue torne out with burning
fleſh-hookes, Fames 1000. tonges ſhall thunder out
Rauillacs name, extoll it, eterniſe it, Cronicle it !
Canoniſe it : oh !

Min.   Downe with this diuell to'th dungeon, there
let him houle.

Rau.   Worlds ſhall applaud my Act, and crowne
my ſoule.   *Exit.*

Plu.   Another.

Omn.   Come, you leane dog.————

Prodigall. Brought in.

Prod.   One drop, a bit.

Plu.   Whats he ? what ſtaruelings this ?

Prod.   One that lacks a medicine for hunger : I am
falne away.

Omn.   From heauen.

Iudg.   To'th common Iayle with him.

Fur.   He muſt feede on beggeries basket : leaue
balling ferra.

Prod.   Shall I be vndon for a little drinke.

Lur.   No, thart vndon for drinking.

Plu.   Starue him away——*Exil Prodigall.*
What was he when he liu'de.

Lur.   A prodigall :
Who (in one yeare,) ſpent on whores, fooles and
    ſlaues,
An Armies maintenance, now begges for cromes, and
    raues
To ſee his ſumptuous buildings, paſtures, woodes,
That ſtood in vplands, dround in Rheniſh floodes.

Plu.   Is here all ?

Shac.   All ! no, the Arch-helhound's here.

Faulx Enters.

Plu.   What Peter Goner's this ?

Fau.   Speake ſoftly, within an inch of giuing fire,
within an inch.

Shac.   Had all thy gray diuells in their higheſt luſt
    ſat,
T'haue litterd furies, they could not haue begot
One to match this : ith' darke he groapd damnation.

Fau.   Now, now.

Shac.   Digd cellars to find where hel ſtood and
    has found it
There was but one villainy vnborne, and he crownd
    it.

Fau.   So : all the billets lye cloſe ; glorious bonfire ? pontificall bonfire ; braue heads to contriue this,
gallant ſoules to conſpire in't, reſolute hand to ſeale
this with my blood, through fire, through flint ; ha, ha,
ha, whither fly my ſelfe to heauen, friends to honour,
none to the halter, enemies to maſſacre, ha, ha, diſmall
tragicall Comedy now ?

Plu.   What does he ?
Shac.   As he thinkes, giuing fire to powder ;
Nere in any land could diuels haue found, fuch
    walkes,
As he was beating out.
Plu.   His name.
Omn.   *Guy Faulx.*
Fau.   Who cals ? damnation ftops throate.
3. *Iud.*   Let it ftop thine.
Fau.   Am I betray'd ? giue fire, now, now, giue fire.
                                            Exit.

Omn.   To burne thine owne foule villaine.
Plu.   Pay him his hire :
He has a defperate rakehels face..
Shac.   Had his plot tane fire,
One realme before any other had doomefday feene,
Kings who in tombes lay at reft had wakened beene,
He was within 12. howers of hewing downe
A whole land at one blow, and at once drowne
In a flood of flames, an Ark roiall with his whole
    fleete,
Of nobilitie and clergy : in a leaden fheete
Law and her children had been hotly wrap'd ;
Millions ere this had in our iayle bin clap'd,
For damned Arts not known now, which had then
Bin rife, but now lye dead (th' Acts with the men.
Plu.   Make much of this our ningle : for the reft
Deliuer 'em to our head-hangman.
Omn.   When ?
Plu.   In a twinckling.
Min.   How applaudes *Pluto*
Our enginous tortures, and moft rigorous doome ?
Plu.   *Minos*, thy doome is iuft ;—But you all-fac'de
    Caitiffs.)
What fifh in your infernall Nets, Drew you vp
Ith *Naples* Court, Citie, and Frierie ?
We charg'de you faile thither : Is mifchiefs Riuer
    there drie ?
Ruff.   Drie, No : Fat preyes for hell we all did
    meete,

In Court, Citie, Countrey, Nay, in euery ſtreete,
In euery houſe, within-him, and without-him.
Hee that wore beſt cloathes, had ſome Diuell about him:
Courtiers from *Naples* hither in ſholes are come,
Some for Ambition, for Flattery, and Enuie ſome:
Some, who (each meale) eate ſubiects vp, and wore
Whole Families in their ſhoo-ſtrings, ſuch, and others
    more,
Being here, haue been examining (euer ſince
They came) by Hells-clarke, (ſpotted-Conſcience.)
   Min. Till the next Seſſions theſe wee muſt deferre.
   Plu. None come fro'th Citie, ſo many bad being
    there!
   Lur. Yes, (King of endles horror) ſee who's here:
Barteruile.
   Plu. Rich-men in hel! they are welcom, whats the
graybeard.
   Bar. One that can buy thee and ten ſuch as thou
art out of thy Sea-coale-pits here. Is not this *New-
caſtle?*
   Lur. No couetous wretch: tis Hell, thy blacke-
ſoules priſon.
   Bar. Soule in priſon! I never had any ſoule to
ſpeake on.
   Lur. Now thou ſhalt finde th'aſt one.
   Bar. Can Angells Bayle mee?
   Min. Not all the wealth which the worlds back
    does beare
Can Bayle thy wretched ſoule hence, Now tis here.
   Bar. A thouſand Pounds.——
   Fur. Where iſt foole?
   Rhad. Thy wealths now gone,
Thy hands ſtill catch at bags, but they gripe none.
   Bar. Whats this?——
   Omn. Ha, ha, ha.
   Æac. Ayre, ſhadowes, things Imaginary:
That is thy Torment now, which was thy Glory.
   Bar. If you giue me bags full of Saw-duſt, in ſtead
of money, my Ghoſt ſhall walke.

3. *Iud*: To thy grim Father of Hell.

Bar. No, to my olde brother, Syr *Achitophell Pinch-gut.*

Plu. Hence with him, the Churl's mad :
In *Lethes*-flood drownd all the wealth hee had.

Bar. My chaine, Let me hang in chaines, fo it bee my Golde chaine ; Theeues, theeues, theeues.   *Exit.*

Min. Throwe him head-long into our boyling-
Lake,
Where molten Golde runnes.

Lur. His thirft it cannot flake,
Seas could not quench his dropfie : Golde to get
Hee would hang a Citie, ftarue a Countrey. Euen
yet
Raues hee for Bonds and incombers : to faue whofe
foule,
(Tho hee fed none liuing) Saw-fages were his dole.

A confufed noyfe to come preffing in.

Omn. What coyle is that ?   *A Noife.*

Enter a Ghoaft, cole-blacke.

Pur. Tis a burning zeale muft confume the wicked, and therefore I will not bee kept out, but will chaftize and correct the foule Fiend.

3. *Iud.* Whats this blacke *Incubus* ?

Shac. An Arch-great Puritane once.

Omn. Ha ! How ! a Puritane ?

Min. An Arch-great Puritane ! How comes thy foule fo little ?

Pur. I did exercife too much with a liuely Spirit.

Plu. Are there any more of his Synagogue ?

Ruff. Yes a whole Hoy-full are Landed.

Omn. Ha !

Plu. Are they all fo blacke as he is ?

Omn. Worfe.

Min. Syrra, why being a Puritane is your foule fo black ?

Pur. Wee were all fmoakt out of our owne Coun-trey, and fent to *Rotterdam.*

Min. How camft thou lame and crooked, why do'ft halt ?

Pur. All the brethren and fifters for the better part are crooked, and halt : for my owne part, I neuer went vpright.

Iudg. And yet a puritane ? hence with him.

Pur. Alacke !
How can I choofe but halt, goe lame, and crooked ?
When I pulld a whole church downe vpon my backe.

Min. Hence with him, he will pull all hell downe too.

A noife to come in.

Pur. Let in the brethren, to confound this wicked affembly.

3. *Iud.* Thruft him out at hell gates.

Plu. Theile confound our kingdome,
If here they get but footing: rife therefore, away ;
Keepe the Iurie of brokers till our next court day.

Min. Adiourne this.

Fur. O yes ! Seffions is deferd
Becaufe of Puritanes, Hell cannot be cleerd.

Plu. Set forward to our Hall paued all with braffe,
Iudges we thanke you : let our officers drinke,
Ith bottome of hells celler, for their good feruice.
Since to this heigth our Empyre vp you reare,
Hell fhall hold triumphes, and (thats don,) prepare,
Agen to walke your circuites o're the earth,
Soules are hells Subiects, and their grones our mirth.

F I N I S.

Epilogue.

IF't be not good, the Diuell is in't, (they fay,)
   The Diuell was in't, this then is no good play
By that conclufion, but hereby is meant,
If for fo many nones, and midnights fpent
To reape three howres of mirth, our harueft-feede
Lyes ftill and rot. The Diuels in't then indeed :
Much Labour, Art, and Wit, make vp a Play
As it does a Ship, yet both are caft away,
(When brauely they haue paft the humorous Seas)
At landing, What black fates curfeth both thefe ?
Sayle it, or finck it, now tis forth, and nere
The Hauen at which it longs t'ariue : if there
It fuffers wrack, the fpitefuller Rockes fhoote forth,
Yet non may bring it home laden with much worth.
By wonted gentle gale, (fweete as the Balme,)
Or by extending your faire liberall Palme,
To fan away all ftormes, if you fee it lowers,
The ayre fhall ring thankes, but the glory's yours.

NOTES AND ILLUSTRATIONS.

PAGE 4.

the other for Weftchefter.

On their way to Ireland : "My refuge is *Ireland* or Virginia ; neceffity cries out, and I will prefently to *Weftchefter*." Cook's *Green's Tu Quoque*, ed. 1622. " Hee came into *Ireland*, where at Dubblin hee was ftrucke lame ; but recovering new ftrength and courage, hee fhip'd himfelfe for England, *landed at Weft Chefter*, whence taking pofte towards London, hee lodg'd at Hockley in the Hole, in his way," &c. Taylor the water poet's *Praife of cleane Linnen,*— *Works*, 1630, p. 170. It may perhaps be neceffary to add, that the ancient city of Chefter is called *Weft* Chefter from its relative fituation, to diftinguifh it from feveral other towns which bear the name of Chefter with fome addition.

PAGE 5.

and your felfe fhall keepe the key of it.

From Shakefpeare :—

 " 'Tis in my memory lock'd,
And you yourfelf fhall keep the key of it."
       Hamlet, act i. fc. 3.

PAGE 10.

you fhall finde me playing at Span-counter.

A pun is intended here : *fpan-counter* being a common game among boys, *counter*, the prifon, to which, if he could procure no bail, Philip was to be configned.

PAGE 11.

Doe you laugh you vnſeaſonable puck-fiſt ?

This word, often uſed by our old writers in the ſenſe of an empty, inſignificant fellow, meant originally a ſort of fungus: "All the ſallets are turn'd to Jewes-ears, muſhrooms, and *Puckfiſts.*" Heywood and Brome's *Lancaſhire Witches,* 1634.

PAGE 12.

Are all the Queſt houſes broken up?

About Chriſtmas, the aldermen and citizens of each ward in the city uſed to hold a queſt to inquire concerning miſ-demeanours and annoyances, brothels, &c. *Queſt-houſes* were the houſes where the queſt was held, and which were uſually the chief watchhouſes. Doll, in her next ſpeech, alludes to the ſhifts made by the ladies when driven out of the city, and their private return when they no longer feared the queſt.

From a paſſage in one of Middleton's plays it appears that gaming was ſometimes carried on there: "Such a day I loſt fifty pound in hugger-mugger at dice, at the *queſt-houſe.*" *Any thing for a quiet life,—Works,* iv. 425, ed. Dyce.

Queſt-houſes generally adjoined churches: "But you may ſay, it is like a farthing candle in a great church: I anſwer, that light will not enlighten the by-chapels of the church, nor *the queſt-houſe,* nor the belfry; neither doth the light move the church, though it enlightens it."—*Philoſophical Letters* by the Ducheſs of Newcaſtle, 1664, p. 189.

Ib.

with a chaine about his neck . . . . . For that, Saint Martins and wee will talke.

So Brathwait:

> "By this hee trauels *to Saint Martins lane,*
> And to the ſhops he goes *to buy a chaine.*"
> *The Honeſt Ghoſt,* &c., 1658, p. 167.

PAGE 13.

double chin.

The characteriſtic of a bawd, according to many of our old dramatiſts:

> "The bawds will be fo fat with what they earn,
> Their chins will hang like udders, by Eafter-eve."
> Middleton's *Chafte Maid in Cheapfide,*—*Works,*
> iv. 32.

PAGE 13.

neuer had the Grincoms :

Or *crincomes,* a cant term for the venereal difeafe : "Grink-comes," fays Taylor, the water poet, "is an Utopian word, which is in Englifh a P. at Paris."—*Works,* 1630, p. 111.

PAGE 15.

WIFE.   *Good Sir, lend me patience.*
MAY.   *I made a fallade of that herbe.*

Patience was the name of an herb : "You may recover it with a fallet of parfly and *the hearbe patience."*—*A pleafant commodie called Looke about you,* 1600.

PAGE 19.

Farewell, Father Snot.

This elegant valediction (after which, in the old copy, is a fhort break) was, perhaps, a parody on, or a quotation from, fome fong.   In *The Wit of a Woman,* 1604, we find,

> " My bufh and my pot
> Cares not a groate
> For fuch a lob-coate,
> *Farewell, Sinior fnot."*

PAGE 20.

the bragging velure-canioned *hobbi-horfes.*

Velure is velvet.

"Cannions, of breeches. G. canóns : on les appele ainsi pource qu'ils font aucunement femblables aux canóns d'artillerie, —becaufe they are like cannons of artillery, or cans or pots."—Minfheu's *Guide into the tongues,* p. 61, ed. 1617.

Strutt explains *canions* to be "ornamental tubes or tags at the ends of the ribbands and laces which were attached to the extremities of the breeches."—*Drefs and Habits,* &c., vol. ii. p. 263.

Canon-hofe, decorated at the knees with a quantity of ribbons, were fafhionable in the time of Charles the Second.

In a MS. copy of a comedy called *The Humourous Lovers*, by the Duke of Newcaftle, among the Harleian MSS., the following fong (not given in the printed copy of the play, 1677) occurs at the beginning of the 4th act :—

> " I conjure thee, I conjure thee,
> By the Ribands in thy Hatt,
> By thy pritty lac'd Cravat,
> By the Ribands round thy Bum,
> Which is brac'd much like a Drum,
> By thy dangling Pantaloons,
> And thy ruffling Port *Cannons,*
> By thy freezeld Perriwige,
> Which does make thee look fo bigg,
> By thy Sword of Silver guilt,
> And the Riband at thy Hilt,—
> Apeare, apear."

PAGE 26.

by this Iron (which is none a gods Angell)

Compare Dekker, *Satiromaftix* :
" I markt, by this candle, *which is none of God's Angels.*"
(See Notes to Vol. II. p. 368.)

PAGE 27.

Mi cara whee, en hellon.

Qy.? Mi gara chwi yn nghalon.

Ib.

there is the moft abominable feere.

The captain does not ufe *abominable* in a bad fenfe, quite the reverfe : fo in Field's *A Woman is a Weathercock,* 1612 :
" *Abraham.* Does fhe fo love me fay you?
" *Pendant.* Yes, yes, out of all queftion the whore does love you *abhominable.*"
Is it neceffary to add that by "*feer*" he means *cheer,* and, a little after, by "*kernicles,*" *chronicles ?*

PAGE 28.

fare-well Sidanien.

"Sidanen, s. f. *dim.* (fidan) that is filken, or made of filk. It is the name of an old tune ; *also an epithet for a fine woman;* and has been applied particularly to Queen Elizabeth."—Owen's *Dictionary of the Welch Language.*

PAGE 33.

I left her at Bofomes Inne.

"Antiquities in this Lane [St. Lawrence Lane] I find none other than that, among many fair Houfes, there is one large Inne for receit of Travellers, called *Bloffoms Inne*, but corruptly *Bofoms Inne*, and hath to fign S. Laurence the Deacon, in a border of Bloffoms or Flowers."—Stow's *Survey of London*, &c., B. iii. p. 40, ed. 1720.

PAGE 34.

he would goe the Iland voiage.

Undertaken againft Hifpaniola, in 1585. The fleet, commanded by Sir Francis Drake, confifted of twenty-one fhips, carrying above two thoufand volunteers. They took poffeffion of St. Domingo.

PAGE 35.

fome noughty packe whome my husband hath fallen in loue with, and meanes to keepe vnder my nofe at his garden houfe.

Garden-houfes were ufed for fuch purpofes : fo in the opening of Barry's *Ram-Alley*, 1611 :

> "what makes he heere,
> In the fkirts of Holborne, fo neere the field,
> *And at a garden-houfe ? a has fome punke,*
> *Upon my life.*"

PAGE 37.

with a cartoofe collour and a pickadell.

A *piccadel* is defcribed as an upright collar with ftiffened plaits : here it feems to mean a fort of edging to the collar.

PAGE 38.

Ile haue you make 12. poefies for a dozen of cheefe trenchers.

Cheefe-trenchers, at the time this play was written, ufed frequently to have pofies infcribed on them. In Dekker's *Honeft Whore, Part Firft,* George quotes fix lines, "as one of our *cheefe-trenchers* fayes very learnedly :" (Vol. II. p. 72.) Compare too Middleton's *No Wit, no Help, like a Woman's ;*

"*L. Gold.* Twelve trenchers, upon every one a month ! January, February, March, April—

Pep. Ay, and their pofies under 'em.

L. Gold. Pray, what fays May ? fhe's the fpring lady.

Pep. [*reads*]

> *Now gallant May, in her array,*
> *Doth make the field pleafant and gay,*" *&c.*

ed. Dyce, v. 40.

Ib.

I had three neft of them giuen mee.

So in the opening of Marfton's *Dutch Courtezan,* 1605 ; "cogging Cocledemoy is runne away with a *neaft of goblets ;*" and fo in Armin's *Two Maides of Moreclacke,* 1609 ;

> "Place your plate, and pile your vitriall boales
> *Neft* upon *neft.*"

The term *neft of goblets* is ftill made ufe of in the Weft Riding of Yorkfhire, to defcribe a large goblet containing many fmaller ones of gradually diminifhing fizes, which fit into each other and fill it up.

PAGE 40.

Pax.

For *pox ;* it was perhaps an affected mode of pronouncing the word. So Heywood and Brome in *The late Lancafhire Witches,* 1634, "*Pax,* I think not on't ;" Brome in the *Joviall Crew,* 1652, "*Pax* o' your fine thing ;" and Middleton, in *Your Five Gallants,* "*Pax* on't, we fpoil ourfelves for want of thefe things at univerfity.—*Works,* ii. 235.

PAGE 41.

the tree in Cuckolds Hauen.

A little below Rotherhithe is a fpot, clofe on the river, called

Cuckold's Point, which is diftinguifhed by a tall pole with a pair of horns on the top. Tradition fays that near this place there lived, in the reign of King John, a miller who had a handfome wife ; that his majefty had an intrigue with the fair dame, and gave the hufband, as a compenfation, all the land on that fide, which he could fee from his houfe, looking down the Thames,— which land, however, he was to poffefs only on the condition of walking on that day (the 18th of October) annually to the fartheft bounds of his eftate with a pair of buck's horns on his head ; and that the miller, having cleared his eyefight, faw as far as Charlton, and enjoyed the land on the above-mentioned terms. (In feveral books which condefcend to notice this ftory we are told that the miller lived at Charlton and faw as far as Cuckold's Point ; but the verfion of it which is here given is what the watermen on the Thames were wont to repeat.)   Horn-fair was long held at Charlton, on the 18th of October, in commemoration of the event.

PAGE 49.

garlick has a white head and a greene ftalke.

So in *The Honeft Lawyer*, 1616; "I'm like a lecke, though I have a gray head, I have a greene," &c.   And fo in various old plays and poems, Chaucer's *Reve's Prologue*, &c.   This piece of wit may be traced to Boccaccio ; " E quagli che contro alla mia età parlando vanno, moftra mal che conoscano che, *perche il porro abbia il capo bianco, che la coda fia verde.*"   *Decamerone,*— Introduction to *Giornata quarta.*

PAGE 50.

as if I were a bawd, no ring pleafes me but a death's head.

The bawds of thofe days, probably from an affectation of piety, ufed to wear rings with death's-heads on them, as feveral paffages from old writers might be adduced to fhow.   But the wearing of fuch rings was not confined to thofe motherly gentlewomen : "the olde Counteffe fpying on the finger of Seignior Cofimo *a Ring with a Death's head ingraven,* circled with this Pofic, Greffus ad vitam, demaunded whether hee adorde the Signet for profit or pleafure : Seignior Cofimo fpeaking in truth as his confcience wild him, told her that it was a favour which a Gentlewoman had beftowed upon him, and that onely hce wore it for her fake." Greene's *Farewell to Follie*, ed. 1617.—Underwood the player bequeathed "to his daughter Elizabeth two feal-rings of gold, *one with a death's-head.*" See his will in Malone's *Hift. Acc. of the Englifh Stage*, p. 216, ed. Bofwell.

PAGE 52.

my white Poet.

White was employed formerly as an epithet to exprefs fondnefs: "*white* boy," "*white* fon," and "*white* girl," occur frequently in our old writers. Lee ufes it in a ftrange paffage of the Dedication of his *Rival Queens* to the Earl of Mulgrave. (Though Mayberry a little after calls Bellamont "my little hoary poet," we are not to conclude that "*white*" in the prefent inftance means *hoary*.)

PAGE 58.

I was a dapper rogue in Portingal voyage.

The *Portugal voyage* was the expedition in 1589, confifting of one hundred and eighty veffels, and twenty-one thoufand men, commanded by Sir Francis Drake and Sir John Norris: it is generally faid to have been undertaken for the purpofe of feating Antonio on the throne of Portugal; but the brave volunteers who compofed it were moft probably excited to the enterprife by the wifh to revenge themfelves on Spain, and by the hopes of gain and glory.

Ib.

the prentices made a riot vpon my glaffe windows, the Shrove-tuefday following.

Shrove-Tuefday was a holiday for apprentices, during which they ufed to be exceedingly riotous, and attempt to demolifh houfes of bad fame:

> " It was the day of all dayes in the yeare,
> That unto Bacchus hath his dedication,
> *When mad-braynd prentifes*, that no men feare,
> *O'rethrow the dens of bawdie recreation.*"
>
> *Pafquils Palinodia*, 1634.

PAGE 59.

Mother Walls cakes.

We learn where this dame refided from the following paffage of Haughton's *Englifh-men for my money*, 1616; "I have the fcent of London-ftone as full in my nofe, as Abchurch-lane of *Mother Walles* pafties."

PAGE 59.

like fquibs that run vpon lynes.

So Marfton, in his *Parafitafter, or the Fawne*, 1606;
" *Page.* There be fquibs, fir, which fquibs running upon lines, like fome of our gawdie gallants, fir, keepe a fmother, fir, with flifhing and flafhing, and in the end, fir, they doe, fir——
Nymphadora. What, fir?
Page. Stink, fir."
In *A Rich Cabinet with Variety of Inventions, &c.*, 1651, by J. White, are inftruétions "How to make your fireworks to run upon a line backward and forward."

PAGE 81.

The Famous Hiftory of Sir Thomas Wyat.

There can be no doubt that *The Famous Hiftory of Sir Thomas Wyat* confifts merely of fragments of two plays,—or rather, a play in Two Parts,—called *Lady Jane*, concerning which we find the following entries in *The Diary of Henflowe;*

" Lent unto John Thare, the 15 of oétobr 1602, to geve unto harey chettell, *Thomas Deckers*, Thomas Hewode, and Mr. Smyth, and Mr. Webfter, in earnefte of aplaye called Ladey Jane, the fome of . . . . ls

" Lent unto Thomas Hewode, the 21 of oétobr 1602, to pay unto *Mr. Dickers*, chettell, Smythe, Webefter and Hewode, in fulle payment of ther play of ladye Jane, the fome of . . . vli xs

" Lent unto John Ducke, the 27 of oétobr 1602, to geve unto *Thomas Deckers*, in earnefte of the 2 pt of Ladye Jane, the fome of . . . vs"

Pp. 242—3, ed. Shakefpeare Soc.

Whether the prefent abridgment of *Lady Jane* was made by Dekker and Webfter (fee its title-page), or by fome other play-wright, cannot be determined ; that it has fuffered cruelly from the hands of the tranfcriber or printer, is certain.—DYCE.

This drama is much mutilated, and its text very defective. It is a very inferior production. There is no difcrimination of cha-racter, no fucceffion of events, and no artful or judicious develop-ment of conduct. There is, however, a gentle and penfive intereft in the forcible fcenes and feparation of Guildford and Lady Jane, and in that mild refignation to their fate, which arifes from their blamelefs and innocent conduct. [Rev.] J. M(itford) in *Gent. Mag.*, June 1833, p. 491.

PAGE 87.

GUI.　*We are led with pompe to prifon.*

Mr. Dyce affigns this fpeech to Lady Jane.

Ib.

Like funerall Coffins, in fome funerall Pompe.

The text of this line is obvioufly corrupt. Mr. Collier (Preface to Coleridge's Lectures, p. cv.) propofes to read "feveral coffins," an emendation adopted by Mr. Dyce in his edition of Webfter.

PAGE 90.

Dying the hauen of Brit. with guiltie blood.

Mr. Dyce reads "Britain." The Rev. J. Mitford (*Gent. Mag.* for June 1833, p. 491) would read "Brute,"—which helps the metre fomewhat, but does not improve the fenfe.

PAGE 93.

if that their Brother dying Iffules, &c.

Mr. Dyce thinks there is manifeftly a line or lines wanting here.

PAGE 94.

That no impeachment *fhould diuert our heartes*
From the impeachment *of the Lady Iane.*

In the fecond line Mr. Dyce has fubftituted " election" for *im-peachment.* The following is his note on the paffage :—

" The old copies have,—

 ' From the *impeachment* of the Lady Jane,'—

the word '*impeachment*' having been repeated from the preceding line by a miftake of the tranfcriber or printer. That the firft '*impeachment*'—i.e. hindrance, let, impediment,—is right, there can be no doubt ; and that in the fecond line '*election*' is the author's word, feems equally certain ; compare what Arundel has faid a little before,—

 ' Are you not griev'd that we have given confent
  To *Lady Jane's election ?*"

(The reading of this paffage propofed by Mr. Mitford (*Gent. Mag.* for June 1833, p. 492),—

 ' That no *impediment* fhould divert our hearts
  From the *impeachment* of the Lady Jane,'—

alters the right word in the firft line, and leaves the wrong one in the fecond.)"

PAGE 95.

Lance perfado, *quarter, quarter.*

Written alfo *lanceprifado, lancepefado, lancepefade,* or *lancepefata;* (Ital. *lancia fpezzata,*) the loweft officer of foot, one who is under the corporal.

" He is a gentleman of no ancient ftanding in the militia, for he draws his pedigree from the time of the wars between Francis I. and his fon, Henry II., kings of France, on the one part ; and the Emperor Charles V., and his brother-in-law, the Duke of Savoy, on the other part. In thofe wars, when a gentleman of a troop of horfe, in any fkirmifh, battle, or rencounter, had broke his lance on the enemy, and loft his horfe in the fcuffle, he was entertained (under the name of a broken lance) by a captain of a foot company as his comrade, till he was again mounted. But as all good orders fall foon from their primitive inftitution, fo in a fhort time our Monfieur Lancepefata (for fo he was called) was forced to defcend from being the captain's comrade, and become the caporal's companion, and affifted him in the exercife of his charge, and therefore was fometimes called by the French, *aide caporal.* But when the caporal grew weary of the comradefhip of his lancepefata, he made him officiate under him, and

for that had fome allowance of pay more than the common
foldier."—Turner's *Pallas Armata*, p. 219—(as quoted by Grofe,
Mil. Ant., v. i., p. 262.)

PAGE 115.

There came but one Dondego *into England, and he made all*
Paules ftinke againe.

i.e. Don Diego.—So Heywood;

> " But for thefe Spaniards, now *you Don Diegoes,*
> *You that made Paules to ftinke."*
>
> *Fair Maid of the Weft,* 1631, Part 1ft, p. 51.

Various other writers allude to the nafty feat of this Don Diego
in St. Paul's Cathedral; and it is very plainly told in a letter
among the Cottonian MSS. (*Jul. C.* iii.), which muft have been
written about the beginning of 1597.

PAGE 123.

Guil.   True, my faire Queene, of forrowe truely fpeake,
Great men like great flies through Lawes cobwebs breake,
But the thinn'ft frame the prifon of the weake.

Mr. Dyce fuggefts the emendation " oft forrow truly fpeaks"
in the firft line.   It is probable that Dekker wrote this fcene,
as the following paffage occurs in one of his plays :—

> " *Jovinelli.*   You muft hang up the lawes.
>
> *Octavio.*   Like cob-webbe in fowle roomes, through which
> great flies
>
> Breake through, the leffe being caught bi'th wing there
> dies."

If this be not a good play the devil is in it, 1612, (page 287.)
But the fimile is derived from ancient wifdom :—"One of the
Seven was wont to fay, that laws were like cob-webs; where the
fmall flies were caught, and the great brake through."   Bacon's
Apophthegms, No. 284.

PAGE 133.

Shall fill with laughter our vaft Theater.

i.e. the Fortune, in Golden or Golding Lane, St. Giles's,

Cripplegate. It was built by Henflowe and Alleyn, in 1599—1600, and was eighty feet fquare on the outfide, and fifty-five feet fquare within. It was deftroyed by fire in 1621.

Page 138.

Falling bands.

Thefe bands, which lay flat upon the drefs from the neck, fucceeded the cumberfome ruff. There is a *jeu de mots* upon the name in Dekker's *If this be not a good Play, the Diuell is in it* (page 315):

> " Tho my collar [choler] ftand
> So hye, it fcarce beares vp this falling band."

" Band," it fhould be oblerved, was formerly fynonymous with "*bond.*"

Page 145.

Well fhot old Adam Bell.

An outlaw, famous for his archery : fee the ballad of *Adam Bel, Clym of the Cloughe and Wyllyam of Cloudefle*, in Ritfon's *Pieces of An. Pop. Poetry.*

Page 147.

yet do you now
Thus baffle *me to my face.*

" Baffle" meant formerly to treat with infult, mockery, or contempt. It is ufed again in this fenfe in Dekker's *If this be not a good Play*, &c. (page 291): " No King on earth baffalls me." Mr. Dyce alfo cites paffages from Nafh and Marmyon.

Page 155.

a blacke fauegard.

i.e. a fort of large petticoat, worn by women over their other clothes, to protect them from foiling.

Page 159.

Saint Antlings-bell.

At St. Antholin's church there ufed to be a lecture early in the morning, which was much frequented by the puritans of the times.

PAGE 161.

I'le try one fpeare againſt your chaſtity
Though it proue too ſhort by the burgh.

" Burgh," or *burre,* is " a broad ring of iron behind the handle" of a tilting lance, "which burre is brought into the fufflue or reſt, when the tilter is ready to run againſt his enimy, or prepareth himſelf to combate or encounter his adverſe party." R. Holme's *Acad. of Armoury.*

PAGE 170.

good phrampell iudes.

" Phrampel," which is written alfo *frampold, frampul,* &c., here appears to fignify *fiery* or *mettlefome.* It generally means vexatious, faucy, pceviſh, &c.

PAGE 173.

quarrelling wedlockes

i.e. wives.

Ib.

al my flanders

So the orig. edition ; but there is hardly any doubt that Mr. Dyce's emendation of " flanderers " is the correct reading.

PAGE 174.

if his ſpirit
Be anſwerable to his vmbles.

i.e. his infide. *Umbles* are the entrails of a deer.

PAGE 176.

I thinke the baby would haue a teate it kyes *ſo.*

" Kyes" for cries, in imitation of the jargon talked by nurfes to infants.

PAGE 177.

it does mee good now to have her fing mee.

There can fcarcely be any doubt that Mr. Dyce's emendation of "fting" is correct.

Ib.

Now fye how you vex me, I cannot abide thefe aperne husbands : fuch cotqueanes, you owerdoe your things, &c.

"Apron husbands :" *i.e.* husbands who follow their wives as if tied to their apron-ftrings. "Cotqueans :" *i.e.* men who meddle with female affairs. The exclamations of Miftrefs Galli-pot evidently refer to fome action on the part of her husband : this portion of the fcene is very adroitly *written*, requiring to be read *entre les lignes* like the dialogue in *La Nuit et le Moment* of Crebillon fils; but how it can have been reprefented publicly on the ftage it is difficult to imagine.

PAGE 178.

as Pan-da-rus *was to* Cref-fida :

So in the old edition, to mark the difficulty with which fuch hard names were read by miftrefs Gallipot.

PAGE 180.

Since laft I faw him twelue moneths three times told,
The Moone hath drawne through her light filuer bow.

In Dekker's *Whore of Babylon* (vol. II. p. 195) we find :
" Fiue Summers haue fcarce *drawn* their glimmering nights
Through the Moons filuer bowe."
It feems, therefore, almoft certain that the fcene in *The Roaring Girle* containing the above lines was written by him and not by Middleton.

PAGE 185.

the bouncing Rampe (*that Roaring Girle my Miftreffe*).

"Ramp :" *i.e.* ramping, rampant creature : "although fhe were a luftie *bounfing rampe*, fomewhat like Gallemalla," &c. G. Harvey's *Pierces Supererogation*, 1593, p. 145.

PAGE 186.

her placket *to the ancient feate of a codpice.*

"Placket" has been varioufly explained—the opening of the petticoat—the forepart of the fhift or petticoat : Nares, in his Gloffary, infifts that it meant only a petticoat, generally an under one.

PAGE 191.

thefe men-midwiues muft bring him to bed i' the counter.

So in Dekker's *Whore of Babylon* (vol. II. p. 213.) "Doe not you know miftreffe, what Serieants are ? . . . why they are certaine men-midwiues, that neuer bring people to bed, but when they are fore in labour, that no body els can deliuer them."

PAGE 200.

haue not many handfome legges in filke ftockins villanous fplay feete for all their great rofes ?

Rofes anciently were worn in fhoes. They were made of ribbons gathered into a knot, and were fometimes of a pre-pofterous fize.

Ib.

an agget fet in a crampe ring.

i.e. a ring, which having been folemnly confecrated on Good Friday, was fuppofed to have the power of preventing the cramp. (See in Waldron's Literary Mufeum, 1792, a reprint of *The Cere-monies of Blefling Cramp-Rings on Good Friday, ufed by the Catholic Kings of England.*

PAGE 202.

till all fplit.

This expreffion occurs in feveral old plays ; and denotes vio-lence of action.

PAGE, 203.

'Faith gib, *are you fpitting, I'le cut your tayle puf-cat for this.*

"Gib" is, properly, a male cat, but is fometimes applied, as a term of reproach to a woman : "She is a tonnyſh gyb" ſays Skelton, in *Elynour Rummyng*, v. 99.

PAGE 203.

y'are beſt get you a mumming.

i.e. a masquing, in which originally the performers uſed geſticulation only, without ſpeaking : miſtreſs Openwork puns on the different meanings of *maſk* and *maſque.*

PAGE 205.

to be made
A ſtale to a common whore?

i.e. a pretence or cover under which he keeps a harlot : the *ſtale,* or *ſtalking-horſe,* was the real or artificial horſe behind which ſportſmen approached their game.

Ib.

I ſweate, wo'ld I lay in cold harbour.

Cold-Harbour, or *Cold-Harborough* was an ancient building, ſituated in the pariſh of All-hallows the Leſs, in Downgate Ward. A good many years before the date of this play, the then Earl of Shrewsbury took it down, and built a number of ſmall tenements in its ſtead, which were let at great rents and ſerved as a retreat for debtors, &c.; the place being conſidered a ſort of ſanctuary, probably becauſe Tunſtall, biſhop of Durham, had reſided there in Henry VIII.'s reign. It appears to have been notorious as a place where marriages were ſolemnized haſtily and without the proper forms; ſuch as the Fleet Priſon and Keith's Chapel were for ſome time before the paſſing of the marriage-act.

Nares citing the above paſſage in his Gloſſary, says that *Cold Harbour* "ſeems to be uſed as a kind of metaphorical term for the grave."

Ib.

Puſh; your Weſterne pug.

"I doubt the ſand-eyde aſſe will kicke like a *Weſterne pugge,*

if I rubbe him on the gall." Greene's *Theeues falling out.*
" Euen the *Weſterne Pugs* receiuing mony here, haue tyed it in a
bag at the end of their barge, and ſo trailed it through the
Thames," &c. Dekker's *Wonderfull Yeare*, 1603.

PAGE 206.

Oh braue girles: worth Gold.

This expreſſion ſeems to have been proverbial: one of Heywood's plays is entitled *The Fair Maid of the Weſt, or A Girle
worth gold* (1631).

Ib.

I'le ride to Oxford, and watch out mine eies, but I'le heare the
brazen head ſpeak.

See *Friar Bacon and Friar Bungay* (firſt printed in 1594) in
Dyce's edition of Greene's Dramatic Works (vol. i. p. 141), and
the extract given (p. 215) from the proſe tract on which that
play is founded, *The Famous Hiſtorie of Friar Bacon*, "How
Fryer Bacon made a Brazen Head to ſpeake, by the which hee
would haue walled England about with Braſſe." The friars loſt
all their labour through the folly of a ſervant named Miles, who
having been ſet to watch the Head while they retired to reſt,
neglected to call them when at laſt it ſpoke.

PAGE 209.

*ſeeing your women are ſo hote, I muſt looſe my haire in their
company I ſee.*

"Alluding," ſays Reed, "to the conſequences of lewdneſs,
one of which, in the firſt appearance of the diſeaſe in Europe,
was the loſs of hair."

Ib.

I pray who playes a knacke to know an honeſt man *in this
company?*

*A Pleaſant Conceited Comedie, called, A knacke to know an
honeſt Man, As it hath beene ſundrie times plaied about the Citie of
London*, was printed in 1596. The author's name is unknown.

PAGE 210.

Get *fethers from thy wings.*

Mr. Dyce fubftitutes "gelt" for *get;* but "is by no means confident that he has reftored the right reading" (Middleton's Works, ii. 527).

Ib.

Play out your game at Irifh *fir : Who winnes?*
MIST. OPEN. *The triall is when fhee comes to* bearing.

A game which differs very flightly from backgammon. The manner of playing it is defcribed in *The Compleat Gamefter.* At page 155—6 (of ed. 1674) the following advice is given :— "*Bear* as faft as you can . . . . . when you *come to bearing,* have a care," &c.

PAGE 211.

Then feeing all bafe defires rak'd vp in duft,
And that to tempt her modeft cares, I fwore, &c.

An intermediate line feems to have dropped out : probably another is wanting after "And yet to try," &c.

Ib.

was it your Megge *of Weftminfters courage.*

Meg of Weftminfter, or long Meg of Weftminfter, was a virago of whom frequent mention is made by our early dramatifts, and indeed, like the heroine of the prefent piece, fhe had the honour of figuring in a play called after her in 1594. At that period, however, fhe is fuppofed to have been dead. She is introduced in an ante-mafque in Ben Jonfon's *Fortunate Ifles.* A quarto tract entitled *The Life of Long Meg of Weftminfter : containing the mad merry prankes fhe played in her life time, not onely in performing fundry quarrels with divers ruffians about London; but alfo how valiantly fhe behaued herfelfe in the warres of Bol-loingne,* was printed (perhaps not for the firft time) in 1635.

PAGE 212.

like a fire-worke to run vpon a line betwixt him and me.

So Dekker, in his *Whore of Babylon :*
"Let vs behold thefe fire-workès, that muft run
Vpon fhort lines of life."

PAGE 212.

away flia I my man, like a fhouell-board fhilling.

i. e., a fhilling ufed at the game of *fhovel-board*, and which was always fmooth, that it might "flide away" eafily.

Ib.

thefe London boote-halers.

Freebooters, plunderers, *halers* of *boot* (profit), or *booty*. Cotgrave explains *picoreur* to be a " *boot-haler* (in a friend's country), a ravening or filching fouldier."

PAGE 213.

Heeres fuch a merry ging.

i. e., gang. This fubftitution of *i* for *a* was common with the Elizabethan writers. The word *ging* or *gyng*, however, is of great antiquity.

PAGE 215.

you skeldering *varlet.*

Skeldring was a cant term for impudent begging, generally applied to vagrants, and often ufed by our early writers. It appears to have been particularly appropriated to thofe vagabonds who wander about under the name of foldiers, borrowing or begging money.

Ib.

The balles of thefe glafiers *of mine (mine eyes).*
See Dekker's *Lanthorne and Candlelight* (1612).

PAGE 216.

A meere whip-Iacke.

In Dekker's *Belman of London* (1608), the defcription of "A Whipiacke" is much the fame as that which Moll gives here.

"An vpright man," "a wilde rogue," "an angler," "a ruffler," "a kinchin mort," and a "wilde del" are alfo fully defcribed in the fame curious tract.

Ib.

hornes for the thumbe.

Pick-pockets were faid to place a cafe, or thimble, of horn on their thumbs, to fupport the edge of the knife in the act of cutting purfes.

PAGE 219.

Now I fee that you are ftal'd to the rogue.

"This done, the Grand Signior called for a Gage of Bowfe, which belike fignified a quart of drinke, for prefently a pot of Ale being put into his hand, he made the yong Squire kneele downe, and powring the full pot on his pate, vttered thefe wordes, I doe *ftall thee to the Rogue* by vertue of this foueraigne Englifh liquor, fo that henceforth it fhall be lawfull for thee to Cant (that is to fay) to be a Vagabond and beg," &c.—Dekker's *Belman of London*, 1608.

PAGE 221.

pacus palabros.

Pocas palabras (Spanifh) *i. e.* few words—an expreffion found under various corrupted forms in our old writers. It is ufually put into the mouths of low people, among whom it feems to have been current :—"With this learned oration the Cobler was tutord : laid his finger on his mouth, and cried *paucus palabros.*"—Dekker's *Wonderfull Yeare*, 1603.

PAGE 226.

The man talkes monthly.

i. e. madly; as if under the influence of the moon.

PAGE 235.

Troia Noua Triumphans. *London Triumphing*, 1612.

The mayoralty pageant here reprinted is one of the rareft of Dekker's works. Nichols, in his *Progreffes, &c., of King James the Firft*, vol. ii. p. 466, fays, "the only copy of this pageant that I know to exift, is one which was fold at Mr. Garrick's sale, April 23rd, 1823. It was bound up with the city pageants of 1626, 1631, 1679, and 1691, and other tracts, and the volume was purchafed for forty guineas by Mr. Thorpe, who has fince parted with it to Mr. Heber." He adds, "I have not yet obtained a tranfcript, but if I am favoured with one in time, it fhall appear in the appendix to this volume." At the fale of Heber's library, this copy formed lot 1631 of part 4, and proved to be imperfect, which was no doubt the reason why Nichols was unable to reprint it according to promise. There are, however, copies in the Bodleian Library and in the British Museum, which are quite perfect, and there is another in the library of the Duke of Devonshire.

"Upon this occasion the lord mayor's banquet was honoured by the presence of Frederick, Count Palatine of the Rhine, then lately arrived to marry Elizabeth, the king's only daughter." 'The Palsgrave dyned in the Guildhall,' as Howe's Chronicle informs us, 'accompanied with the Archbishop of Canterbury, the Lord Bishop of London, and divers earls and barons, and during the whole dinner the Palsgrave and the Lord Archbishop entertained the time with sundry discourses in Latine. To this great feast Prince Henry was also invited, and would have bin there, but he was sicke and could not come.

"After dinner, the lord mayor and his brethren, in the behalfe of the cittie, and cittizens of London, for testimonie of hearty welcome and their love, presented the Palsgrave with a very large bason and eure of silver, richly guilded, and curiously wrought; and two great guilded livery pots.' The present is described in the city records as :—'a bason and ewer gilt, weighing 234oz. 3grs.; one paire of dansk potts, chast and chefeld, weighing 513½oz. ½gr., having the armes of the city, and the wordes, 'Civitas London,' engraved thereon in divers places."

Mr. Chamberlain, in a letter to Sir Dudley Carleton, gives us a still better account of this entertainment, and adds some very interesting particulars of the previous pageantry; his words are : "the Count Palatine and his company, after they had seen the shew in Cheapside, went to Guildhall, and were there feasted and welcomed by Sir John Swinnerton, the new-made lord mayor, and were presented toward the end of the dinner, in the name of the city, with a fair standing cup, a curious basin and ewer, with two large livery pots, weighing together 1200 ounces, to the value of almost £500. The Merchant Adventurers had sent him a present of wine the Saturday before, to the value of 100 marks. He behaved himself very courteously, and in very good fashion at the feast, and would needs go and salute the lady mayoress and her train where she sat. The shew was somewhat extraordinary, with four or five pageants, and other devices; and the day was fair enough on land, but great winds

on the water had like to have marred all ; for divers of the companies were in great danger and pain to run their barges on
ground, and fome to turn back, fo that my lord mayor with much
ado came almoft alone to Weftminfter.' "—*Nichols's Progreſſes of
James I.*

Sir John Swinnerton was a man of confiderable note in his
day. He was a merchant of great wealth, and when fheriff in
1603, went with the mayor and principal citizens to meet King
James on his journey from Theobalds to London, and was knighted
with the other aldermen at Whitehall, in July following. In
1612 he accufed the farmers of the cuftoms of defrauding the
king of more than 70,000 a year, "but upon ripping up the
matter they went away acquitted, and he commended for his
good meaning to the king's fervice." During his mayoralty the
jurifdiction over the Thames and Medway, as enjoyed by the
mayor of London, was finally fettled ; and on Michaelmas day
1613, he attended with Sir Thomas Middleton, that day elected
mayor for the enfuing year, at the opening of the New River
head, "to fee the great ciftern, and firft iffuing of the ftrange
river thereunto, which was then made free denizen of London."
—Delaune, *Prefent State of London*, 1681.

PAGE 241.

Peale of Chambers.

In Edward Sharpham's comedy, *The Fleire*, 1610, is the following allufion to thefe noify falutations :—" He has taught my
lady to make fireworks, they can deal in chambers already, as
well as all the gunnes that make them fly off with a train at
Lambeth, when the Mayor and Alderman land at Weftminfter."

PAGE 242.

Painted cloath and browne paper.

This rather contemptuous notice of preceding pageants is
curious. Pafteboard was ufed in the conftruction of the giants
and other figures in continental fhows, and the Chefter giants
that were made on the reftoration of Charles the Second
were formed of that material ; but it would appear from the
charges for deal-boards and nails in their conftruction, that a
frame work of wood was ufed as a fuperftructure. There is an
entry of one fhilling and fourpence "for arfenic to put into the
pafte, to fave the giants from being eaten by the rats."

How the "living beafts" who drew this pageant were "queintly difguifed like dolphins and mermaids," we are not told, but in 1298, horfes difguifed "like luces of the fea," are mentioned in the civic pageant, on the victory over the Scots at Falkirk.

The objection to "the trouble and peftering of Porters" urged by Dekker, feems to have been pretty generally felt by the City poets : several notices occur in their pamphlets of their attempts to rid themfelves of the annoyance. Webfter, in his *Monuments of Honor*, 1624, defcribes the principal pageant, *The Chariot of Honor*, as drawn by four horfes, "for porters would haue made it moue tottering and improperly." The porters, however, ftood their ground well, for they are noticed by Jordan in his pageant for 1679, and were hired ftill later.

PAGE 243.

troopes of Swannes.

The Thames was "much beautified" in the early times by myriads of fwans, that principally belonged to the city companies ; and it was the cuftom to go up the river annually, and mark thefe fwans on the beak with the peculiar fign ufed by the company who claimed them. This ceremony was called fwan-upping, becaufe it was the duty of the official vifitors to take *up*, and mark the birds upon the beak, whence comes the modern name of fwan-hopping given to the voyage as ftill performed. The Vintners' and Dyers' companies are now the chief proprietors of the Thames fwans, next to her Majefty. In Yarrell's *Hiftory of Britifh Birds* are engraved the ancient fwan-marks of thefe companies during the reign of Elizabeth (from Kempe's *Lofely Manufcripts*), and the modern marks as ftill ufed, along with many others ; with fome curious information on this head. Hone, in his *Every-day Book* (vol. ii. p. 958) has printed entire the *Order for Swannes*, a rare tract of 1570, which fhows how highly they were then eftimated, and how carefully they were protected. Leland, the antiquary, in one of his rareft works, *Cygnea Cantio, a Swan's Song*, imagines a Thames fwan failing down the river from Oxford to Greenwich, defcribing, as fhe paffes along, all the towns, caftles, and other places of note within her view.

Page 248.

Ryot and Calumny in the shapes of Gyants.

From this paffage it appears that other gigantic figures than thofe of Gogmagog and Corineus appeared in the fhows occafionally. The giants exhibited this year were not merely conftructed for impofing effect, but were emblematic characters forming an important portion of the poet's invention.

Page 249.

Barrathrum.

i. e., abyfs, hell, bottomlefs gulf. See alfo page 351, "rareft diuell that euer hould in *Barathrum.*"

Page 251.

thy margent quoate.

An allufion to the general cuftom, at this time, of printing in the margins of books a brief note, guiding the reader to the fact written of in the body of the work, or elfe to the author quoted as an authority. The works of Prynne are remarkable fpecimens of this cuftom, and give much point to Milton's faying, "that he had ever his wits befide him in the margin, to be befide his wits in the text."

Page 255.

Stop, ftony *her.*

Probably a mifprint for "ftay," which is the word given in the fpeech at p. 249, of which this is a repetition. "Stony" certainly mars the metre, if not the fenfe ; though as regards the latter, it might be an abbreviated form of *aftonifh* (ftartle).

Page 354.

Is there a King to be murdred, whilest he does ftand
Coloffus-like, fupporting a whole land,
And when by his fall that Land moft feares a wracke,
Send forth this diuell ; his name is Rauillac.

The affaffination of King Henry IV. of France by Rauaillac took place on the 14th May, 1610, the day of the queen's coronation. It was an event therefore quite frefh in the memory of thofe who witneffed the performance of this play.

<table>
<tr><td>n</td><td>C C</td></tr>
</table>

Ravaillac is defcribed by Mr. Eyre Evans Crowe, in his *Hif-tory of France* (III. 378, 379) as "a half crazy fchoolmafter of Angoulême, who left his home at one time with the wild idea of perfuading the king to abandon his purpofes of war and tolerance of the Proteftants. Driven back by hunger and deftitution, the idea of regicide took firm hold of him, and he again left Angoulême at Eafter, 1610, with the determination to flay the king if he could nut fpeak with him. The *facre*, as the coronation was called, took place with all due magnificence early in the day. Henry fought fome repofe on his couch after it, but was uneafy, and could not fleep, tormented by aftrologic predictions of ill, and by his own mind giving unufual weight to fuch prefentiments. To relieve the dulnefs of the hour he refolved to pay a vifit to Sully at the arfenal. Even in this he hefitated ; but at length fet forth in his coach. It was a vehicle without doors or panels, the roof fupported on pillars, the intervals filled by curtains, which for the moment had been tied up or removed. The Rue de la Ferronnerie being obftructed by carts, the foot attendants left the carriage, to make their way round by the market ; and the guards did anything but guard it. There was nothing, therefore, to prevent Ravaillac mounting on the wheel and ftriking his knife into the king's breaft. Henry had fcarcely time to exclaim, "I am wounded," when the affaffin ftruck another blow, which penetrated the heart. Henry the Fourth breathed his laft."

PAGE 356.

Guy Faulx.

The confpiracy of Guy Fawkes was detected, and Fawkes taken in the vaults, Nov. 5, 1605. Guy Fawkes and feven others executed, Jan. 30, 1606.

END OF THIRD VOLUME.